# THE LOEB CLASSICAL LIBRARY

FOUNDED BY JAMES LOEB

EDITED BY

## G. P. GOOLD

# GREEK IAMBIC POETRY

## LCL 259

# GREEK IAMBIC POETRY

## FROM THE SEVENTH TO THE FIFTH CENTURIES BC

EDITED AND TRANSLATED BY

## DOUGLAS E. GERBER

HARVARD UNIVERSITY PRESS
CAMBRIDGE, MASSACHUSETTS
LONDON, ENGLAND
1999

*First published 1999*

LOEB CLASSICAL LIBRARY® is a registered trademark
of the President and Fellows of Harvard College

Library of Congress Cataloging-in-Publication Data

Greek iambic poetry : from the seventh to the fifth centuries BC
/ edited and translated by Douglas E. Gerber.
p.   cm.—(The Loeb classical library ; 259)
Includes bibliographical references.
ISBN 0-674-99581-3
1. Iambic poetry, Greek—Translations into English.
I. Gerber, Douglas E.   II. Series.
PA3623.E44G74   1999
881′0108—dc21          98-20803

# CONTENTS

CONTENTS

# PREFACE

This volume aims at providing a text and translation of the main iambic poets contained in the second edition of M. L. West's two-volume *Iambi et Elegi Graeci* (Oxford 1989 and 1992). Omitted, however, are papyrus fragments too lacunose to provide anything intelligible, poets whose iambic fragments are included elsewhere in the Loeb Classical Library (e.g., Anacreon), and because of limitations of space the minor poets Aeschines, Aristoxenus, Asopodorus, and Euclides. Half-brackets are inserted only when it is important to indicate what is actually attested in the papyrus. I have not attempted to include all the testimonia, but only those which are significant. Similarly the apparatus criticus is reduced to what I have judged most important. In some instances a fragment is cited or referred to in several sources, but only the most important are given. The reader can find the others in West's edition. The numbering of the fragments follows West, that of the testimonia is my own. In my translations I have attempted to provide an English rendering which represents the Greek as closely as possible without being stilted or ambiguous.

It remains to express my deep gratitude to Professors

## PREFACE

Christopher Brown, Robert Renehan, and Emmet Robbins, who read and commented on substantial portions, and to Robert Fowler, George Goold, and Jeffrey Henderson, who provided assistance on a variety of details. Their generosity and expertise are much appreciated.

University of Western Ontario          Douglas E. Gerber

To Dianne
amicae carissimae et fortissimae

# INTRODUCTION

The etymology of the word iambus is unclear, but there is no doubt that ἴαμβος as a metrical term (◡ –) is secondary and that in origin it described a type of poetry. This is indicated by Archilochus fr. 215, the earliest example of the word, where it can hardly refer exclusively to meter, whatever its precise force may be, and by the fact that the word could be used of trochaic tetrameters (e.g., fr. 111). Significant too is test. 3 (A col. III.38) where on a particular occasion Archilochus' poetry was described as ἰαμβι-κώτερον, "too iambic," clearly a reference to content rather than to meter (see below).

What type of poetry then does iambus signify?[1] Plutarch in his *Life of Cato* 7 states that Cato "betook himself to iambic verse, and heaped much scornful abuse upon Scipio, adopting the bitter tone of Archilochus, but avoiding his license and puerility" (Loeb translation). 'Scornful

---

[1] The nature and purpose of archaic iambic poetry have been examined in some detail by Christopher Brown in his contribution (pp. 13-88) to D. E. Gerber (ed.), *A Companion to the Greek Lyric Poets* (Leiden 1997), and my brief account here is deeply indebted to his analysis. His notes contain all the relevant bibliography, except for one item which came to our attention too late for inclusion, Krystyna Bartol's *Greek Elegy and Iambus. Studies in Ancient Literary Sources* (Poznań 1993).

INTRODUCTION

abuse,' 'bitter tone,' and (sexual) 'license': these are terms
which are frequently used to describe iambus in general
and in particular the poetry of Archilochus and Hipponax.
The purpose of such poetry, however, is a more complex
issue. With Hipponax, a century later than Archilochus, it
appears that the purpose was primarily one of entertain-
ment, although this assessment might well change if we
had more information at our disposal. But with Archilo-
chus there is evidence to assist us in reaching at least some
tentative conclusions. Particularly revealing is the evi-
dence of cult. A figure called Iambe appears in the Ho-
meric *Hymn to Demeter* (perhaps late seventh century)
and indulges in insulting language, thereby causing the
grieving goddess to laugh (vv. 202-204). Demeter does not
play a prominent role in the surviving verses of Archilo-
chus. She and Persephone appear in fr. 323, a fragment
which West judges spurious, but test. 65 suggests that
Archilochus' family had some connection with the worship
of Demeter, and there is ample evidence that Demeter
was a major deity in Paros.[2] Insulting or obscene language
($αἰσχρολογία$), so typical of iambus, was a common fea-
ture of festivals of Demeter.[3] In the *Hymn to Demeter* this
insulting language is directed towards a goddess, a behav-
iour which is the opposite of what is normal in addressing a
deity. Such inversion figures in other cults as well and, as
Brown points out (p. 41), its purpose "is to re-affirm and
strengthen the traditional structures of society and even

[2] See N. J. Richardson, *The Homeric Hymn to Demeter* (Ox-
ford 1974), commentary on v. 491.
[3] Richardson pp. 213-17.

2

the natural world. Normality is reinforced by experiencing its opposite."

In addition to the cult worship of Demeter we should consider the possible connection between early iambus and Dionysus. One type of song especially associated with Dionysus is the dithyramb, a word which appears to contain the same root as iambus, and both Dionysus and dithyramb are present in fr. 120. Drunkenness too is present in the fragment and the early dithyramb seems to have been a riotous affair. There is ample evidence that phallic rites were a common feature of the worship of Dionysus and this association is almost certainly found in fr. 251. The source of this fragment is the inscription of Mnesiepes (test. 3) and the inscription goes on, unfortunately in a highly mutilated condition, to state that something, presumably the verses just cited, was "too iambic." Apparently as a result of this criticism the citizens suffered a variety of disasters, until the Delphic oracle told them to appease the anger of Dionysus by honouring Archilochus. "Too iambic" cannot here refer to meter, since fr. 251, whatever its meter, is clearly not iambic. It must refer to the content of the fragment, in all likelihood to its obscenity. Whether the verses also contained insulting language cannot be determined.

It seems a reasonable deduction from all this that in festivals honouring both Demeter and Dionysus there were cult songs of an insulting and/or obscene nature and that from these a poetic genre, what we can call 'literary iambus,' was developed. What role Archilochus played in this development is unknown, but it may have been significant.

When we turn to the question how early iambus was delivered, we have at our disposal only the evidence of much later sources. According to Pseudo-Plutarch, for example, "Archilochus introduced the practice whereby some iambics were spoken to musical accompaniment and others sung" (test. 47), but this is surely a deduction "based on the practice of later artists" (West, *Studies* 33). Musical instruments are mentioned in Archilochus (e.g., pipe and lyre in fr. 93a), but nowhere is there an indication that any instrument accompanied his verses. The more lyrical nature of epodes suggests that they were not simply recited and the same may be true for trochaic tetrameters and perhaps for iambic trimeters as well.

With regard to the occasion for the delivery of iambus, we are again lacking secure evidence from the extant verses, but it seems safe to say that one at least of the main occasions was the symposium.[4] The other was presumably festivals. Such is in fact the occasion named in the inscription of Mnesiepes (test. 3) just before fr. 251. We are told that Archilochus could be among those whose works were performed at poetic contests (test. 34; cf. also Plato *Ion* 531a and test. 67) and the same was said of Semonides (test. 4), but in the case of Archilochus it is not clear what meter (or meters) was involved nor is there any evidence that Archilochus himself participated in poetic competition.

[4] Much has been written in recent years on the symposium and it must suffice here to refer the reader to O. Murray (ed.), *Sympotica* (Oxford 1990), and O. Murray and M. Tecusan (edd.), *In vino veritas* (London 1995).

## INTRODUCTION

### *Archilochus*

Archilochus was born on Paros, an island in the Cyclades, in the first half of the seventh century (testt. 5-11). His father, Telesicles, was involved in the Parian colonization of Thasos, an island in the north Aegean close to Thrace, and Archilochus' poetry contains numerous references to Thasos and to hostilities between the colonists and Thracian tribes. His poetry also attests to hostilities between Paros and neighbouring Naxos. Many sources record that Archilochus was engaged to marry Neoboule, daughter of Lycambes, that the latter broke off the engagement, and that Lycambes, Neoboule, and one or more additional daughters hanged themselves as a result of the poet's bitter invective against them (see testt. 19-32). Several fragments record the invective, but none the suicide, and it is possible that this was based on verses, no longer extant, which asserted that suicide was the family's only recourse in light of Lycambes' actions. I see no reason to doubt the general veracity of Archilochus' feud with Lycambes, but Brown, who discusses the evidence in considerable detail (pp. 50-69), is surely right to see more than a purely personal response on the part of Archilochus. It must suffice here to quote his conclusion (p. 69): "Consideration of the Lycambes poetry has also provided some support for our earlier contention that the function of ἴαμβος was similar to that of the religious occasion in which it developed. Lycambes is revealed as an oath-breaker and thus a menace to society; the daughters are exposed as sexually incontinent and so deserving of opprobrium. By subjecting his enemies to invective Archilochus seeks to protect the

community. However personal the insult, Archilochus
treats his feud with Lycambes as a matter of public con-
cern, and this public aspect seems to lie very near the heart
of ἴαμβος."

Lycambes was not the only object of the poet's invec-
tive. In fact Archilochus was viewed as early as Pindar
(test. 35) as the archetypal poet of blame and according to
Critias (test. 33) this was directed against friends and ene-
mies alike. The fragmentary nature, however, of what has
survived does not allow us to determine the extent to
which blame figured in his poetry. For example, before the
publication of P. Oxy. 2310 we had only v. 2 of fr. 25 and it
is only the papyrus which allows us to see that the poem
contains invective.

There is some evidence that Archilochus belonged to a
family involved in the cult worship of Demeter and Diony-
sus (see above and Brown 45-47) and long after the poet's
death he was the recipient of heroic honours. An Archilo-
cheion was established in Paros, and some of the inscrip-
tions set up in it have been found (testt. 3-4). Archilochus
was also the subject of two comedies, an Ἀρχίλοχος by
Alexis and an earlier Ἀρχίλοχοι by Cratinus, and he is
represented anachronistically as Sappho's lover in Diphi-
lus' Σαπφώ. Unlike the other two major iambographers,
Semonides and Hipponax, whose works were assembled in
two books each by the Alexandrians, Archilochus is cited
by such terms as elegiacs, trimeters, tetrameters, and ep-
odes rather than by book number. For ancient works writ-
ten on Archilochus see testt. 63-64.

## INTRODUCTION

### Semonides

Although the evidence for Semonides' date is much less substantial than that for Archilochus', such evidence as there is points to the middle of the seventh century (testt. 1-3). Originally from Samos, he was involved in the colonization of Amorgos, an island at the eastern edge of the Cyclades. According to the *Suda* he composed elegiac as well as iambic poetry, but elsewhere he is cited as an iambographer, and only iambic verses have survived. The one elegiac fragment that some assigned to him has now been shown to be the work of Simonides (frr. 19-20 *IEG²*). Although our sources regularly refer to the iambic poet as Simonides, the grammarian Choeroboscus (test. 5) states that the proper spelling is Semonides. Whether this is correct or not, the distinction in spelling avoids confusion with the much better known lyric poet of the fifth century.

Except for frr. 1 and 7, nothing exceeding three verses has survived. Fr. 1 shows that iambics could also be used for serious meditation on life's vicissitudes, a topic more commonly reserved for elegiacs. Fr. 7, the longest iambic poem we have from the archaic period, describes ten types of wives, all of whom are said to be derived from different animals except for two which owe their origin to earth and sea. Only the last in the series, the bee woman, is praised and it is clear that only she enhances her husband's household. What follows, however, seems to indicate that all wives are a bane and Semonides may be suggesting to his audience that the bee woman is a mirage or at least extremely rare. Although the misogyny of fr. 7 is an appropriate topic for iambics, the tone is more reminiscent of

Hesiod than of Archilochus. Fr. 7 seems to be derived in part from beast fable, as do some of the other fragments, and the fable appears in both Archilochus and Hesiod. In contrast to Archilochus, however, there is in Semonides' remains none of the Parian poet's harsh invective or obscenity.

## Hipponax

Hipponax can be assigned with some confidence to the middle of the sixth century (testt. 1-2). A native of Ephesus, he was banished by the city's tyrants and settled in Clazomenae. Ancient sources and several of the poet's fragments attest to bitter invective directed against the sculptors Bupalus and Athenis, especially the former, ostensibly because they caricatured his appearance. Although we have a substantial number of fragments, many are lacunose scraps of papyrus and brief citations of rare words by lexicographers. In spite of this, however, Hipponax is revealed as a forceful poet whose verses contain many colourful, foreign, rare, and obscene words. He is especially fond of depicting the lower levels of society and several fragments attest to his interest in composing parody, primarily of epic poetry. Like Archilochus he employed a variety of meters, but unlike the Parian poet his iambic trimeters usually end in a spondee rather than an iambus, thereby creating a limping effect; hence the term choliambic or lame iambic given to this meter. He was also not above combining iambic and dactylic meters in the same verse (e.g., fr. 35).

Hipponax was much admired by the Alexandrians, especially Callimachus and Herodas, both of whom imitated his meter and style, and his virulent invective was the subject of several poems in the *Palatine Anthology* (testt. 7-10).

## *Minor Poets*

Not enough of the remaining poets in this volume has survived to enable us to form much of an impression of their works.

Ananius, homeland unknown, seems to have been roughly a contemporary of Hipponax, and the two poets are sometimes confused (see n. 4 on fr. 1). Both composed in choliambics and both occasionally included ischiorrhogic lines (see test. 2), the latter apparently being commoner in Ananius than in Hipponax. The only fragment of any length (fr. 5) is in trochaic tetrameters, ten verses on the best season of the year to eat certain meats and seafood.

Susarion of Megara, probably late 6th and/or early 5th century B.C., is credited in several sources with having invented comedy. Nothing, however, has survived, except for one iambic fragment which can hardly be from a comedy. On Susarion see especially West, *Studies* 183-84.

Hermippus of Athens, like Susarion, was also a comic and iambic poet (latter part of the 5th century), but much more has been preserved, especially of his comedies. The few iambic and trochaic fragments extant, in particular frr. 4 and 5, are characterized by puns and rare words.

Scythinus of Teos, perhaps 5th century, was both an iambic poet and a writer of prose. Only one fragment of his poetry has survived.

Among the Adespota there are several fragments which could be assigned to Anacreon (1, 3, 39), Archilochus (35, 38), and Hipponax (51, 52).

# BIBLIOGRAPHY

The following list contains works cited either by author's name alone or by author together with a short title. Other works referred to are cited in sufficient detail as they appear in the notes. Journals are cited by the abbreviations given in *L'Année Philologique*. For further bibliography see D. E. Gerber, "Early Greek Elegy and Iambus 1921-1989," *Lustrum* 33 (1991) 7-225 and 401-409.

Bossi = F. Bossi, *Studi su Archiloco*² (Bari 1990)

Chaniotis = A. Chaniotis, *Historie und Historiker in den griechischen Inschriften: epigraphische Beiträge zur griechischen Historiographie* (Stuttgart 1988)

Degani = E. Degani, *Hipponactis Testimonia et Fragmenta* (Leipzig 1983, 1991²)

Degani, *Studi* = E. Degani, *Studi su Ipponatte* (Bari 1984)

Henderson = J. Henderson, *The Maculate Muse. Obscene Language in Attic Comedy* (New Haven 1975, New York 1991²)

*IEG* = M. L. West, *Iambi et Elegi Graeci* (Oxford; vol. 1 2nd ed. 1989, vol. 2 2nd ed. 1992)

Masson = O. Masson, *Les fragments du poète Hipponax. Edition critique et commentée* (Paris 1962)

Miralles-Pòrtulas = C. Miralles & J. Pòrtulas, *Archilochus and the Iambic Poetry* (Rome 1983)

# BIBLIOGRAPHY

Mosshammer = A. A. Mosshammer, *The Chronicle of Eusebius and Greek Chronographic Tradition* (Lewisburg 1979)

Pellizer-Tedeschi = E. Pellizer & G. Tedeschi, *Semonide. Introduzione, testimonianze, testo critico, traduzione e commento* (Rome 1990)

*SEG = Supplementum Epigraphicum Graecum*

Slings = J. M. Bremer, A. M. van Erp Taalman Kip, S. R. Slings, *Some Recently Found Greek Poems* (Leiden 1987)

Tarditi = G. Tarditi. *Archiloco. Introduzione, testimonianze sulla vita e sull'arte, testo critico, traduzione* (Rome 1968)

West, *Studies* = M. L. West, *Studies in Greek Elegy and Iambus* (Berlin 1974)

# GREEK IAMBIC POETRY

# ARCHILOCHUS

## TESTIMONIA

### Inscriptions

**1** Inscriptio, *SEG* 14.565

Γλαύκου εἰμὶ μνῆμα τοῦ Λεπτίνεω·
ἔθεσαν δέ με οἱ Βρέντεω παῖδες.

**2** Inscriptio (*CEG* 2.674 Hansen)

Ἀρχίλοχος Πάριος Τελεσικλέος ἐνθάδε κεῖται,
τὸ Δόκιμος μνημήιον ὁ Νεοκρέωντος τόδ᾽ ἔθηκεν.

# ARCHILOCHUS

## TESTIMONIA

### *Inscriptions*

**1** Inscription

I am the memorial of Glaucus, son of Leptines;
the sons of Brentes made me.[1]

[1] The inscription, found in Thasos and dated to the late 7th
century, was first published (with full discussion) by J. Pouilloux
in *BCH* 79 (1955) 75-86. It was written boustrophedon in four
lines (I have printed a transliterated text) and clearly refers to the
Glaucus whom Archilochus mentions several times (see n. 1 on fr.
15).

**2** Inscription

Archilochus of Paros, son of Telesicles, lies here;
this memorial for him was set up by Dokimos, son of Neo-
    kreon.[1]

[1] This inscription, found in Paros and dated to the middle of
the 4th century, was first published by A. K. Orlandos in *PAAH*
(1960) 255-56. It was written on a capital, a photograph of which
can be seen in *Archiloque*, Entretiens sur l'antiquité classique 10
(Geneva 1964) facing p. 44.

IAMBIC POETRY

**3** Mnesiepis inscriptio, *SEG* 15.517

*The inscription, found in the valley of the river Elita (hence the designation E) in Paros, was first published by N. M. Kondoleon in Ἀρχαιολογικὴ Ἐφημερίς (1952, appeared in 1955) 32-95. Dated to the 3rd century* B.C., *it was inscribed on at least two orthostats but is only partially preserved. Each stone contained four columns with 57 lines per column. Of col. I on stone A (= E₁) only a few letters on the right side remain; col. II is almost entirely legible; col. III is missing lines 1-5, then we have the first two*

A(E₁), col. I

1 κ]αὶ ὅτε    2 τῶν Π]αρίων

col. II

Μνησιέπει ὁ θεὸς ἔχρησε λῶιον καὶ ἄμεινον εἶμεν
ἐν τῶι τεμένει, ὃ κατασκευάζει, ἱδρυσαμένωι
βωμὸν καὶ θύοντι ἐπὶ τούτου Μούσαις καὶ
Ἀπόλλ[ω]ν[ι]
Μουσαγέται καὶ Μνημοσύνει· θύειν δὲ καὶ καλλι-
5    ερεῖν Διὶ Ὑπερδεξίωι, Ἀθάναι Ὑπερδεξίαι,
Ποσειδῶνι Ἀσφαλείωι, Ἡρακλεῖ, Ἀρτέμιδι
Εὐκλείαι.
Πυθῶδε τῶι Ἀπόλλωνι σωτήρια πέμπειν.
Μνησιέπει ὁ θεὸς ἔχρησε λῶιον καὶ ἄμεινον εἶμεν
ἐν τῶι τεμένει, ὃ κατασκευάζει, ἱδρυσαμένωι
10    βωμὸν καὶ θύοντι ἐπὶ τούτου Διονύσωι καὶ
Νύμφαις

16

**3** Inscription of Mnesiepes

*letters of each of three lines of poetry (= fr. 299, omitted here), and of the rest only 1 to 12 letters per line on the left side remain; col. IV is entirely missing. Of stone B (= E₂) we can read only about one-third on the left side of col. I. The inscription must have been originally set up in the Archilocheion, a precinct established in honour of the poet. I have printed the text essentially as it appears in* SEG *(omitting the most exiguous parts), except that for the oracle in A col. III, lines 47-50, I have printed Parke's tentative restoration. There is an extensive apparatus in Chaniotis 28-29 and a bibliographic survey in* Lustrum *33 (1991) 33-36.*

A(E₁) col. I

and when . . . of the Parians . . .

col. II

The god declared to Mnesiepes that it was preferable and better to set up an altar in the precinct which he was constructing and to sacrifice on it to the Muses and Apollo Mousagetes and Mnemosyne, and also to sacrifice and obtain favourable omens from Zeus Hyperdexios, Athena Hyperdexia, Poseidon Asphaleios, Heracles, and Artemis Eukleia, and to send thank-offerings to Apollo at Pytho.

The god declared to Mnesiepes that it was preferable and better to set up an altar in the precinct which he was constructing and to sacrifice on it to Dionysus and the Nymphs and the Seasons, and also to sacrifice and obtain

καὶ Ὥραις· θύειν δὲ καὶ καλλιερεῖν Ἀπόλλωνι
Προστατηρίωι, Ποσειδῶνι Ἀσφαλείωι, Ἡρακλεῖ.
Πυθῶδε τῶι Ἀπόλλωνι σωτήρια πέμπειν.
Μνησιέπει ὁ θεὸς ἔχρησε λῶιον καὶ ἄμεινον εἶμεν
15   τιμῶντι Ἀρχίλοχον τὸμ ποιητάν, καθ᾽ ἃ ἐπινοεῖ.
      χρήσαντος δὲ τοῦ Ἀπόλλωνος ταῦτα τόν τε
          τόπον
      καλοῦμεν Ἀρχιλόχειον καὶ τοὺς βωμοὺς
          ἱδρύμεθα
      καὶ θύομεν καὶ τοῖς θεοῖς καὶ Ἀρχιλόχωι καὶ
      τιμῶμεν αὐτόν, καθ᾽ ἃ ὁ θεὸς ἐθέσπισεν ἡμῖν.
20   περὶ δὲ ὧν ἠβουλήθημεν ἀναγράψαι, τάδε παρα-
      δέδοταί τε ἡμῖν ὑπὸ τῶν ἀρχαίων καὶ αὐτοὶ
          πεπρα-
      γματεύμεθα. λέγουσι γὰρ Ἀρχίλοχον ἔτι
          νεώτερον
      ὄντα πεμφθέντα ὑπὸ τοῦ πατρὸς Τελεσικλέους
      εἰς ἀγρόν, εἰς τὸν δῆμον, ὃς καλεῖται Λειμῶνες,
25   ὥστε βοῦν καταγαγεῖν εἰς πρᾶσιν, ἀναστάντα
      πρωίτερον τῆς νυκτός, σελήνης λαμπούσης,
      [ἄ]γειν τὴμ βοῦν εἰς πόλιν. ὡς δ᾽ ἐγένετο
          κατὰ τὸν
      τόπον, ὃς καλεῖται Λισσίδες, δόξαι γυναῖκας
      [ἰ]δεῖν ἀθρόας. νομίσαντα δ᾽ ἀπὸ τῶν ἔργων
          ἀπιέναι
30   αὐτὰς εἰς πόλιν προσελθόντα σκώπτειν, τὰς δὲ
      δέξασθαι αὐτὸν μετὰ παιδιᾶς καὶ γέλωτος καὶ

favourable omens from Apollo Prostaterios, Poseidon
Asphaleios, and Heracles, and to send thank-offerings to
Apollo at Pytho.

The god declared to Mnesiepes that it was preferable
and better to honour the poet Archilochus in accordance
with his intentions.

Since Apollo declared these things, we call the place
the Archilocheion and we set up altars and we sacrifice
both to the gods and to Archilochus and we honour him in
accordance with the god's oracular response to us. Con-
cerning the matters which we wished to inscribe, these
have both been handed down to us by men of old and we
have elaborated on them ourselves. They say that when
Archilochus was still a young man he had been sent by his
father Telesicles into the country, to the district which is
called Leimones, to bring a cow for sale. He got up before
the end of night, while the moon was shining, and was
bringing the cow to town, and when he was at a place
which is called Lissides, he thought he saw a group of
women. Believing that they were on their way from their
work to the town, he approached and bantered with them.
They received him with jesting and laughter and asked if

[ἐ]περωτῆσαι, εἰ πωλήσων ἄγει τὴμ βοῦν·
  φήσαντος δὲ
[εἰ]πεῖν, ὅτι αὐταὶ δώσουσιν αὐτῶι τιμὴν ἀξίαν.
[ῥη]θέντων δὲ τούτων αὐτὰς μὲν οὐδὲ τὴμ
  βοῦν οὐκέτι
35  [φ]ανερὰς εἶναι, πρὸ τῶν ποδῶν δὲ λύραν
  ὁρᾶν αὐτόν.
  καταπλαγέντα δὲ καὶ μετά τινα χρόνον ἔννουν
[γ]ενόμενον ὑπολαβεῖν τὰς Μούσας εἶναι τὰς
  φανείσας
[καὶ] τὴν λύραν αὐτῶι δωρησαμένας· καὶ ἀνελό-
[μ]ενον αὐτὴν πορεύεσθαι εἰς πόλιν καὶ τῶι
  πατρὶ
40  [τὰ] γενόμενα δηλῶσαι. τὸν δὲ Τελεσικλῆν ἀκού-
[σ]αντα καὶ τὴν λύραν ἰδόντα θαυμάσαι· καὶ
  πρῶτομ
  μὲν ζήτησιν ποιήσασθαι τῆς βοὸς κατὰ πᾶσαν
[τ]ὴν νῆσον καὶ οὐ δύνασθαι εὑρεῖν· ἔπειθ'
  ὑπὸ τῶν
[π]ολιτῶν θεοπρόπον εἰς Δελφοὺς εἰρημένον
  μετὰ
45  [Λυ]κάμβου χρησόμενον ὑπὲρ τῆς πόλεως
  προθυμό-
[τ]ερον ἀποδημῆσαι, βουλόμενον καὶ περὶ τῶν
[α]ὐτοῖς συμβεβηκότων πυθέσθαι·
  ἀφικομένων δὲ
[κ]αὶ εἰσιόντων αὐτῶν εἰς τὸ μαντεῖον τὸν θεὸν
  εἰπεῖν Τελεσικλεῖ τὸν χρησμὸν τόνδε·

20

he was bringing the cow to sell it. When he said he was, they replied that they would themselves give him a fitting price. After these words were spoken, neither they nor the cow were any longer visible, but before his feet he saw a lyre. He was astounded and when he recovered his senses after a while he assumed that it was the Muses who had appeared to him and that they had given him the lyre. He picked it up, went to the town, and revealed to his father what had happened. When Telesicles heard the story and saw the lyre, he was amazed. First he conducted a search for the cow throughout the whole island and was unable to find it. Then, having been chosen by the citizens to go with Lycambes to Delphi to consult the oracle on behalf of the city, he was more eager to make the trip because he wanted to inquire about what had happened to them. After their arrival and entrance to the oracular seat the god gave Telesicles the following response:

50 [Ἀ]θάνατός σοι παῖς καὶ ἀοίδιμος, ὦ Τελεσίκλεις,
ἔσται ἐν ἀνθρώποισιν, ὃς ἂμ πρῶτός σε προσείπει
νηὸς ἀποθρώσκοντα φίλην εἰς πατρίδα γαῖαν.
παραγενομένων δ' αὐτῶν εἰς Πάρον τοῖς Ἀρτε-
μισίοις πρῶτον τῶν παίδων Ἀρχίλοχον ἀπαν-
55 τήσαντα προσειπεῖν τὸμ πατέρα· καὶ ὡς ἦλθον
οἴκαδε, ἐρωτήσαντος τοῦ Τελεσικλέους, εἴ τι τῶν
ἀναγκαίων ὑπάρχει, ὡς ἂν ὀψὲ τῆς ἡμέρας

col. III

12 ἀοιδ[ιμ     14 λύραν     15 Ἀρχιλο[χ
16 ἐν ἀρχε[ῖ     17 τεῖ δ' ἑορ[τεῖ     18 παρ' ἡμῖν
19 φασὶν Ἀρ[χίλοχον     20 [αὐτο]σχεδιασ[
21 τινας τῶν π[     22 διδάξαντα     23 τὰ]
παραδεδομ[ένα     24 κεκοσμημέ[ν
25 κή]ρυκος εἰς π[     27 καὶ συνακολο[υθ
28 των καὶ ἄλλω[ν     28-29 κατασκευ]ασθέντων
τὰ μ[     30 πα]ρὰ τοὺς ἑταίρου[ς

31-35 = fr. 251

36 λεχθέντων [δὲ τούτων     37 ὡς κακῶς ἀκ[ου
38 ἰαμβικώτερο[ν     39 οὐ κατανοήσ[αντας
40 τῶν] καρπῶν, ἢν τα[     41 τὰ] ῥηθέντα εἰς τὴ[ν
42 ἐν τεῖ κρίσει μ[     42-43 μετ' οὐ πολὺν] χρόνον
γίνεσθ[αι     43-44 ἀσθενεῖς] εἰς τὰ αἰδοῖα
45 τὴν πόλιν τινὰς     46 τὸν δὲ θεὸν

47 Τίπτε δίκαις ἀν[όμοις κεχρημένοι ἠδὲ βίηφι
ἤλθετε πρὸς Π[υθὼ λοιμοῦ λύσιν αἰτήσαντες;

Immortal and renowned in song among men, Telesicles, will be whichever son of yours first speaks to you as you leap from your ship onto your beloved homeland.

When they arrived in Paros at the festival of Artemis, Archilochus was the first of the sons to meet and speak to his father. And when they returned home and Telesicles asked if any of the necessities (for the festival) were at hand, since it was late in the day

## col. III

. . . renowned in song . . . lyre . . . Archilochus . . . in the beginning . . . at the festival . . . among us . . . they say that Archilochus . . . improvised . . . some of the . . . taught . . . what had been handed down . . . decorated . . . herald to . . . and accompanied . . . and of others . . . equipped(?) . . . to the (his) companions . . . (fr. 251) . . . (when these things) had been said . . . that(?) ill-spoken of . . . too iambic[1] . . . not understanding . . . of fruits . . . what had been spoken to the . . . in the judgement . . . (after a short) time became . . . impotent . . . the city some . . . and the god (gave the following oracle?):

Why have you (who use illegal) judgements (and force) come to P(ytho to ask for a release from the

οὐκ ἔστιν πρὶν [Βάκχον ἀμείλιχον ἐξιλάσασθαι,
50    εἰς ὅ κεν Ἀρχίλ[οχον Μουσῶν θεράποντα τίητε.

51 ἀπαγγελθ[έντων δὲ τούτων
52 μιμνησκομ[     52-53 τῶν ἐ]κείνου ῥη[μάτων
54 τὰ] διημαρ[τημένα     55 Διον[υσ

B(E₂) col. I

1 νομίσειεν ἄν τις Ἀρχίλ[οχον    2 καὶ ἐξ
ἄλλων  πο[λλῶν  μαρτυρίων    3 ἀνα]γράφειν
μακρόν· ἐν ὀ[λίγοις    4 δηλωσόμε[θα
4-5 πολέμου γάρ ποτε ἡμῖν πρὸς τοὺς Να]ξίους
ἰσχυροῦ ὄντος  6 ὑπὸ τῶν πολ[ι]τῶ[ν  7 περὶ αὐτῶν
8 ὡς ἔχει πρὸ[ς    9 πατρίδος καὶ ὑπ[ὸ
10 καὶ ἐνεφάνισεν    11 καὶ παρεκάλε[σεν
12 βοηθεῖν ἀπροφασ[ίστως    13 καὶ λέγει περὶ
αὐτῶν    14 νῦν πάντες

15-44 = fr. 89

45 εὐξαμένωι οὖν    45-46 ὑπή]κουσαν οἱ θεοὶ
κα[ὶ    47 τὰς] εὐχάς· πάντες    48 γε]νόμενον
αὐτὸν ε[    49 ἐν ταῖς μάχαις    50 ἐκ τῆς
χώρας κ[    51 ὕστερόν τε χρόν[ωι    52 καὶ
τῶν πολιτῶν    53 ταις πεντηκοντ[
54 τούτων ἐπιπλε[    55 ἀνδραγαθοῦντα κα[
56 ἀποκτείναντα    57 τὰς δὲ καὶ δυομεν (δυο-
μέν[ας?)

51-57 = fr. 90

24

pestilence)? It is not possible (to appease harsh Bacchus) until (you honour) Archilochus (servant of the Muses).

When (this) was announced . . . remembering . . . the words of that one [i.e., the god] . . . the errors . . . Dionysus . . .

### B(E₂) col. I

One might think that Archilochus . . . also from much additional (evidence) . . . long to inscribe; in (a few words) . . . we will show . . . (when we were once engaged) in a hard-fought (war) with the Naxians . . . by the citizens . . . concerning them . . . how it was with(?) . . . of homeland and by . . . and showed . . . and summoned . . . to help without hesitation . . . and says about them . . . now all . . . (fr. 89) . . . and so to his prayer . . . the gods gave ear and . . . the prayers; all . . . him being . . . in the battles . . . from the land . . . later . . . and of the citizens . . . with fifty (fifty-oared ships?) . . . of these sailing against(?) . . . acting bravely . . . having killed . . . and also the (sinking ships?) . . .

[1] Or "in too iambic a manner." This seems to refer to the contents of fr. 251, presumably its obscene language (see Introduction).

IAMBIC POETRY

4 Sosthenis inscriptio, *IG* XII 5 n. 445 (+ Suppl. pp. 212-14; W. Peek, *ZPE* 59 (1985) 13-22)

A col. Ia

[ἀναγέγραφε] γὰ̣ρ̣ [Δ]ημέας οὐ μόνον περὶ
Π̣ά̣[ρου, ἀλλὰ καὶ]
[περὶ ὧν πέπρ]α̣κται ὑπὸ Ἀρχιλόχου καὶ τῆς
Ἀρχιλόχ[ου περὶ πάν]-
[τας τοὺς θεοὺ]ς̣ εὐσ‹ε›βείας καὶ τῆς περὶ τὴν
πατ[ρίδα σπου]-
[δῆς· ἀνέμνησ]ε γὰρ τῶν πεπραγμένων ὑ[πὸ τοῦ
ποιη]-
5    [τοῦ πολ]λῶν καὶ μεγάλων ἀγαθῶν [ἐκ τῶν
. . . . .]
. . . . ς τοῦ ἀνηγαγωχότας ταῦτα εἰς αὑ[τὸν τὸν
Ἀρχί]-
[λοχον]. ἀναγέγραφεν δὲ ὁ Δημέας ἕκαστα τ[ῶν
πεπραγμέ]-
[νω]ν καὶ γεγραμμένων ὑπὸ Ἀρχιλόχου κατ᾽
[ἄρχοντα]
ἕκαστον καὶ ἦρκται ἀπὸ ἄρχοντος πρῶτον
Εὐρ[. . . . . , ἐφ᾽ οὗ]
10   λέγει πεντηκόντορο‹ν› Μιλησίων πρέσβεις
ἄγ[ουσαν]
καὶ ἀνακομιζομένη‹ν› ἐγ Μιλήτου διαφθαρῆνα[ι
ἐν ‹τῶι› πορθμῶι]
τῶι Ναξιακῶι καὶ σωθῆναι ἕνα τινὰ αὐτῶν, ὧι
ὄ[νομα Κοίρα]-

26

**4** Inscription of Sosthenes

*The inscription, dated to c. 100 B.C., was first published in 1900 by Hiller von Gaertringen and presumably was once in the Archilocheion along with the inscription of Mnesiepes (test. 3). It consists of two orthostats, but much is now illegible and in addition the execution is much more careless than that of the Mnesiepes inscription. The author of the inscription was a certain Sosthenes who recorded an account of Archilochus' deeds made by Demeas and arranged chronologically by Parian archons. Included are several poems of Archilochus (frr. 7, 7a, 93a, 94-98, 192), mostly of martial content. I have printed the first 20 lines as they appear in SEG 15 n. 518, but much is uncertain. For most of the rest I have followed West's edition of Archilochus and Peek in ZPE 59 (1985) 13-22. There is an extensive apparatus in Chaniotis 64-66.*

## A col. Ia

For Demeas (has written an account) not only about Paros (but also about the deeds done) by Archilochus and the piety of Archilochus (towards all the gods) and his (zeal) for his country. For he (mentioned) the many deeds done (by the poet) and great benefits . . . who ascribed them to (Archilochus himself). Demeas has written an account of each (of the deeds done) and written about by Archilochus, dating them according to each (archon), and he has begun first with the archon Eur(-, at which time) he says that a fifty-oared ship bringing Milesian ambassadors and returning from Miletus was destroyed (in the strait) of Naxos and that one person, whose (name was Koira)nos,

νος, ὑπὸ δελφῖνος ἀναλημφθέντα καὶ ἐκπεσόν[τα
εἰς τὸν]
τ[ῶ]ν Συρίων [αἰ]γι[αλὸ]ν εἴς τι σ[π]ήλαιον
συνφυ[γεῖν καὶ]
15    ἐκεῖθεν αὖτ[ις ἐλθεῖν εἰς] τὴν ἰδίαν. τὸ δὲ
σπ[ήλαιον]
ἔτι νῦν ὑ[πάρχει καὶ ἀπ' ἐκ]είνου Κοιράνει[ον
καλεῖ]-
[τ]αι, κ[αὶ ναίει ὁ Ποσειδῶν ὁ Ἵ]ππιος ἔντ[οσθε,
καθ]-
[άπερ ὁ ποιητὴς ποιεῖται αὐτο]ῦ μνήμη[ν λέγων
οὗ]-
τ[ω· πεντήκοντ' ἀνδρῶν λίπε Κοίρα]νον Ἱππ[ιος
Ποσει]-
20    [δ]ῶ[ν. καὶ μετὰ ταῦτα γίγνεται πάλι]ν
ἄρ[χων(?) . . .]

perierunt 21-39

40                              ]φονδετοσ[          χρή]-
μ]ατα τοὺς Θρᾳκ[ας λέ]γουσιν Πάριοι ἑαυ[τοῖς
ἀποκαθιστάνα[ι πάλι]ν. διασαφεῖ δὲ τ[οῦτο
τ. αὐτὸς ᾳ[

43-49 = fr. 93a

                              ὅτι τοὺς Θρᾷκας
50    ἀποκτείναντες αὐτοὶ οἱ μὲν αὐτῶν ὑπὸ Παρί-
ων ἀπώλοντο, οἱ δ' εἰς τὰς Σάπας ⟨φυγόντες⟩
ὑπὸ τῶν Θρᾳ-

was saved. Lifted up by a dolphin and cast (on to the) shore
of the Syrians into a cave he escaped (and) from there he
(made his way) back (to) his own land. The cave still (ex-
ists) now (and is called) Koiraneion after him. (And Posei-
don) Hippios (dwells) within, as (the poet makes) mention
(in the following words): "out of fifty men Poseidon
Hippios spared Koiranos" (= fr. 192). (And after this Eur-
was archon again). (lines 21-39 missing). . . the Parians said
that the Thracians were to restore to them (the gold). And
(this the poet) himself makes clear, (saying): (fr. 93a), be-
cause after the Parians themselves had slain the Thracians
some of them were killed by the Parians and others, (hav-
ing fled) to Sapae [or: to the Sapaeans], were killed by the

κ]ων. μετὰ ταῦτα πάλιν γίνεται ἄρχων Ἀμ-
φ[ί]τιμος· καὶ ἐν τούτοις διασαφεῖ πάλιν ὡς
ἐνίκησαν καρτερῶς τοὺς Ναξίους, λέγων
55    ο]ὕτω·

   55-59 = fr. 94

col. IVa
δηλοῖ ὁ ποιητὴς [ἐν τούτοις

   1-6 = fr. 95

6-8    ὅτι δὲ Γλαῦκ[ος - - - ἀπῆρεν εἰς Θά]σον μάχηι
      κρατησ[άντων - - -]
      δηλοῖ ὁ ποιητὴ[ς ἐν τούτοις·

   8-13 = fr. 96

      - -]αν τῆς εἰς τὴν Θάσο[ν - - - ]τησε καὶ παρ᾽
14-22    ἑταί[ρας - - -]νης γαύρας
      ἡττ[ή]θη τολ[μ]ηι [ - - -]πλ[. .]ς τοιαῦτα ἤ[κ]οντες
      [- - -] . . . . .ν ἀσπίσιν
      [κα]ρτε[ρ]ία [ - - -].ν τῆς Θάσου και[. . .] απα[- -
      -]το ἐκεῖ. ὅτι δ᾽ ἀλη[θῆ - - -]
      ὑπὲρ ταύτης τῆς π[ - - -] τάδε·

   22 = fr. 97

23-27    ἔ]πειτα γυναῖκας ει[ - - -]λαι τι[. .]ς τῆς πύλης
      ἔ[τ]ρεχον εἰς [ - - -] ἐκ τῆς
      Θάσο[υ - - -]ν· ὅτι δ᾽ ἀλη[θ]ῆ [ - - - ] σημ[.]αει
      τιν[ - - -]

30

Thracians. After this Amphitimus was archon again. And in these verses he makes clear again that they soundly defeated the Naxians, speaking as follows: (fr. 94)

## col. IVa

The poet makes clear (in these verses): (fr. 95). And that Glauc(us departed for Tha)sos (when the Thracians) were victorious in battle . . . the poet makes clear (in these verses): (fr. 96) . . . (fr. 97) . . . (fr. 98)[1]

[1] I have not attempted to translate what precedes frr. 97 and 98, but there is clearly mention of Thasos, fighting, and women. West's fr. 97a appears in the mutilated section between 97 and 98 and has been omitted.

lineae 28-41 mutilae et omissae
42-58 = fr. 98

B col. (Vb?)

1-4 = frr. 7, 7a

5 ναυμαχίαι μαχομ[     6 ἀνὴ]ρ ἀγαθός,
πολλοὺς     7 ὑπὸ τῶν ἐναντίων
8 ἐτελ]εύτησεν· οἱ δὲ Πάριοι     9 φυγὴν δύο
μὲν αὐτῶν     10 κατεπόντι]σαν, τὰς δὲ λοιπὰς
11 πάλιν εἰς τὴν Πά[ρον     12 μετὰ τ]αῦτα
τὸν Ἀρχίλοχον     13 μεγαλοπρεπῶς ἔθα[ψαν
14 ]ου ποιησάμενοι τὰ ὑ[πὸ     15 ἤ]δεσαν,
οὐκ ὀργισθέντες     16 φαῦλον κατὰ τῆς
πόλε[ως

col. VII

3 μητρὸς αὐτῆς     8 τῆς πατρίδος καὶ Ἀρχι-
λόχου ἐνταῦθα π[

12     Τίς σὲ τὸν ἐμ πέτρηι Μουσῶν θεράποντ᾽
       ἐχάραξεν,
    παῖ Τελεσικλῆος κοῦρε, καταγλαΐσας;
    λέξω δή σοι ἐγὼ μάλ᾽ ἐτήτυμα, εἰ σὺ μὴ οἶδας·
15     ἐσθλὸς ἐὼν ἀρετῆς τ᾽ οὐχ ὑπολειπόμενος
    Σωσθεὺς Προσθένου υἱὸς ἐμὴν πολ[ύυ]μ[νον
       ἀοι]δὴν
    τιμῶν ἀεν[άων] αἶσαν ὑπεσπάσατο.

18 Σωφροσύνας οἴακα[     21 Πάρος.

B col. (Vb?)

(frr. 7, 7a) . . . fighting in a sea battle . . . brave (man), many
. . . by the opponents . . . he died; and the Parians . . . flight
two of their (ships) . . . they (sank) and the rest . . . back to
Pa(ros) . . . (after) this Archilochus . . . they buried magni-
ficently . . . deeming(?) the . . . they knew, not angry . . .
derogatory against the city

col. VII

. . . of the mother of her [of the mother herself?] . . . of his
country and of Archilochus there . . .

Who inscribed you, servant of the Muses, on a stone
      glorifying you, son of Telesicles?
I will tell you quite truthfully, if you do not know.
      Sostheus,[2] son of Prosthenes, a noble man and
not falling short of excellence, has filched my much
      celebrated poetry as his portion of everlasting
      honour.

Ruler of Wisdom[3] . . . Paros.

[2] An abbreviated form of Sosthenes for metrical convenience.
See A. J. Gossage, "The Family of Prosthenes at Paros," *RhM* 94
(1951) 213-21.      [3] Explained by some as denoting an official
position held by Sosthenes.

# IAMBIC POETRY

## Chronology

**5** Tatian. *ad Graecos* 31 (p. 58 Whittaker)

ἕτεροι δὲ κάτω τὸν χρόνον ὑπήγαγον, σὺν Ἀρχιλόχῳ γεγονέναι τὸν Ὅμηρον εἰπόντες· ὁ δὲ Ἀρχίλοχος ἤκμασε περὶ ὀλυμπιάδα τρίτην καὶ εἰκοστήν, κατὰ Γύγην τὸν Λυδόν, ὕστερον τῶν Ἰλιακῶν ἔτεσι πεντακοσίοις.

**6** Proclus ap. Phot. *bibl.* (v.158.27 Henry)

ἰάμβων δὲ ποιηταὶ Ἀρχίλοχός τε ὁ Πάριος ἄριστος καὶ Σιμωνίδης ὁ Ἀμόργιος ἤ, ὡς ἔνιοι, Σάμιος, καὶ Ἱππῶναξ ὁ Ἐφέσιος· ὧν ὁ μὲν πρῶτος ἐπὶ Γύγου, ὁ δὲ ἐπ᾽ Ἀργαίου τοῦ Μακεδόνος, Ἱππῶναξ δὲ κατὰ Δαρεῖον ἤκμαζε.

Ἀργαίου Clinton, Ἀμύντου Sylburg, Ἀνανίου cod.

**7** Hdt. 1.12

. . . Γύγης τοῦ καὶ Ἀρχίλοχος ὁ Πάριος κατὰ τὸν αὐτὸν χρόνον γενόμενος ἐν ἰάμβῳ τριμέτρῳ ἐπεμνήσθη.

34

## Chronology

**5** Tatian, *Address to the Greeks*

Others brought down Homer's date, saying that he was a contemporary of Archilochus. And the latter flourished in about the 23rd Olympiad (688-685),[1] at the time of Gyges[2] the Lydian, 500 years after the Trojan War.

[1] The same dating is given by Syncellus, *chron.* 340 (p. 211.17 Mosshammer), Eusebius, *praep. ev.* 10.11.4 (i.596 Mras), and Cyril, *contra Iulianum* 1.14 (p. 132 Burguière & Évieux), whereas Olympiad 29.1 (664-663) is given by Eusebius ap. Hieron. (p. 94b Helm), and 665-664 in the Armenian version (ii.86 Schöne-Petermann). On the complex chronographic tradition see Moss-hammer pp. 210-17.        [2] Cf. fr. 19 with n. 1.

**6** Proclus in Photius, *Library*

Of the iambic poets Archilochus of Paros was the best, then Semonides of Amorgos or, as some say, of Samos, and Hipponax of Ephesus. The first of these flourished in the time of Gyges, the second in the time of Argaeus[1] of Macedon, and Hipponax in the time of Darius.[2]

[1] Ruled 684-647. See Degani, *Studi* 85 n. 5.        [2] Ruled 522-486.

**7** Herodotus, *Histories*

. . . Gyges whom Archilochus of Paros, a contemporary, mentioned in iambic trimeters.[1]

[1] Some consider everything after Gyges' name a later insertion.

# IAMBIC POETRY

**8** Clem. *Strom.* 1.131.7-8

Ξάνθος δὲ ὁ Λυδὸς (*FGrHist* 765 F 30) περὶ τὴν ὀκτωκαιδεκάτην ὀλυμπιάδα, ὡς δὲ Διονύσιος (*FGrHist* 231 F 3) περὶ τὴν πεντεκαιδεκάτην, Θάσον ἐκτίσθαι, ὡς εἶναι συμφανὲς τὸν Ἀρχίλοχον μετὰ τὴν εἰκοστὴν ἤδη γνωρίζεσθαι ὀλυμπιάδα· μέμνηται γοῦν καὶ τῆς Μαγνήτων ἀπωλείας προσφάτως γεγενημένης. Σιμωνίδης μὲν οὖν κατὰ Ἀρχίλοχον φέρεται, Καλλῖνος δὲ πρεσβύτερος οὐ μακρῷ· τῶν γὰρ Μαγνήτων ὁ μὲν Ἀρχίλοχος ἀπολωλότων, ὁ δὲ εὐημερούντων μέμνηται.

**9** Ps.-Plut. *de musica* 5.1133a

μετὰ δὲ Τέρπανδρον καὶ Κλονᾶν Ἀρχίλοχος παραδίδοται γενέσθαι.

**10** Cic. *Tusc. disp.* 1.1.3

Homerus fuit et Hesiodus ante Romam conditam, Archilochus regnante Romulo.

**8** Clement of Alexandria, *Miscellanies*

Xanthus of Lydia records that Thasos was founded about
the 18th Olympiad (708-705), but about the 15th (720-
717) according to Dionysius,[1] with the result that clearly
Archilochus was already known after the 20th (700-697).
At any rate he mentions the destruction of the Magnesians
as a recent occurrence. Semonides is assigned to the time
of Archilochus, but Callinus is a little older, since he men-
tions the Magnesians as prosperous whereas Archilochus
mentions their destruction.[2]

[1] Presumably Dionysius of Halicarnassus.     [2] See fr. 20
and Strabo ad loc.

**9** Pseudo-Plutarch, *On Music*

Tradition has it that Archilochus came after Terpander[1]
and Clonas.

[1] For the various dates assigned to Terpander see Campbell's
Loeb *Greek Lyric* ii.294-99, and Mosshammer 226-33. In 1132e
ps.-Plutarch cites Glaucus of Rhegium for the same chronolo-
gical relationship between Archilochus and Terpander, whereas
Phaenias of Eresos (fr. 33 Wehrli) makes Terpander younger.

**10** Cicero, *Tusculan Disputations*

Homer and Hesiod lived before the founding of Rome,
Archilochus during the reign of Romulus.[1]

[1] A period of 37 years after about the middle of the 8th century
(Cic. *de re publica* 2.10.17, 2.30.52).

# IAMBIC POETRY

**11** Corn. Nepos ap. Aul. Gell. *Noct. Att.* 17.21.8

Archilochum autem Nepos Cornelius tradit Tullo Hostilio
Romae regnante iam tunc fuisse poematis clarum et no-
bilem.

## Death

**12** *Suda* (i.376.11 Adler) = Aelian. fr. 80 Hercher

ὅτι τῶν σπουδαίων οὐδὲ θανόντων οἱ θεοὶ λήθην τίθεν-
ται. Ἀρχίλοχον γοῦν ποιητὴν γενναῖον τἄλλα, εἴ τις
αὐτοῦ τὸ αἰσχροεπὲς καὶ τὸ κακορρῆμον ἀφέλοι, καὶ
οἱονεὶ κηλίδα ἀπορρύψαι, ὁ Πύθιος ἠλέει τεθνεῶτα καὶ
ταῦτα ἐν τῷ πολέμῳ, ἔνθα δήπου ξυνὸς Ἐνυάλιος. καὶ
ὅτε ἧκεν ὁ ἀποκτείνας αὐτόν, Καλώνδας μὲν ὄνομα,
Κόραξ δὲ ἐπώνυμον, τοῦ θεοῦ δεόμενος ὑπὲρ ὧν ἐδεῖτο,
οὐ προσήκατο αὐτὸν ἡ Πυθία ὡς ἐναγῆ, ἀλλὰ ταῦτα
δήπου τὰ θρυλούμενα ἀνεῖπεν. ὁ δὲ ἄρα προεβάλλετο
τὰς τοῦ πολέμου τύχας καὶ ἔλεγεν, ὡς ἧκεν ἐς
ἀμφίβολον ἢ δρᾶσαι ἢ παθεῖν, ὅσα ἔπραξε, καὶ ἠξίου
μὴ ἀπεχθάνεσθαι τῷ θεῷ εἰ τῷ ἑαυτοῦ δαίμονι ζῇ, καὶ
ἐπηρᾶτο, ὅτι μὴ τέθνηκε μᾶλλον ἢ ἀπέκτεινε. καὶ
ταῦτα ὁ θεὸς οἰκτείρει καὶ αὐτὸν κελεύει ἐλθεῖν εἰς
Ταίναρον, ἔνθα Τέττιξ τέθαπται, καὶ μειλίξασθαι τὴν
τοῦ Τελεσικλείου παιδὸς ψυχὴν καὶ πραῦναι χοαῖς.
οἷς ἐπείσθη, καὶ τῆς μήνιδος τῆς ἐκ τοῦ θεοῦ ἐξάντης
ἐγένετο.

ARCHILOCHUS

**11**  Nepos in Aulus Gellius, *Attic Nights*

Cornelius Nepos records that as early as the reign of Tullus Hostilius[1] at Rome Archilochus was famous and celebrated for his poetry.

[1] Traditionally dated to 673-642.

## Death

**12**  *Suda* = Aelian

Not even in death do the gods forget the good. At any rate Archilochus, a noble poet in other respects if one were to take away his foul mouth and slanderous speech and wash them away like a stain, was pitied by the Pythian after his death, even though this occurred in battle where doubtless the war god is impartial.[1] And when his slayer, named Calondas[2] but with the nickname Corax, came and made certain requests of the god, the Pythia did not give him admittance on the ground that he was polluted and spoke those words which are no doubt common knowledge.[3] But he put forward as a plea the fortunes of war, said that what he had done was a question of kill or be killed, begged that he not incur the god's hatred if he lived according to his own destiny, and cursed himself for not preferring death to killing. And the god took pity on him for this and bade him go to Taenarus where Tettix had been buried and appease the soul of the son of Telesicles and soothe him with libations. He obeyed and became free of the god's anger.

[1] Cf. fr. 110.        [2] Callondes in Plutarch (test. 13).
[3] They are cited by Galen (test. 14).

39

**13** Plut. *de sera num. vind.* 17.560e

ὁ γὰρ ἀποκτείνας ἐν τῇ μάχῃ τὸν Ἀρχίλοχον ἐκαλεῖτο
Καλλώνδης, ὡς ἔοικεν, ἦν δ᾽ αὐτῷ Κόραξ ἐπωνύμιον.
ἐκβληθεὶς δὲ τὸ πρῶτον ὑπὸ τῆς Πυθίας ὡς ἱερὸν
ἄνδρα τῶν Μουσῶν ἀνῃρηκώς, εἶτα χρησάμενος λι-
ταῖς τισι καὶ προστροπαῖς μετὰ δικαιολογίας ἐκε-
λεύσθη πορευθεὶς ἐπὶ τὴν τοῦ Τέττιγος οἴκησιν
ἱλάσασθαι τὴν τοῦ Ἀρχιλόχου ψυχήν. τοῦτο δ᾽ ἦν ὁ
Ταίναρος· ἐκεῖ γάρ φασιν ἐλθόντα μετὰ στόλου Τέτ-
τιγα τὸν Κρῆτα πόλιν κτίσαι καὶ κατοικῆσαι παρὰ τὸ
ψυχοπομπεῖον.

**14** Galen. *protrept.* 9.22 (i.118.3 Marquardt)

ὁ δ᾽ αὐτὸς οὗτος θεὸς καὶ τὸν Ἀρχίλοχον τεθνεῶτα
φαίνεται τιμῶν οὐ τὰ μέτρια. τὸν γοῦν φονέα
βουλόμενον εἰσελθεῖν εἰς τὸν νεὼν αὐτοῦ διεκώλυσεν
εἰπών· "Μουσάων θεράποντα κατέκτανες, ἔξιθι νηοῦ."

**15** Heracl. Lemb. π. πολιτείων (p. 22 Dilts)

Ἀρχίλοχον τὸν ποιητὴν Κόραξ ὄνομα ἔκτεινε, πρὸς
ὅν φασιν εἰπεῖν τὴν Πυθίαν, "ἔξιθι νηοῦ," τοῦτον δ᾽
εἰπεῖν· "ἀλλὰ καθαρός εἰμι, ἄναξ, ἐν χειρῶν γὰρ νόμῳ
ἔκτεινα."

**16** Dio Chrys. 33.11-12

καὶ μὴν ὅσῳ τὸ λοιδορεῖν καὶ τὴν ἀβελτερίαν τὴν

**13** Plutarch, *On the slowness of divine vengeance*

The one who slew Archilochus in the battle was called Callondes, as it seems, but his nickname was Corax. At first he was expelled by the Pythia on the ground that he had killed a man sacred to the Muses, but then after resorting to certain prayers and entreaties together with pleas of justification, he was ordered to go to the dwelling of Tettix and propitiate the soul of Archilochus. This was Taenarus, since they say that Tettix the Cretan came with a fleet and founded a city by the place where souls are conjured up.

**14** Galen, *Exhortation to learning*

This same god clearly holds Archilochus in no moderate honour after his death. At any rate when his slayer wished to enter Apollo's temple, he prevented him with the words: "You killed the servant of the Muses; depart from the temple."

**15** Heraclides Lembus, *On Constitutions*

A man named Corax killed the poet Archilochus and they say that the Pythia said to Corax, "Leave the temple," and that he replied, "But, lord, I am undefiled, since I killed him in hand-to-hand combat."

**16** Dio Chrysostom, *Orations*

And indeed how much better it is to revile and to reveal

IAMBIC POETRY

ἑκάστου καὶ τὴν πονηρίαν φανερὰν ποιεῖν κρεῖττόν
ἐστι τοῦ χαρίζεσθαι διὰ τῶν λόγων καὶ τοῖς ἐγκωμίοις
θρύπτειν τοὺς ἀκούοντας, οὐχ ἥκιστα ἐκεῖθεν εἴσεσθε.
δύο γὰρ ποιητῶν γεγονότων ἐξ ἅπαντος τοῦ αἰῶνος,
οἷς οὐδένα τῶν ἄλλων ξυμβάλλειν ἄξιον, Ὁμήρου τε
καὶ Ἀρχιλόχου, τούτων Ὅμηρος μὲν σχεδὸν πάντα
ἐνεκωμίασε . . . Ἀρχίλοχος δὲ ἐπὶ τὴν ἐναντίαν ἦκε, τὸ
ψέγειν, ὁρῶν, οἶμαι, τούτου μᾶλλον δεομένους τοὺς
ἀνθρώπους, καὶ πρῶτον αὐτὸν ψέγει. τοιγαροῦν μόνος
καὶ μετὰ τὴν τελευτὴν καὶ πρὶν ἢ γενέσθαι τῆς μεγί-
στης ἔτυχε μαρτυρίας παρὰ τοῦ δαιμονίου. τὸν μέν γε
ἀποκτείναντα αὐτὸν ὁ Ἀπόλλων ἐξελαύνων ἐκ τοῦ νεὼ
Μουσῶν αὐτὸν ἀνεῖπε θεράποντα ἀνῃρηκέναι. καὶ τὸ
δεύτερον, ὡς ἀπελογεῖτο ἐν πολέμῳ λέγων ἀποκτεῖναι,
πάλιν Μουσῶν θεράποντα ἔφη τὸν Ἀρχίλοχον. τῷ
πατρὶ δὲ αὐτοῦ χρωμένῳ πρὸ τῆς γενέσεως ἀθάνατόν
οἱ παῖδα γενήσεσθαι προεῖπεν.

**17** Aristides *or.* 46 (ii.380 Dindorf)

οὐδέ γε . . . (scil. Ἀπόλλων) τὸν ἀποκτείναντα Ἀρχί-
λοχον, ὃς τὸ πάντων ἔξοχον καὶ δυσχερέστερον εἶδος
τῆς ποιήσεως μετεχειρίζετο, τοὺς ἰάμβους, ἐξεῖργεν
ἂν τοῦ νεὼ φάσκων οὐκ εἶναι καθαρόν, καὶ ταῦτ' ἐν
πολέμῳ τοῦ φόνου συμβάντος. ἀλλ' ὅμως ἐτίμησε τὸν
Ἀρχίλοχον καὶ Μουσάων γε θεράποντα προσεῖπεν,
ἀλλ' οὐκ ἀνθρώπων διάκονον οὐδενός. οὐ τοίνυν οὐδ'
Ἀρχίλοχος περὶ τὰς βλασφημίας οὕτω διατρίβων

each person's stupidity and baseness than to court favour through one's words and corrupt listeners with praise, you will learn best from what follows. For of the two poets who for all time deserve to be compared with no other, namely Homer and Archilochus, Homer praised nearly everything . . . But Archilochus went to the opposite extreme, to censure, seeing, I suppose, that men are in greater need of this, and first of all he censures himself. Consequently, he alone, both after his death and before his birth, won the highest commendation from heaven. In fact Apollo drove his slayer from the temple, asserting that he had killed a servant of the Muses. And a second time, when the slayer defended himself by stating that he had killed him in war, Apollo again said that Archilochus was a servant of the Muses. And when the father of Archilochus consulted the oracle before his birth, Apollo proclaimed that he would have an immortal son.[1]

[1] Cf. test. 3, col. ii.50.


**17** Aelius Aristides, *Orations*

Nor (if it was a bad thing) would Apollo keep from his temple the slayer of Archilochus who practised a form of poetry that stands out from all others and is rather disagreeable, the lampoon, asserting that his slayer was impure even though the killing took place in war. Nevertheless Apollo honoured Archilochus and called him a servant of the Muses and not in the service of any man. Therefore even Archilochus who was so involved in defamation did not slander the best and most distinguished of the

IAMBIC POETRY

τοὺς ἀρίστους τῶν Ἑλλήνων καὶ τοὺς ἐνδοξοτάτους
ἔλεγε κακῶς, ἀλλὰ Λυκάμβην καὶ Χαρίλαον (Liebel
pro Χειδὸν) καὶ τὸν δεῖνα τὸν μάντιν, καὶ τὸν Περι-
κλέα τὸν καθ᾽ αὑτόν, οὐ τὸν πάνυ, καὶ τοιούτους
ἀνθρώπους ἔλεγε κακῶς.

**18** Oenomaus (pp. 71-72 Hammerstaedt) ap. Euseb.
  *praep. ev.* 5.32.2-33.9

φέρε δὲ τούτοις προσθῶμεν καὶ δι᾽ ὧν αὖθις ὁ Ἀπόλ-
λων θαυμάζει τὸν Ἀρχίλοχον, ἄνδρα παντοίαις κατὰ
γυναικῶν αἰσχρορρημοσύναις καὶ ἀρρητολογίαις, ἃς
οὐδ᾽ ἀκοῦσαί τις σώφρων ἀνὴρ ὑπομείνειεν, ἐν τοῖς
οἰκείοις ποιήμασι κεχρημένον . . . (33.1)

  Ἀθάνατός σοι παῖς καὶ ἀοίδιμος, ὦ Τελεσίκλεις,
  ἔσσετ᾽ ἐν ἀνθρώποις·

ὁ δὲ παῖς ἦν Ἀρχίλοχος . . . (33.5) τί ποτ᾽ οὖν ἦν τοῦτο
δι᾽ ὃ σοι Ἀρχίλοχος ἔδοξεν ἄξιος εἶναι τοῦ οὐρανοῦ;
. . . (33.8) οὐκ ἀπεικότως ἄρα σοι καὶ Μουσῶν
θεράπων ἔδοξεν εἶναι, καὶ ὁ φονεὺς αὐτοῦ οὐκ ἄξιος
εἶναι τῆς πρὸς ὑμᾶς τοὺς θεοὺς εἰσόδου οὐδὲ τῆς παρ᾽
ὑμῶν φωνῆς, ἄνδρα φωνάεντα ἀποκτείνας. οὔκουν
ἄδικος ἡ πρὸς τὸν Ἀρχίαν ἀπειλὴ οὐδ᾽ ἄκαιρος ἡ
Πυθία τιμωροῦσα Ἀρχιλόχῳ τῷ πάλαι νεκρῷ καὶ
κελεύουσα ἐξιέναι τοῦ ναοῦ τὸν ἐναγῆ· "Μουσάων"
γὰρ ἀπέκτεινεν "θεράποντα."

44

Greeks, but he slandered Lycambes, Charilaus,[1] so-and-so the seer,[2] Pericles[3]—his contemporary, not the famous one—and such men.

[1] Cf. frr. 167-171.    [2] Cf. frr. 182 f.    [3] Cf. fr. 16 with note 1.

**18** Oenomaus in Eusebius, *Evangelical Preparation*

Come, let us add to these oracles those in which Apollo again shows his admiration for Archilochus, a man who in his own poems makes use of every kind of foul and unspeakable language against women, language which no man of discretion would even bear to hear . . .

Immortal and renowned in song among men will be your son, Telesicles.[1]

The son was Archilochus . . . What then was it that made Archilochus seem to you to be worthy of heaven? . . .[2] It is not unreasonable then that he seemed to you to be a servant of the Muses and that his slayer was not worthy of entrance to you, the gods, or of hearing your voice, since he had killed a man endowed with voice. Therefore, not unjust was the threat to Archias[3] and not inappropriate the vengeance of the Pythia for Archilochus, long since dead, and the command for the accursed one to leave the temple. For he had killed "the servant of the Muses."

[1] Cf. test. 3, col. ii.50-51.    [2] The first part of fr. 294 belongs here.    [3] Presumably an error for Calondas (test. 12) or Callondes (test. 13), perhaps resulting from confusion with the Archias of fr. 293.

*Lycambes and His Daughters*

**19** P.Dublin inv. 193a (ed. Bond, *Hermathena* 80 [1952] 3-11) = *SH* 997

col. i

εἰς τὰς τοῦ Λυκά]μβεω παρθένους

        ] πρὸς βίην λαλεύσας
        ]εις ὁδῖτα
        Λυκ]άμβεω θύγατρες
5        ]υς λίθος πολίτης
        ]..αμετρ᾽ ἰάμβωι
        α]ψάμεσθα δειρὰς
           ]σηις ἐς ἡμᾶς
           ]σι καὶ γῆ

col. ii

ω[
αφημ[
καὶ λειρίοισι . . .[
περισφυροι . . .[
5  οὐδ᾽ εἴχομε[
αλλημε[
καπνευ[
ηδεν[
εφρον[
10 πραπ[
κοσμ[

*Lycambes and His Daughters*

**19** Dublin papyrus (late 3rd cent. B.C.)

(On the) virgin daughters of Lycambes

### col. i

(Behold the maidens who died?) violently, saying[1] . . . wayfarer . . . daughters of Lycambes . . . country's(?) stone[2] . . . immoderately in iambics . . . we fastened our necks (in nooses?) . . . to (against?) us . . . both (and?) earth[3]

### col. ii[4]

. . . and lily[5] . . . about the ankles[6] . . . and we were not able(?) . . . but one (of us)(?) . . . and lifeless(?) . . . the other(?) . . .[7]

---

[1] The daughters of Lycambes are represented as speaking from the grave (in iambic tetrameters catalectic). [2] Perhaps a way of referring to the Parian marble under which they were buried. [3] Part of an oath? [4] Col. ii is probably part of the same poem. [5] More probably an adjective modifying (e.g.) eyes or voice than a noun. [6] Either a compound adjective or noun, perhaps in the dative plural, or a prepositional phrase. Cf. fr. 206. [7] The beginnings of the last three verses seem to refer to intellect and adornment.

---

i 6 ἄμετρ᾽?     9 μαρτυροῦ]σι Bond
ii 4 περίσφυροι, περισφύροι[σι, περὶ σφυροῖ[σι, περὶ σφύρ᾽ οἱ[
     6 ἀλλ᾽ ἡ μὲ[ν ?     7 κἄπνευ[σεν Bond, κἄπνευ[στος
Peek     8 ἡ δ᾽ ?

# IAMBIC POETRY

**20** *Anth. Pal.* 7.351 = *HE* 1555-64 (Διοσκορίδου)

Οὐ μὰ τόδε φθιμένων σέβας ὅρκιον αἵδε
  Λυκάμβεω,
αἳ λάχομεν στυγερὴν κληδόνα, θυγατέρες
οὔτε τι παρθενίην ᾐσχύναμεν οὔτε τοκῆας
οὔτε Πάρον, νήσων αἰπυτάτην ἱερῶν,
5  ἀλλὰ καθ᾽ ἡμετέρης γενεῆς ῥιγηλὸν ὄνειδος
  φήμην τε στυγερὴν ἔφλυσεν Ἀρχίλοχος.
Ἀρχίλοχον, μὰ θεοὺς καὶ δαίμονας, οὔτ᾽ ἐν
  ἀγυιαῖς
εἴδομεν οὔθ᾽ Ἥρης ἐν μεγάλῳ τεμένει.
εἰ δ᾽ ἦμεν μάχλοι καὶ ἀτάσθαλοι οὐκ ἂν ἐκεῖνος
10  ἤθελεν ἐξ ἡμέων γνήσια τέκνα τεκεῖν.

**21** *Anth. Pal.* 7.352 = *HE* 4742-49 (ἀδέσποτον vel
Μελεάγρου)

Δεξιτερὴν Ἀίδαο θεοῦ χέρα καὶ τὰ κελαινὰ
  ὄμνυμεν ἀρρήτου δέμνια Περσεφόνης,
παρθένοι ὡς ἔτυμον καὶ ὑπὸ χθονί· πολλὰ δ᾽ ὁ
  πικρὸς
αἰσχρὰ καθ᾽ ἡμετέρης ἔβλυσε παρθενίης
5  Ἀρχίλοχος· ἐπέων δὲ καλὴν φάτιν οὐκ ἐπὶ καλὰ
  ἔργα, γυναικεῖον δ᾽ ἔτραπεν ἐς πόλεμον.
Πιερίδες, τί κόρῃσιν ἐφ᾽ ὑβριστῆρας ἰάμβους
  ἐτράπετ᾽, οὐχ ὁσίῳ φωτὶ χαριζόμεναι;

**20** *Palatine Anthology* (Dioscorides)

We here, the daughters of Lycambes who gained a hateful reputation, swear by the reverence in which this tomb of the dead is held that we did not shame our virginity or our parents or Paros, pre-eminent among holy islands, but Archilochus spewed forth frightful reproach and a hateful report against our family. We swear by the gods and spirits that we did not set eyes on Archilochus either in the streets or in Hera's great precinct. If we had been lustful and wicked, he would not have wanted to beget legitimate children from us.

**21** *Palatine Anthology* (anonymous or Meleager)

We swear by the right hand of the god Hades and the dark bed of Persephone whom none may name that we are truly virgins even beneath the earth. But bitter Archilochus spewed forth much that is shameful against our virginity. He turned the fine utterance of his verses to war with women rather than to noble deeds. Muses, why did you direct his violent iambics against girls, favouring an impious man?

# IAMBIC POETRY

**22** *Anth. Pal.* 7.71 = FGE 197-202 (Γαιτουλίχου)

Σῆμα τόδ᾽ Ἀρχιλόχου παραπόντιον, ὅς ποτε
  πικρὴν
Μοῦσαν Ἐχιδναίῳ πρῶτος ἔβαψε χόλῳ,
αἱμάξας Ἑλικῶνα τὸν ἥμερον. οἶδε Λυκάμβης,
μυρόμενος τρισσῶν ἄμματα θυγατέρων.
5  ἠρέμα δὴ παράμειψον, ὁδοιπόρε, μή ποτε τοῦδε
κινήσῃς τύμβῳ σφῆκας ἐφεζομένους.

**23** *Anth. Pal.* 7.69 (Ἰουλιανοῦ)

Κέρβερε, δειμαλέην ὑλακὴν νεκύεσσιν ἰάλλων,
ἤδη φρικαλέον δείδιθι καὶ σὺ νέκυν·
Ἀρχίλοχος τέθνηκε· φυλάσσεο θυμὸν ἰάμβων
δριμύν, πικροχόλου τικτόμενον στόματος.
5  οἶσθα βοῆς κείνοιο μέγα σθένος, εὖτε Λυκάμβεω
νηῦς μία σοι δισσὰς ἤγαγε θυγατέρας.

**24** Eust. in Hom. *Od.* 11.277 (1684.45)

ἰστέον δὲ ὅτι πολλῶν προσώπων ἁψαμένων βρόχους
ἐπὶ λύπαις ἔπαθον οὕτω κατὰ τὴν παλαιὰν ἱστορίαν
καὶ αἱ Λυκαμβίδαι ἐπὶ τοῖς Ἀρχιλόχου ποιήμασι, μὴ
φέρουσαι τὴν ἐπιφορὰν τῶν ἐκείνου σκωμμάτων· ἦν
γὰρ ὁ ἀνὴρ δεινὸς ὑβρίζειν· ὅθεν καὶ παροιμία ἐπὶ
τῶν οὕτω σκώπτειν εὐφυῶν τό, Ἀρχίλοχον πεπάτηκας,
ὡς εἴ τις εἴπῃ, σκορπίον ἢ ὄφιν ἢ κακὴν ἄκανθαν.

**22** *Palatine Anthology* (Gaetulicus)

This tomb beside the sea belongs to Archilochus who was the first to dip a bitter Muse in Echidna's gall and to stain mild Helicon with blood. Lycambes attests to it, bewailing the hanging of his three[1] daughters. Wayfarer, pass by quietly, lest you stir up the wasps that settle on his tomb.

[1] The only source to record three daughters. Cf. test. 23.

**23** *Palatine Anthology* (Julian, Prefect of Egypt)

Cerberus, whose barking strikes the shades with terror, now even you must fear a horrifying shade: Archilochus is dead. Be on your guard against the pungent iambic wrath engendered by the bitter anger of his tongue. You know the mighty potency of his outbursts, since a single boat brought Lycambes' two daughters.

**24** Eustathius on Homer, *Odyssey*

It should be recognized that many people have hanged themselves out of grief and that according to the ancient account the daughters of Lycambes did so because of Archilochus' poetry, since they could not bear the onslaught of his gibes. For the man was skilful at insulting, and hence "you have stepped on Archilochus" is a proverb with reference to those who are adept at such gibes, as if one were to say that you have stepped on a scorpion or snake or painful thorn.

**25**  Hor. *epod.* 6.11-14

cave cave, namque in malos asperrimus
  parata tollo cornua,
qualis Lycambae spretus infido gener
  aut acer hostis Bupalo.

**26**  Pseudacronis schol. ad loc. (i.404 Keller)

Lycambes habuit filiam Neobulen. hanc cum Archilochus
in matrimonium postulasset, promissa nec data est a patre.
hinc iratus Archilochus in eum maledicum carmen scrip-
sit; quo tanto est dolore compulsus ut cum filia vitam la-
queo finiret.

  Lycambes filiam suam promisit Archilocho daturum
uxorem, quod postea denegavit. qua de causa iratus Archi-
lochus carmina scripsit in Lycamben et eius filias, ita ut ex
dolore carminum eius filiae laqueo vitam finirent.

**27**  Hor. *epist.* 1.19.23-31

            Parios ego primus iambos
      ostendi Latio, numeros animosque secutus
25    Archilochi, non res et agentia verba Lycamben.
      ac ne me foliis ideo brevioribus ornes,
      quod timui mutare modos et carminis artem,
      temperat Archilochi Musam pede mascula Sappho,
      temperat Alcaeus, sed rebus et ordine dispar,

**25** Horace, *Epodes*

Beware, beware, for with the utmost ferocity I lift my ready horns against evildoers, just like the scorned son-in-law of treacherous Lycambes or the impassioned enemy[1] of Bupalus.

[1] Hipponax.

**26** Pseudo-Acron on the passage

Lycambes had a daughter Neoboule. When Archilochus sought her hand in marriage, she was promised by her father but not given to him. In anger at this Archilochus wrote an abusive poem against him and the latter was so grief-stricken that he hanged himself along with his daughter.

Lycambes promised to give Archilochus his daughter as wife and afterwards refused. Because of this Archilochus in anger wrote poems against Lycambes and his daughters, as a result of which his daughters in grief hanged themselves.

**27** Horace, *Epistles*

I was the first to show Latium the iambics of Paros, following the rhythms and spirit of Archilochus, but not the subject matter and words that assailed Lycambes. And lest you adorn me with a scantier wreath because I was afraid to change the measures and verse form, manly[1] Sappho shapes her Muse by the rhythm of Archilochus, as does Alcaeus, though his subject matter and arrangement are different, since he does not seek a father-in-law to smear

30      nec socerum quaerit, quem versibus oblinat atris
        nec sponsae laqueum famoso carmine nectit.

**28**  Ov. *Ibis* 53-54

        postmodo, si perges, in te mihi liber iambus
            tincta Lycambeo sanguine tela dabit.

**29**  Schol. C ad loc. (p. 10 La Penna)

Lycambes Neobulen, filiam suam, Archilocho desponsavit
et dotem promisit; quam quia postea negavit, Archilochus
in iambico metro invectivam in ipsum fecit et tam turpia
de eo dixit quod ipsum et uxorem et filiam ad laqueos coe-
git: maluerunt enim mori quam sub turpibus obprobriis
vivere.

**30**  Ov. *Ibis* 521-24

        utque repertori nocuit pugnacis iambi,
            sic sit in exitium lingua proterva tuum.
        utque parum stabili qui carmine laesit Athenin
            invisus pereas deficiente cibo.

        523 Athenas codd., corr. Alciatus

**31**  Schol. ad loc. (pp. 156 sq. La Penna)

Archilochus propter filiam Hipponactis Lycambi datam,
quam antea desponsaverat ipsi Archilocho, commotus ad
iram composuit in eum, scilicet Lycamben, invectiones

with malevolent verses nor does he weave a noose for his bride-to-be with defaming poetry.

[1] See Sappho test. 17 (Campbell).

**28** Ovid, *Ibis*

Afterwards, if you continue, my unrestrained iambics will launch against you shafts tinged with the blood of Lycambes.

**29** Scholia on the passage

Lycambes betrothed his daughter Neoboule to Archilochus and promised a dowry. Because afterwards he refused, Archilochus abused him in the iambic meter and said such vile things about him that he forced him, his wife, and his daughter to hang themselves; for they preferred to die rather than live subjected to vile reproaches.

**30** Ovid, *Ibis*

And as it harmed the inventor of the combative iambus, so may a violent tongue bring about your death. And like him who injured Athenis[1] with his halting verses, may you perish, hated and starved.

[1] Hipponax's enemy.

**31** Scholia on the passage

Because the daughter of Hipponax whom he had previously betrothed to Archilochus had been given to Lycambes,[1] Archilochus was moved by anger to compose invective in the iambic meter against him, i.e., Lycambes, and

iambico metro scriptas, quibus eum coegit ad mortem . . .
postea autem lingua sua sibi fuit in exitium.

Archilochus, iamborum inventor, postquam Lycamben
coegerat ad suspendium, ab amicis eius persecutus, se ip-
sum interfecit.

Archilochus, inventor iambi, propter linguae suae pra-
vitatem, missus est in exilium.

Archilochus ab inimicis suis interfectus fuit, quia fecit
contra eos invectiones iambico metro.

**32**  Mart. 7.12.5-8

quid prodest, cupiant cum quidam nostra videri,
    si qua Lycambeo sanguine tela madent,
vipereumque vomat nostro sub nomen virus,
    qui Phoebi radios ferre diemque negat?

### The Verdict of Antiquity

**33**  Critias 88 B 44 D.-K. ap. Aelian. *V.H.* 10.13 (= fr.
    295 West)

αἰτιᾶται Κριτίας Ἀρχίλοχον ὅτι κάκιστα ἑαυτὸν εἶπεν.
εἰ γὰρ μή, φησίν, ἐκεῖνος τοιαύτην δόξαν ὑπὲρ ἑαυτοῦ
ἐς τοὺς Ἕλληνας ἐξήνεγκεν, οὐκ ἂν ἐπυθόμεθα ἡμεῖς
οὔτε ὅτι Ἐνιποῦς υἱὸς ἦν τῆς δούλης, οὔθ᾽ ὅτι κατα-
λιπὼν Πάρον διὰ πενίαν καὶ ἀπορίαν ἦλθεν ἐς Θάσον,
οὔθ᾽ ὅτι ἐλθὼν τοῖς ἐνταῦθα ἐχθρὸς ἐγένετο, οὐδὲ μὴν
ὅτι ὁμοίως τοὺς φίλους καὶ τοὺς ἐχθροὺς κακῶς ἔλεγε.

this drove him to death . . . Afterwards, however, Archilochus' own tongue destroyed him.

After Archilochus, the inventor of iambics, forced Lycambes to hang himself, he was pursued by the latter's friends and killed himself.

Because of his vicious tongue Archilochus, the inventor of iambics, was sent into exile.

Archilochus was killed by his enemies, because he composed invective in the iambic meter against them.

1 A highly garbled version. See Degani, *Studi* 107 n. 175.

## 32 Martial, *Epigrams*

What does it avail me when certain people wish to pass off as mine whatever shafts drip with the blood of Lycambes, and one who admits that he cannot stand the rays of the sun and the light of day spews forth his viper's venom under my name?

### *The Verdict of Antiquity*

## 33 Critias in Aelian, *Historical Miscellanies*

Critias censures Archilochus because he spoke very ill of himself.[1] For if, he says, Archilochus had not made public among the Greeks such an opinion of himself, we should not have learned that he was the son of Enipo, a slave-woman,[2] that because of poverty and difficult straits he left Paros and went to Thasos, that upon his arrival he became an enemy of the inhabitants, and in addition that he spoke ill of friends and enemies alike.[3] And furthermore, he says,

πρὸς δὲ τούτοις, ἦ δ' ὅς, οὔτε ὅτι μοιχὸς ἦν ᾔδειμεν ἄν,
εἰ μὴ παρ' αὐτοῦ μαθόντες, οὔτε ὅτι λάγνος καὶ
ὑβριστής, καὶ τὸ ἔτι τούτων αἴσχιον, ὅτι τὴν ἀσπίδα
ἀπέβαλεν. οὐκ ἀγαθὸς ἄρα ἦν ὁ Ἀρχίλοχος μάρτυς
ἑαυτῷ τοιοῦτον κλέος ἀπολιπὼν καὶ τοιαύτην ἑαυτῷ
φημήν. ταῦτα οὐκ ἐγὼ Ἀρχίλοχον αἰτιῶμαι, ἀλλὰ
Κριτίας.

**34**  Heraclitus 22 B 42 D.-K. ap. D.L. 9.1

τόν τε Ὅμηρον ἔφασκεν ἄξιον ἐκ τῶν ἀγώνων ἐκ-
βάλλεσθαι καὶ ῥαπίζεσθαι καὶ Ἀρχίλοχον ὁμοίως.

**35**  Pind. *Pyth.* 2.52-56

       ἐμὲ δὲ χρεὼν
φεύγειν δάκος ἀδινὸν κακαγοριᾶν.
εἶδον γὰρ ἑκὰς ἐὼν τὰ πόλλ' ἐν ἀμαχανίᾳ
ψογερὸν Ἀρχίλοχον βαρυλόγοις ἔχθεσιν
πιαινόμενον·

**36**  Callim. fr. 380 Pf.

 εἵλκυσε δὲ δριμύν τε χόλον κυνὸς ὀξύ τε κέντρον
  σφηκός, ἀπ' ἀμφοτέρων δ' ἰὸν ἔχει στόματος.

we should not have known that he was an adulterer, if we had not learned it from him, nor that he was lecherous and arrogant, nor what is still more shameful than this, that he threw away his shield.[4] Therefore, by leaving behind such a report and such an account of himself Archilochus was not a good witness on his own behalf. It is Critias who censures him for this, not I.

[1] Cf. test. 16.     [2] This statement, along with at least some of those that follow, is very probably an erroneous deduction based on a faulty understanding of Archilochus' poetry.
[3] Among his friends we should presumably number Pericles (cf. fr. 16 with n. 1) and Glaucus (cf. fr. 15 with n. 1); the most obvious enemy is Lycambes.     [4] Cf. fr. 5.

**34**  Heraclitus in Diogenes Laertius, *Lives of the Philosophers*

He said that Homer deserved to be banished from the contests and flogged, and Archilochus likewise.

**35**  Pindar, *Pythians*

But I must shun the deep bite of slander. For at a far remove I have seen fault-finding Archilochus many times in his helplessness fattening himself on harsh words of hatred.

**36**  Callimachus

Archilochus drew in (?) the dog's pungent bile and the wasp's sharp sting, and he has his mouth's venom from both.

59

# IAMBIC POETRY

**37** Theocr. *epig.* 21 Gow = *HE* 3434-39 (*Anth. Pal.* 7.664)

Ἀρχίλοχον καὶ στᾶθι καὶ εἴσιδε τὸν πάλαι ποιητὰν
τὸν τῶν ἰάμβων, οὗ τὸ μυρίον κλέος
διῆλθε κἠπὶ νύκτα καὶ ποτ' ἀῶ.
ἦ ῥά νιν αἱ Μοῦσαι καὶ ὁ Δάλιος ἠγάπευν
  Ἀπόλλων,
5    ὡς ἐμμελής τ' ἐγένετο κἠπιδέξιος
ἔπεά τε ποιεῖν πρὸς λύραν τ' ἀείδειν.

**38** "Long." *de subl.* 13.3

μόνος Ἡρόδοτος Ὁμηρικώτατος ἐγένετο; Στησίχορος
ἔτι πρότερον ὅ τε Ἀρχίλοχος, πάντων δὲ τούτων
μάλιστα ὁ Πλάτων . . .

**39** "Long." *de subl.* 33.5

Ἐρατοσθένης ἐν τῇ Ἠριγόνῃ (διὰ πάντων γὰρ ἀμώ-
μητον τὸ ποιημάτιον) Ἀρχιλόχου πολλὰ καὶ ἀνοι-
κονόμητα παρασύροντος, κἀκείνης τῆς ἐκβολῆς τοῦ
δαιμονίου πνεύματος ἣν ὑπὸ νόμον τάξαι δύσκολον,
ἆρα δὴ μείζων ποιητής;

**37**  Theocritus, *Epigrams*

Stop and look upon Archilochus, the iambic poet of old, whose vast fame has spread from the sun's rising to its setting. In truth the Muses and Delian Apollo loved him, so musical was he and skilful in composing verses and singing them to the lyre.[1]

1 Cf. also *Anth. Pal.* 4.1.37-38 and 9.185.

**38**  "Longinus," *On Sublimity*

Was Herodotus alone the most Homeric? No, earlier still there were Stesichorus and Archilochus,[1] and more Homeric than any of these was Plato . . .

1 The author may be thinking of such passages as frr. 131 and 134 which are closely modeled on Homer. Cf. also frr. 219-221. Comparisons between Homer and Archilochus are implied by testt. 16, 34, 41, 63. Cf. also *Anth. Pal.* 7.674 and 11.20.

**39**  "Longinus," *On Sublimity*

Was Eratosthenes, whose little poem *Erigone* is absolutely faultless, a superior poet to Archilochus who sweeps along much that is ill-arranged in that outpouring of the divine spirit which with difficulty is made subordinate to the rule of law?[1]

1 On the passage as a whole see D. A. Russell's edition of "Longinus" (pp. 158 f.).

# IAMBIC POETRY

**40** Plut. *de curiositate* 10.520a-b

φέρε γάρ, εἴ τις ἐπιὼν τὰ συγγράμματα τῶν παλαιῶν ἐκλαμβάνοι τὰ κάκιστα τῶν ἐν αὐτοῖς, καὶ βιβλίον ἔχοι συντεταγμένον, οἷον Ὁμηρικῶν στίχων ἀκεφάλων καὶ τραγικῶν σολοικισμῶν καὶ τῶν ὑπ᾽ Ἀρχιλόχου πρὸς τὰς γυναῖκας ἀπρεπῶς καὶ ἀκολάστως εἰρημένων, ἑαυτὸν παραδειγματίζοντος, ἆρ᾽ οὐκ ἔστι τῆς τραγικῆς κατάρας ἄξιος, "ὄλοιο θνητῶν ἐκλέγων τὰς συμφοράς;" (fr. adesp. trag. 388 K.-S.)

**41** Philostr. VS 6.620 (ii.119 Kayser)

ἐσπούδαζε δὲ καὶ ἀπὸ Ἀρχιλόχου καλῶν τὸν μὲν Ὅμηρον φωνὴν σοφιστῶν, τὸν δὲ Ἀρχίλοχον πνεῦμα.

**42** Orig. *c. Celsum* 3.25 (ii.58.15 Borret)

καὶ ἐν τοῖς χρησμοῖς δὲ τοῦ Πυθίου εὕροις ἂν προστασσόμενά τινα οὐκ εὔλογα. ὧν δύο ἐπὶ τοῦ παρόντος παραθήσομαι . . . ἀλλὰ καὶ Μουσῶν θεράποντα εἰπὼν τὸν Ἀρχίλοχον, ἄνδρα ἐν κακίστῃ καὶ ἀσελγεστάτῃ ὑποθέσει ἐπιδειξάμενον τὴν ἑαυτοῦ ποιητικὴν καὶ ἦθος ἀσελγὲς καὶ ἀκάθαρτον παραστήσαντα, ὅσον ἐπὶ τῷ θεράποντα εἶναι Μουσῶν, νομιζομένων εἶναι θεῶν, εὐσεβῆ τινα ἀνηγόρευσεν. οὐκ οἶδα δὲ εἰ καὶ ὁ τυχὼν τὸν εὐσεβῆ φήσει μὴ πάσῃ κεκοσμῆσθαι μετριότητι καὶ ἀρετῇ, καὶ κόσμιος τοιαῦτα λέγοι ἄν, ὁποῖα περιέχουσιν οἱ μὴ σεμνοὶ τοῦ Ἀρχιλόχου ἴαμβοι.

**40** Plutarch, *On being a busybody*

Come now, if someone were to go through the writings of the ancients, pick out the worst that is in them and compile a book, for example, of Homer's headless verses and solecisms in tragedy and the unseemly and lewd utterances directed towards women whereby Archilochus makes a spectacle of himself, is he not deserving of the curse found in a tragedy, "May you be damned for singling out the misfortunes of mortals"?

**41** Philostratus, *Lives of the Sophists*

He (sc. Hippodromus[1]) was also a serious student of Archilochus, calling Homer the voice of the sophists, but Archilochus their breath.

[1] A sophist active from the latter part of the 2nd cent. A.D. to the early part of the 3rd.

**42** Origen, *Against Celsus*

And even among the oracles of the Pythian you can find some injunctions that are not reasonable. For the present I shall cite two of them . . . But also by calling Archilochus a servant of the Muses, a man who displayed his poetic skill in a subject matter that is extremely base and lewd and who revealed a character that is licentious and impure, in so far as he was a servant of the Muses, who are judged to be goddesses, Apollo proclaimed him to be a man of piety. I do not know whether the common person will say that the man of piety is not adorned with every moderation and virtue and whether a decent person would speak such things as the irreverent iambics of Archilochus encompass.

**43** Iulian. Imp. *or.* 7.207b-c

ὁ δὲ μετὰ τοῦτον Ἀρχίλοχος ὥσπερ ἥδυσμά τι περι-
τιθεὶς τῇ ποιήσει, μύθοις ‹οὐκ› ὀλιγάκις ἐχρήσατο
ὁρῶν, ὡς εἰκός, τὴν μὲν ὑπόθεσιν, ἣν μετῄει, τῆς
τοιαύτης ψυχαγωγίας ἐνδεῶς ἔχουσαν, σαφῶς δὲ
ἐγνωκὼς ὅτι στερομένη μύθου ποίησις ἐποποιία μόνον
ἐστίν, ἐστέρηται δέ, ὡς ἂν εἴποι τις, ἑαυτῆς· οὐ γὰρ
ἔτι λείπεται ποίησις· ἡδύσματα ταῦτα παρὰ τῆς ποιη-
τικῆς Μούσης ἐδρέψατο, καὶ παρέθηκέ γε αὐτὸς
τούτου χάριν, ὅπως μὴ σιλλογράφος τις, ἀλλὰ ποιη-
τὴς νομισθείη.

**44** Philostr. *imag.* 1.3 (ii.298 Kayser)

φοιτῶσιν οἱ μῦθοι παρὰ τὸν Αἴσωπον, ἀγαπῶντες
αὐτὸν ὅτι αὐτῶν ἐπιμελεῖται. ἐμέλησε μὲν γὰρ καὶ
Ὁμήρῳ μύθου καὶ Ἡσιόδῳ, ἔτι δὲ καὶ Ἀρχιλόχῳ πρὸς
Λυκάμβην· ἀλλ’ Αἰσώπῳ πάντα τὰ τῶν ἀνθρώπων
ἐκμεμύθωται.

**45** Quint. *inst. orat.* 10.1.60

summa in hoc vis elocutionis, cum validae tum breves
vibrantesque sententiae, plurimum sanguinis atque ner-
vorum, adeo ut videatur quibusdam, quod quoquam mi-
nor est, materiae esse non ingenii vitium.

**43** The Emperor Julian, *Speeches*

And Archilochus after him (sc. Hesiod) not infrequently made use of fables, putting a seasoning as it were round his poetry, because he presumably saw that the subject matter which he was pursuing needed such an attractiveness and because he knew clearly that poetry deprived of fable is merely versification and lacks, one might say, its real self, since poetry no longer remains. He culled these seasonings from his poetic Muse and served them up himself in order that he might be deemed a poet, not some writer of lampoons.

**44** Philostratus, *Pictures*

Fables gather about Aesop, loving him because he is devoted to them. For although both Homer and Hesiod took an interest in fable, and Archilochus as well in his verses against Lycambes, Aesop has put into his fables all aspects of human life.

**45** Quintilian, *Principles of Oratory*

We find in him (sc. Archilochus) the greatest force of expression, sententious statements that are not only vigorous but also terse and vibrant, and a great abundance of vitality and energy, to the extent that in the view of some his inferiority to anyone results from a defect of subject matter rather than poetic genius.

# IAMBIC POETRY

**46** Val. Max. 6.3, ext. 1 (p. 291 Kempf)

Lacedaemonii libros Archilochi e civitate sua exportari
iusserunt, quod eorum parum verecundam ac pudicam
lectionem arbitrabantur: noluerunt enim ea liberorum
suorum animos imbui, ne plus moribus noceret quam
ingeniis prodesset. itaque maximum poetam, aut certe
summo proximum, quia domum sibi invisam obscenis
maledictis laceraverat, carminum exilio multarunt.

*Meter*

**47** Ps.-Plut. *de musica* 28.1140f-1141b (p. 124 Lasserre)

ἀλλὰ μὴν καὶ Ἀρχίλοχος τὴν τῶν τριμέτρων ῥυθμο-
ποιίαν προσεξεῦρε καὶ τὸν εἰς τοὺς οὐχ ὁμογενεῖς
ῥυθμοὺς ἔντασιν καὶ τὴν παρακαταλογὴν καὶ τὴν
περὶ ταῦτα κροῦσιν. πρώτῳ δ᾽ αὐτῷ τά τ᾽ ἐπῳδὰ
καὶ τὰ τετράμετρα καὶ τὸ κρητικὸν καὶ τὸ προσο-
διακὸν ἀποδέδοται, καὶ ἡ τοῦ ἡρῴου αὔξησις, ὑπ᾽
ἐνίων δὲ καὶ τὸ ἐλεγεῖον· πρὸς δὲ τούτοις ἥ τε τοῦ
ἰαμβείου πρὸς τὸν ἐπιβατὸν παίωνα ἔντασις καὶ ἡ τοῦ
ηὐξημένου ἡρῴου εἴς τε τὸ προσοδιακὸν καὶ τὸ
κρητικόν. ἔτι δὲ τῶν ἰαμβείων τὸ τὰ μὲν λέγεσθαι
παρὰ τὴν κροῦσιν τὰ δ᾽ ᾄδεσθαι Ἀρχίλοχόν φασι
καταδεῖξαι, εἶθ᾽ οὕτω χρήσασθαι τοὺς τραγικοὺς
ποιητάς. Κρέξον δὲ λαβόντα εἰς διθύραμβον ἀγαγεῖν.
οἴονται δὲ καὶ τὴν κροῦσιν τὴν ὑπὸ τὴν ᾠδὴν τοῦτον

66

**46** Valerius Maximus, *Memorable Deeds and Sayings*

The Spartans ordered the works of Archilochus to be removed from their state, since they believed that their text was shameful and indecent.[1] They did not want the minds of their children to be defiled by it, lest it harm their morals more than it benefited their talents. Accordingly, by banishing his poetry they punished the best of poets, or at least the next to best, because he had ripped to shreds with foul abuse a house hateful to him.

[1] Cf. Plutarch's introduction to fr. 5.

*Meter*

**47** Pseudo-Plutarch, *On Music*

Furthermore, Archilochus in addition devised the rhythmical pattern of the (iambic) trimeter, combinations involving heterogeneous rhythms, recitative, and the instrumental music associated with this. And he is the first to be credited with epodes, (trochaic) tetrameters, the cretic, the prosodiac, and the augmented heroic verse, and according to some the elegiac couplet as well,[1] and in addition the combination of iambic verse with the epibatic paeon and that of the augmented heroic verse with the prosodiac and the cretic. Furthermore, they say that Archilochus introduced the practice whereby some iambics were spoken to musical accompaniment and others sung, and that afterwards the tragic poets made use of this procedure, as did Crexus who took it over and applied it to the dithyramb. And it is also thought that Archilochus was the first to invent musical accompaniment that is under the

IAMBIC POETRY

εὑρεῖν, τοὺς δ' ἀρχαίους πάντας πρόσχορδα κρούειν.

**48** Orion *etym*. s.v. ἔλεγος (col. 58.8 Sturz)

εὑρετὴ‹ν› δὲ τοῦ ἐλεγείου οἱ μὲν τὸν Ἀρχίλοχον, οἱ δὲ Μίμνερμον, οἱ δὲ Καλλῖνον παλαιότερον.

**49** Hermog. π. ἰδεῶν (p. 319.23 Rabe)

ὁ δὲ Ἀρχίλοχος αὐτὸ καὶ σαφέστερον ἐποίησε καὶ γοργότερον· οἱ γὰρ τετράμετροι αὐτῷ διὰ τοῦτ' οἶμαι καὶ γοργότεροι καὶ λογοειδέστεροι τῶν ἄλλων εἶναι δοκοῦσι, διότι τροχαϊκῶς σύγκεινται· τρέχει γὰρ ὡς ὄντως ἐν τούτοις ὁ ῥυθμός.

**50** Mar. Vict. (= Aphthonius), *Gramm. Lat.* vi.104.7 Keil

nam perfecto poetae levia et sonora sectanda sunt; quae autem fragosa et aspera, dicis causa, non ut imitentur, sed ut vitentur, noscenda sunt. quorum, sicut et aliorum complurium, auctor et parens fertur Archilochus singularis artificii in excogitandis ac formandis novis metris, qui primus epodos excitavit alios breviores, alios longiores, detrahens unum pedem seu colum metro, ut illi subiceret id quod ex ipso detractum esse videbatur.

melody, whereas all the earlier poets used musical accompaniment in unison with the voice.[2]

[1] See Orion below.  [2] For the terminology used throughout this passage see A. Barker, *Greek Musical Writings* I (Cambridge 1984) 234 f.

## 48 Orion, *Lexicon*

Some say that the elegiac couplet originated with Archilochus, others with Mimnermus, and others with Callinus at an earlier time.

## 49 Hermogenes, *On Types of Style*

Archilochus demonstrated this (sc. the effect of trochees) even more clearly and more rapidly. His tetrameters in my opinion seem to be more rapid and more prosaic than those of others because they are composed of trochees; for the rhythm literally runs in these verses.

## 50 Marius Victorinus (= Aphthonius), *Grammar*

For a consummate poet the metrical breaks should be smooth and melodious; those which are uneven and harsh should be learned for the sake of form, not so that they might be imitated but so that they might be avoided. The originator and parent of the latter, as of several others also, is said to have been Archilochus, who had a unique talent for devising and forming new meters and who was the first to construct epodes, some shorter, some longer, withdrawing one foot or colon from the meter, so that what seemed to be withdrawn from it might be placed underneath.[1]

[1] The source then cites Hor. *Odes* 4.7.1-2 as an example.

**51-60**

*The grammarians record a variety of meters used by Archilochus. For what follows I restrict myself to citing the sources and to providing the metrical patterns attested therein. See also the meters prefixed to frr. 168-171, 172-181, 182-187, 188-192, 193-194, 195, 196-196a, 197. Additional metrical testimonia can be found in Tarditi pp. 212-16.*

**51** Terent. Maur., *Gramm. Lat.* vi.379.1801-1808 Keil

**52** Diom., *Gramm. Lat.* i.516.13 Keil

**53** Mar. Vict. (= Aphthonius), *Gramm. Lat.* vi.122.23 Keil

**54** Id., vi.142.31

**55** Id., vi.143.3

**56** Id., vi.143.5

**57** Diom., *Gramm. Lat.* i.509.3 Keil

**51** Terentianus Maurus, *On Meters* (= fr. 198 West)

–∪∪ –∪∪ –∪∪ –∪∪ –∪∪ ––
    –∪∪ –∪∪ –[1]

[1] The meter of Hor. *Odes* 4.7.

**52** Diomedes, *Grammar* (= fr. 199 West)

×–∪–×–∪–|–∪∪ –∪∪ –[1]

[1] The meter of Hor. *Epod.* 13.2, where a dactylic hexameter precedes.

**53** Marius Victorinus (= Aphthonius), *Grammar* (= fr. 314 West)

– $\overline{∪∪}$ – $\overline{∪∪}$ – $\overline{∪∪}$ – ∪∪ –∪ –∪–

**54** The same (= fr. 315 West)

∪∪ –∪∪ –|–∪ –∪ ––

**55** The same (= fr. 316 West)

×–∪ – |–∪∪–

**56** The same (= fr. 317 West)

∪∪ –∪∪ –∪∪ –∪∪ – |×–∪ –∪ ––

**57** Diomedes, *Grammar* (= fr. 318 West)

–∪∪ –∪ ––[1]

[1] The meter of Hor. *Odes* 1.8.1.

**58**  Id., i.510.11

**59**  Id. (ex Varrone), i.515.14

**60**  Id., i.516.4

## Miscellaneous

**61**  Diphilus (fr. 71 K.-A.) ap. Ath. 13.599d

Δίφιλος ὁ κωμῳδιοποιὸς πεποίηκεν ἐν Σαπφοῖ δρά-
ματι Σαπφοῦς ἐραστὰς Ἀρχίλοχον καὶ Ἱππώνακτα.

**62**  Callim. (fr. 544 Pf.) ap. Eust. in Hom. *Il.* 6.135
(ii.262.2 V.d.Valk)

τοῦ ‹∪› μεθυπλῆγος φροίμιον Ἀρχιλόχου

Ἀντιλόχου Eust., corr. Ruhnken

**63**  Heracl. Pont. (fr. 178 Wehrli) ap. D. L. 5.87

. . . Περὶ Ἀρχιλόχου καὶ Ὁμήρου α′β′.

**58** The same (= fr. 319 West)

‒‒‒∪∪‒|‒∪∪‒|‒∪∪ ‒∪ ‒[1]

> [1] The meter of Hor. *Odes* 1.18.

**59** The same (= fr. 320 West)

‒∪∪ ‒∪∪ ‒∪∪ ‒

**60** The same (= fr. 321 West)

‒‒∪∪ ‒‒

## *Miscellaneous*

**61** Diphilus in Athenaeus, *Scholars at Dinner*

The comic poet Diphilus in his play *Sappho* represented Archilochus and Hipponax as lovers of Sappho.

**62** Callimachus in Eustathius on Homer, *Iliad*

the prelude of Archilochus smitten with wine[1]

> [1] Cf. fr. 120.

**63** Heraclides Ponticus in Diogenes Laertius, *Lives of the Philosophers:* Diogenes lists among the writings of Heraclides a work entitled

On Archilochus and Homer, in two books.

**64** Hesychii Milesii vita Aristotelis (p. 16 Rose, 87 Düring)

Ἀπορήματα Ἀρχιλόχου Εὐριπίδου Χοιρίλου ἐν βιβλίοις γ΄.

**65** Paus. 10.28.3

Τέλλις μὲν ἡλικίαν ἐφήβου γεγονὼς φαίνεται, Κλεό-βοια δὲ ἔτι παρθένος, ἔχει δὲ ἐν τοῖς γόνασι κιβωτὸν ὁποίας ποιεῖσθαι νομίζουσι Δήμητρι. ἐς μὲν δὴ τὸν Τέλλιν τοσοῦτον ἤκουσα ὡς ὁ ποιητὴς Ἀρχίλοχος ἀπόγονος εἴη τρίτος Τέλλιδος, Κλεόβοιαν δὲ ἐς Θάσον τὰ ὄργια τῆς Δήμητρος ἐνεγκεῖν πρώτην ἐκ Πάρου φασίν.

**66** Steph. Byz. s.v. Θάσος (p. 303 Meineke)

ὅτι δὲ καὶ Ἀερία ἡ Θάσος, δῆλον ἐκ τοῦ χρησμοῦ τοῦ δοθέντος πατρὶ τοῦ Ἀρχιλόχου·

ἄγγειλον Παρίοις, Τελεσίκλεες, ὥς σε κελεύω νήσῳ ἐν Ἠερίῃ κτίζειν εὐδείελον ἄστυ.

**67** Ath. 14.620c

Χαμαιλέων δὲ ἐν τῷ περὶ Στησιχόρου (fr. 28 Wehrli)

**64** Hesychius of Miletus, *Life of Aristotle*

Problems in Archilochus, Euripides, and Choerilus in three books.[1]

[1] The list of Aristotle's writings given by Diogenes Laertius does not include this work. Both Apollonius Rhodius (Athenaeus 10.451c) and Aristophanes of Byzantium (fr. 367 Slater) wrote on the "grieving message-stick" of fr. 185.2. See Slater's edition of Aristophanes (pp. 132 f.). Aristarchus (Clem. *Strom.* 1.21.117) wrote a commentary on Archilochus.

**65** Pausanias, *Description of Greece*

Tellis appears to be in his late teens, Cleoboea as still a girl and she has on her knees a chest of the sort that they are accustomed to make for Demeter. With regard to Tellis I heard only that he was the grandfather of Archilochus and they say that Cleoboea was the first to introduce the rites of Demeter to Thasos from Paros.[1]

[1] Pausanias is describing a painting by Polygnotus, part of which depicts Tellis and Cleoboea on Charon's boat.

**66** Stephanus of Byzantium, *Lexicon of Place Names*

It is clear from the oracle given to Archilochus' father that Thasos was also called Aeria:
> Announce to the Parians, Telesicles, that I bid you found a conspicuous city in the island Eeria.[1]

[1] The same oracle is recorded in Euseb. *praep. ev.* 6.7.8.

**67** Athenaeus, *Scholars at Dinner*

Chamaelion in his *On Stesichorus* says that not only

IAMBIC POETRY

καὶ μελῳδηθῆναί φησιν οὐ μόνον τὰ Ὁμήρου ἀλλὰ
καὶ τὰ Ἡσιόδου καὶ Ἀρχιλόχου, ἔτι δὲ Μιμνέρμου καὶ
Φωκυλίδου. Κλέαρχος δ' ἐν τῷ προτέρῳ περὶ γρίφων
(fr. 92 Wehrli)· τὰ Ἀρχιλόχου, φησίν, Σιμωνίδης ὁ
Ζακύνθιος ἐν τοῖς θεάτροις ἐπὶ δίφρου καθήμενος
ἐρραψῴδει.

FRAGMENTA

*1-17. Elegi*

**1** Ath. 14.627c

Ἀρχίλοχος γοῦν ἀγαθὸς ὢν ποιητὴς πρῶτον ἐκαυ-
χήσατο τῷ δύνασθαι μετέχειν τῶν πολιτικῶν ἀγώνων,
δεύτερον δὲ ἐμνήσθη τῶν περὶ τὴν ποιητικὴν ὑπαρ-
χόντων αὐτῷ, λέγων·

  εἰμὶ δ' ἐγὼ θεράπων μὲν Ἐνυαλίοιο ἄνακτος
    καὶ Μουσέων ἐρατὸν δῶρον ἐπιστάμενος.

Plut. *Phocion* 7.6

καὶ γὰρ τῶν ἀνδρῶν ἐκείνων ἕκαστος ἐφαίνετο κατὰ
τὸν Ἀρχίλοχον

  ἀμφότερον θεράπων μὲν Ἐνυαλίοιο θεοῖο
    καὶ Μουσέων ἐρατῶν δῶρον ἐπιστάμενος.

ARCHILOCHUS

Homer's verses were set to music, but also those of Hesiod and Archilochus and also Mimnermus and Phocylides. And Clearchus says in the first of his two works *On Riddles* that Simonides of Zacynthus used to recite the verses of Archilochus while sitting on a stool in the theatres.

## FRAGMENTS

### 1-17. Elegiac Poems

**1** Athenaeus, *Scholars at Dinner*

At any rate Archilochus who was a fine poet boasted first of his ability to participate in civic struggles and mentioned second his talent for poetry, saying:

> I am the servant of lord Enyalius[1] and skilled in the lovely gift of the Muses.

Plutarch, *Life of Phocion*

In fact each of these men showed himself to be, in the words of Archilochus,

> both a servant of the god Enyalius and skilled in the gift of the lovely Muses.[2]

[1] God of war.　　[2] Plutarch's text is inferior. He has removed the first-person reference to avoid conflict with his introductory ἕκαστος, "each."

**2** Ath. 1.30f

Ἀρχίλοχος τὸν Νάξιον τῷ νέκταρι παραβάλλει (fr. 290)· ὃς καί πού φησιν·

ἐν δορὶ μέν μοι μᾶζα μεμαγμένη, ἐν δορὶ δ'
οἶνος
Ἰσμαρικός· πίνω δ' ἐν δορὶ κεκλιμένος.

1-2 Synes. epist. 130 (p. 717 Hercher, 223 Garzya), Suda s.v. ὑπνομαχῶ (iv.666.6 Adler) et s.v. Ἰσμαρικὸς οἶνος (ii.669.25)

1 μοι Synes., τοι Suda, om. Ath.

**3** Plut. Theseus 5.2-3

οἱ δ' Ἄβαντες ἐκείραντο πρῶτοι τὸν τρόπον τοῦτον
. . . ὄντες πολεμικοὶ καὶ ἀγχέμαχοι καὶ μάλιστα δὴ
πάντων εἰς χεῖρας ὠθεῖσθαι τοῖς ἐναντίοις μεμαθηκό-
τες, ὡς μαρτυρεῖ καὶ Ἀρχίλοχος ἐν τούτοις·

οὔτοι πόλλ' ἐπὶ τόξα τανύσσεται, οὐδὲ θαμειαὶ
σφενδόναι, εὖτ' ἂν δὴ μῶλον Ἄρης συνάγῃ
ἐν πεδίῳ· ξιφέων δὲ πολύστονον ἔσσεται ἔργον·
ταύτης γὰρ κεῖνοι δάμονές εἰσι μάχης
5    δεσπόται Εὐβοίης δουρικλυτοί.

4 δαήμονες codd. (δαίμονες recc. duo), corr. Fick
5 Εὐβοίας codd., corr. Schneidewin

**2** Athenaeus, *Scholars at Dinner*

Archilochus compares Naxian wine to nectar (fr. 290) and he also says somewhere:

> On board ship I have kneaded barley bread, on board ship Ismarian wine,[1] and I drink it while reclining on board ship.[2]

[1] From Ismaros in Thrace.     [2] The meaning of ἐν δορί is much disputed and the phrase is often translated "on my spear," but see Bossi 68-76 and n. 3 on fr. 4. If "on board ship" is incorrect, it is probably best to translate by "under arms."

**3** Plutarch, *Life of Theseus*

The Abantes[1] were the first to cut their hair short in this manner . . . since they were warlike and fought at close quarters and had learned better than all others to press forward into hand-to-hand combat with their enemies, as Archilochus attests in these verses:

> Not many bows will be stretched nor will there be numerous slings, whenever Ares brings together the press of battle on the plain; it will be the woeful work of swords. This is the warfare in which those spear-famed lords of Euboea are skilled.[2]

[1] A tribe in Euboea (see *Il.* 2.536-45).     [2] Often assumed to refer to the Lelantine War between Eretria and Chalcis, but there is much uncertainty. See V. Parker, *Untersuchungen zum Lelantischen Krieg und verwandten Problemen der frühgriechischen Geschichte* (Stuttgart 1997).

**4** P. Oxy. vi.854

φρα[
  ξεινοι[
δεῖπνον δ᾽ ου[
5     οὔτ᾽ ἐμοὶ ωσαι[
ἀλλ᾽ ἄγε σὺν κώ[θωνι θοῆς διὰ σέλματα νηὸς
  φοίτα καὶ κοίλ[ων πώματ᾽ ἄφελκε κάδων,
ἄγρει δ᾽ οἶνον |ἐρυθρὸν ἀπὸ τρυγός· οὐδὲ γὰρ
  ἡμεῖς
νηφέμεν |ἐν φυλακῇ τῇδε δυνησόμεθα.

Ath. 11.483d

μνημονεύει αὐτοῦ (sc. τοῦ κώθωνος) καὶ Ἀρχίλοχος ἐν
ἐλεγείοις ὡς ποτηρίου, οὕτως· "ἀλλ᾽ ἄγε—δυνησό-
μεθα," ὡς τῆς κύλικος λεγομένης κώθωνος.

  2 φρά[ζεο Lasserre     9 νήφειν μὲν Ath., νήφειν ἐν
Musurus

**5** Plut. instit. Lac. 34.239b (excidit v. 3, αὐτὸν—μέλει)

Ἀρχίλοχον τὸν ποιητὴν ἐν Λακεδαίμονι γενόμενον
αὐτῆς ὥρας ἐδίωξαν, διότι ἐπέγνωσαν αὐτὸν πεποι-
ηκότα ὡς κρεῖττόν ἐστιν ἀποβαλεῖν τὰ ὅπλα ἢ ἀπο-
θανεῖν·

ἀσπίδι μὲν Σαΐων τις ἀγάλλεται, ἣν παρὰ
  θάμνῳ,

80

**4** Oxyrhynchus papyrus (2nd c. AD)

Observe(?)[1] ... strangers(?) ... a meal ... nor for
me ... But come, make many a trip with a cup
through the thwarts[2] of the swift ship, pull off the
covers of the hollow casks, and draw the red wine
from the lees; we won't be able to stay sober on this
watch.[3]

Athenaeus, *Scholars at Dinner*

Archilochus in his elegies refers to the κώθων as a cup,
thus (vv. 6-9), where the κώθων is like what is called a
κύλιξ.

[1] A paragraphus and coronis in the margin show that a new
poem began here. Nothing of what precedes is legible.
[2] Or "across the deck."    [3] Some connect frr. 2 and 4 (see
Bossi on fr. 2).

**5** Plutarch, *Ancient Customs of the Spartans*

When the poet Archilochus arrived in Sparta, they drove
him out at once, because they learned that in his poetry he
had said that it was better to throw away one's arms than
to be killed:

Some Saian[1] exults in my shield which I left—a

ἔντος ἀμώμητον, κάλλιπον οὐκ ἐθέλων·
αὐτὸν δ᾽ ἐξεσάωσα. τί μοι μέλει ἀσπὶς ἐκείνη;
ἐρρέτω· ἐξαῦτις κτήσομαι οὐ κακίω.

1-3 (—ἐξέφυγον θανάτου τέλος) Sext. Emp. *Pyrrh. hypot.*
3.216; (—ἐξεσάωσα) Ar. *Pax* 1298-99, 1301 (ubi schol. Ἀρχι-
λόχου ἐστὶ τὸ δίστιχον κτλ.). 1-2 Strabo 10.2.17, 12.3.20;
Vita Arati (p. 77.1 Maass). 3-4 (—ἐρρέτω) Olympiod. in Pl.
*Gorg.* (p. 141.1 Westerink); Elias *proleg. philos.* 8 (*Comm. in
Arist. Graeca* xviii.22.21); Ps.-Elias in Porph. *isagogen* 12.19 (p.
16 Westerink)

1 ἀσπίδα . . . ἀνείλετο (ἀγείλετο, ἀνείλατο, ἀφείλατο) τὴν
Strabo περὶ θάμνον Strabo 12.3.20 3 αὐτὸς δ᾽ ἐξέφυγον
θανάτου τέλος Sext. Emp., ψυχὴν δ᾽ Aristophanes (def. V. Di
Benedetto, *Eikasmos* 2 [1991] 13-27, fort. recte), αὐτόν μ᾽ fere
Neoplatonici τί μοι μέλει; ἀσπὶς ἐκείνη ἐρρέτω malunt quidam
4 ἐξαῦθις Plut. (-ῆς cod. unus), corr. Schaefer

**6** Schol. Soph. *El.* 96, "φοίνιος Ἄρης οὐκ ἐξένισεν"

ἀντὶ τοῦ οὐκ ἀπέκτεινεν. ξένια γὰρ Ἄρεως τραύματα
καὶ φόνοι. καὶ Ἀρχίλοχος·

ξείνια δυσμενέσιν λυγρὰ χαριζόμενοι

*Suda* s.vv. ἐξένισεν (ii.307.1 Adler) et ξένια καὶ ξενίζω
(iii.493.1)

χαριζόμενος *Suda* utroque loco

faultless weapon—beside a bush against my will. But I saved myself. What do I care about that shield? To hell with it! I'll get one that's just as good another time.

[1] A Thracian tribe.

**6** Scholiast on Sophocles, *Electra*

"murderous Ares did not present his guest-gifts"[1] instead of 'did not kill.' For the guest-gifts of Ares are wounds and slaughter. Cf. Archilochus:

favouring the enemy with guest-gifts of grief

[1] Electra's lament is that Agamemnon was killed by his wife rather than in war.

## IAMBIC POETRY

**7** Fragmentum Sosthenis inscriptionis (v. test. 4), ed. W. Peek, *ZPE* 59 (1985) 14

> ἐ]πὶ δυσμεν[έας
> ἀ]μείλιχον ἐν [
> ]ευάμενος.

**7a** πο[λλῶν δ᾽ ἀθυμησάντων πάλιν λέ]γει·

ἐξ ἐλάφων ν[

(7) 1 ἴτω πᾶς ἐ]πὶ Peek, ἦι᾽ ἐ]πὶ Slings    2 ἄλκιμον ἦτορ ἔχων καὶ ἀ]μείλιχον ἐν [φρεσὶ θυμόν West, ἐν [φρεσὶν ἦτορ Slings    3 ἀλ]ευάμενος Treu, σ]ευάμενος Slings    (7a) ν[όον ἔσχετ᾽ ἐνὶ φρεσί Peek

**8** Schol. Ap. Rhod. 1.824 (p. 71 Wendel), "θεσσάμενοι"

ἐξ αἰτήσεως ἀναλαβόντες, αἰτήσαντες· θέσ‹σασ›θαι γὰρ τὸ αἰτῆσαι καὶ ἱκετεῦσαι . . . καὶ Ἀρχίλοχος·

> πολλὰ δ᾽ εὐπλοκάμου πολιῆς ἁλὸς ἐν πελάγεσσι
> θεσσάμενοι γλυκερὸν νόστον ∪ −∪∪ −

Ἀρχίλοχος cod. L, Ἀντίλοχος P

**9** P. Oxy. xxiii.2356a et Plut. *quomodo aud. poet.* 6.23b

(quae praecedunt v. ad fr. 108) ὅταν δὲ τὸν ἄνδρα τῆς ἀδελφῆς ἠφανισμένον ἐν θαλάσσῃ καὶ μὴ τυχόντα νομίμου ταφῆς θρηνῶν λέγει μετριώτερον ἂν τὴν συμφορὰν ἐνεγκεῖν,

**7** Fragment of the inscription of Sosthenes

> . . . against the enemy . . . implacable in (heart?) . . .
> avoiding(?)

**7a** (and when many were disheartened he says again):

> from deer[1] . . .

[1] Perhaps an image for lack of courage. Cf. fr. 280.

**8** Scholiast on Apollonius Rhodius

θεσσάμενοι means 'getting upon request, requesting,'
since θέσσασθαι means 'to ask for, to beg for' . . . Cf.
Archilochus:

> and praying often (earnestly?) to the fair-haired
> (goddess)[1] on the expanse of the white-capped sea
> for a sweet homecoming

[1] Many treat "fair-haired" as an epithet of the sea.

**9** Oxyrhynchus papyrus (2nd c. AD)[1] and Plutarch, *How
the young man should study poetry*

But when Archilochus, lamenting his sister's husband who
had been lost at sea and had not obtained funeral rites, says
that he would have borne the disaster[2] with greater moder-
ation,

IAMBIC POETRY

εἰ κείνου κεφαλὴν καὶ χαρίεντα] μέλεα
Ἥφαιστος καθαροῖσιν ἐν εἵμασιν] ἀμφεπον[ήθη,

τὸ πῦρ οὕτως, οὐ τὸν θεὸν προσηγόρευκε.

**10** P.Oxy. 2356b

   2 ]θια δέ σφεας      4 ἐξ]απίνης γὰρ
6 ]ᾳ γυναικῶν

**11** Plut. *quomodo aud. poet.* 12.33a-b

πάλιν ὁ Ἀρχίλοχος οὐκ ἐπαινεῖται λυπούμενος μὲν ἐπὶ
τῷ ἀνδρὶ τῆς ἀδελφῆς διεφθαρμένῳ κατὰ θάλασσαν,
οἴνῳ δὲ καὶ παιδιᾷ πρὸς τὴν λύπην μάχεσθαι δια-
νοούμενος. αἰτίαν μέντοι λόγον ἔχουσαν εἴρηκεν·

οὔτε τι γὰρ κλαίων ἰήσομαι, οὔτε κάκιον
θήσω τερπωλὰς καὶ θαλίας ἐφέπων.

1-2 Tzetz. *alleg. Hom.* Ω 130 sq. (quae praecedunt v. ad
fr. 215)

   2 θαλίαν Boissonade (θάλειαν Tzetzes)

**12** Schol. Aesch. *PV* 616 (p. 166 Herington), "δωρεάν"

τὸ "δωρεά" ἐπὶ συμφορᾶς λαμβάνεται. καὶ Ἀρχί-
λοχος·

if Hephaestus had tended to his head and lovely
limbs wrapped in pure white raiment,

he meant by this not the god, but fire.

[1] This contains the remnants of 18 verses, too tattered to be
translated. Plutarch's lines occurred in vv. 10-11.     [2] It is pos-
sible that frr. 9-13 (or 8-13) come from the same poem or at least
refer to the same disaster.

**10** Oxyrhynchus papyrus

2 them          4 for suddenly          6 of women

**11** Plutarch, *How the young man should study poetry*

Again, Archilochus is not praised for intending to fight
with wine and amusements the grief he felt over the loss of
his sister's husband at sea. He has, however, given a reason-
able explanation:

for I shall cure nothing by weeping nor shall I make
matters worse by pursuit of pleasures and festivities

**12** Scholiast on Aeschylus, *Prometheus Bound*

The word δωρεά ('gift') is used for misfortune, as by Ar-
chilochus:

†κρύπτομεν† ἀνιηρὰ Ποσειδάωνος ἄνακτος
   δῶρα.

1 κρύπτωμεν ‹δ'› Liebel (-ῶμεν cod. V)   Ποσειδάωνος
Liebel: -δῶνος cod. Φ, -δῶνα (et ἄνακτα) M

**13** Stob. 4.56.30

Ἀρχιλόχου·

   κήδεα μὲν στονόεντα, Περίκλεες, οὔτε τις ἀστῶν
      μεμφόμενος θαλίης τέρψεται οὐδὲ πόλις·
   τοίους γὰρ κατὰ κῦμα πολυφλοίσβοιο θαλάσσης
      ἔκλυσεν, οἰδαλέους δ' ἀμφ' ὀδύνης ἔχομεν
5    πνεύμονας. ἀλλὰ θεοὶ γὰρ ἀνηκέστοισι κακοῖσιν,
      ὦ φίλ', ἐπὶ κρατερὴν τλημοσύνην ἔθεσαν
   φάρμακον. ἄλλοτε ἄλλος ἔχει τόδε· νῦν μὲν ἐς ἡμέας
      ἐτράπεθ', αἱματόεν δ' ἕλκος ἀναστένομεν,
   ἐξαῦτις δ' ἑτέρους ἐπαμείψεται. ἀλλὰ τάχιστα
10    τλῆτε, γυναικεῖον πένθος ἀπωσάμενοι.

4 ἀμφ' ὀδύνῃ ἴσχομεν cod. S, ἴσχομεν ἀμφ' ὀδύνῃ Par. 1985,
corr. Gaisford      9 ἑταίρους S, corr. Frobenius

**14** Orion *etym.* col. 55.22 Sturz (sine versibus *Et. Gen.*,
   *Et. Mag.*)

ἐπίρρησις· ὁ ψόγος, καὶ ἡ κακηγορία· ἔνθεν λοιπὸν
καὶ ἐπίρρητος. Ἀρχίλοχος ἐν ἐλεγείοις·

   Αἰσιμίδη, δήμου μὲν ἐπίρρησιν μελεδαίνων

let us conceal(?) the painful gifts of lord Poseidon[1]

[1] If the context is that given in Plutarch's introduction to frr. 9 and 11, the verb cannot mean 'bury.' Perhaps 'keep silent about.'

**13** Stobaeus, *Anthology*

From Archilochus:

> There will be no disapproval of our mourning and lamentation, Pericles, when any citizen or even state takes pleasure in festivities, since such fine men did the wave of the loud-roaring sea wash over, and our lungs are swollen from pain. But, my friend, for incurable woes the gods have set powerful endurance as an antidote. This woe comes to different people at different times. Now it has turned upon us and we bewail a bloody wound, but later it will pass to others. Come, endure with all haste, thrusting aside womanly mourning.

**14** Orion, *Lexicon*

ἐπίρρησις means 'blame' or 'slander;' moreover, from there comes also ἐπίρρητος. Cf. Archilochus in his elegiacs:

> No one, Aesimides, will experience very many de-

οὐδεὶς ἂν μάλα πόλλ᾽ ἱμερόεντα πάθοι.

1 Αἰσιμήδη δηλοῦμεν cod., corr. Elmsley    ἐπίρρησι cod.,
corr. Ruhnken

**15** Arist. *Eth. Eudem.* 7.1236a33

τούτων (sc. τῶν φιλιῶν) ἡ μὲν διὰ τὸ χρήσιμόν ἐστιν ἡ
τῶν πλείστων φιλία· διὰ γὰρ τὸ χρήσιμοι εἶναι φιλοῦ-
σιν ἀλλήλους, καὶ μέχρι τούτου, ὥσπερ ἡ παροιμία·

Γλαῦκ᾽, ἐπίκουρος ἀνὴρ τόσσον φίλος ἔσκε
μάχηται.

τὸν σοφὸν φίλον codd., corr. Fritzsche    ἔστε Fick

**16** Stob. 1.6.3

πάντα Τύχη καὶ Μοῖρα, Περίκλεες, ἀνδρὶ
δίδωσιν.

**17** Syrianus in Hermog. (i.6.12 Rabe)

καὶ ἐν Μιλήτῳ ὁ θεός· "οὐδὲν ἄνευ καμάτου πέλει
ἀνδράσιν εὐπετὲς ἔργον" (Ps.-Phocyl. 162)· καὶ πάλιν·

πάντα πόνος τεύχει θνητοῖς μελέτη τε βροτείη.

cf. Io. Sicel. in Hermog. (*Rhet. Gr.* vi.96.5 Walz)

lights, if he is concerned about the people's censure.

**15** Aristotle, *Eudemian Ethics*

Of these friendships the one that is based on usefulness is the friendship of most people; for they are friends of one another only as long as they are useful, as the proverb goes:

> Glaucus, an ally is a friend only as long as he fights.[1]

[1] Generally assigned to Archilochus because of the name Glaucus (cf. frr. 48.7; 105.1; 117; 131.1; test. 1).

**16** Stobaeus, *Anthology*

> Fortune and Destiny, Pericles, give a man everything.[1]

[1] Assigned by some to Archilochus because of the name Pericles (cf. fr. 13.1, introduction to fr. 124a, and test. 17).

**17** Syrianus on Hermogenes

And in Miletus the god (Apollo) says: "nothing is easily accomplished by men without toil;" and again:

> Hard work and human effort accomplish everything
> for mortals.[1]

[1] Assigned to Archilochus by John of Sicily, but rejected by some on metrical grounds (τέ βρ).

*18-87. Trimetri*

**18** Eust. in Hom. *Il.* 5.31 (ii.15.24 V.d.Valk) = Herodian. (ii.639.24 Lentz)

κλίνεται δὲ καὶ ὡς σπονδειακόν, Ἄρης Ἄρου· ὅθεν
κατὰ Ἰάδα διάλεκτον ἐπεκτείνας Ἀρχίλοχος ἔφη ἐν
τοῖς τριμέτροις

παῖδ᾽ Ἄρεω μιηφόνου

**19** Plut. *de tranqu. animi* 10.470b-c

εἶθ᾽ οὕτως ἀεὶ τῶν ὑπὲρ ἑαυτοὺς ἐνδεεῖς ὄντες οὐδέποτε
τοῖς καθ᾽ ἑαυτοὺς χάριν ἔχουσιν.

οὔ μοι τὰ Γύγεω τοῦ πολυχρύσου μέλει,
οὐδ᾽ εἷλέ πώ με ζῆλος, οὐδ᾽ ἀγαίομαι
θεῶν ἔργα, μεγάλης δ᾽ οὐκ ἐρέω τυραννίδος·
ἀπόπροθεν γάρ ἐστιν ὀφθαλμῶν ἐμῶν.

"Θάσιος γὰρ ἦν ἐκεῖνος." ἄλλος δέ τις Χῖος, ἄλλος δὲ
Γαλάτης ἢ Βιθυνὸς οὐκ ἀγαπῶν εἰ . . .

Arist. *Rhet.* 3.17.1418b28

εἰς δὲ τὸ ἦθος, ἐπειδὴ ἔνια περὶ αὑτοῦ λέγειν ἢ
ἐπίφθονον ἢ μακρολογίαν ἢ ἀντιλογίαν ἔχει, καὶ περὶ
ἄλλου ἢ λοιδορίαν ἢ ἀγροικίαν, ἕτερον χρὴ λέγοντα
ποιεῖν, ὅπερ Ἰσοκράτης ποιεῖ ἐν τῷ Φιλίππῳ καὶ ἐν
τῇ Ἀντιδόσει, καὶ ὡς Ἀρχίλοχος ψέγει· ποιεῖ γὰρ τὸν

## ARCHILOCHUS

### *18-87. Iambic Trimeters*

**18**  Eustathius on Homer, *Iliad*

It is also declined as a spondee, Ἄρης Ἄρου, and hence
by extending it in accordance with the Ionic dialect Archi-
lochus said in his trimeters

> son of bloodthirsty Ares

**19**  Plutarch, *On tranquillity of mind*

Accordingly, since they always lack what is beyond them,
they are never grateful for what befits their station.

> The possessions of Gyges[1] rich in gold are of no con-
> cern to me, not yet have I been seized with jeal-
> ousy of him, I do not envy the deeds of the gods, and
> I have no love of tyranny. That is beyond my sights.

"Yes, since he was a Thasian," someone will say. Yet others,
a Chian, Galatian, or Bithynian, are not content if . . .

Aristotle, *Rhetoric*

And with regard to character, since to say some things
about oneself results in jealousy or longwindedness or con-
troversy and since to say some things about another results
in abuse or boorishness, it is necessary to represent an-
other as speaker, as Isocrates does in *Philippus* and in *An-
tidosis*, and as Archilochus censures. For he represents the

93

IAMBIC POETRY

πατέρα λέγοντα περὶ τῆς θυγατρὸς ἐν τῷ ἰάμβῳ
"χρημάτων—ἀπώμοτον" (fr. 122.1), καὶ τὸν Χάρωνα
τὸν τέκτονα ἐν τῷ ἰάμβῳ οὗ ἡ ἀρχή "οὔ μοι τὰ
Γύγεω."

2 ἀγάζομαι Plut. codd. S²V    3 ἐρῶ codd., corr.
Schneidewin

**20** Heracl. Lemb. π. πολιτείων 50 (p. 30 Dilts)

οὗτοι δι᾽ ὑπερβολὴν ἀτυχημάτων πολλὰ ἐκακώθησαν.
καί που καὶ Ἀρχίλοχός φησι·

κλαίω τὰ Θασίων, οὐ τὰ Μαγνήτων κακά.

Strabo 14.1.40

καὶ τὸ παλαιὸν δὲ συνέβη τοῖς Μάγνησιν ὑπὸ Τρηρῶν
ἄρδην ἀναιρεθῆναι, Κιμμερικοῦ ἔθνους, εὐτυχήσαντας
πολὺν χρόνον, τῷ δ᾽ ἑξῆς ἔτει Μιλησίους κατασχεῖν
τὸν τόπον. Καλλῖνος μὲν οὖν (fr. 3) ὡς εὐτυχούντων ἔτι
τῶν Μαγνήτων μέμνηται καὶ κατορθούντων ἐν τῷ
πρὸς τοὺς Ἐφεσίους πολέμῳ, Ἀρχίλοχος δὲ ἤδη
φαίνεται γνωρίζων τὴν γενομένην αὐτοῖς συμφοράν,
κλαίειν <φάσκων τὰ> (add. West) Θασίων οὐ τὰ
Μαγνήτων κακά. ἐξ οὗ καὶ τὸ νεώτερον εἶναι τοῦ
Καλλίνου τεκμαίρεσθαι πάρεστιν.

cf. Ath. 12.525c, Clem. Strom. 1.131.7-8 (= test. 8)

τὰ Θασίων Tyrwhitt, θαλασσῶν Heracl., θάσων, θᾶσσον,
θείων codd. Strabonis

94

father as speaking about his daughter in the iambic poem (fr. 122.1) and Charon the carpenter in the iambic poem whose beginning is "The possessions of Gyges are of no (concern) to me."

[1] Gyges ruled over Lydia 687-652.

**20** Heraclides Lembus, *On Constitutions*

They (sc. the Magnesians) were greatly afflicted because of excessive misfortunes. And somewhere Archilochus says:

> I bewail the woes of the Thasians, not those of the Magnesians.

Strabo, *Geography*

And in ancient times it happened that the Magnesians, who had long been prosperous, were utterly destroyed, and that in the following year the Milesians took possession of the place. Now Callinus mentions the Magnesians as still prosperous and as successful in their war with the Ephesians, but Archilochus is clearly already aware of the disaster that befell them, (since he says that) he bewails the woes of the Thasians, not those of the Magnesians. As a result one may infer that he is later than Callinus.[1]

[1] But only a short period may have elapsed between the two poets' references to the Magnesians.

**21** Plut. *de exilio* 12.604c

ἀλλ' ἡμεῖς, καθάπερ Ἀρχίλοχος τῆς Θάσου τὰ καρ-
ποφόρα καὶ οἰνόπεδα παρορῶν διὰ τὸ τραχὺ καὶ
ἀνώμαλον διέβαλε τὴν νῆσον εἰπών·

> ἥδε δ' ὥστ' ὄνου ῥάχις
> ἕστηκεν ὕλης ἀγρίης ἐπιστεφής,

οὕτω τῆς φυγῆς πρὸς ἓν μέρος τὸ ἄδοξον ἐντεινόμενοι
παρορῶμεν τὴν ἀπραγμοσύνην κτλ.

2 ἀγρίας Plut., corr. Liebel

**22** Ath. 12.523d

καὶ Ἀρχίλοχος δὲ ὁ ποιητὴς ὑπερτεθαύμακε τὴν
χώραν τῶν Σιριτῶν διὰ τὴν εὐδαιμονίαν. περὶ γοῦν
τῆς Θάσου λέγων ὡς ἥσσονός φησιν·

> οὐ γάρ τι καλὸς χῶρος οὐδ' ἐφίμερος
> οὐδ' ἐρατός, οἷος ἀμφὶ Σίριος ῥοάς.

ὠνομάσθη δὲ ἡ Σῖρις, ὡς μὲν Τίμαιός φησιν (*FGrHist*
566 F 52) καὶ Εὐριπίδης ἐν Δεσμώτιδι Μελανίππῃ (fr.
496 N.) ἀπὸ γυναικός τινος Σίριδος, ὡς δὲ Ἀρχίλοχος
ἀπὸ ποταμοῦ.

**23** P. Oxy. xxii.2310 fr. 1 col. i.1-21, ed. Lobel

5                                   γὰρ ἐργματ[
                                    ιχα..ω[

**21** Plutarch, *On exile*

But just as Archilochus disregarded the fruitful fields and vineyards of Thasos and attacked the island because of its ruggedness and unevenness, saying,

> this (island) stands like the backbone of an ass, cov-
> ered with a wild forest,

so we, concentrating on one aspect of exile, the absence of fame, overlook the absence of politics etc.

**22** Athenaeus, *Scholars at Dinner*

And the poet Archilochus had great admiration for the land of the Sirites because of its prosperity. At any rate, speaking about Thasos as an inferior place, he says:

> for it is not at all a fair, desirable, or lovely land, like
> that round about the stream of Siris.[1]

According to Timaeus and Euripides in his *Melanippe Bound* it was called Siris after a woman named Siris, but according to Archilochus after a river.

[1] Athenaeus is referring to Siris on the gulf of Tarentum, but Archilochus' acquaintance with this area is surprising and some argue for a reference to a river, elsewhere called Syros, which flows into the Propontis.

**23** Oxyrhynchus papyrus (mid 2nd c. AD)[1]

. . . for deeds . . . I replied: "Lady, have no fear of

97

τὴν δ' ἐγὼνταμειβόμ[ην·
"γύνα[ι], φάτιν μὲν τὴν πρὸς ἀνθρώπω[ν κακὴν
μὴ τετραμήνηις μηδέν· ἀμφὶ δ' εὔφ[ρονι,
10      ἐμοὶ μελήσει· [θ]υμὸν ἵλαον τίθεο.
ἐς τοῦτο δή τοι τῆς ἀνολβίης δοκ[έω
ἥκειν; ἀνήρ τοι δειλὸς ἆρ' ἐφαινόμην,
οὐ]δ' οἷός εἰμ' ἐγὼ [α]ὐτὸς οὐδ' οἴων ἄπο.
ἐπ]ίσταμαί τοι τὸν φιλ[έο]ν[τα] μὲν φ[ι]λεῖν,
15      τὸ]ν δ' ἐχθρὸν ἐχθαίρειν τε [κα]ὶ κακο[
μύ]ρμηξ. λόγωι νυν τ[ῶιδ' ἀλη]θείη πάρ[α.
πό]λιν δὲ ταύτη[ν ...].[....ἐ]πιστρέ[φεα]ι[
οὔ]τοι ποτ' ἄνδρες ἐξε[πόρθη]σαν, σὺ δ[ὲ
ν]ῦν εἷλες αἰχμῆι κα[ὶ μέγ' ἐ]ξήρ(ω) κ[λ]έος.
20      κείνης ἄνασσε καὶ τ[υραν]νίην ἔχε·
π[ο]λ[λοῖ]σ[ί θ]η[ν ζ]ηλωτὸς ἀ[νθρ]ώπων ἔσεαι."

8 κακὴν Lobel      9 εὔφ[ρονι Bossi, εὐφ[ρόνηι West
10 τιθεῦ pap., corr. West      11 ἀνολβείης pap., corr. Chan-
traine      13 [α]ὐτὸς Lobel, [ο]ὗτος West      14 φ[ι]λέειν
pap., corr. West      15 κακο[στομέειν Lobel, κακο[ῖς δακεῖν
Bossi, alii alia      16 Μύ]ρμηξ aliqui      τ[ῶιδ' ἀλη]θείη
Lobel      18 οὔ]τοι Lobel, ἐχθ]ροί Bossi, alii alia, cetera
Lobel      19 ν]ῦν West      μέγ' ἐ]ξῆρα[ς Lobel, -αο Adrados,
-ω West      20 suppl. Lobel      21 π[ο]λ[λοῖ]σ[ι Peek,
θ]η[ν West

**24** P. Oxy. 2310 fr. 1 col. i.22-39, ed. Lobel

]νηἳ σὺν σ[μ]ικρῆι μέγαν
πόντον περῆσ]ας ἦλθες ἐκ Γορτυνίης

the evil rumour that people spread. As for kindly report(?),[2] that will be my concern. Make your heart propitious. Do you think I have reached such a degree of misfortune? I seem to you then to be a base man, not the sort of person I am and my ancestors were. Indeed I know how to repay love with love and hatred with hate and biting abuse(?) like an ant. There is truth then in what I say. You move about this city (which?) men have never sacked, but now you have captured it with the spear and you have won great glory. Rule over it and retain your dominance; in truth you will be the envy of many people."

[1] Some treat frr. 23 and 24 as one poem (no paragraphus is visible), but it is difficult to reconcile their subject matter. For the many attempts to explain both fragments (also 25 and 26), see Bossi 88-113.     [2] West's supplement "as for a (or the) night" is suitable if, as he argues (*Studies* 118-20), the poem is erotic and if there was an earlier reference in the poem to night. For another interpretation see Luppe, *APF* 41 (1995) 20-23, who also argues that a new poem commences at v. 11.

**24**  Same papyrus

. . .(after crossing) the large (sea) in a small ship you arrived from the region of Gortyn[1] . . . I am glad of

]σ ουτιτ γεπεστάθη[[ν]]

        ]καὶ τόδ᾽ ἁρπαλ[ί]ζομ[αι]

5      κρ]ηγύης ἀφίκ[

      ]λμοισιν εξ[........].ς

      ]χειρα καὶ π[αρ]εστ[ά]θης

      ]ουσας· φ[ο]ρτίων δέ μοι μέ[λ]ει

ἥκιστα,      ] ος εἰτ᾽ ἀπώλετο

10           ]ν ἐστι μηχανή

     δ᾽ ἂν ἄλ]λον οὗτιν᾽ εὑροίμην ἐγώ

     εἰ σ]ὲ κῦμ᾽ ἁλὸς κατέκλυσεν

ἢ      ].ν χερσὶν αἰχμητέων ὕπο

     ἤ]βην ἀγλ[α]ὴν ἀπ[ώ]λεσ[α]ς.

15  νῦν δ᾽    ]θεῖ καί σε θε[ὸς ἐρ]ρύσατο

      ].[.]. κἀμὲ μουνωθέντ᾽ ἰδ..

      ]ν, ἐν ζόφωι δὲ κείμενο⟨ς⟩

     αὖτις] ἐ[ς] φά[ος κ]ατεστάθην.

2 suppl. Adrados     5 Lasserre     7 Adrados
9 init. West     11 Steffen et φίλον vel γαμβρὸν init. West
12 Peek et τοιοῦτον init. West     13 init. Peek
15 init. Schiassi     18 Peek

**25** P. Oxy. 2310 fr. 1 col. i.40-48, ed. Lobel

      ]τις ἀνθρώπου φυή,

ἀλλ᾽ ἄλλος ἄλλωι κα]ρδίην ἰαίνεται.

     ].τ[.]. Μελησά[νδρω]ι σάθη

     ]ε βουκόλωι Φαλ[αγγ]ιωι.

5  τοῦτ᾽ οὔτις ἄλλ]ος μάντις ἀλλ᾽ ἐγὼ εἶπέ σοι·

this . . . you came on a good (ship?) . . . (a god held over you?) his hand and you got here . . . I am (not at all) concerned about the cargo . . . whether it was lost (or) . . . there is a means . . . I could not find another . . . (if?) the waves of the sea had washed over you (or) . . . at the hands of spearmen . . . you had lost the splendid prime of your youth. (But as it is) . . . and a god saved you . . . and me left alone . . . prostrate in the gloom . . . I am restored to the light of day.

1 Presumably the Gortyn in Crete.

**25**  Same papyrus[1]

. . . human nature, but different people are warmed at heart by different things . . . for Melesa(nder) prick . . . for the herdsman Phal(ang)ios.[2] I, (no other) prophet, proclaimed (this) to you . . . for to

]γάρ μοι Ζεὺς πατὴρ 'Ολυμπίων
ἔ]θηκε κἀγαθὸν μετ' ἀνδράσι
οὐ]δ' ἂν Εὐρύμας διαψέγο[ι

2 Schol. Hom. Od. 14.228, Sext. Emp. adv. math. 11.44, Clem.
Strom. 6.7.3-5

2 ἀλλ' Clem., om. Sext. et schol. Hom.      ἄλλῳ ἐπ' ἔργῳ
Sext.      κραδίην Clem., schol. Hom., v.l. in Sext.
3,4 suppl. West      5 τοῦτ' West, οὔτις ἄλλ]ος Lobel
8 init. Lobel, fin. Lasserre

**26**  P. Oxy. 2310 fr. 1 col. ii, ed. Lobel

5      ὦναξ "Απολλον, καὶ σὺ τοὺς μὲν αἰτίους
πήμαινε καί σφας ὄλλυ' ὥσπερ ὀλλύεις,
ἡμέας δὲ.[

Macr. Sat. 1.17.9-10

alii cognominatum Apollinem putant ὡς ἀπολλύντα τὰ
ζῷα: exanimat enim et perimit animantes, cum pestem
intemperie caloris immittit, ut Euripides in Phaethonte
(224-25 Diggle) . . . item Archilochus: "ἄναξ—ὀλλύεις."

5 ωνξ.π..[ pap., ἄναξ Macr.      6 πημαιν[ pap., σήμαινε
Macr. (πημ- corr. Camerarius)      σφας codd. primarii, σφεας
rec. unus      7 Lobel

**29**  P. Oxy. 2310 fr. 4, ed. Lobel

2 αρθμιάδεω      4 γάρ εἰς      5 ἀνθ]ρώπων ἔτι
7 ]ειδ' ὅπηι δύνε[αι      8 θαυμαστός εἰς

me Zeus father of the Olympians . . . made and good
among men . . . (nor) would Eurymas³ find fault.

¹ We have the beginning of the poem, since above v. 1 the
papyrus preserves meager traces of ink which do not leave enough
room for a trimeter and so suggest a title. ² Presumably two
men are named who find erotic pleasure in different parts of
the body. There may be a contrast between homosexual and het-
erosexual preferences. ³ "Eurymas annoyed Castor with
malicious accusations against Polydeuces" (West, *Studies* 122).

**26** Same papyrus

You too, lord Apollo, bring ruin upon the guilty and
destroy them as you do, but us . . .¹

Macrobius, *Saturnalia*

Others think that Apollo got his name because he destroys
(ἀπολλύντα) living creatures; for he deprives of life and
kills the living when he sends a pestilence as a result of
excessive heat, as in Euripides' *Phaethon* . . . Similarly Ar-
chilochus.

¹ The two emendations required to make Macrobius' citation
agree with the papyrus do not inspire confidence that both texts
are the same. Traces of 4 verses before and 8 after what is printed
here are discernible in the papyrus.

**29** Same papyrus

. . . Arthmiades(?) . . . for you are . . . men(?) still
. . . where(ver) you can . . . you are astounding

# IAMBIC POETRY

**30** Ps.-Ammonius *de adfin. vocab. diff.* 431 (p. 111 Nickau)

ῥόδον καὶ ῥοδωνιὰ καὶ ῥοδῇ διαφέρει. ῥόδον μὲν γὰρ τὸ ἄνθος, ῥοδωνιὰ δὲ ὁ τόπος, ῥοδῇ δὲ τὸ φυτόν. Ἀρχίλοχος·

ἔχουσα θαλλὸν μυρσίνης ἐτέρπετο
ῥοδῆς τε καλὸν ἄνθος.

cf. schol. Theocr. 4.45 (p. 147.12 Wendel), *Et. Gen.* (p. 29 Calame), *Et. Mag.* 441.48, Ath. 2.52f, Eust. in Hom. *Od.* 24.341 (1963.48)

1 μυρρίνης schol. Theocr., *Et. Mag.*; μυρίνης *Et. Gen.*

**31** Synes. *laudatio calvitii* 11.75b (ii.211.12 Terzaghi)

οὐκοῦν ἅπαντες οἴονταί τε καὶ λέγουσιν αὐτοφυὲς εἶναι σκιάδειον τὴν κόμην· καὶ ὁ κάλλιστος ποιητῶν Ἀρχίλοχος ἐπαινέσας αὐτήν, ἐπαινεῖ μὲν οὖσαν ἐν ἑταίρας σώματι, λέγει δὲ οὕτως·

ἡ δέ οἱ κόμη
ὤμους κατεσκίαζε καὶ μετάφρενα.

2 κατασκιάζει codd., corr. Bentley

**32** *Et. Gen.* (p. 25 Calame) = *Et. Mag.* 324.17 (quae praecedunt v. ad fr. 46)

καὶ πάλιν

διὲξ τὸ μύρτον,

104

**30** Pseudo-Ammonius, *On similar but different words*

ῥόδον, ῥοδωνιά, and ῥοδῆ are different. ῥόδον is the rose flower, ῥοδωνιά the rose garden, and ῥοδῆ the rose bush. Cf. Archilochus:

> she took delight in holding a sprig of myrtle and the lovely flower of the rose bush

**31** Synesius, *Praise of baldness*

Therefore all think and say that hair is a natural sunshade. And Archilochus, the finest of poets, when he praises the hair, praises it on the body of a courtesan, speaking as follows:

> and her hair cast a shade over her shoulders and back[1]

[1] Many combine this with fr. 30.

**32** *Etymologicum Genuinum* and *Magnum*

And again

> right through the myrtle spray,[1]

ἀντὶ τοῦ διὰ τὸ μύρτον (σημαίνει δὲ τὴν μυρσίνην).

**33** Ps.-Luc. *amores* 3 (iii.86.24 Macleod)

ἔναγχος γοῦν διηγουμένου σου τὸν πολὺν ὡς καὶ παρ'
Ἡσιόδῳ κατάλογον ὧν ἀρχῆθεν ἠράσθης ἱλαραὶ μὲν
τῶν ὀμμάτων αἱ βολαὶ τακερῶς ἀνυγραίνοντο, τὴν
φωνὴν δ' ἴσην τῇ Λυκάμβου θυγατρὶ λεπτὸν ἀφη-
δύνων ἀπ' αὐτοῦ τοῦ σχήματος εὐθὺς δῆλος ἦς οὐκ
ἐκείνων μόνων ἀλλὰ καὶ τῆς ἐπ' αὐτοῖς μνήμης ἐρῶν.

**34** Ap. Dysc. *de adverb.* (*Gramm. Gr.* ii.i.i.161)

ὅτι γὰρ τὰ τοιαῦτα διὰ τοῦ ῑ (sc. γράφεται) σαφὲς μὲν
καὶ ἐκ τῶν διαλέκτων . . . καὶ ἔτι τῆς παρεπομένης
ἔσθ' ὅτι συστολῆς, ὅπερ ἴδιον τῶν διχρόνων. τὸ γοῦν
Ἀρχιλόχειον συνεστάλη,

αμισθὶ γάρ σε πάμπαν οὐ διάξομεν.

**35** *Et. Gen.* (p. 35 Calame); *Et. Gud.* col. 339.30 Sturz;
*Et. Mag.* 530.28

κορωνός· ὁ γαῦρος καὶ ὑψαυχενῶν . . . Ἀρχίλοχος·

with διέξ instead of διά (by μύρτον he means myrtle spray).

[1] Probably here a metaphor for the female genitals.

## 33 Pseudo-Lucian, *Affairs of the Heart*

Just now at any rate, when in Hesiodic fashion you were going through the long catalogue of your loves from the beginning, the merry glances of your eyes grew meltingly moist, and giving a delicate sweetness to your voice so that it matched that of Lycambes' daughter you made it immediately clear from your very manner that you were in love not just with them but also with your memory of them.

## 34 Apollonius Dyscolus, *On adverbs*

For that such words are written with a long iota is clear from the dialects . . . And yet sometimes shortening occurs, as is characteristic of syllables with variable length. At any rate Archilochus shortened the iota,

for on no account will we ferry[1] you without payment

[1] Probably a metaphor for sexual intercourse, perhaps placed in the mouths of the daughters of Lycambes.

## 35 *Etymologicum Genuinum, Gudianum,* and *Magnum*

κορωνός means proud and with neck held high . . . Cf. Archilochus:

βοῦς ἐστιν ἥμιν ἐργάτης ἐν οἰκίῃ,
κορωνός, ἔργων ἴδρις, οὐδαρ( )

1 ἥμιν pro ἡμῖν West     2 οὐδαρ Et. Gen. A, οὐδαμῶς Et.
Gen. B (om. Gud., Mag.), οὐδ' ἀροῦν κακός tent. West, alii alia

**36** Harpocr. s.v. παλίνσκιον (p. 200 Keaney)

Ἰσαῖος μὲν ἐν τῷ πρὸς ὀργεῶνας (fr. 112 Sauppe, 26
Thalheim) "μήτε παλίνσκιον γίγνεσθαι τὸ χωρίον,"
ἀντὶ τοῦ σύσκιον, Ἀρχίλοχος δὲ τριμέτροις

πρὸς τοῖχον ἐκλίνθησαν ἐν παλινσκίῳ

ἀντὶ τοῦ ἐν σκοτεινῷ, καὶ Σοφοκλῆς Ἰνάχῳ (fr. 289
Radt) "χειμῶνι σὺν παλινσκίῳ" ἀντὶ τοῦ ζοφερῷ.

ἐκινήθησαν codd., corr. Toup

**37** Porphyrius in Hom. Il. 9.90 (p. 134 Schrader)

τὸν αὐτὸν τρόπον καὶ τὸν Λαέρτου οἶκον (Od. 24.208)
περιέχεσθαι πανταχόθεν (sc. φησὶν Δωρόθεος ὁ
Ἀσκαλωνίτης) ὑπὸ τοῦ κλισίου, κατὰ μέσον ᾠκο-
δομημένον. τὸ γὰρ περιθεῖν τοῦτο δηλοῖ, οἷον καὶ
Ἀρχίλοχος δηλοῖ ποιήσας

τοῖον γὰρ αὐλὴν ἕρκος ἀμφιδέδρομεν.

**38** Schol. A Hom. Il. 11.786 (iii.280 Erbse), "γενεῇ μὲν
ὑπέρτερός ἐστιν Ἀχιλλεύς"

ὅτι Ἀρχίλοχος ὑπερτέραν τὴν νεωτέραν ἐδέξατο·

we have in the stable[1] a work-ox, proud, a skilled
worker, and not . . .

[1] Or "house," if the ox is a metaphor. For a possible sexual
connotation of the word for 'work,' cf. fr. 208.

**36** Harpocration, *Lexicon of the Ten Attic Orators*

Isaeus in *Against the members of a religious association*
uses παλίνσκιον instead of σύσκιον, "and that the plot of
land not be thickly shaded," and Archilochus in his trime-
ters uses it instead of σκοτεινῷ,

they leaned against a wall in the shadow,[1]

and Sophocles in *Inachus* uses it instead of ζοφερῷ, "with a
gloomy winter."

[1] West suggests a reference to the daughters of Lycambes and
the precinct of Hera (see test. 20).

**37** Porphyry on Homer, *Iliad*

Dorotheus of Ascalon[1] says that in the same way the house
of Laertes was surrounded on all sides by the lean-to(?),
with the house built in the middle. For περιθεῖν makes this
clear, as Archilochus also makes clear when he composed

for such an enclosure runs round the courtyard[2]

[1] Grammarian of the 1st cent. A.D.      [2] West tentatively
suggests that frr. 36-37 be combined.

**38** Scholiast A on Homer, *Iliad* ("Achilles is superior in
birth")

For Archilochus uses ὑπερτέρα to mean νεωτέρα:

οἵην Λυκάμβεω παῖδα τὴν ὑπερτέραν,

ἀντὶ τοῦ τὴν νεωτέραν.

οἵην? Maas, σχοίην Jurenka    Λυκάμβεος cod., corr. Elmsley

**39** Ath. 3.122b

Κηφισόδωρος γοῦν ὁ Ἰσοκράτους τοῦ ῥήτορος μα-
θητὴς ἐν τῷ τρίτῳ τῶν πρὸς Ἀριστοτέλην λέγει ὅτι
εὕροι τις ἂν ὑπὸ τῶν ἄλλων ποιητῶν ἢ καὶ σοφιστῶν
ἓν ἢ δύο γοῦν πονηρῶς εἰρημένα, οἷα παρὰ μὲν Ἀρχι-
λόχῳ τὸ πάντα ἄνδρα ἀποσκολύπτειν, Θεοδώρῳ δὲ (fr.
754 SH) τὸ κελεύειν μὲν πλέον ἔχειν, ἐπαινεῖν δὲ τὸ
ἴσον, Εὐριπίδῃ δὲ (Hipp. 612) τὸ τὴν γλῶτταν ὀμωμο-
κέναι φάναι.

**40** Schol. Ar. Pac. 1148 (p. 164 Holwerda), "παρδακὸν τὸ
χωρίον"

δίυγρον. οὕτω γὰρ καὶ Ἀρχίλοχος,

παρδακὸν δ᾽ ἐπείσιον,

καὶ παρὰ Σιμωνίδῃ τῷ Ἀμοργίῳ (fr. 21)

παρδοκὸν δι᾽ ἐπιοῖον cod., corr. Hecker; fort. παρδακῶν δ᾽
ἐπεισίων, cf. fr. 67.11 et Hesych. παρδάκων· διύγρων

only the superior daughter of Lycambes,

instead of younger.[1]

[1] In the Homeric passage ὑπέρτερος was incorrectly taken to mean 'younger' and Archilochus was cited, also incorrectly, in support. Archilochus meant physically or morally superior or less probably, with West (*Studies* 123), that she had the 'upper' position in sexual intercourse. Some assign the line to the lost beginning of fr. 196a.

**39** Athenaeus, *Scholars at Dinner*

At any rate Cephisodorus, the pupil of the orator Isocrates, says in the third book of his *Against Aristotle* that one can find at least one or two vulgar sayings in other poets or even sophists, such as in Archilochus the ἀποσκολύπτειν[1] every man, in Theodorus the urging to acquire more while praising equality, and in Euripides the saying that the tongue has sworn.

[1] The verb can mean both 'to pull back the foreskin' and 'to injure' in a variety of ways (cf. fr. adesp. iamb. 45). The precise form of Archilochus' words cannot be determined. For a full discussion see Bossi 123-26.

**40** Scholiast on Aristophanes, *Peace* ("the area is sodden")

παρδακόν means 'wet,' as in Archilochus,

a moist pubis,

and in Semonides of Amorgos.

111

IAMBIC POETRY

**41** Schol. Arat. 1009 (p. 481.13 Martin), "ἀπτερύονται"

ἢ . . . ἀντὶ τοῦ διασείουσι τὰς πτέρυγας ὑποστρέψαν-
τες· διακινοῦσι δὲ τὰς πτέρυγας ἤτοι ὑφ᾽ ἡδονῆς,
τὴν κοίτην καταλαβόντες, ἢ τὴν ἐκ τοῦ ἀέρος δια-
τινάσσοντες ἰκμάδα. καὶ παρ᾽ Ἀρχιλόχῳ ἡ ὑφ᾽ ἡδονῆς
σαλευομένη †κορώνη ὥσπερ

κηρύλος
πέτρης ἐπὶ προβλῆτος ἀπτερύσσετο

ὥσπερ: ὥστε Wilamowitz, ὡς Edmonds

**42** Ath. 10.447b

τὸν δὲ κρίθινον οἶνον καὶ βρῦτόν τινες καλοῦσιν, ὡς
Σοφοκλῆς ἐν Τριπτολέμῳ (fr. 610 Radt) "βρῦτον δὲ
χερσαῖον †οὗ δυεῖν†," καὶ Ἀρχίλοχος·

ὥσπερ αὐλῷ βρῦτον ἢ Θρέϊξ ἀνὴρ
ἢ Φρὺξ ἔμυζε· κύβδα δ᾽ ἦν πονεομένη.

1 init. ⟨ἡ δ᾽⟩ Lattimore, alii alia    Θρᾶιξ cod., corr. Wila-
mowitz    2 ἔβρυζε cod., corr. Wilamowitz    πονευμένη
cod., corr. Fick

**43**

ἡ δέ οἱ σάθη
×–∪ –×    ὥστ᾽ ὄνου Πριηνέως
κήλωνος ἐπλήμυρεν ὀτρυγηφάγου.

112

**41** Scholiast on Aratus, *Phaenomena*

or . . . by the word ἀπτερύονται is meant that they flap
their wings upon their return. They flap their wings either
from pleasure at reaching their nest or because they are
shaking off moisture from the air. And in Archilochus the
crow[1] bouncing around from pleasure like

> a kingfisher flapped its wings on a protruding rock

[1] West (*Studies* 123-24) may well be right in treating κορώνη
as a corruption for something like πόρνη ('prostitute') or κόρη
('girl') and the protruding rock as an erect penis.

**42** Athenaeus, *Scholars at Dinner*

Some call barley wine βρῦτον, as Sophocles in *Triptole-
mus*, "beer of the mainland . . . ," and Archilochus:

> she was sucking like a Thracian or Phrygian sucking
> beer through a tube, and she was bent over working
> hard[1]

[1] The fragment almost certainly describes a woman engaged
in fellatio.

**43** his prick . . . swelled like that of a Prienian grain-fed
breeding ass[1]

[1] The meter is uncertain (many do not assume a lacuna and
adopting Bergk's emendation treat the meter as a combination of
iambic trimeter and dimeter) and a few argue for two separate
fragments (see Bossi 132-35 and W. Luppe, *Hermes* 123 [1995]
247-49). Priene lay across the bay north of Miletus.

# IAMBIC POETRY

*Et. Gud.* (i.230.15 de Stefani)

ἀτρύγετος· ἄκαρπος . . . τρύγη δέ ἐστιν ὁ Δημη-
τριακὸς καρπός. Ἀρχίλοχος· "οἱ δέ οἱ σάθη ὅση τ᾽
ὄνου κήλωνος ὀτρυγηφάγου," περιττεύοντος τοῦ ο, ὡς
καὶ ὀκρυόεις.

cf. *Et. Gen.* (pp. 17, 23, 38, 40 Calame), *Et. Mag.* 167.21, *Et.
Sym.* cod. V (Gaisford ad *Mag.* 271.26), Eust. in Hom. *Il.* 15.27
(iii.696.22 V.d.Valk), Hesych. s.vv. ἀτρυγηφάγου et ὀτρυγη-
φάγου

Eust. in Hom. *Od.* 8.335 (1597.28)

κήλων καὶ λάγνης (ἢ λάγνος διὰ τοῦ ο) καὶ οἰφόλης
καὶ Τιτὰν καὶ μάχλος· ὧν αἱ χρήσεις παρὰ τοῖς πα-
λαιοῖς, οἵ φασιν ὡς κήλων μὲν πεποίηται ἀπὸ τῶν
ὀχευτῶν ὄνων. Ἀρχίλοχος· "ὥστ᾽ ὄνου Πριηνέως κή-
λωνος ἐπλήμυρον."

cf. Suet. *de blasph.* (p. 49 Taillardat)

1 ἡ δέ οἱ Schneidewin, οἱ δέ οἱ *Et. Gud.*, οἰδέοι Gallavotti
2 ὥστ᾽ Eust., ὅση τ᾽ fere Etymologica, ὡσεί τ᾽ Bergk ut sit
dimeter    3 ἐπλήμυρον Eust., corr. Bergk

**44** Ar. *Lys.* 1254 sqq.

ἀμὲ δ᾽ αὖ Λεωνίδας ἆγεν ἇπερ τὼς κάπρως θάγοντας
οἰῶ τὸν ὀδόντα, πολὺς δ᾽ ἀμφὶ τὰς γένυας ἀφρὸς
ἤνσεεν, πολὺς δ᾽ ἁμᾷ κὰτ τῶν σκελῶν {ἀφρὸς} ἵετο.

114

*Etymologicum Gudianum*

ἀτρύγετος means 'without fruit' . . . and τρύγη is the fruit of Demeter. Cf. Archilochus, οἱ . . . ὀτρυγηφάγου, with pleonastic omicron as in ὀκρυόεις.

Eustathius on Homer, *Odyssey*

κήλων and λάγνης (or λάγνος with omicron) and οἰφόλης and Τιτάν and μάχλος: these words are used by the ancients who say that κήλων comes from asses kept for breeding purposes. Cf. Archilochus, ὥστ᾽ . . . ἐπλήμυρον.

**44** Aristophanes, *Lysistrata*

And Leonidas led us, sharpening our teeth I imagine like wild boars, and much foam billowed round our jaws and much also poured down our legs.

Schol. ad loc. (p. 54 Hangard)

πρὸς τὸ παρὰ τῷ Ἀρχιλόχῳ,

  πολλὸς δ' ἀφρὸς ἦν περὶ στόμα.

πολὺς codd., corr. Porson


**45** Phot. *lex.* s.v. κύψαι (i.362 Naber)

ἀντὶ τοῦ ἀπάγξασθαι. Ἀρχίλοχος·

  κύψαντες ὕβριν ἀθρόην ἀπέφλυσεν.

ἀπέφλοσαν cod., corr. Schleusner


**46** Schol. A Hom. *Il.* 9.7 (ii.398.2 Erbse), "παρέξ"

. . . μετὰ γοῦν τῆς διά οὖσα ἡ ἐξ οὐ τρέπει τὸ ξ·

  διὲξ σωλῆνος εἰς ἄγγος.


*Et. Gen.* (p. 25 Calame) = *Et. Mag.* 324.14 = Herodian. (ii.402.29 Lentz)

ἐκ Ῥώμης· ἡ ἐξ πρόθεσις, ὅταν αὐτῇ σύμφωνον ἐπιφέρηται, τρέπει τὸ ξ εἰς κ. δεῖ δὲ προσθεῖναι χωρὶς εἰ μὴ εὑρεθῇ ἡ ἐξ πρόθεσις μετὰ τῆς διά παρέλκουσα, οἷον ὡς παρ' Ἀρχιλόχῳ, "διὲξ σωλῆνος," καὶ πάλιν (sequitur fr. 32).

Scholiast on the passage

This refers to the passage in Archilochus,

> and there was much foam round the mouth[1]

[1] West translates "her mouth" and includes the fragment among those of an erotic nature, but the mouth cannot be identified.

**45** Photius, *Lexicon*

κύψαι for ἀπάγξασθαι ('to hang oneself'). Cf. Archilochus:

> stooped over they spewed out all their insolence[1]

[1] The interpretation of the fragment is much disputed. For a full discussion see Bossi 135-37.

**46** Scholiast on Homer, *Iliad* ("alongside")

. . . At any rate when it is combined with διά the preposition ἐξ does not change the ξ:

> right through the pipe into the container[1]

[1] Probably a reference to ejaculation, with 'pipe' standing for penis and 'container' for vagina.

*Etymologicum Genuinum* and *Magnum*

From (ἐκ) Rome: the preposition ἐξ, whenever a consonant follows, changes the ξ to κ, but not, one must add, if the preposition ἐξ is found lengthened with διά, as in Archilochus, "right through the pipe," and again (fr. 32).

**47** P. Oxy. xxxvii.2811 fr. 5.3-6

"στυπάζει" Ἀμμ[ώνιος ]. στύπ[ει] παίε[ι] ξυλοκοπή-
σω[ν. τοιοῦ]τόν ἐστ[ι] καὶ τ[ὸ] παρ' Ἀρχιλόχω[ι·

.]ε παρθένοι
θυρέων ἀπεστύ[παζ]ον.

cf. *Et. Gen.* (pp. 15, 39, 44 Calame), *Et. Mag.* 120.3, 633.30,
731.45, schol. Ap. Rhod. 1.1117

1 μ]ε (vel αἱ δ]ὲ ) Bossi, σ]ὲ West     2 θυρέων, θύραισιν,
ὀρέων, οὐρέων etym.

**48** P. Oxy. xxii.2311 fr. 1a, ed. Lobel

5     τροφὸς κατ.[ ⌊ἐσμυριχμένας κόμας
      καὶ στῆθος, ⌊ὡς ἂν καὶ γέρων ἠράσσατο
      ὦ Γλαῦκ.[

15 ἐρχ[ε.]θ[        18 ἐβουλόμην
19 ἀπαγγελου[      20 ψιῆισιν[
21 φοιτᾶν·     22 πᾶσαι     23 ἔρδειν·
25 ἀκάτια· καὶ β[     27 πολλῶν       32 ἐγὼ

Ath. 15.688c
τῷ δὲ τοῦ μύρου ὀνόματι πρῶτος Ἀρχίλοχος κέχρηται
λέγων "οὐκ ἂν μύροισι γραῦς ἐοῦσ' ἠλείφετο" (fr. 205)·
καὶ ἀλλαχοῦ δ' ἔφη "ἐσμυριχμένας—ἠράσσατο."

5 κατῆ[γεν West     ἐσμυριχμένας Fick, ἐσμυρισμένας
Ath. cod. A (μυριχμένας cod. B); huc fort. spectat Hesych. ἐσ-

**47** Oxyrhynchus papyrus (early 2nd c. A.D.)

στυπάζει according to Amm(onius[1] . . .) means 'hits with a stump,' 'seeking to beat with a club.' Such is the passage in Archilochus:

> . . . the maidens[2] were driving me (you?) away from the door with cudgels

[1] A grammarian of the 2nd c. B.C.      [2] "Perhaps virgin priestesses of Hera" (West, *Studies* 125). Cf. test. 20.

**48** Oxyrhynchus papyrus (mid 2nd c. A.D.)

> . . . their nurse (brought?) them,[1] with scented hair and breasts, so that even an old man would have been enamoured of them. O Glaucus . . . come . . . I wanted . . . from a messenger(?) . . . frolic(?) . . . to roam about . . . all . . . to do . . . light vessels(?);[2] and . . . of many . . . I . . .

Athenaeus, *Scholars at Dinner*

Archilochus is the first to use the word μύρον ('perfume'), saying: (fr. 205). And also elsewhere he said: "with scented hair . . . enamoured of them."

[1] Perhaps the daughters of Lycambes. Some deny any connection between the papyrus and the fragment cited by Athenaeus.
[2] Or "shoes"(?).

---

μυριχμέναι· μεμυρισμέναι (= fr. adesp. iamb. 61)      κόμην West

**49** P. Oxy. 2311 fr 1b, ed. Lobel

γυνὴ τ[
5  ἔχθιστε[
   καὶ πατ[
   φιλῆτα ν[ύκτωρ περὶ πόλιν πωλεόμενε·
   οὔτ᾽ ὦ[

Eust. in Hom. *Od.* 20.185 (1889.1)

φιλήτου δὲ τοῦ εἰρημένου χρῆσις μὲν παρά τε Ἡσιόδῳ
(*Op.* 375), καὶ παρὰ Ἀρχιλόχῳ ἐν τῷ "φιλήτα—
πωλευμένῳ," ἤγουν κλέπτῃ νυκτιλόχῳ.

7 φιλήτα—πολευμένῳ Eust.: πωλ Liebel, -μενε anon.
8 ὦ[ν Lobel

**51** P. Oxy. xxii.2312 fr. 1, ed. Lobel

3 νῦν      4 πνοαὶ φερ[      6 ἐρετ[

**54** P. Oxy. 2312 fr. 4

]μεν ἡλι[
]ιδε μὲν δυ[
]δ᾽ ἐγὼ γεραιτ[ερ
].ν.[.]ς ἐδεξάμην[
5     ]αὐχέν᾽· ἥδε δ᾽ αζ[

**49**  Same papyrus[1]

> . . . woman . . . most hateful . . . and father(?) . . . you
> thief who prowls about the city at night; nor . . .

Eustathius on Homer, *Odyssey*

The use of the aforesaid φιλήτης is found in Hesiod (*Op.*
375) and in Archilochus in his "thief—at night," that is, a
thief lying in wait at night.

> [1] Perhaps from the same poem as fr. 48 and so the subject
> matter may be the Lycambides. Some see no connection between
> the papyrus and the fragment cited by Eustathius.

**51**  Oxyrhynchus papyrus (late 2nd or early 3rd c. A.D.)

> . . . now . . . breezes . . . oars(?) . . .

**54**  Same papyrus[1]

> . . . I older . . . I received . . . neck; and (but?) she

]ν δὲ δὴ π[ει]ρήσεται·[
]ἄλλοτ’, ὦ καχ[.....]ε
Λυκά]μβα· μηδεμ[.]γουν[
]ειε· λωβητ[.]ν πυθ[
10                ]κακ[ ]. φαι[
]ν λύρην π[
]οσεστι φιλ[
]θα· τηνδ[
]υσεβουλο[
15               ]δε παρθέ[ν
]χε και μ[
].μοσω.[
                 ]χεξ[

5 de ἄζ[υγα (fr. 262) cogit. Lobel      6 suppl. West
8 init. Lobel      μηδέ μ[’ ἢ] γουν[άζεο tent. West
9 λωβητ[ὸ]ν vel -την Lobel      14 o]ὺ̂ς ἐβουλό[μην vel o]ὔ σε
βούλο[μαι tent. West

**57** P. Oxy. 2312 fr 5a

]ταφρος αμ[
]κται πᾶσα· φι[
]ἀγρίουσκι[
]ασα μαιν[
5                ]κεωσαγ.[
]υνοηῃ[
Δω]ταδεω πατρ[
]πάντα δ’ ἠείδ[ει
]ραφεῖσα· τὰ[

122

. . . she will be penetrated(?) . . . at another time
oh . . . Lycambes(?); and do not entreat me(?) . . .
outraged (outrageous)(?) . . . lyre . . . whom I
wanted(?)[2] . . . maiden . . .

[1] Apparently we have a combination of abuse directed against
Lycambes and a description of an erotic encounter with one of his
daughters.     [2] Or "I do not want you"(?).

**57** Same papyrus

. . . ditch(?), foam(?) . . . all . . . wild . . . mad(?) . . .
Dotades(?)[1] . . . knew everything(?) . . .

[1] I.e., Lycambes, if the supplement, based on Hesychius, is
correct.

---

1 τάφρος vel τ᾽ ἀφρὸς Lobel     7 suppl. Lobel cl. Hesych.
Δωτάδης· Δώτου υἱός, ὁ Λυκάμβας

**58** P. Oxy. 2312 frr. 6 + 7 + 8

5              ]γίνετα[ι ...]θυμίης
              ]διατελε[ ]προσω[.....]ε
              ]τε δηϊων[....]ρθ[
          ο]ὐκ ἀποτρ[
          τ]έχνην πᾶσα[ν
10        ]ὀφρύκ[νησ]το[ν
    .....]ν ἐμεωυτο[
    ἄιδων] ὑπ᾽ αὐλητῆι[ρος

5 προ]θυμίης Lobel        10 West ex Hesych. ὀφρύκνη-
στον· ἐρυθριῶντα

**60** P. Oxy. 2312 fr. 9

2 ]ρων λυκ[    6 ὦ τρι]σμακά[ριος ὅστις
7 τοι]αῦτα τέκ[να

2 Λυκ[αμβ Lobel        6-7 suppl. West

**66** *Epimer. Hom.* (p. 322 Dyck)

φύω . . . , ἀφ᾽ οὗ οὐδέτερον τὸ φυτόν· . . . (*Il.* 18.57),
ἀφ᾽ οὗ ἡ φύσις· . . . (*Od.* 10.303), ἀφ᾽ οὗ τὸ φῦμα

    μηρῶν μεταξύ

Ἀρχίλοχος.

ARCHILOCHUS

**58** Same papyrus

... becomes ... eagerness(?) ... enemy ... not ...
every skill ... blushing(?) ... myself ... singing to
the accompaniment of a piper[1] ...

[1] Both the scholiast to Aristophanes, *Birds* 1426, and to *Iliad*
18.492 cite the last three words as an example of ὑπό instead of
μετά.

**60** Same papyrus

... Lycambes(?) ... (oh) thrice-blessed[1] (who) ...
such children ...

[1] Perhaps sarcastic.

**66** *Homeric Parsings*

φύω ('grow'), from which are derived the neuter φυτόν
('plant'), φύσις ('nature'), and φῦμα ('growth'),

between the thighs,

as in Archilochus.[1]

[1] Although some form of φῦμα clearly occurred in the vicinity
of the citation, iambic meter and a connection with fr. 67 need not
be assumed. A metaphor for the penis seems likely.

**67** P. Oxy. 2312 fr. 14

$$
\begin{array}{r}
].\tau о\mu\eta\iota \\
]\lambda\acute{\eta}\sigma о\mu\alpha\iota\cdot \\
\dot{\epsilon}\sigma\theta\lambda\grave{\eta}\nu \ \gamma\grave{\alpha}\rho \ \ddot{\alpha}\lambda\lambda\eta\nu \ о\^{\iota}\delta\alpha \ \tau о\iota о\acute{\upsilon}|\tau о\upsilon \ \phi\upsilon\tau о\^{\upsilon} \\
\ddot{\iota}\eta\sigma\iota\nu \quad\quad\quad ]\delta о\kappa\acute{\epsilon}\omega \\
]\kappa\alpha\kappa\acute{\alpha}\cdot \\
\dot{\epsilon}]\pi\acute{\iota}\phi\rho\alpha\sigma\alpha\iota\cdot \\
]\acute{\eta}\sigma о\mu\alpha\iota \\
]о\upsilon \ \lambda\acute{\iota}\nu о\upsilon \\
]\tau\alpha\theta\eta \\
]\nu\dagger\mu\epsilon\nu о\iota\nu\iota\omega[ \\
].\epsilon\iota\sigma\iota\omega[
\end{array}
$$

(lines 5 and 10 numbered in left margin)

Schol. Theocr. 2.48/49d (p. 281.19 Wendel), "ἱππομανὲς φυτόν"

ἴσως φυτὸν αὐτὸ ἔφη ὁ Θεόκριτος οἰονεὶ φῦμα, ἀπὸ τοῦ φύεσθαι ἐν τοῖς πώλοις, ὥς φησιν Ἀριστοτέλης (H. A. 6.22.577a9). λέγει γὰρ καὶ Ἀρχίλοχος τὸ φῦμα φυτόν· "ἐσθλὴν—†εἴκασιν."

4 ἴησιν Schneidewin, εἴκασιν codd.   10 μενοινέων?
Peek   11 ἐ]πεισίω[ι tent. Lobel

**67** Same papyrus as for fr. 51

... surgery(?) ... for I know another good cure for such a growth[1] ... I seem ... evil ... devise ... flax(?) ... desiring eagerly(?) ... pubic area(?)[2] ...

Scholiast on Theocritus

Perhaps by φυτόν Theocritus meant φῦμα, from a growth on horses, as Aristotle says. For Archilochus also uses φυτόν for φῦμα: "I know ... growth."

[1] Presumably an erect penis which intercourse will 'cure.'
[2] Some treat fr. 40 as belonging here.

**82** P. Oxy. xxii.2319 fr. 4, ed. Lobel

$$]π[. .]χεται[ι$$
$$]εθων$$
$$]ακ[. .]ρίης$$
$$]νώξυνες σάθης$$
5      $$]ην ἐγὼ δίκην$$
$$]οσεστάθης$$
$$].οισιν ἤρκεσας·$$
$$]μελες ἀρκέσειν$$
$$]. ἐλάγχανες$$
10      $$].ματι·$$
$$]θενειάδη[ ]$$
$$εκ]αλλιννας πόλιν[$$
$$]α γὰρ φρονεῖς[$$

### 88-167. Tetrametri

**88** Anon. Ambros. de re metr. (*Anecd. Varia Graeca* p. 223.2 Studemund)

τροχαῖος δὲ ἐκλήθη ὅτι τροχαλὸν ἔχει τὸν ρυθμόν· καὶ γὰρ ὁ Ἀρχίλοχος ἐπὶ τῶν θερμῶν ὑποθέσεων αὐτῷ κέχρηται, ὡς ἐν τῷ

Ἐρξίη, πῇ δηῦτ᾽ ἄνολβος ἀθροΐζεται στρατός;

cf. *Anecd. Chis.* (p. 206.5 Studemund), Hephaest. *Ench.* 6.2, schol. Hephaest. (p. 271.6 et 21 Consbruch), *Et. Gen.* (p. 26 Calame), *Et. Symeon.* (Gaisford ad *Et. Mag.* 376.51), *Et. Mag.* 376.52

**82** Oxyrhynchus papyrus (mid 2nd c. A.D.)

. . . you were stimulating(?) . . . of (my?) prick . . . I (was demanding?) justice . . . you stood(?) . . . you warded off(?) . . .to ward off(?) . . . it was your lot . . . you beautified(?) the city . . . for you understand . . .

*88-167. Trochaic Tetrameters*

**88** Anonymous, *On Meter*

The trochee got its name because the rhythm rolls along (cf. test. 49). For Archilochus has used it on the subject of hasty intentions, as in his

Erxies,[1] to what end (how? where?) is the hapless army assembling this time?

[1] Mentioned also in fr. 89.28. The Etymologica implausibly derive the name from ῥέζειν ('to do') and hence meaning ὁ πρακτικός, 'the man of action.' See Bossi 149.

**89** Mnesiepis inscriptio B (E₂) col. I 15-44 (v. test. 3)

ἀμφικαπνίουσιν[
νηυσίν, ὀξεῖαι δ[
δηΐων, αὐαίνετ[αι
ἠλίωι, θράσος τε[
5     οἳ μέγ᾽ ἱμείροντες[
Ναξίων δῦναι φ.[
καὶ φυτῶν τομὴν[
ἄνδρες ἴσχουσιν[
τοῦτό κεν λεὼι μ[
10    ὡς ἀμηνιτεὶ παρηι[
καὶ κασιγνήτων .[
τέων ἀπέθρισαν[
ἤριπεν πληγῆισιδ[
ταῦτά μοι θυμὸς[
15    νειόθεν .οβ...δε[
ἀλλ᾽ ὅμως θανον[
γνῶθί νυν, εἴ τοι[
ῥήμαθ᾽ ὃς μέλλε[ι
οἱ μὲν ἐν Θάσωι.[
20    καὶ Τορωναίην[
οἱ δ᾽ ἐν ὠκείηισ[ι
και...ἐκ Πάρου τ[
καὶ κασιγνη[τ
θυμὸς αλ.[
25    πῦρ ὃ δὴ νῦν ἀμφι.[
ἐν προαστίωι κε[

**89** Inscription of Mnesiepes

They will surround with smoke . . . ships, piercing
(cries?, rays of the sun?) . . . of the enemy, is (are?)
being parched . . . by the sun, and boldness . . . who
greatly desiring . . . of the Naxians to get into . . . and
a cutting down of trees . . . men hold back . . . this
would on the army . . . so that without anger . . . and
of brothers . . . of whom (which) they cut off . . . fell
under blows . . . these things my heart . . . from its
depths . . . but nevertheless dead . . . know then if
. . . words who is going to . . . some in Thasos . . . and
Torone[1] . . . and others in swift (ships) . . . from
Paros . . . and brothers . . . heart . . . fire which now
round . . . in the suburb . . . they despoil the land . . .

γῆν ἀεικίζουσιν[
Ἐρξίη, καταδραμ[
τῶ 's ὁδὸν στελλ[
30    μηδὲ δεξιοὺς επ[

**90**  (v. test. 3, B col. I 51-57)

**91**  P. Lit. Lond. 55 (vv. 1-46) + P. Oxy. xxii.2313 fr. 10 (vv. 2-13)

                   ]ον παθεῖν
                 ν]ήπιοι φρένα
                 ]τ̣' ἀκήρατος
               ]σημάντορες
5             αἰ]χμητὴς ἐών
                  ]ευμενος·
               ]δρης τελεῖν
              ο]μνύων, ὅτε
               ]ν ἀκούσεαι
10               α]ντίον·
                   ]πολει·
                    ]έχειν
                  ]σμενος
         μηδ' ὁ Τα]ντάλου λίθος
15  τῆσδ' ὑπὲρ νήσου κρεμάσθω]      ]ς̣ ἔχων

16-23: omisi

παντ[.....]ηνες γεν̣έσθαι̣[

Erxies,² ravaging(?) . . . therefore(?) preparing for
a journey . . . and do not (wait for?) favourable
(omens?) . . .

¹ A town on the southern end of the central peninsula of Chal-
cidice, southwest of Thasos.     ² See note on fr. 88.

**91** London and Oxyrhynchus papyri (3rd c. B.C. and 1st
or 2nd c. A.D.)

. . . to suffer . . . foolish at heart . . . pure (gold?) . . .
commanders . . . being a spearman . . . to complete
. . . swearing, when . . . you will give ear . . . opposite
(against?) . . . city(?) . . . to have(?) . . . let the stone
of Tantalus not hang over this island¹ . . . having . . .

25 φαίνο[μαι ‸.]τωνδ᾽ εν μ̣.[
   εἰ γὰρ ω[‸‸‸‸‸].‸ν μ.[.]..[
   χωρὶς α̣[‸‸‸]ντε̣.α̣.ζ[
   συνια[‸‸‸]ω̣.ιων[.]‸.α̣.[
   ειτοδ̣[.]ν̣[.].(.)ον̣.(.)νεθ̣ειμ̣‸‸[

30 ἐς μέσον, τάλαντα δὲ Ζεὺ[ς] εχ[
   μήτε τῶν καινῶν μετωπασμ[
   γῆ φόνωι χλκ̣.ον̣δενηεδ̣[

33-46: omisi

Plut. *praec. gerendae reip.* 6.803a

δέχεται δ᾽ ὁ πολιτικὸς λόγος δικανικοῦ μᾶλλον καὶ
γνωμολογίας καὶ ἱστορίας καὶ μύθους καὶ μεταφορὰς,
αἷς μάλιστα κινοῦσιν οἱ χρώμενοι μετρίως καὶ κατὰ
καιρόν, ὡς . . . Ἀρχίλοχος, "μηδ᾽—κρεμάσθω."

   cf. schol. Pind. *Ol.* 1.91a (i.37.22 Dr.), Paus. 10.31.12

   2 sscr. ομοιοι π]αισιν P. Lond.      7 fort. Οἰσύ]δρης (cf.
fr. 92)      9 ακουσεαι P. Oxy., ]υσεται P. Lond.
25 φαίνο[μαι Blass      30 vel ἔλκ[εν West      31 vel κλίνων
West

**92** Comm. in Callim., P. Univ. Mediol. 18 col. v 9 (fr. 104
   Pf.), "Οἰσύδρεω Θρήϊκος ἐφ᾽ αἵματι πολλὰ Θάσοιο"

φησὶν Παρίους Οἰσύδρην τὸν Θρᾶκα φονεύσαντας
διαπολιορκηθῆναι Θασι[‸‸] ἔ]ως τὸ ἀρέσκον Βεισάλ-
ταις [ἐ]πιτίμιο[ν] τείνειν ἔχρησεν ὁ θεός· οἱ δετει-

ARCHILOCHUS

to become . . . I seem . . . would that . . . apart . . . into the middle, and Zeus (held?) the scales . . . nor the front-line(?) of the new(?) . . . the earth with blood . . .

Plutarch, *Precepts of Statecraft*

And political oratory, much more than that used in a court of law, admits maxims, historical and mythical tales, and metaphors, by means of which those who use them moderately and at the appropriate time move their audience exceedingly, as . . . did Archilochus, "let the stone of Tantalus not hang over this island."

1 The scholiast on Pindar cites Alcaeus (fr. 365 V.), Alcman (fr. 79 *PMGF*) and Archilochus as sources for the stone hanging over Tantalus. The island is presumably Thasos, since the tattered end of the fragment seems to include a mention of it.

**92** Milan papyrus on Callimachus, "because of the murder of the Thracian Oesydres many (misfortunes befell the people of?) Thasos"

He says that because the Parians murdered the Thracian Oesydres they were besieged . . . until(?) the god declared that they pay the penalty that was satisfactory to the Bisal-

135

χο.[...]χαυνοθ..[.....]Θασίοις ἐρωτωισι [....]ειν
.η.[.......]πέμπειν πα[

**93a** Sosthenis inscriptio A col. Ia 43-49 (v. test. 4)

ωντολα.[ ]ειπεασ[...]ιων πάϊς Πεισιστράτου
5  ἄνδρας ..(.)ωλεῦντας αὐλὸν καὶ λύρην ἀνήγαγεν
ἐς Θάσον κυσὶ Θρέϊξιν δῶρ' ἔχων ἀκήρατον
χρυσόν, οἰκείωι δὲ κέρδει ξύν' ἐποίησαν κακά—

5 [εὖ ν]ωμῶντας Leo    ἀνήγαγεν Jensen: -γον vel -γων
lapis    6 εις lapis, corr. Lasserre    Θρηιξιν lapis, corr.
Hiller v. Gaertringen    7 οικειως lapis, corr. Wilamowitz

**93b** Paus. 7.10.6

καὶ ἐπί τε ⟨Σαπαίους καὶ⟩ Σαπαίων τὸν βασιλέα
Ἀβρούπολιν στράτευμα ἀγαγὼν (ὁ Περσεὺς) ἐποίη-
σεν ἀναστάτους, Ῥωμαίων συμμάχους ὄντας. Σα-
παίων δὲ τούτων καὶ Ἀρχίλοχος ἐν ἰάμβῳ (v.l. -ίῳ, sc.
-είῳ) μνήμην ἔσχε.

**94** Inscriptio eadem A col. Ia 55-59 + P. Oxy. xxii.2313 fr.
2 (v. test. 4)

                    τῶν δ' Ἀθηναίη μάχηι
ἵλαος παρασταθεῖσα παῖς ἐρικτύπου Διὸς
καρδίην ὤρινεν †αὐτῆς τῆς πολυκλαύτου λεώ
.[..]υτων[..]αλλα κείνης ἡμέρης ἐπὶ χθ[όν]α

tae[1] . . . Thasians . . . to send

[1] A Thracian tribe. Pfeiffer on Callim. fr. 104 suggests an allusion to Archilochus' account of fighting on Thasos. The name Oesydres may occur in fr. 91.7.

**93a** Inscription of Sosthenes

. . . the son of Pisistratus brought back men well-versed(?) in pipe and lyre to Thasos, bearing pure gold for Thracian dogs; but for personal profit they did public harm—[1]

[1] I have omitted scraps of three preceding verses. After the fragment of Archilochus the inscription goes on to mention some Parians who were killed by the Thracians at Sapae and it is to this that fr. 93b may refer.

**93b** Pausanias, *Description of Greece*

And after leading an army against the Sapaeans, Rome's allies, and their king Abroupolis, Perseus drove them from their land. And Archilochus also mentioned these Sapaeans in his iambics.

**94** Same inscription

In their battle Athena, daughter of loud-thundering Zeus, standing propitiously by their side, roused the hearts . . . of the much-lamented army[1] . . . in the course of that day over the land other . . . ; for so

5  ἄλλον †ἤ̣ειϲεν· τόϲουϲ γὰρ ἐξεχώρηϲεν γύαϲ
   νηλε[....]παντοϲ· ἀλλὰ θεῶν Ὀλυμπίων νόωι
   νη[

**95** Inscriptio eadem A col. IVa 1-6

      ]δ' ἐπὶ ϲτρατ..[
   νῦν ἐεργμέν.[
   πημεϲωϲερ.[
5  ἀλκίμωι ϲ[

4 πῆ μ' ἔϲωϲ' Ἑρμ[ῆϲ Zieliński (cl. Hor. *Carm.* 2.7.13)

**96** Inscriptio eadem A col. IVa 8-13

            Γλαῦκε, τίϲ ϲε θεῶν νό]ον
   καὶ φρέναϲ τρέψ[αϲ
   γῆϲ ἐπιμνήϲαιο τ[ῆϲδε
   δει]νὰ τολμήϲαϲ μεθ[
5  –∪ –] ἣν εἷλεϲ αἰχμῆι καὶ λ[
   –∪ –×–]ϲον {δ} ἔϲκεν καὶ χαλ[

1 Γλαῦκε et νό]ον Hiller v. Gaertringen, cetera West
3 fin. West    4 init. Hiller v. G.

**97** Inscriptio eadem A col. IVa 22

   χειλίουϲ γὰρ ἄν[δ]ρας̣ [.]κ̣[

χιλιουϲ lapis, corr. Diehl       [ἤ̣]κ̣[αν Peek

much land did it give up . . . ; but the mind of the
Olympian gods . . .

1 Of the various emendations for αὐτῆς τῆς perhaps the most
attractive is αὖτις (West) γῆς (Steffen), "roused again the hearts
of the much-lamented land's army."

**95** Same inscription

. . . army (general?) . . . now hemmed in(?) . . . how
Hermes saved me(?) . . . brave . . .

**96** Same inscription

(Glaucus, which one of the gods) turning your mind
and thoughts . . . may you remember this land . . .
daring dangerous deeds . . . you captured with the
spear and . . .

**97** Same inscription

for (they sent?) a thousand men . . .

**98** Inscriptio eadem, A col. IVa 42-58 (vv. 1-17); P. Oxy.
2313 fr. 3a (vv. 12-21)

```
                              ]τ’ ἢ κέρδει ν[ ∪ –
                           ]εταξυι[ – ∪ –
                           ]σὺν δενι[ ∪ –
                           ]λ’ ἀμφὶ δ[ – ∪ –
5                          ]ων δούρατ’ ἐκπ[ × – ∪ –
                       ]ε τῶν δ’ ἐδάμν[αμ]εν ν[όον
                       παῖς] Ἀθηναίη Διός
     ἀμφ[ὶ] δ’ ὑψ[ηλὰς ἐπάλξεις ἤρ]κεσαν πρὸ
         π[α]τρίη[s]
     χρημ[              κ]εῖτο πύργος ἀμφα[ή]ς,
10   θαυ[μ]α[         ] ἐκ λίθων ἐδε[ίμαμ]ε[ν
     – ∪ – ἄν]δ[ρ]ε[s] αὐτοὶ Λεσβίω[...]ει[
     – ∪ – τῶ]ν δ’ ἀ[μ]φ[ιθ]έντες χερσὶν ο[....]δια
     ιμενωι.[ ]ων ἐσο[.(.)]σει Ζεὺς Ὀλυμπίω[ν ]ο.ι[
     – ∪ αἰχμ]ῆ[ι]σιν θοῆισι πημονὴν ἐπήγομ[εν
15   ει.εθ[ ]ότ’ ἀμφὶ πύργον ἔστασαν πονε[όμενοι
     κλίμακας, μ]έγαν δ’ ἔθεντο θυμὸν ἀμφε[
     βαρὺ δ’ ὑπεβρ]όμε[ι σίδ]ηρον εἱμένη καλ[
             ἀ]μειπτή· πολλὰ δ’ ἐρρύ[η βέλεα
             ]φαρέτραι δ’ οὐκέτ’ ἔκρυ[πτον φόνον
20   ]σαν ἰῶν· οἱ δ’ ἐπε[
     στρέψα]ντες ἶνας καὶ ταν[ύσσαντες βιούς
```

6 ἐδάμν[αμ]εν Slings    ν[όον Peek    7 παῖς] Maas
8 ὑψ[ηλὰς ἐπάλξεις West    ἤρ]κεσαν Maas    π[α]τρίη[s
Peek    10 fin. Hiller v. G.    14 αἰχμ]ῆ[ι]σιν Tarditi

**98** Same inscription + Oxyrhynchus papyrus[1]

. . . profit . . . spears . . . we were breaking their spirit
. . . Athena daughter of Zeus; round about the lofty
battlements they warded off in defence of their
homeland . . . there was set a tower visible on all
sides, a marvel(?) . . . from stones we built . . . men
of Lesbos . . . putting round their arms(?) . . . Zeus
the Olympians' . . . we were inflicting misery with
our swift spears . . . when(?) round about the tower
they strenuously set ladders, their spirits high . . .
loud crashed the ironclad . . . alternating(?); and
missiles streamed in abundance . . . and the quivers
no longer kept slaughter concealed . . . of arrows;
but they . . . twisting sinews and drawing bows . . .

[1] Except for v. 5 I have printed and translated West's text, but it
must be emphasized that many of the supplements and readings
are highly uncertain, and that 1-4 may be prose.

---

15 τ]όт' vel ὅτ'    εστασαν pap., ιστασαν lapis    fin. Hiller
v. G.    16 init. West    17 init. West    σίδ]ηρον Peek
18 ἐρρύ[η Peek    βέλεα West    19 fin. West
21 Peek et West

**101** Plut. *Galba* 27.9

ὡς δέ φησιν Ἀρχίλοχος,

εἰκοσι γὰρ νεκρῶν πεσόντων, οὓς ἐμάρψαμεν
   ποσίν,
χείλιοι φονῆές εἰμεν,

οὕτως τότε πολλοὶ τοῦ φόνου μὴ συνεφαψάμενοι,
χεῖρας δὲ καὶ ξίφη καθαιμάσσοντες, ἐπεδείκνυντο καὶ
δωρεὰς ᾔτουν.

2 χίλιοι codd., corr. Fick     ἐσμεν codd., corr. Renner

**102** Strabo 8.6.6

καὶ Ἀπολλόδωρος δὲ (*FGrHist* 244 F 200) μόνους τοὺς
ἐν Θετταλίᾳ καλεῖσθαί φησιν Ἕλληνας· "Μυρμιδόνες
δ᾽ ἐκαλεῦντο καὶ Ἕλληνες" (*Il.* 2.684)· Ἡσίοδον μέντοι
καὶ Ἀρχίλοχον ἤδη εἰδέναι καὶ Ἕλληνας λεγομένους
τοὺς σύμπαντας καὶ Πανέλληνας. τὸν μὲν περὶ τῶν
Προιτίδων λέγοντα ὡς Πανέλληνες ἐμνήστευον αὐτάς
(fr. 130 M.-W.), τὸν δὲ ὡς

Πανελλήνων ὀϊζὺς ἐς Θάσον συνέδραμεν.

nonnulli ὡς ex Strabone Archilocho tribuunt

**101**  Plutarch, *Life of Galba*

But as Archilochus says,

> a thousand of us are the slayers of the seven who fell
> dead, overtaken by us in pursuit,

similarly then many who had no part in the murder blood-
ied their hands and swords and showed them to Otho,
asking for rewards.

**102**  Strabo, *Geography*

And Apollodorus says that only those in Thessaly are called
Greeks: "The Myrmidons were also called Greeks." He
says, however, that Hesiod and Archilochus already knew
that they were collectively spoken of as Greeks and as All-
Greeks, the former saying with regard to the daughters of
Proetus that All-Greeks were their suitors and the latter
that

> the misery of All-Greeks has rushed to Thasos

**105** Heracl. *Alleg. Hom.* 5.2

ὁ γὰρ ἄλλα μὲν ἀγορεύων τρόπος, ἕτερα δὲ ὧν λέγει
σημαίνων, ἐπωνύμως ἀλληγορία καλεῖται· καθάπερ
Ἀρχίλοχος μὲν ἐν τοῖς Θρᾳκικοῖς ἀπειλημμένος δει-
νοῖς τὸν πόλεμον εἰκάζει θαλαττίῳ κλύδωνι, λέγων
ὧδέ πως·

Γλαῦχ', ὅρα· βαθὺς γὰρ ἤδη κύμασιν ταράσσεται
πόντος, ἀμφὶ δ' ἄκρα Γυρέων ὀρθὸν ἵσταται νέφος,
σῆμα χειμῶνος, κιχάνει δ' ἐξ ἀελπτίης φόβος.

2 cf. Theophrast. *de signis temp.* (fr. 6.45 Wimmer), Plut. *de
superstit.* 8.169b, Syrian. in Hermog. (i.73.8 Rabe), Cic. *ad Att.*
5.12.1

2 γυρέων, γυρῶν, γυρεῦον, γυρεύωρν Plut., γύρεον fere
codd. Heracliti, ΤΗΡΕΟΝ vel ΤΝΡΕΟΝ fere codd. Ciceronis

**106** P. Lit. Lond. 54, ed. Milne

                    ]νται νῆες ἐν πόντωι θοαί
                π]ολλὸν δ' ἱστίων ὑφώμεθα
            λύσαν]τες ὅπλα νηός· οὐρίην δ' ἔχε
                ]ρους, ὄφρα σεο μεμνεώμεθα
5               ]άπισχε, μηδὲ τοῦτον ἐμβάληις
                ]ν ἵσταται κυκώμενον
                ]χης· ἀλλὰ σὺ προμήθεσαι
                        ]υμος

2 suppl. Körte      3 suppl. Diehl

ARCHILOCHUS

**105** Heraclitus, *Homeric Allegories*

Allegory derives its name from the device whereby one thing is said but another meant. In exactly this way Archilochus, embroiled in Thracian troubles, likens the war to a storm at sea, speaking, I think, as follows:

> Look, Glaucus! Already waves are disturbing the deep sea and a cloud stands straight round about the heights of Gyrae,[1] a sign of storm; from the unexpected comes fear.

[1] Either the promontory on Tenos or a mythological allusion to the rocks on which the Lesser Ajax met his death (*Od.* 4.500 ff.).

**106** London papyrus (3rd c. B.C.)

> . . . swift ships on the sea . . . let us lower much of the sails . . . loosening the ship's tackle; and keep the wind favourable . . . so that we may remember you . . . hold off, and do not hurl this . . . stands churned up . . . but take thought . . .[1]

[1] Authorship and meter are uncertain. Some treat the meter as iambic and argue for a Hellenistic date, while others assign the fragment to Archilochus, either as a sequel to fr. 105 or as a separate poem.

**107** Plut. *quaest. conv.* 3.10.2.658b (διὰ τί τὰ κρέα σήπεται μᾶλλον ὑπὸ τὴν σελήνην ἢ τὸν ἥλιον)

τὴν γὰρ σελήνην ἠρέμα χλιαίνουσαν ἀνυγραίνειν τὰ σώματα, τὸν δ᾽ ἥλιον ἀναρπάζειν μᾶλλον ἐκ τῶν σωμάτων τὸ νοτερὸν διὰ τὴν πύρωσιν· πρὸς ὃ καὶ τὸν Ἀρχίλοχον εἰρηκέναι φυσικῶς·

> ἔλπομαι, πολλοὺς μὲν αὐτῶν Σείριος καθανανεῖ
> ὀξὺς ἐλλάμπων.

**108** Plut. *quomodo aud. poet.* 6.23a

χρῶνται τοῖς τῶν θεῶν ὀνόμασιν οἱ ποιηταὶ ποτὲ μὲν αὐτῶν ἐκείνων ἐφαπτόμενοι τῇ ἐννοίᾳ, ποτὲ δὲ δυνάμεις τινάς, ὧν οἱ θεοὶ δοτῆρές εἰσι καὶ καθηγεμόνες, ὁμωνύμως προσαγορεύοντες. οἷον εὐθὺς ὁ Ἀρχίλοχος, ὅταν μὲν εὐχόμενος λέγῃ·

> κλῦθ᾽ ἄναξ Ἥφαιστε, καί μοι σύμμαχος
>     γουνουμένῳ
> ἵλαος γενέο, χαρίζεο δ᾽ οἷά περ χαρίζεαι,

αὐτὸν τὸν θεὸν ἐπικαλούμενος δῆλός ἐστιν· ὅταν δέ κτλ. (quae sequuntur v. ad fr. 9)

2 γενοῦ codd., corr. Fick    χαρίζεται codd. nonnulli

**107** Plutarch, *Table Talk* (why flesh rots more under the moon than under the sun)

For the moon with its slight warmth softens corpses, whereas the sun instead takes up the moisture from corpses because of the burning heat. In light of this Archilochus has spoken scientifically:

> many of them, I expect, will be dried up by the Dog Star's[1] fierce rays

[1] Not the sun, as Plutarch states, but the brightest star in the constellation Dog (Canis). See D. Kidd, *Aratus, Phaenomena* (Cambridge 1997) 305-10.

**108** Plutarch, *How the young man should study poetry*

When the poets employ the names of the gods, sometimes their intent is to refer to the gods themselves and sometimes they call by the same name certain properties of which the gods are the givers and in which they are preeminent. To take the first example that comes to mind, when Archilochus prays with the words,

> Lord Hephaestus, give ear to my entreaty, be my propitious ally and grant the kind of favour that you grant,

it is clear that he is calling upon the god himself; but when . . . (see on fr. 9).

**109** Ar. *Pax* 603 sq.

ὦ σοφώτατοι γεωργοί, τἀμὰ δὴ ξυνίετε
ῥήματ᾽, εἰ βούλεσθ᾽ ἀκοῦσαι τήνδ᾽ ὅπως
ἀπώλετο.

Schol. ad loc. (p. 95 Holwerda)

πρὸς ταῦτα καὶ Κρατῖνος ἐν Πυτίνῃ πεποίηκεν (fr. 211
K.-A.) "ὦ λιπερνῆτες πολῖται, τἀμὰ δὴ ξυνίετε." ἔστι
δὲ πρὸς τὰ Ἀρχιλόχου·

⟨ὦ⟩ λιπερνῆτες πολῖται, τἀμὰ δὴ συνίετε
ῥήματα.

1 ὦ add. Liebel    ξυνίετε schol., corr. Bergk    2 vel
ῥήματ᾽

**110** Clem. *Strom.* 6.6.1 (quae praecedunt v. ad fr. 127)

καθάπερ ἀμέλει κἀκεῖνο τὸ ἔπος, "ξυνὸς ἐννάλιος· καί
τε κτανέοντα κατέκτα" (*Il.* 18.309), μεταποιῶν αὐτὸς
ὧδέ πως ἐξήνεγκεν·

†ἔρξω· ἐτήτυμον γὰρ ξυνὸς ἀνθρώποις Ἄρης.

Ἐρξίων Bergk, Ἐρξίην Tarditi, ἔρξον οὖν Deuticke (ὡς vel
ὦν vel ὦδ᾽ Hoffmann)    ἀνθρώποισιν cod., corr. Brunck

**109** Aristophanes, *Peace*

"Farmers most wise,[1] take note of my words if you wish to hear how Peace has disappeared."

Scholiast on the passage

With reference to this Cratinus in *Pytine* has composed: "Indigent citizens, take note of my words." And this comes from Archilochus:

Indigent[2] citizens, take note of my words.[3]

[1] σοφώτατοι ('most wise') is apparently an error for λιπερνῆτες.     [2] The etymology of λιπέρνης and λιπερνήτης was much debated. See P. Hummel, *Philologus* 141 (1997) 145-48.     [3] Perhaps an encouragement to emigrate to Thasos.

**110** Clement of Alexandria, *Miscellanies*

Just as doubtless adapting the well-known verse, "the war god is impartial and slays the would-be slayer," he came out with something like the following:

Erxies(?);[1] for in truth Ares is impartial towards men

[1] Some form of the name Erxies (cf. frr. 88 and 89.28) seems likely.

**111** Pergit Clemens

ἔτι κἀκεῖνο μεταφράζων· "νίκης ἀνθρώποισι θεῶν ἐν
†πείρᾳ κεῖται" (cf. *Il.* 7.102 νίκης πείρατ᾽ ἔχονται ἐν
ἀθανάτοισι θεοῖσι) διὰ τοῦδε τοῦ ἰάμβου δῆλός ἐστι·

καὶ νέους θάρσυνε· νίκης δ᾽ ἐν θεοῖσι πείρατα.

θαρρῦναι Clem., corr. Elmsley

**112** P. Oxy. xxii.2314 col. i + 2313 fr. 27 (coniunxit
Dervisopoulos)

```
            ]ηρας· ἔλπομαι γάρ, ἔλπομαι
              ἀ]νόλβο[ι]ς ἀμφαϋτήσει
                  στρατός
            ].αγγες κοιτον ἀρκαδοσσονον
5       ].α, πολλὰ δ᾽ ἔλπονται νέοι
            ].α· διὰ πόλιν Κουροτρόφος
            ]τατα[ ]εθ.....αεισεται
            ]....ν...αν ἀγκάσεαι
       ]τοιχει.[ ]...τονοχλο· βητεται
10          ]ν· τέωι προσέρχεται [.]εθε
            ]ως Ἀφροδίτηι <δὴ> φίλος
            ]χων ἅτ᾽ ὄλβιος
            ]ερον[
```

3 ]νολβο σι pap., corr. Lobel: vel ἄνολβος?      4 Ἀρκάδ᾽
ὅσσ᾽ ὄνον Latte      5 θέλγονται Lobel dubitans
11 <δὴ> add. Treu

**111** Clement continues

Moreover he is clearly adapting in iambic meter the well-known verse, "the . . . of victory for men depends on the gods":[1]

> and encourage the young, but the accomplishment
> of victory rests with the gods

[1] Clement's citation is corrupt and it is uncertain what passage he had in mind.

**112** Oxyrhynchus papyri[1]

> . . . for I expect, I expect . . . the host[2] will raise a
> shout round about the wretched (the wretched host
> will raise a shout?) . . . like(?) an Arcadian ass[3] . . .
> the young men have high expectations . . . through
> the city Kourotrophos[4] . . . you will lift up your arms
> . . . to whom approaches . . . dear to Aphrodite . . .
> as if blessed . . .

[1] The subject matter may be a sarcastic description of a wedding.    [2] Not necessarily military.    [3] Proverbial for simplemindedness, if the scholiast to Callim. fr. 1.43 Pf. is to be interpreted in this way.    [4] Nurse of the young (Aphrodite?).

**113** P. Oxy. xxii.2314 col. ii

7    ἀρχὸς εὖ μαθ[ὼ]ν ἄκοντι τ[
πειρέαι; λίην λιάζεις κυρ[
ἴσθι νυν, τάδ᾽ ἴσθι…γγο[

7 ἄρχ᾽ ὃς Lobel    μαθ[ὼ]ν Peek    τ[ί? West
8 πειρέαι (πείρω) editores, πειρέαι (πειρῶμαι) West    λιαν
pap., corr. Tarditi

## 114

οὐ φιλέω μέγαν στρατηγὸν οὐδὲ διαπεπλιγμένον
οὐδὲ βοστρύχοισι γαῦρον οὐδ᾽ ὑπεξυρημένον,
ἀλλά μοι σμικρός τις εἴη καὶ περὶ κνήμας ἰδεῖν
ῥοικός, ἀσφαλέως βεβηκὼς ποσσί, καρδίης
πλέως.

Dio Chrys. 33.17

ὁ δὲ Ἀρχίλοχος, ὅν φημι τῷ Ἀπόλλωνι ἀρέσαι, περὶ
στρατηγοῦ λέγων οὕτω φησίν· "οὐ φιλέω—ὑπεξυρη-
μένον," ἀλλά μοι, φησίν, εἴη ῥαιβός, ἀσφαλῶς βεβη-
κὼς καὶ ἐπὶ κνήμαισιν δασύς. μὴ οὖν αὐτὸν οἴεσθε
στρατηγὸν μὲν μὴ ἀγαπᾶν οἷον εἴρηκε, μηδ᾽ ἐν
σώματος μεγέθει καὶ κόμῃ τίθεσθαι τὸ τοῦ στρατηγοῦ
ὄφελος, πόλιν δ᾽ ἂν ἐπαινέσαι ποτὲ εἰς ταῦτα ὁρῶντα,
ποταμοὺς καὶ βαλανεῖα καὶ κρήνας καὶ στοὰς καὶ
πλῆθος οἰκιῶν καὶ μέγεθος; κόμῃ γὰρ ἀτεχνῶς καὶ
βοστρύχοις ταῦτα ἔοικεν. ἀλλ᾽ ἔμοιγε δοκεῖ μᾶλλον

**113** Oxyrhynchus papyrus (3rd c. A.D.)

A commander[1] well versed in the javelin, (why?) do you make trial of . . .?[2] You are too enthusiastic . . . know then, know this . . .

[1] Or a proper name (Archus).    [2] In West's view (*Studies* 129-30) the subject is marriage and a "thrusting weapon" (*sensu erotico*) is being contrasted with a throwing spear.

**114**

I have no liking for a general who is tall, walks with a swaggering gait, takes pride in his curls, and is partly shaven. Let mine be one who is short, has a bent look about the shins, stands firmly on his feet, and is full of courage.

Dio Chrysostom, *Discourses*

But Archilochus who, I say (cf. test. 16), found favour with Apollo, speaks as follows about a general (vv. 1-2). Rather, he says, let mine be bowlegged, with a firm stand, and with thick hair on his shins. Therefore do not think that Archilochus, who did not love the sort of general he has described and did not reckon a general's usefulness by the size of his body and by his hair, would ever have praised a city with an eye on these features, rivers, baths, fountains, porticoes, multitude of houses and vast size, since these things are simply like curls. But to me at least it seems that

ἂν τούτων προκρῖναι σμικράν τε καὶ ὀλίγην σωφρό-
νως οἰκουμένην κἂν ἐπὶ πέτρας.

Galenus in Hippocr. π. ἄρθρων (xviii (1) 604 Kühn)

. . . ὥστε καὶ αὐτῶν τῶν κατὰ φύσιν ἐχόντων τοὺς
ῥαιβοὺς ἢ ῥοικοὺς ὀνομαζομένους ἀσφαλέστερόν τε
καὶ δυσανατρεπτότερον ἵστασθαι τῶν ἀκριβῶς ἐχόν-
των τὰ σκέλη ὀρθά. δηλοῦται δὲ τοῦτο κἀξ ὧν Ἀρχί-
λοχος εἶπεν· "οὐ φιλέω—πλέως."

ibid. p. 537

τὸ μὲν γὰρ διὰ τοῦ κ λεγόμενον ῥοικὸν οἶδα καὶ παρὰ
Θεοκρίτῳ γεγραμμένον ἔνθα φησί· (4.49), καὶ παρ'
Ἀρχιλόχῳ "ἀλλά—πλέως."

cf. Erotian. p. 112.11 Nachmanson, schol. Theocr. 4.49a (p.
148.19 Wendel)

Pollux 2.192

ῥαιβοὺς δὲ καλοῦσιν, οἷς καμπύλα εἰς τὸ ἔνδον τὰ
σκέλη, βλαισοὺς δὲ οἷς τὸ ἀπὸ τῶν γονάτων εἰς τὸ
ἔξω ἀπέστραπται. καὶ τὸ μὲν Ἀρχίλοχος, τὸ δὲ Ξενο-
φῶν λέγει (de re equ. 1.3)

1 διαπεπλεγμένον Dio, -πεπηγμένον Gal., corr. Hem-
sterhuys          3 σμικρός Erotian., μικρός Gal.     κατὰ
κνήμην schol. Theocr., ἐπὶ κνήμασιν δασύς Dio     4 ῥαιβός
Dio, Pollux

instead of these things he would have preferred a city that is small in size and population and is wisely governed, even if it is on a rock.

## Galen on Hippocrates, *On Joints*

. . . with the result that those who have bent or curved legs, as they are called, stand more firmly and are more difficult to overturn than those who have perfectly straight legs. This is clear from what Archilochus said (vv. 1, 3-4).

## Galen as above[1]

For I know that ῥοικός is also written with a kappa in Theocritus (4.49) and in Archilochus (vv. 3-4).

[1] The texts of Galen are with minor corrections those preserved in the oldest MS, Laurentianus gr. Plut. 74.7 (from which the others are derived), except that in the second citation there is a lacuna in the MS between ῥοι- and -οκρίτῳ. I am indebted here to my colleague, Paul Potter.

## Pollux, *Vocabulary*

They call ῥαιβοί those whose legs are curved inward and βλαισοί those whose area from the knees is turned outward. Archilochus speaks of the former, Xenophon of the latter.

**115** 'Herodian.' *de figuris* (*Rhet. Gr.* viii.598.16 Walz, iii.97.8 Spengel)

πολύπτωτον δέ, ὅταν ἤτοι τὰς ἀντονομασίας ἢ τὰ ὀνόματα εἰς πάσας τὰς πτώσεις μεταβάλλοντες διατιθώμεθα τὸν λόγον, ὡς παρὰ Κλεοχάρει· . . . ἔστι δὲ τὸ τοιοῦτον σχῆμα καὶ παρά τισι τῶν ποιητῶν, ὡς παρ' Ἀρχιλόχῳ καὶ Ἀνακρέοντι. παρὰ μὲν οὖν Ἀρχιλόχῳ·

νῦν δὲ Λεώφιλος μὲν ἄρχει, Λεωφίλου δ'
    ἐπικρατεῖν,
Λεωφίλῳ δὲ πάντα κεῖται, Λεώφιλον δ' †ἄκουε.

παρὰ δὲ Ἀνακρέοντι ἐπὶ τριῶν (fr. 359 *PMG*).

1 Λεωφίλου et Λεώφιλος ἐπικρατεῖ codd., corr. West, ἐστὶ κράτος Murru    2 πάντ' ἀνεῖται Bergk    Λεώφιλον, -ε, -ος codd.

**116** Ath. 3.76b

τῶν δ' ἐν Πάρῳ τῇ νήσῳ—διάφορα γὰρ κἀνταῦθα γίνεται σῦκα τὰ καλούμενα παρὰ τοῖς Παρίοις αἰμώνια . . .—Ἀρχίλοχος μνημονεύει λέγων οὕτως·

ἔα Πάρον καὶ σῦκα κεῖνα καὶ θαλάσσιον βίον.

**115** 'Herodian', *On Figures of Speech*

There is polyptoton whenever we arrange what is said by changing all the cases of pronouns or nouns, as in Cleochares: . . . Such a figure is found also in some of the poets as in Archilochus and Anacreon. In Archilochus:

> Now Leophilus is in charge, power rests with Leophilus, everything depends on Leophilus, and . . . Leophilus.[1]

And in Anacreon with three cases.

[1] In the example omitted from 'Herodian' above, the name Demosthenes appears in the order nom., gen., dat., acc. and voc., and it is likely that the same sequence is present in Archilochus, but no satisfactory emendation for the end of the fragment has been proposed.

**116** Athenaeus, *Scholars at Dinner*

The figs on the island of Paros—for there too there are excellent ones, called *haimonia* by the Parians . . .—are mentioned by Archilochus who speaks as follows:

> Good-bye to Paros and those figs and life on the sea

**117** Schol. (b)T Hom. *Il.* 24.81 (v.536 Erbse), "βοὸς κέρας"

οἱ δὲ νεώτεροι κέρας τὴν συμπλοκὴν τῶν τριχῶν ὁμοίαν κέρατι.

τὸν κεροπλάστην ἄειδε Γλαῦκον.

Ἀρχίλοχος.

**118** Plut. *de E apud Delphi* 5.386d

"εἰ γὰρ {ὤφελον}," φησὶν ἕκαστος τῶν εὐχομένων· καὶ Ἀρχίλοχος·

εἰ γὰρ ὡς ἐμοὶ γένοιτο χεῖρα Νεοβούλης θιγεῖν.

χειρὶ Elmsley

**119** Schol. Eur. *Med.* 679, "ἀσκοῦ με τὸν προὔχοντα μὴ λῦσαι πόδα"

ἀσκὸν τοίνυν λέγει τὸν περὶ τὴν γαστέρα τόπον. Ἀρχίλοχος·

καὶ πεσεῖν δρήστην ἐπ' ἀσκόν, κἀπὶ γαστρὶ
    γαστέρα
προσβαλεῖν μηρούς τε μηροῖς,

"δρήστην" λέγων οἷα δράσαντά τι.

προσβάλλειν cod., corr. Matthiae

**117**  Scholiast on Homer, *Iliad* ("horn of an ox")

Later authors use the word horn to describe the horn-like
intertwining of the hair.

> sing of Glaucus who arranges his hair in horns

So Archilochus.

**118**  Plutarch, *On the E at Delphi*

"Would that" says everyone who prays. Cf. Archilochus:

> Would that I might thus touch Neoboule on her
> hand[1]

[1] Or "touch Neoboule with my hand," if Elmsley's emenda-
tion, accepted by a number of critics, is adopted.

**119**  Scholiast on Euripides, *Medea* ("that I was not to
loosen the projecting foot of the wineskin")

By ἀσκός he means the region of the stomach. Cf. Archi-
lochus,

> and to fall upon her wineskin[1] that works for hire[2]
> and to thrust belly against belly, thighs against
> thighs,[3]

meaning by δρήστην one who did some work.

[1] Metaphor for the genital area.      [2] Cf. fr. 208, but
δρήστην may be subject of the infinitive, the "labourer" as a
metaphor for penis.      [3] Many combine frr. 118 and 119.

**120** Ath. 14.628a

Φιλόχορος δέ (*FGrHist* 328 F 172) φησιν ὡς οἱ παλαιοὶ
σπένδοντες οὐκ αἰεὶ διθυραμβοῦσιν, ἀλλ᾽ ὅταν σπέν-
δωσι, τὸν μὲν Διόνυσον ἐν οἴνῳ καὶ μέθῃ, τὸν δ᾽
Ἀπόλλωνα μεθ᾽ ἡσυχίας καὶ τάξεως μέλποντες. Ἀρχί-
λοχος γοῦν φησιν·

> ὡς Διωνύσοι᾽ ἄνακτος καλὸν ἐξάρξαι μέλος
> οἶδα διθύραμβον οἴνῳ συγκεραυνωθεὶς φρένας.

1 Διονύσοιο cod., corr. Bentley: Διωνύσου Hermann

**121** Ath. 5.180d-e

οὐ γὰρ ἐξάρχοντες οἱ κυβιστητῆρες (*Il.* 18.606 = *Od.*
4.19), ἀλλ᾽ ἐξάρχοντος τοῦ ᾠδοῦ πάντες ὠρχοῦντο. τὸ
γὰρ ἐξάρχειν τῆς φόρμιγγος ἴδιον. διόπερ ὁ μὲν
Ἡσίοδός φησιν ἐν τῇ Ἀσπίδι (205) "θεαὶ δ᾽ ἐξῆρχον
ἀοιδῆς Μοῦσαι Πιερίδες," καὶ ὁ Ἀρχίλοχος·

> αὐτὸς ἐξάρχων πρὸς αὐλὸν Λέσβιον παιήονα.

**122** Stob. 4.46.10 (Ἀρχιλόχου) + P. Oxy. xxii.2313 fr. 1a,
ed. Lobel

> χρημάτων ἄελπτον οὐδέν ἐστιν οὐδ᾽ ἀπώμοτον
> οὐδὲ θαυμάσιον, ἐπειδὴ Ζεὺς πατὴρ Ὀλυμπίων
> ἐκ μεσαμβρίης ἔθηκε νύκτ᾽, ἀποκρύψας φάος
> ἡλίου †λάμποντος, λυγρὸν† δ᾽ ἦλθ᾽ ἐπ᾽
>     ἀνθρώπους δέος

**120** Athenaeus, *Scholars at Dinner*

And Philochorus says that when the ancients pour liba-
tions they do not always sing dithyrambs, but whenever
they pour libations, they do so singing of Dionysus amid
wine and drunkenness, Apollo quietly and with good
order. Archilochus at any rate says:

> for[1] I know how to take the lead in the dithyramb,
> the lovely song of lord Dionysus, my wits thunder-
> struck with wine[2]

[1] Possibly ὡς belongs to Athenaeus ("that").     [2] Cf.
test. 62.

**121** Athenaeus, *Scholars at Dinner*

For it was not the tumblers who took the lead, but they
all danced while the singer led, since taking the lead is
the lyre's proper function. That is why Hesiod says in the
*Shield*, "and the divine Muses of Pieria were taking the
lead in the song," and Archilochus:

> I myself taking the lead in the Lesbian paean to the
> pipe's accompaniment

**122** Stobaeus, *Anthology*, and Oxyrhynchus papyrus[1]

From Archilochus:

> Nothing is to be unexpected or sworn impossible or
> marvelled at, now that Zeus father of the Olympians
> has made night out of the noonday, hiding away the
> light of the shining sun,[2] and clammy(?) fear came

5    ἐκ δὲ τοῦ καὶ πιστὰ πάντα κἀπίελπτα γίνεται
ἀνδράσιν· μηδεὶς ἔθ' ὑμέων εἰσορέων θαυμαζέτω
μηδ' ἐὰν δελφῖσι θῆρες ἀνταμείψωνται νομὸν
ἐνάλιον, καί σφιν θαλάσσης ἠχέεντα κύματα
φίλτερ' ἠπείρου γένηται, τοῖσι δ' ὑλέειν ὄρος.

10                  Ἀρ]χηνακτίδης
                       ]ητου πάϊς
                     ]τυθη γάμωι

cf. Arist. *Rhet.* 3.17.1418b28 et schol. ad loc. (*Comm. in Arist. Graeca* xxi(2).255.31), Plut. *de facie lun.* 19.931e; v. ad fr. adesp. iamb. 59

1 δ' post χρημάτων Arist. codd. recc.        3 μεσημβρίας Stob., corr. Hoffmann    4 λαμπόν, τοσοῦτον Mähly, ὑγρὸν Valckenaer, ὠχρὸν Bentley, αὖον Kamerbeek, αἰνὸν Marcovich 5 οὐκ ἄπιστα Stob., καὶ πιστὰ Liebel    6 ὑμῶν Stob., corr. Renner    7 ἵνα Stob., ἐὰν Valckenaer    8 σφι Stob., corr. Gaisford    9 ἡδὺ ἦν (sic) Stob., ] ειν pap., ὑλέειν Lobel (ὑλήειν Bergk)

**124**  Ath. 1.7f-8b

ὅτι περὶ Περικλέους φησὶν Ἀρχίλοχος ὁ Πάριος ποιητὴς ὡς ἀκλήτου ἐπεισπαίοντος εἰς τὰ συμπόσια

    (a)              Μυκονίων δίκην.

δοκοῦσι δ' οἱ Μυκόνιοι διὰ τὸ πένεσθαι καὶ λυπρὰν νῆσον οἰκεῖν ἐπὶ γλισχρότητι καὶ πλεονεξίᾳ διαβάλλεσθαι . . .

over people. From now on men can believe and
expect anything; let none of you any longer marvel
at what you see, not even if wild animals take on a
briny pasturage in exchange with dolphins and the
crashing waves of the sea become dearer to them
than the land, the wooded mountain dearer to dol-
phins . . . Archeanactides[3] . . . child of . . . marriage
. . .

[1] According to Aristotle (see on fr. 19) Archilochus here repre-
sents a father as speaking about his daughter.　　　[2] Gener-
ally taken to be the eclipse of 648, but some prefer that of 689 or
711.　　　[3] Identity unknown. Some explain him as the one to
whom Lycambes gave Neoboule in marriage after breaking off
her engagement to the poet. The papyrus continues for a further
five verses, but only ἀν]δράσιν ('men') can be translated.

**124** Athenaeus, *Scholars at Dinner*

Archilochus, the poet of Paros, speaks of Pericles[1] as burst-
ing into drinking parties uninvited

    (a) like the people of Myconos

It seems that the Myconians had a bad name for stinginess
and greed because of their poverty and because they lived
on a wretched island . . .

IAMBIC POETRY

(b)      πολλὸν δὲ πίνων καὶ χαλίκρητον μέθυ,
οὔτε τῖμον εἰσενείκας ‹– ∪ – × – ∪ –›
οὐδὲ μὲν κληθεὶς ‹∪ –×› ἦλθες οἷα δὴ φίλος,
ἀλλά σεο γαστὴρ νόον τε καὶ φρένας παρήγαγεν
5   εἰς ἀναιδείην,

Ἀρχίλοχός φησιν.

(b) 1 μεθύων codd., corr. Casaubon      2 εἰσήνεγκας
codd., corr. Kaibel      3 ‹Περίκλεις› post κληθεὶς suppl.
Diehl, alii alia      4 σευ codd., corr. West

**125** Ath. 10.433e

τὸ δίψος γὰρ πᾶσιν ἰσχυρὰν ἐπιθυμίαν ἐμποιεῖ τῆς
περιττῆς ἀπολαύσεως. διὸ καὶ Σοφοκλῆς φησι (fr. 763
Radt)· "διψῶντι γάρ τοι πάντα προσφέρων σοφὰ / οὐκ
ἂν πλέον τέρψειας ἢ πιεῖν διδούς." καὶ ὁ Ἀρχίλοχος·

μάχης δὲ τῆς σῆς, ὥστε διψέων πιεῖν,
ὡς ἐρέω.

**126** Theophilus ad Autolycum 2.37 (p. 94 Grant)

ἤδη δὲ καὶ τῶν ποιητῶν τινες ὡσπερεὶ λόγια ἑαυτοῖς
ἐξεῖπον ταῦτα καὶ εἰς μαρτύριον τοῖς τὰ ἄδικα
πράσσουσιν, λέγοντες ὅτι μέλλουσι κολάζεσθαι . . .
ὁμοίως καὶ Ἀρχίλοχος

(b) Although you consumed a large quantity of un-
mixed wine, you did not contribute to the cost . . .
nor again did you come invited . . . as though a
friend, but your belly led astray your mind and wits
to shamelessness,[2]

Archilochus says.

[1] Cf. test. 17.       [2] The number and location of the lacunae
are uncertain: see Bossi 181-83.

## 125  Athenaeus, *Scholars at Dinner*

For thirst arouses in everyone a strong desire for abundant
satisfaction. Therefore Sophocles says: "though you offer a
thirsty man every wise saying, you cannot please him more
than by giving him something to drink." And Archilochus
says:

as when I am thirsty for drink, so I long to do battle
with you.[1]

[1] The context may be either erotic or martial.

## 126  Theophilus, *To Autolycus*

Now some of the poets made these statements as if they
were oracles for themselves and as testimony against those
who act unjustly . . . similarly Archilochus:

ἐν δ' ἐπίσταμαι μέγα,
τὸν κακῶς ‹μ'› ἔρδοντα δεινοῖς ἀνταμείβεσθαι
κακοῖς.

2 μ' add. Hecker    δρῶντα cod., corr. Turyn    δέννοις
Herzog

**127** Clem. *Strom.* 6.6.1

αὖθίς τε ὁ Ἀρχίλοχος τὸ Ὁμηρικὸν ἐκεῖνο μεταφέρων,
"ἀασάμην, οὐδ' αὐτὸς ἀναίνομαι· ἀντί νυ πολλῶν" (*Il.*
9.116), ὧδέ πως γράφει·

ἤμβλακον. καί πού τιν' ἄλλον ἤδ' †ἄτη 'κιχήσατο.

ἡ ἀάτη (cum syniz.) Meineke, ἄση Bentley, ἀρὴ Liebel, ἄλη
vel ἄγη Hermann, ἡ δύη Wilamowitz

**128** Stob. 3.20.28

Ἀρχιλόχου·

θυμέ, θύμ', ἀμηχάνοισι κήδεσιν κυκώμενε,
†ἀναδευ δυσμενῶν† δ' ἀλέξεο προσβαλὼν ἐναντίον
στέρνον †ἐνδοκοισιν† ἐχθρῶν πλησίον
    κατασταθεὶς
ἀσφαλέως· καὶ μήτε νικέων ἀμφάδην ἀγάλλεο,
5  μηδὲ νικηθεὶς ἐν οἴκῳ καταπεσὼν ὀδύρεο,
ἀλλὰ χαρτοῖσίν τε χαῖρε καὶ κακοῖσιν ἀσχάλα
μὴ λίην, γίνωσκε δ' οἷος ῥυσμὸς ἀνθρώπους
    ἔχει.

but one great thing I know, to repay with terrible
harm one who does me harm

**127** Clement of Alexandria, *Miscellanies*

And again Archilochus, adapting that Homeric line "I was
infatuate and I myself admit it; worth many," writes some-
what as follows:

I erred, and perhaps this infatuation(?) has come
upon another

**128** Stobaeus, *Anthology*

From Archilochus:

My heart, my heart, confounded by woes beyond
remedy, rise up(?) and defend yourself, setting your
breast against your foes(?) as they lie in ambush(?)
and standing steadfastly near the enemy. Do not ex-
ult openly in victory and in defeat do not fall down
lamenting at home, but let your rejoicing in joy-
ful times and your grief in bad times be moderate.
Know what sort of pattern governs mankind.

---

1 Dion. Hal. *de comp. verb.* 106 (ii.69.9 et 171.22 Us.-Rad.)
2 Hesych. ἔνδοκος· ἐνέδρα       6-7 Apost. 18.8a (*Paroem.
Gr.* ii.718)

2 ἄνα δέ Liebel, ἄνα σύ Pfeiffer, ἀνὰ δ᾽ ἔχεν (vel ἀναδύευ)
μένων δ᾽ Bergk, δυσμενέων Lasserre       3 δοκοῖσιν codd. SA,
δόκοισιν M, ἐνδόκοισιν Valckenaer (cf. Hesych. supra),
λόχοισιν Klinger       4 νικῶν codd., corr. Lasserre
6 ἄσχαλλε SA, Apost., ἄσχαλε M, corr. Grotius

**129** Arist. *Pol.* 7.7.1328a1

πρὸς γὰρ τοὺς συνήθεις καὶ φίλους ὁ θυμὸς αἴρεται
μᾶλλον ἢ πρὸς τοὺς ἀγνῶτας, ὀλιγωρεῖσθαι νομίσας.
διὸ καὶ Ἀρχίλοχος προσηκόντως τοῖς φίλοις ἐγκαλῶν
διαλέγεται πρὸς τὸν θυμόν·

σὺ γὰρ δὴ παρὰ φίλων ἀπάγχεαι.

οὐ codd., corr. Schneider     παρὰ Par. 1858 et versio
Guilielmi de Moerbeka, περὶ ceteri     ἀπάγχεαι, ἀπέγχεαι,
ἀπάγχε(τ)ο, ἀπέγχεο codd.

**130** Stob. 4.41.24

Ἀρχιλόχου·

τοῖς θεοῖς †τ᾽ εἰθεῖάπαντα· πολλάκις μὲν ἐκ κακῶν
ἄνδρας ὀρθοῦσιν μελαίνῃ κειμένους ἐπὶ χθονί,
πολλάκις δ᾽ ἀνατρέπουσι καὶ μάλ᾽ εὖ βεβηκότας
ὑπτίους, κείνοις ⟨δ᾽⟩ ἔπειτα πολλὰ γίνεται κακά,
5    καὶ βίου χρήμῃ πλανᾶται καὶ νόου παρήορος.

1 τιθεῖν ἅπαντα Jacobs, τέλεια Hommel, πείθοι᾽ West, alii
alia     4 κινοῦσ᾽ codd., κλίνουσ᾽ Valckenaer (postea inter-
pungens), κείνοις Blaydes ⟨δ᾽⟩ add. West     post h. v.
lacunam stat. Meineke

**129** Aristotle, *Politics*

For one's heart, when it thinks it is being slighted, rises up more against friends and acquaintances than against strangers. Therefore when Archilochus accuses his friends it is fitting that he address his heart:

   for you are being strangled by your friends

**130** Stobaeus, *Anthology*

From Archilochus:

   Everything is . . . for (to, by) the gods. Often when
   men are lying prostrate on the dark earth they raise
   them upright from their misery, and often they
   overturn on their backs even those whose stance was
   very firm. Then much misery is theirs and a man
   wanders about in need of livelihood and distraught
   in mind.

**131** Stob. 1.1.18

τοῖος ἀνθρώποισι θυμός, Γλαῦκε Λεπτίνεω πάϊ,
γίνεται θνητοῖς, ὁποίην Ζεὺς ἐφ' ἡμέρην ἄγῃ.

cf. Ps.-Plut. *de vita et poesi Hom.* (B) 155 (vii.424.24 Bernardakis), Theon, *Progymn.* (*Rhet. Gr.* i.152.24 Walz, ii.62.22 Spengel), Sext. Emp. *adv. math.* 7.127, Diog. Laert. 9.71, *Sud.* s.v. Πυρρώνειοι (iv.278.28 Adler), Syrian. in Hermog. (i.30.24 Rabe), *Rhet. Gr.* vii.934.9 Walz

1 θυμός Ps.-Plut., Theon, Stob.: νόος vel νοῦς (ex *Od.* 18.136) Diog. L., *Suda*, Syrian., *Rhet.*     2 ὁποίην Sext.: ὁκοίην Diog. L., *Suda*, Syrian., *Rhet.* v.l. (οἰκοίην Stob.): ὁκοῖον Ps.-Plut., Theon, *Rhet.* cod. unus     ἄγῃ Stob., Syrian. v.l.: ἄγει cett.

**132** Ps.-Plat. *Eryxias* 397e

ὁποῖοι γὰρ ἄν τινες ὦσιν οἱ χρώμενοι, τοιαῦτα καὶ τὰ πράγματα αὐτοῖς ἀνάγκη εἶναι. καλῶς δέ, ἔφη, δοκεῖ μοι καὶ τὸ τοῦ Ἀρχιλόχου πεποιῆσθαι·

καὶ φρονέουσι τοῖ' ὁποίοις ἐγκυρέωσιν ἔργμασιν.

cf. Stob. 4.31.117, Apostol. 12.97d, Heracl. 22 B 17 D.-K.

ὁκοίοις codd., corr. Wilamowitz     ἐρύμασιν codd., ἔργμασιν Stob., Apostol.

**133** Stob. 4.58.4

Ἀρχιλόχου·

οὔτις αἰδοῖος μετ' ἀστῶν †καὶ περίφημος† θανὼν
γίνεται· χάριν δὲ μᾶλλον τοῦ ζοοῦ διώκομεν

**131** Stobaeus, *Anthology*

Glaucus, son of Leptines,[1] the mood of mortals varies with the day that Zeus brings on

[1] See test. 1.

**132** Pseudo-Plato, *Eryxias*

For of whatever sort friends are, such must their actions be. And, he said, it seems to me that the line of Archilochus was well composed:

and their thoughts match whatever events they encounter[1]

[1] Jacobs plausibly combined fr. 132 with 131 and many have followed him.

**133** Stobaeus, *Anthology*

From Archilochus:

Once dead no one is held in respect among the citizens even though he be powerful(?).[1] Instead we the

⟨οἳ⟩ ζοοί, κάκιστα δ᾽ αἰεὶ τῷ θανόντι γίνεται.

1 καίπερ ἴφθιμος Porson, οὐδε π. Hiller      2-3 ζο- pro ζω-
Porson      3 ⟨οἳ⟩ anon. ap. Gaisford      δ᾽ αἰεὶ idem, δέει
cod. M (δὲ S)

**134** Schol. Hom. *Od.* 22.412, "οὐχ ὁσίη κταμένοισιν ἐπ᾽
ἀνδράσι εὐχετάασθαι"

ἔνθεν καὶ Ἀρχίλοχός φησιν·

οὐ γὰρ ἐσθλὰ κατθανοῦσι κερτομεῖν ἐπ᾽
ἀνδράσιν.

**135-166** Frag. pap. minora (P. Oxy. 2313)

**139** P. Oxy. xxii.2313 fr. 5

⟩χ᾽ ἀσπιδ[
⟩ν ἴσην τὴν[
⟩δ[..]χθεὶς ἔργον[
⟩δ᾽ ἐστὶν οὐδεὶς τέκμ[αρ
5          ⟩ς ἔντος δηϊοισεμ[
⟩ν ἀκόντων δοῦπον ου[
⟩ευ[.]ονα[.]ει τήνδεκαλ[
⟩βων ῥήματ᾽ οὐκετ[
⟩γὰρ [ο]ὐδὲν εἰδόσ[ιν

3 δ[αϊ]χθεὶς tent. West      9 εἰδόσ[ιν West

living curry the favour of the living and the dead are always the worst off.

[1] With Porson's emendation; with Hiller's, "nor is he celebrated."

**134** Scholiast on Homer, *Odyssey* ("it is not sanctioned by divine law to boast over the dead")

Hence Archilochus says:

for it is not good to jeer at the dead

**135-166** Scraps of an Oxyrhynchus papyrus (Those containing nothing of significance have been omitted.)

**139** Oxyrhynchus papyrus

. . . shield . . . equal . . . (slain?) . . . deed . . . there is no (no one) . . . end (sign?) . . . weapon . . . enemy . . . thud of javelins . . . words no longer . . . for knowing nothing . . .

**140** P. Oxy. 2313 fr. 6

1 αὐ]χένα σχεθών     3 κ]αρτερὸν
6 ]ενην ἔχων     7 ].αρμονέων
9 ]δόμους

**142** P. Oxy. 2313 fr. 8a

3 ]ν Ἰμβρίου     4 ]ạ σχέθοι     9 ]χρεώ
11 ]ς ἔλπομα[ι     13 ].ους ἔπεις
15 ]ροις ἔχων

9 "χρεώ potius quam χρέω (imperat.)" West

**144** P. Oxy. 2313 fr. 9

1 νέος     2 ]κίνει ταλαν[τ     4 τερπε[

2 κίνει imperat. vel ἐ]κίνει imperf.

**145** P. Oxy. 2313 frr. 11 + 12

7 ἐν ζοοῖσιδ[     9 ]ης ἀλκῆς λ̣[

**146** P. Oxy. 2313 fr. 13

5
]προσβαλόντε[ς .]σ[
].ν ξεινίων φειδοίατ[ο
]ων ἀθρόοι γενοίμεθ[α
]σης τεύχεσιν πεφρ[
]σφας ἀμφικουρίη λάβ[

**140** Same papyrus

. . . holding the neck (aslant?) . . . mighty . . . having
. . . agreements(?) . . . homes . . .


**142** Same papyrus

. . . Imbrian . . . may he(?) hold . . . need . . . I expect
. . . you are busying yourself with[1] . . . having . . .

[1] Probably a compound verb with tmesis (ἀμφέπεις, διέπεις
etc.).


**144** Same papyrus

. . . young . . . move (moved) the scales . . . delight(s)
. . .


**145** Same papyrus

. . . among the living . . . defence (prowess) . . .

**146** Same papyrus

. . . striking against . . . were sparing of guest-
gifts(?)[1] . . . we were all together . . . fortified(?) by
arms . . . capture by encirclement(?) . . .

[1] Cf. fr. 6.

---

8 πεφρ[αγμ- Lobel

**148**  P. Oxy. 2313 fr. 15

   2 δ]έννος ὕβριν      4 ]ρους ἀλκίμους

   2 Lobel     4 κού]ρους Peek

**151**  P. Oxy. 2313 fr. 17

   2 ]υ γαμ[     3 ]άδεω[

   2 ο]ὐ γάμ[ου Peek    3 Δωτ]άδεω Peek

**152**  P. Oxy. 2313 fr. 21

   2 γυναῖ]κα βινέων[

   2 Peek

**163**  P. Oxy. 2313 fr. 34

   2 τρισο]ιζυρη[

   2 Lasserre, qui cum fr. 228 coniunxit

**166**  P. Oxy. 2313 fr. 38

   3 ἱμ]ερτὴ Πάρ[ος

   3 Lobel

**148**  Same papyrus

. . . abuse . . . insolence(?) . . . stout-hearted
(youths?) . . .


**151**  Same papyrus

. . . (no?) marriage . . . Dotades(?)[1]

[1] See note on fr. 67.


**152**  Same papyrus

. . . fucking a woman . . .


**163**  Same papyrus

. . . thrice-wretched (city?) . . .


**166**  Same papyrus

. . . longed-for Paros . . .

**167** Ath. 10.415d

περὶ δὲ Θυὸς τοῦ Παφλαγόνων βασίλεως, ὅτι καὶ
αὐτὸς ἦν πολυφάγος, προειρήκαμεν . . . Ἀρχίλοχος
δὲ ἐν τετραμέτροις Χαρίλαν εἰς τὰ ὅμοια διαβέβλη-
κεν, ὡς οἱ κωμῳδιοποιοὶ Κλεώνυμον καὶ Πείσανδρον.

cf. test. 17

*168-204. Epodi*

**168-171**

× – ⏑⏑ – ⏑⏑ – –

– ⏑ – ⏑⏑ – –

Hephaest. *Ench.* 15.1-3

γίνεται δὲ καὶ ἀσυνάρτητα, ὁπόταν δύο κῶλα μὴ
δυνάμενα ἀλλήλοις συναρτηθῆναι μηδὲ ἔνωσιν ἔχειν
ἀντὶ ἑνὸς μόνου παραλαμβάνηται στίχου. πρῶτος δὲ
καὶ τούτοις Ἀρχίλοχος κέχρηται. πῇ μὲν γὰρ ἐποίη-
σεν ἔκ τε ἀναπαιστικοῦ ἐφθημιμεροῦς καὶ τροχαϊκοῦ
ἡμιολίου τοῦ καλουμένου ἰθυφαλλικοῦ "Ἐρασμο-
νίδη—γελοῖον." τοῦτο δὲ οἱ μετ᾽ αὐτὸν οὐχ ὁμοίως
αὐτῷ ἔγραψαν. οὗτος μὲν γὰρ τῇ τε τομῇ δι᾽ ὅλου
κέχρηται {τοῦ ἐφθημιμεροῦς}, καὶ σπονδείους παρέλα-
βεν ἐν τῷ ἀναπαιστικῷ κώλῳ, οἷον "ἀστῶν—πολλοί."
οἱ δὲ μετ᾽ αὐτὸν τῇ μὲν τομῇ ἀδιαφόρως ἐχρήσαντο,
ὥσπερ Κρατῖνος (fr. 360 K.-A.)·

**167**  Athenaeus, *Scholars at Dinner*

With regard to Thys, king of the Paphlagonians, we have
already said that he was a glutton . . . And Archilochus in
his tetrameters attacked Charilaus on the same grounds,[1]
just as the comic poets attacked Cleonymus and Pisander.

[1] Probably from the same poem as fr. 168 in spite of the refer-
ence to tetrameters. See note 5 on frr. 168-171.


*168-204. Epodes*

**168-171**


Hephaestion, *Handbook of Meters*

And there are also unconnected meters, whenever two
cola which cannot be connected with each other and form
a unity are used instead of one single line.[1] Archilochus
was the first to use these too, since in some places he
composed out of the anapaestic hephthemimer[2] and the
trochaic hemiolion[3] called ithyphallic Ἐρασμονίδη—
γελοῖον (fr. 168.1-2). But those who came after him did
not write this in the same way as he did, since he used the
caesura throughout[4] and he introduced spondees in the
anapaestic colon, as in ἀστῶν—πολλοί (fr. 170), whereas
those who came after him used the caesura indiscrimi-

χαῖρ᾽ ὦ μέγ᾽ ἀχρειόγελως ὅμιλε ταῖς ἐπίβδαις,
τῆς ἡμετέρας σοφίας κριτὴς ἄριστε πάντων . . .

. . . καὶ μέντοι καὶ τοὺς σπονδείους παρῃτήσαντο τοὺς
ἐν τῷ μέσῳ.

Ib. 8.7 de paroemiaco

πρῶτος δὲ Ἀρχίλοχος ἐχρήσατο τῷ μεγέθει τούτῳ ἐν
τοῖς τετραμέτροις προτάξας αὐτὸ τοῦ ἰθυφαλλικοῦ. τὸ
γὰρ "Ἐρασμονίδη Χαρίλαε" ἐφθημιμερές ἐστιν ἀνα-
παιστικόν. ἐχρήσατο δὲ τῷ πρώτῳ ποδὶ καὶ ἰάμβῳ,
ὡς καὶ ἐκ τοῦ παραδείγματός ἐστι δῆλον, καὶ σπον-
δείῳ, "Δήμητρί τε χεῖρας ἀνέξων."

**168**

Ἐρασμονίδη Χαρίλαε,
    χρῆμά τοι γελοῖον
ἐρέω, πολὺ φίλταθ᾽ ἑταίρων,
    τέρψεαι δ᾽ ἀκούων.

nately, as in Cratinus: "all hail, throng that laughs untimely on the day after the festival, best of all judges of our poetic skill" . . . and they also avoided spondees in the middle.

Hephaestion (on the paroemiac)

But Archilochus was the first to use this (metrical) length, placing it in front of the ithyphallic in his tetrameters.[5] For Ἐρασμονίδη Χαρίλαε (fr.168.1) is an anapaestic hephthemimer. But for the first foot he used both an iambus, as is clear from the example, and a spondee, Δήμητρί τε χεῖρας ἀνέξων (fr. 169).

[1] There is disagreement on whether these unconnected meters should be printed as one line or two.     [2] Literally, 'consisting of seven half parts,' i.e., three and a half feet.
[3] Literally, 'a half and a whole.' By 'whole' Hephaestion here means a pair of trochees.     [4] I.e., word-end always occurred after the hephthemimer.     [5] Ancient sources sometimes use this term for epodes.

**168**

Charilaus, son of Erasmon,[1] by far the dearest of my companions, I shall tell you something funny and you will be delighted to hear it.

Hephaest. *Ench.* 15.2 ut supra; 1 etiam 8.7, 15.4

Hephaest. *Ench.* 15.6

ὑπονοήσειε δ᾽ ἄν τις καὶ τρίτην διαφορὰν εἶναι τῷ
Ἀρχιλόχῳ πρὸς τοὺς μετ᾽ αὐτόν, καθ᾽ ἣν ἀναπαιστῷ
δοκεῖ τῷ πρώτῳ χρῆσθαι· "ἐρέω—ἀκούων," "φιλέειν—
διαλέγεσθαι," ᾧ οὐκ ἐχρήσαντο ἐκεῖνοι. φαίνεται δὲ
οὐδ᾽ αὐτὸς κεχρημένος· δύναται γὰρ ἀμφότερα κατὰ
συνεκφώνησιν εἰς ἴαμβον περιίστασθαι.

1-2 cum 3-4 coniunxit Koen

**169** Hephaest. *Ench.* 8.7 ut supra

Δήμητρί τε χεῖρας ἀνέξων.

**170** Hephaest. *Ench.* 15.2 ut supra

ἀστῶν δ᾽ οἱ μὲν κατόπισθεν
ἦσαν, οἱ δὲ πολλοί.

2 ἦσαν Meineke

**171** Hephaest. *Ench.* 15.6 (v. ad fr. 168)

φιλεῖν στυγνόν περ ἐόντα
μηδὲ διαλέγεσθαι.

φιλέειν Hephaestion

182

Hephaestion as above (vv. 1-2)

Hephaestion

One might suspect that Archilochus has also a third differ-
ence from those who came after him, in that he seems to
use an anapaest in the first foot ἐρέω—ἀκούων (fr. 168.3-
4), φιλέειν—διαλέγεσθαι (fr. 171), which they did not
use. But it is clear that he himself did not use it either, since
both can be turned into an iambus by synecphonesis.

[1] No doubt a coined patronymic which might be rendered as
'Darlingson.'

**169** Hephaestion as above

and about to lift up hands to Demeter

**170** Hephaestion as above

some of the citizens were behind, but the majority
. . .

**171** Hephaestion (on fr. 168)

to be his friend, hateful though he is, and (but?) not
to converse

# IAMBIC POETRY

**172-181** Fabula de Vulpe et Aquila

× – ∪ – × – ∪ – × – ∪ –
× – ∪ – × – ∪ –

Aesop. *fab.* 1 (Perry)

ἀετὸς καὶ ἀλώπηξ φιλίαν πρὸς ἀλλήλους ποιησάμενοι
πλησίον ἑαυτῶν οἰκεῖν διέγνωσαν, βεβαίωσιν φιλίας
τὴν συνήθειαν ποιούμενοι. καὶ δὴ ὁ μὲν ἀναβὰς
ἐπί τι περίμηκες δένδρον ἐνεοττοποιήσατο, ἡ δὲ εἰσ-
ελθοῦσα εἰς τὸν ὑποκείμενον θάμνον ἔτεκεν. ἐξελ-
θούσης δέ ποτε αὐτῆς ἐπὶ νομήν, ὁ ἀετὸς ἀπορῶν
τροφῆς καταπτὰς εἰς τὸν θάμνον καὶ τὰ γεννήματα
ἀναρπάσας μετὰ τῶν ἑαυτοῦ νεοττῶν κατεθοινήσατο.
ἡ δὲ ἀλώπηξ ἐπανελθοῦσα, ὡς ἔγνω τὸ πραχθέν, οὐ
μᾶλλον ἐπὶ τῷ τῶν νεοττῶν θανάτῳ ἐλυπήθη ὅσον ἐπὶ
τῇ ἀμύνῃ· χερσαία γὰρ οὖσα πτηνὸν διώκειν ἠδυνάτει.
διόπερ πόρρωθεν στᾶσα, ὃ μόνον τοῖς ἀδυνάτοις καὶ
ἀσθενέσιν ὑπολείπεται, τῷ ἐχθρῷ κατηρᾶτο. συνέβη
δὲ αὐτῷ τῆς εἰς τὴν φιλίαν ἀσεβείας οὐκ εἰς μακρὰν
δίκην ὑποσχεῖν. θυόντων γάρ τινων αἶγα ἐπ' ἀγροῦ,
καταπτὰς ἀπὸ τοῦ βωμοῦ σπλάγχνον ἔμπυρον
ἀνήνεγκεν· οὗ κομισθέντος ἐπὶ τὴν καλιὰν σφοδρὸς
ἐμπεσὼν ἄνεμος ἐκ λεπτοῦ καὶ παλαιοῦ κάρφους
λαμπρὰν φλόγα ἀνῆψε. καὶ διὰ τοῦτο καταφλεχθέντες
οἱ νεοττοί, καὶ γὰρ ἦσαν ἔτι <ἀ>πτῆνες {ἀτελεῖς}, ἐπὶ
τὴν γῆν κατέπεσον, καὶ ἡ ἀλώπηξ προσδραμοῦσα ἐν
ὄψει τοῦ ἀετοῦ πάντας αὐτοὺς κατέφαγεν.

**172-181** Fable of the Fox and the Eagle

Aesop, *Fable*

An eagle and a fox became friends and decided to live near each other, thinking that their friendship would be strengthened by cohabitation. And so the eagle flew up into a very tall tree and made its nest, while the fox went into a thicket that lay beneath and gave birth. One day, when the fox had gone out to forage, the eagle, at a loss for food, flew down into the thicket and seizing the cubs dined on them along with its nestlings. The fox, upon returning and realizing what had been done, was more distressed by the inability to exact vengeance than by the death of its cubs, since as a land animal it was unable to pursue one that had wings. Therefore, standing far away, it cursed its enemy, the only thing left for the powerless and weak. And it happened that the eagle soon paid the penalty for its sacrilege against friendship. Some people were sacrificing a goat in the countryside and the eagle flying down carried off from the altar a burning entrail. When it had been brought to the nest, a strong gust of wind kindled a bright flame from the thin and aged straw. Because of this the nestlings were set on fire and since they were not yet capable of flight they fell to the ground. The fox ran up within sight of the eagle and devoured them all.

**172**

πάτερ Λυκάμβα, ποῖον ἐφράσω τόδε;
    τίς σὰς παρήειρε φρένας
ἧς τὸ πρὶν ἠρήρησθα; νῦν δὲ δὴ πολὺς
    ἀστοῖσι φαίνεαι γέλως.

Schol. Hermog., *Rhet. Gr.* vii.820.17 Walz

ἔστι δὲ ἀεὶ τὸ ἐπῳδὸν βραχύτερον τοῦ πρὸ αὐτοῦ
στίχου συλλαβὰς τέσσαρας, οἷον στίχος μὲν ὁ πρῶ-
τος, ἤγουν στροφὴ ἤτοι κῶλον, οἷον "πάτερ—τόδε,"
εἶτα τὸ ἐπῳδόν, "τίς—φρένας," εἶτα ἀντίστροφος ἤτοι
κῶλον, "ἧς—πολύς," εἶτα πάλιν ἐπῳδόν, "ἀστοῖσι—
γέλως."

  1-2 Hephaest. *de poem.* 7.2 (v. ad fr. 182)

  3 ἠρήρεισθα schol. Hermog., corr. Bergk

**173**  Orig. *c. Celsum* 2.21 (i.314 Borret)

τίς γὰρ οὐκ οἶδεν ὅτι πολλοὶ κοινωνήσαντες ἁλῶν καὶ
τραπέζης ἐπεβούλευσαν τοῖς συνεστίοις; καὶ πλήρης
ἐστὶν ἡ Ἑλλήνων καὶ βαρβάρων ἱστορία τοιούτων
παραδειγμάτων· καὶ ὀνειδίζων γε ὁ Πάριος ἰαμβο-
ποιὸς τὸν Λυκάμβην μετὰ ἅλας καὶ τράπεζαν συν-
θήκας ἀθετήσαντά φησι πρὸς αὐτόν

ὅρκον δ᾽ ἐνοσφίσθης μέγαν
ἅλας τε καὶ τράπεζαν.

ARCHILOCHUS

**172**

Father Lycambes, what did you mean by this? Who
unhinged your wits which previously were sound?
Now you seem to the townspeople a source of much
laughter.[1]

Scholiast on Hermogenes

The epodic line is always four syllables shorter than the
line before it,[2] such as, for example, the first line (or stro-
phe or colon) πάτερ—τόδε (v. 1), then the epodic line
τίς—φρένας (v. 2), then the antistrophic line or colon
ἧς—πολύς (v. 3), and then again the epodic line
ἀστοῖσι—γέλως (v. 4).

[1] These verses seem to have begun the poem.　　[2] As a
generalization this is clearly untrue.

**173** Origen, *Against Celsus*

For who does not know that many who have shared salt
and table have conspired against their fellow diners? And
the history of the Greeks and barbarians is full of such
examples. It is in fact the reproach which the iambic poet
of Paros levels against Lycambes for having broken an
agreement after salt and table:

you have turned your back on salt and table by
which you swore a solemn oath

# IAMBIC POETRY

**174** Herenn. Philo *de diversis verborum significationibus*
(pp. 142 sq. Palmieri)

αἶνος καὶ παροιμία διαφέρει. ὁ μὲν γὰρ αἶνός ἐστι
λόγος μυθικὸς ἐκφερόμενος ἀπὸ ἀλόγων ζῴων ἢ
φυτῶν πρὸς ἀνθρώπων παραίνεσιν, ὥς φησι Λουκίλ-
λιος ὁ Ταρραῖος ἐν τῷ πρώτῳ Περὶ παροιμιῶν. οἷον
ἀπὸ μὲν ἀλόγων ζῴων ὡς παρ᾽ Ἀρχιλόχῳ,

> αἶνός τις ἀνθρώπων ὅδε,
> ὡς ἄρ᾽ ἀλώπηξ καἰετὸς ξυνεωνίην
>     ἔμειξαν,

καὶ τὰ ἑξῆς.

Ap. Dysc. *de coniunct*. (*Gramm. Gr.* I.i.223.24)

ἆρα. οὗτος κατὰ πᾶσαν διάλεκτον, ὑπεσταλμένης τῆς
κοινῆς καὶ τῆς Ἀττικῆς, "ἦρα" λέγεται . . . Ἀρχίλοχος
μέντοι κοινότερον ἔφη "ὡς—ξυνωνίην."

2 ξυνωνίην vel -αν codd., corr. Fick    3 ἔμιξαν ἤ, καθ᾽
ἑτέραν γραφήν, ἔθεντο Eust. in Hom. *Od.* 14.508 (1768.58),
ἔμειξαν Fick

**175** P. Oxy. xxii.2315 fr. 1, ed. Lobel

× – ∪ ἐς παῖ]δας φέρων
        δαῖ]τα δ᾽ οὐ καλὴν ἐπ[ὶ
× – ∪ ἀπτ]ῆνες δύο
× – ∪ – × ].γῆ[ς] ἐφ᾽ ὑψηλῶι π[άγωι
5    × – ∪ – ]νεοσσιῆι

188

**174** Herennius Philo, *On the Different Meanings of
Words*

Fable and proverb differ. For the fable is a mythical tale
delivered by animals or plants as advice to humans, as
Lucillius[1] of Tarrha says in his first book *On Proverbs*. An
example involving animals is in Archilochus,

> There is a fable men tell as follows, that a fox and an
> eagle joined in friendship, etc.[2]

Apollonius Dyscolus, *On Conjunctions*

In every dialect except Koine and Attic ἆρα occurs in the
form ἦρα . . . Archilochus, however, is more in keeping
with Koine when he said (v. 2).

[1] Ammonius (p. 5 Nickau) has Lucius (Λούκιος) and Eustathius Lucillus (Λούκιλλος). The latter is probably the correct
form.  [2] Philo proceeds immediately to a second example
from Archilochus (fr. 185).

**175** Oxyrhynchus papyrus (early 2nd c. A.D.)

> . . . (the eagle) carrying to its young . . . and for the
> unlovely meal (eagerly waited?) two fledgelings . . .
> on the land's lofty crag (where they had their?) nest[1]

× – ∪ – ]προύθηκε, τὴν δ[ × – ∪ –
× – ∪ – ].εχο.[ ∪ –
× – ∪ – ]α̣δε̣..[ ∪ – × – ∪ –
× – ∪ – × ]φωλα̣[δ –

1 suppl. Lasserre      2 δαῖ]τα Lasserre      κἀκηνοπ[
pap., sscr. λ et ε: ἔπ[ι Lobel, fort. recte      3 ὥρμησαν suppl.
West (vix apte, ut opinor)      ἀπτ]ῆνες Lobel      4 π[άγῳ
West      9 West

**176** Atticus fr. 2 (p. 41 des Places)

μιᾷ γὰρ ὁδῷ βαδίζοντα, ἥτις ἄγειν πέφυκεν ἐπί τι τῶν
μικρῶν καὶ ταπεινῶν, οὐκ ἔστιν ἐλθεῖν ἐπὶ τὰ μείζω
καὶ ἐν ὕψει κείμενα.

> ὁρᾷς ἵν᾽ ἐστὶ κεῖνος ὑψηλὸς πάγος,
>     τρηχύς τε καὶ παλίγκοτος;
> ἐν τῷ κάθηται, σὴν ἐλαφρίζων μάχην.

ἐπὶ τοῦτον τὸν ὑψηλὸν πάγον τὸ δριμὺ καὶ πανοῦργον
ἐκεῖνο θηρίον ἀνελθεῖν ἀδύνατον· ἵνα δ᾽ εἰς ταὐτὸν
ἔλθῃ τοῖς ἀετοῦ γεννήμασιν ἀλώπηξ, ἢ τύχῃ τινὶ δεῖ
χρησαμένους ἐκείνους πονηρᾷ καταπεσεῖν εἰς γῆν,
τῶν οἰκίων αὐτοῖς φθαρέντων, ἢ φύσασαν αὐτὴν ἃ μὴ
πέφυκε φύειν "λαιψηρὰ κυκλῶσαι πτερά" (cf. fr.
181.11), καὶ οὕτως ἀρθεῖσαν ἐκ γῆς ἀναπτέσθαι πρὸς
τὸν ὑψηλὸν πάγον.

1 ἐστὶν ἐκεῖνος codd., corr. Schneidewin      3 κάθημαι
Meineke

190

... the eagle set before (them the fox's cubs?) and
... the den ...

1 In the margin opposite "nest" there is a scholium containing
the word πυρός 'fire' (cf. fr. 180).

**176** Atticus

For if one follows a single path which is to lead to some-
thing insignificant and paltry, it is not possible to reach
greater goals set on the heights.

Do you see where that lofty crag is, rugged and
hostile? On it (the eagle) sits, making light of your
assault.[1]

To climb this lofty crag was an impossibility for that shrewd
and sly creature. In order for the fox to get to the same
place as the eagle's nestlings, either they had to meet up
with some mischance and fall to the ground, their nest
destroyed, or the fox, contrary to its nature, had "to wheel
on nimble wings" and rising from the earth in this way fly
up to the lofty crag.

1 Perhaps the fox is addressing herself.

**177** Stob. 1.3.34

ὦ Ζεῦ, πάτερ Ζεῦ, σὸν μὲν οὐρανοῦ κράτος,
σὺ δ' ἔργ' ἐπ' ἀνθρώπων ὁρᾷς
λεωργὰ καὶ θεμιστά, σοὶ δὲ θηρίων
ὕβρις τε καὶ δίκη μέλει.

1-4 Clem. *Strom.* 5.127.1, Euseb. *praep. ev.* 13.13.54

2 ἀνθρώπους Clem., Euseb.    3 καθέμιστας Stob., καὶ
ἃ θέμις Clem., τε καὶ ἀθέμιστα Euseb., corr. Matthiae et Liebel

**178** Porphyrius in Hom. *Il.* 24.315 (p. 275.1 Schrader)

εἴωθε δὲ καὶ ὁ Ἀρχίλοχος μελάμπυγον τοῦτον καλεῖν
(sc. τὸν μέλανα αἰετόν)·

μή τευ μελαμπύγου τύχῃς.

ἄλλος γὰρ ὁ πύγαργος, ἄλλος δὲ ὁ μέλας ὅλος.

Tzetz. in Lyc. 91 (ii.50.23 Scheer), "πύγαργον"

εἰσὶ γὰρ μελάμπυγοι ⟨καὶ⟩ πύγαργοι εἴδη ἀετῶν κατ'
Ἀρχίλοχον . . . ὁ δὲ δειλὸς πάλιν πύγαργος λέγεται,
ὡς λευκὴν ἔχων τὴν πυγήν, ἐκ τοῦ ἐναντίου τῇ
παροιμίᾳ, "οὔπω μελαμπύγῳ τετύχηκας" . . . Θεία δὲ ἡ
Ὠκεανοῦ τοῖς ἰδίοις τοῦτο παισὶν εἶπε περὶ τοῦ Ἡρα-
κλέος, "οὔπω μελαμπύγῳ τετυχήκατε."

Zenob. Athous 2.85 (Miller, *Mélanges* 367)

μελαμπύγῳ συνέτυχες· παρὰ Ἀρχιλόχῳ κεῖται. ὁ γὰρ

192

**177** Stobaeus, *Anthology*[1]

Zeus, father Zeus, yours is the rule in heaven, you oversee men's deeds, wicked and lawful, and both the violence and the justice of beasts are your concern.[2]

[1] Stobaeus ascribes the fragment to Aeschylus, Clement to Archilochus.    [2] No doubt spoken by the fox.

**178** Porphyry on Homer, *Iliad*

Archilochus too used to call this (sc. the black eagle) black-rumped:

lest you encounter one that is black-rumped[1]

For another is white-rumped and another all black.

Tzetzes on Lycophron, "white-rumped"

For according to Archilochus there are black-rumped and white-rumped varieties of eagles ... The cowardly one is called white-rumped, since its rump is white, in contrast to the proverb "not yet have you encountered the black-rumped" ... And Theia, daughter of Oceanus, said this to her own children, "not yet have you encountered the black-rumped."

Zenobius of Athos

"You have met with the black-rumped." This is found in

IAMBIC POETRY

Ἡρακλῆς καὶ λάσιος καὶ μελάμπυγος ἐγένετο.
λέγουσι δὲ ὅτι τῶν Κερκώπων ἡ μήτηρ προύλεγεν
αὐτοῖς τὸν μελάμπυγον φυλάξασθαι· μετὰ δὲ ταῦτα
συλληφθέντες ὑπὸ τοῦ Ἡρακλέος καὶ δεθέντες τοὺς
πόδας πρὸς ἀλλήλους ἐκ τῶν ὤμων αὐτοῦ τὰς κεφαλὰς
κρεμαμένας εἶχον· ὁρῶντες δὲ αὐτὸν μελάμπυγον
ἐγέλασαν. καὶ τὴν πρόφασιν ἐρωτηθέντες τῆς μητρὸς
τὴν πρόρρησιν εἶπον, καὶ οὕτω φιλανθρωπίας ὥς
φασιν ἔτυχον.

Hesych.

μή τευ μελαμπύγου τύχοις· μή τινος ἀνδρείου καὶ
ἰσχυροῦ τύχοις.

τύχης Porph., alii; τύχοις Hesych., alii

**179** *Et. Mag.* 32.26

αἰηνές· τὸ δεινὸν καὶ πολύστονον. Ἀρχίλοχος·

προύθηκε παισὶ δεῖπνον αἰηνὲς φέρων.

**180** Schol. Ar. *Ach.* 278 (p. 48 Wilson), "ἐν τῷ φεψάλῳ"

ἐν τῷ καπνῷ. φέψαλοι γὰρ οἱ σπινθῆρες . . . καὶ παρὰ
Ἀρχιλόχῳ δὲ κεῖται·

πυρὸς δ' ἐν αὐτῷ φεψάλυξ.

δ' ἦν schol., corr. Schneidewin

194

Archilochus. For Heracles was hairy and black-rumped. And they say that the mother of the Cercopes warned them to be on their guard against the black-rumped. Afterwards, when they were seized by Heracles and their feet were tied together, they had their heads hanging from his shoulders. And seeing his black rump they burst into laughter. When asked the reason they told him their mother's warning, and so, it is said, they met with kind treatment.

Hesychius, *Lexicon*

May you not encounter one who is black-rumped: may you not encounter one who is strong and powerful.

[1] Most of the many sources (see Bossi 191-96) connect this fragment with the tale of Heracles and the Cercopes, but the words are appropriate in the mouth of the fox, warning the eagle that it may encounter one who is stronger (in this case, Zeus).

**179** *Etymologicum Magnum*

αἰηνές: terrible and lamentable, as in Archilochus:

(the eagle) carried and set before its young a woeful meal

**180** Scholiast on Aristophanes, *Acharnians* ("in the sparks")

In the smoke, for φέψαλοι are sparks . . . And the word is also found in Archilochus:

a spark of fire (was) in it

IAMBIC POETRY

**181** P. Oxy. xxii.2316, ed. Lobel

> ].τάτην[
> μ]έγ᾽ ἠείδει κακ[όν
> 5      φ]ρέ[ν]ας
> ].δ᾽ ἀμήχανον τ.[
> ]ακον·
> ].ᾳνων μεμνημένοςͅ[
> ].ῃν κλύσας
> 10      κέ]λευθον ὠκέως δι᾽ αἰθέρος[
> λαυψηρὰ κυ]κλώσας πτερά
> ]ͅν ἡσ̣.̣.· σὸς δὲ θυμὸς ἔλπεται

11 cf. Atticum (ad fr. 176), Plut. *de garrul.* 10.507a, Plut. *amat.* 3.750b

4 init. suppl. Lasserre, fin. Peek      8 ὀρ]φανῶν Lobel 9 κ[.]ύσας pap., sscr. λ      10 init., de τάμνων cogit. Lobel

**182-187**

× – ∪ – × – ∪ – × – ∪ –
–∪∪ –∪∪ –

**182** Hephaest. *de poem.* 7.2 (p. 71 Consbruch)

εἰσὶ δὲ ἐν τοῖς ποιήμασι καὶ οἱ ἀρρενικῶς οὕτω καλούμενοι ἐπῳδοί, ὅταν μεγάλῳ στίχῳ περιττόν τι ἐπιφέρηται, οἷον "πάτερ—φρένας (fr. 172.1-2), καὶ ἔτι

**181**  Oxyrhynchus papyrus (3rd c. A.D.)

. . . (the eagle?) became aware of the great disaster
. . . heart . . . helpless . . . mindful of . . . washing
away(?) . . . (cleaving?) a path swiftly through the air,
wheeling on nimble wings . . . your heart expects . . .

**182**  Hephaestion, *On Poems*

And there are also in poetry the so-called epodes (ἐπῳδοί)
with masculine termination, whenever some surplus is
added to a long line, such as (fr. 172.1-2) and also

εὖτε πρὸς ἆθλα δῆμος ἠθροΐζετο,
    ἐν δὲ Βατουσιάδης.

1 εὖ τι vel εὖ τοι codd., corr. Bentley          ἄεθλα codd., corr.
Fick

**183**

Σελληΐδεω

Hesych. Σελληΐδεω· Σελ<λ>έως υἱός, ὁ μάντις, Βατου-
σιάδης τὸ ὄνομα.

**184** Plut. *de primo frig.* 14.950e

οὐ γὰρ εἰς τοὐναντίον ἀλλ᾽ ὑπὸ τοῦ ἐναντίου φθείρεται
τῶν ἀπολλυμένων ἕκαστον, ὥσπερ τὸ πῦρ ὑπὸ τοῦ
ὕδατος εἰς τὸν ἀέρα . . . ὁ δ᾽ Ἀρχίλοχος ἐπὶ τῆς
τἀναντία φρονούσης οὐ κακῶς εἶπε·

    τῇ μὲν ὕδωρ ἐφόρει
δολοφρονέουσα χειρί, θητέρῃ δὲ πῦρ.

**185-187** Fabula de Vulpe et Simio

Aesop. *fab.* 81 (Perry)

ἐν συνόδῳ τῶν ἀλόγων ζῴων πίθηκος ὀρχησάμενος

when the people gathered for the games, and among them Batousiades[1]

[1] See fr. 183.

## 183

of the son of Selleus[1]

Hesychius, *Lexicon* s.v. Σελληίδεω: son of Selleus, the seer named Batousiades.

[1] Probably a mock patronymic with reference to the Selloi, prophets of Zeus at Dodona (cf. *Il.* 16.234 f.). Aristides (test. 17) states that Archilochus "slandered Lycambes, Charilaus, so-and-so the seer . . ." In general see Bossi 207-210.

**184** Plutarch, *The Principle of Cold*

For when anything is destroyed, it does not perish into its opposite but by the action of its opposite, as fire perishes into air by the action of water . . . And Archilochus expressed himself well on a woman who had opposing thoughts:

with deceitful intent she was carrying water in one hand, fire in the other

**185-187** Fable of the Fox and the Monkey

Aesop, *Fable*

A monkey danced in a gathering of animals and having

καὶ εὐδοκιμήσας βασιλεὺς ὑπ' αὐτῶν ἐχειροτονήθη.
ἀλώπηξ δὲ αὐτῷ φθονήσασα, ὡς ἐθεάσατο ἔν τινι
πάγῃ κρέας κείμενον, ἀγαγοῦσα αὐτὸν ἐνταῦθα ἔλεγεν
ὡς εὑροῦσα θησαυρὸν αὐτὴ μὲν οὐκ ἐχρήσατο, γέρας
δὲ αὐτῷ τῆς βασιλείας τετήρηκε, καὶ παρῄνει αὐτῷ
λαμβάνειν. τοῦ δὲ ἀμελήτως ἐπιόντος καὶ ὑπὸ τῆς
παγίδος συλληφθέντος, αἰτιωμένου τε τὴν ἀλώπεκα
ὡς ἐνεδρεύσασαν αὐτῷ, ἐκείνη ἔφη "ὦ πίθηκε, σὺ δὲ
τοιαύτην πυγὴν (ita Buchholtz: τύχην codd.) ἔχων τῶν
ἀλόγων ζῴων βασιλεύεις;"

**185** Herenn. Philo (v. ad fr. 174)

καὶ πάλιν ὅταν λέγῃ

> ἐρέω τιν' ὕμιν αἶνον, ὦ Κηρυκίδη,
> ἀχνυμένη σκυτάλη,

εἶτ' ἐπιφέρει·

> πίθηκος ᾔει θηρίων ἀποκριθεὶς
> μοῦνος ἀν' ἐσχατιήν,
> τῷ δ' ἄρ' ἀλώπηξ κερδαλῆ συνήντετο,
> πυκνὸν ἔχουσα νόον.

**186** *Et. Gen.* (p. 44 Calame) = *Et. Mag.* 715.44

σκανδάλιθρον· τὸ πέτευρον τῶν παγίδων . . . ἔστι δὲ

won their esteem was elected king by them. A fox was
envious and when he saw meat lying in a trap he led the
monkey there and told him he had found a treasure. He
said that he had not made use of it himself but had kept
watch over it as a prerogative of royalty, and he urged him
to take it. When the monkey thoughtlessly approached, he
was caught in the trap, and when he accused the fox of
having laid an ambush for him, the latter replied: "Mon-
key, with a rump like that, are you king of the animals?"

**185** Herennius Philo (continuing immediately after
citing fr. 174)

And again when he says

A grieving message stick,[1] I shall tell you people a
fable, Cerycides.[2]

Then he continues:

A monkey was on his way alone in the outback apart
from the animals, when a crafty fox with guileful
mind met him.

[1] Some of the sources record the dative, but this is difficult to
construe. It seems more likely that the phrase is in apposition to
the subject of the verb than to the vocative. In general, see S.
West, *CQ* 38 (1988) 42-48, and n. 1 on test. 64.    [2] Probably
a mock patronymic, 'Herald's son.'

**186** *Etymologicum Genuinum* and *Magnum*

σκανδάλιθρον: the spring of traps . . . and it is the bent

τὸ ἐν τῇ παγίδι καμπύλον ξύλον ᾧ ἐρείδεται. Ἀρχί-
λοχος δὲ ῥόπτρον ἔφη, οἷον

ῥόπτρῳ ἐρειδόμενον.

**187** Ar. *Ach.* 119-20

ὦ θερμόβουλον πρωκτὸν ἐξυρημένε,
τοιόνδε δ᾽, ὦ πίθηκε, τὸν πωγῶν᾽ ἔχων κτλ.

Schol. ad loc. (p. 25 Wilson)

καὶ τοῦτο παρῴδηκεν ἐκ τῶν Ἀρχιλόχου ἐπ‹ῳδ›ῶν"

τοιήνδε δ᾽, ὦ πίθηκε, τὴν πυγὴν ἔχων.

**188-192**

– ⏑⏑ – ⏑⏑ – ⏑⏑ – ⏑⏑ | – ⏑ – ⏑ – –
× – ⏑ – × |– ⏑ – ⏑ – –

**188** P. Colon. 58.36-40, ed. Merkelbach-West, ZPE 14
(1974) 97

οὐκέ|θ᾽ ὁμῶς θάλλεις ἁπαλὸν χρόα· κάρφετα|ι
γὰρ ἤδη
ὄγμο|ς· κακοῦ δὲ γήραος καθαιρεῖ
.....] ἀφ᾽ ἱμερτοῦ δὲ θορὼν γλυκὺς ἵμερος
π[ροσώπου
.....]κεν· ἦ γὰρ πολλὰ δή σ᾽ ἐπῆιξεν
5    πνεύμ]ατα χειμερίων ἀνέμων, μάλα πολλάκις δ᾽
ε[

wood in the trap on which it presses. Archilochus called it
ῥόπτρον, as in

pressing on the trap spring

**187** Aristophanes, *Acharnians* 119-20

"You who have shaved your hot-desiring arse-hole,
and, you monkey, with a beard like yours . . ."

Scholiast on the passage

And this is a parody of Archilochus' epodes:

monkey, with a rump like yours

**188** Cologne papyrus (2nd c. A.D.)

No longer does your skin have the soft bloom that it
once had; now your furrow[1] is withered, the . . . of
ugly old age is taking its toll, and sweet loveliness
(has gone?) with a rush from your lovely face. For
in truth many a blast of wintry winds has assaulted
you, and many a time . . .

[1] I.e., the sexual vitality of youth. See C. G. Brown, *QUCC* n.s.
50 (1995) 29-34.

---

cf. Hephaest. *Ench.* 6.3 (v. 1), *Ench.* 5.3 (v. 2), Atil. Fortunat.
(*Gramm. Lat.* vi.298.6 Keil)

2 ὄγμος Hephaest., ολμον Atil., ὄγμοις Snell      κακὸν Atil.
3 πήματ'] suppl. Slings      4 βέβη]κεν Lebek

**189** Ath. 7.299a

Ὁμήρου δὲ εἰπόντος "τείροντ᾽ ἐγχέλυές τε καὶ ἰχθύες"
(*Il.* 21.353), ἀκολούθως ἐποίησε καὶ Ἀρχίλοχος·

πολλὰς δὲ τυφλὰς ἐγχέλυας ἐδέξω.

οἱ δὲ Ἀττικοί, ὡς Τρύφων φησί (fr. 21 Velsen), τὰς
ἑνικὰς χρήσεις ἐπιστάμενοι διὰ τοῦ υ τὰς πληθυντικὰς
οὐκέτι ἀκολούθως ἐπιφέρουσιν.

ἐγχέλως Wilamowitz

**190** Hephaest. *Ench.* 15.8 (p. 50 Consbruch)

γίνεται δὲ ὁ τελευταῖος τῆς τετραποδίας διὰ τὴν ἐπὶ
τέλους ἀδιάφορον καὶ κρητικός·

καὶ βήσσας ὀρέων δυσπαιπάλους, οἷος ἦν ἐφ᾽
ἥβης.

ἐπ᾽ v.l.

**191** Stob. 4.20.43

Ἀρχιλόχου·

τοῖος γὰρ φιλότητος ἔρως ὑπὸ καρδίην ἐλυσθεὶς
πολλὴν κατ᾽ ἀχλὺν ὀμμάτων ἔχευεν,
κλέψας ἐκ στηθέων ἀπαλὰς φρένας.

**189** Athenaeus, *Scholars at Dinner*

When Homer said, "the eels and fishes were in distress,"
Archilochus also composed accordingly:

> you received many blind eels[1]

But although Attic writers, as Tryphon says, know the singular with upsilon, they no longer follow this practice in the plural.[2]

[1] Probably erotic, 'you received (in your body) many penises.'
[2] It seems clear that Athenaeus cites Archilochus as a parallel for the Homeric declension. To avoid the synizesis in -υας West adopts Wilamowitz's emendation, but probably the synizesis should be tolerated.

**190** Hephaestion, *Handbook of Meters*

And the last foot of the tetrapody, because the syllable at the end is indifferent, becomes also a cretic:

> and rugged[1] mountain glens,[2] such was I[3] in my
> youth

[1] The adjective is judged corrupt by those who reject a cretic in this position.    [2] Treated by West (*Studies* 134 f.) as a metaphor for a woman's body.    [3] Or "he in his youth."

**191** Stobaeus, *Anthology*

From Archilochus:

> For such a desire for sex coiled itself up under my
> heart, poured a thick mist down over my eyes, and
> stole the weak wits from my breast.

# IAMBIC POETRY

**192** Plut. *sollert. anim.* 36.984f

ἐκ δὲ τούτου καὶ τὰ περὶ Κοίρανον ὄντα μυθώδη πίστιν
ἔσχε. Πάριος γὰρ ὢν τὸ γένος ἐν Βυζαντίῳ δελφίνων
βόλον ἐνσχεθέντων σαγήνῃ καὶ κινδυνευόντων κατα-
κοπῆναι πριάμενος μεθῆκε πάντας. ὀλίγῳ δὲ ὕστερον
ἔπλει πεντηκόντορον ἔχων, ὥς φησι, Μιλησίων (Rohde
ex Aeliano, λῃστῶν Plut.) ἄνδρας ἄγουσαν· ἐν δὲ τῷ
μεταξὺ Νάξου καὶ Πάρου πορθμῷ τῆς νεὼς ἀνατρα-
πείσης καὶ τῶν ἄλλων διαφθαρέντων ἐκεῖνον λέγουσι
δελφῖνος ὑποδραμόντος αὐτῷ καὶ ἀνακουφίζοντος
ἐξενεχθῆναι τῆς Σικύνθου (Σικίνου Palmerius pro
ignoto Σικύνθου, alii alia) κατὰ σπήλαιον ὃ δείκνυται
μέχρι νῦν καὶ καλεῖται Κοιράνειον. ἐπὶ τούτῳ δὲ
λέγεται ποιῆσαι τὸν Ἀρχίλοχον·

> πεντήκοντ᾽ ἀνδρῶν λίπε Κοίρανον ἵππιος
> Ποσειδέων.

ἐπεὶ δὲ ὕστερον ἀποθανόντος αὐτοῦ τὸ σῶμα πλησίον
τῆς θαλάττης οἱ προσήκοντες ἔκαιον, ἐπεφαίνοντο
πολλοὶ δελφῖνες παρὰ τὸν αἰγιαλόν, ὥσπερ ἐπι-
δεικνύντες ἑαυτοὺς ἥκοντας ἐπὶ τὰς ταφὰς καὶ παρα-
μείναντες ἄχρις οὗ συνετελέσθησαν.

cf. test. 4

Ποσειδῶν Plut., corr. Schneidewin

206

**192** Plutarch, *The Cleverness of Animals*

As a result of this the fabulous story about Koiranos gained credence. A Parian by birth he bought in Byzantium a catch of dolphins that had been entangled in a net and were in danger of being carved up, and he set them all free. Shortly afterward he was sailing, they say, in a penteconter carrying men from Miletus. In the strait between Naxos and Paros the ship capsized and although the others drowned they say that a dolphin raced under Koiranos, lifted him up and carried him opposite a cave in Sicynthos(?). The cave is pointed out up to the present and is called Koiraneion. And it is said that on this man Archilochus composed the line:

out of fifty men Poseidon Hippios spared Koiranos

And when later he died and his relatives were burning his body near the sea, many dolphins appeared along the shore, as though showing that they had come for his funeral and were waiting until it had been completed.[1]

[1] The story is also told by Phylarchus (*FGrHist* 81 F 26) and Aelian (*H.A.* 8.3), but without mentioning Archilochus. Phylarchus makes Koiranos a Milesian and places the shipwreck off Myconos.

**193, 194**(?)

– ‾‾ – ‾‾ – ‾‾ – ‾‾ – ∪∪ – –

× – ∪ – × – ∪ –

**193** Stob. 4.20.45

Ἀρχιλόχου·

δύστηνος ἔγκειμαι πόθῳ,
ἄψυχος, χαλεπῇσι θεῶν ὀδύνῃσιν ἕκητι
πεπαρμένος δι᾽ ὀστέων.

**194** Grammaticus ap. Nauck, *Lexicon Vindob.* p. 269

βακχεία, καὶ

ἔξωθεν ἕκαστος
ἔπινεν, ἐν δὲ βακχίη,

Ἀρχίλοχος.

ἔωθεν et βακχίῃσιν Bergk ut sit simile fragmentorum 168-
171, βακχίη Welcker

**195** Hephaest. *Ench.* 7.2 (p. 21 Consbruch)

καὶ τὸ τετράμετρον (δακτυλικὸν) εἰς δισύλλαβον
καταληκτικόν, ᾧ πρῶτος μὲν ἐχρήσατο Ἀρχίλοχος ἐν
ἐπῳδοῖς·

φαινόμενον κακὸν οἴκαδ᾽ ἄγεσθαι,

**193** Stobaeus, *Anthology*

From Archilochus:

> I am in the throes of desire, miserable and life-
> less, pierced through my bones with grievous pangs
> thanks to the gods.

**194** Anonymous Grammarian

βακχεία, and in Archilochus,

> outside each one was drinking, and inside (there
> was?) bacchic revelry[1]

[1] Colometry uncertain. The grammarian is concerned with
words that can be spelled differently, in this instance words that
can end either in -εία or in -ία.

**195** Hephaestion, *Handbook of Meters*

And the dactylic tetrameter[1] with disyllabic close, first
used by Archilochus in epodes:

> to bring home for oneself a manifest evil,[2]

ὕστερον δὲ καὶ Ἀνακρέων τούτῳ τῷ μέτρῳ καὶ ὅλα ᾄσματα συνέθηκεν.

**196-196a**

× – ∪ – × – ∪ – × – ∪ –

– ∪∪ – ∪∪ –

× – ∪ – × – ∪ –

**196** Hephaest. *Ench.* 15.9 (p. 50 Consbruch)

τρίτον δ᾿ ἐστὶ παρ᾿ Ἀρχιλόχῳ ἀσυνάρτητον ἐκ δακτυλικοῦ πενθημιμεροῦς καὶ ἰαμβικοῦ διμέτρου ἀκαταλήκτου·

ἀλλά μ᾿ ὁ λυσιμελής, ὦταῖρε, δάμναται πόθος.

**196a** P. Colon. 58.1-35, ed. Merkelbach-West, *ZPE* 14 (1974) 97-112

πάμπαν ἀποσχόμενος·
ἶσον δὲ τολμ[
εἰ δ᾿ ὦν ἐπείγεαι καί σε θυμὸς ἰθύει.
ἔστιν ἐν ἡμετέρου
5      ἢ νῦν μέγ᾿ ἱμείρε[ι
καλὴ τέρεινα παρθένος· δοκέω δέ μι[ν
εἶδος ἄμωμον ἔχειν·
τὴν δὴ σὺ ποίη[σαι φίλην."

and later Anacreon composed even whole poems in this meter.[3]

1 Diomedes (*Gramm. Lat.* i.520.15 Keil) states that Horace's seventh ode, consisting of a dactylic hexameter followed by a tetrameter, is in the Archilochian meter, and presumably this tetrameter was also preceded by a hexameter.      2 Possibly a wife.      3 Hephaestion quotes Anac. fr. 394.

**196** Hephaestion, *Handbook of Meters*

A third asynartete in Archilochus is formed from a dactylic penthemimer and an acatalectic iambic dimeter:

but, my friend, limb-loosening desire overwhelms me[1]

1 Perhaps vv. 2-3 of fr. 196a.

**196a** Cologne papyrus (2nd c. A.D.)[1]

". . . holding off completely; and endure (I shall endure?) . . . likewise.

But if you are in a hurry and desire impels you, there is in our house one who now greatly longs for (marriage?),

a lovely tender maiden.[2] In my opinion she has a faultless form; make her your (loved one)."

τοσαῦτ' ἐφώνει· τὴν δ' ἐγῶνταμει[βόμην·
10 "'Αμφιμεδοῦς θύγατερ,
ἐσθλῆς τε καὶ [
γυναικός, ἣν νῦν γῆ κατ' εὐρώεσσ' ἔ[χει,
τ]έρψιές εἰσι θεῆς
πολλαὶ νέοισιν ἀνδ[ράσιν
15 παρὲξ τὸ θεῖον χρῆμα· τῶν τις ἀρκέσε[ι.
τ]αῦτα δ' ἐφ' ἡσυχίης
εὖτ' ἂν μελανθῆ[ι
ἐ]γώ τε καὶ σὺ σὺν θεῶι βουλεύσομεν.
π]είσομαι ὥς με κέλεαι·
20 πολλόν μ' ε[
θρ]ιγκοῦ δ' ἔνερθε καὶ πυλέων ὑποφ[
μ]ή τι μέγαιρε, φίλη·
σχήσω γὰρ ἐς ποη[φόρους
κ]ήπους· τὸ δὴ νῦν γνῶθι. Νεοβούλη[ν
25 ἄ]λλος ἀνὴρ ἐχέτω·
αἰαῖ, πέπειρα, δὶς ⌊τόση,
ἄν]θος δ' ἀπερρύηκε παρθενήιον
κ]αὶ χάρις ἣ πρὶν ἐπῆν·
κόρον γὰρ ουκ[
30 ..]ης δὲ μέτρ' ἔφηνε μαινόλις γυνή.
ἐς] κόρακας ἔπεχε·
μὴ τοῦτ' εφ.ιταν[
ὅ]πως ἐγὼ γυναῖκα τ[ο]ιαύτην ἔχων
γεί]τοσι χάρμ' ἔσομαι·
35 πολλὸν σὲ βούλο[μαι

212

Such were her words, and I replied: "Daughter of Amphimedo, a worthy and (prudent?)

woman, whom now the mouldy earth holds, many are the delights the goddess[3] offers young men

besides the sacred act;[4] one of these will suffice. But at leisure, whenever . . has become dark,[5]

you and I will deliberate on these matters with heaven's help. I shall do as you bid me. (You arouse in me?) a strong (desire?).

But, my dear, do not begrudge my . . . under the coping and the gates. For I shall steer towards the grassy

garden;[6] be sure now of this. As for Neoboule, let (some?) other man have her. Ugh, she's overripe, twice your age,

and her girlhood's flower has lost its bloom as has the charm which formerly was on it. For (her desire is?) insatiable,

and the sex-mad woman has revealed the full measure of her (infatuation?). To hell with her! (Let) no (one bid?) this,

that I have such a wife and become a laughing-stock to my neighbours. I much prefer (to have?) you,

σὺ] μὲν γὰρ οὔτ᾽ ἄπιστος οὔτε διπλόη,
ἢ δ]ὲ μάλ᾽ ὀξυτέρη,
πολλοὺς δὲ ποιεῖτα[ι φίλους·
δέ]δοιχ᾽ ὅπως μὴ τυφλὰ κἀλιτήμερα
40    σπ]ουδῆι ἐπειγόμενος
τὼς ὥσπερ ἡ κ[ύων τέκω."
τοσ]αῦτ᾽ ἐφώνεον· παρθένον δ᾽ ἐν ἄνθε[σιν
τηλ]εθάεσσι λαβών
ἔκλινα· μαλθακῆι δ[έ μιν
45    χλαί]νηι καλύψας, αὐχέν᾽ ἀγκάληις ἔχω[ν,
...]ματι παυ[σ]αμ̣έ̣νην
τὼς ὥστε νεβρ[
μαζ]ῶν τε χερσὶν ἠπίως ἐφηψάμην
...]ρ̣έφηνε̣ νέον
50    ἥβης ἐπήλυσιν χρόα
ἅπαν τ]ε̣ σῶμα καλὸν ἀμφαφώμενος
....]ον ἀφῆκα μένος
ξανθῆς ἐπιψαύ[ων τριχός.

1 ανασχ sscr. πο    2 τόλμ[ησον Snell, τολμ[ήσω West
5 fin. γάμου M.-W., σ᾽ ἔχειν Slings    8 Ebert-Luppe
11 [σαόφρονος Marcovich    15 cf. Hesych. παρὲξ τὸ
θεῖον χρῆμα· ἔξω τῆς μίξεως    16 ἐπησυχιησ pap.
20 ἐ[πορνύεις πόθον Slings    21 ὑποφ[θάνειν West,
ὑποφ[λύσαι Slings et Latacz    24 fin. δέ τις M.-W.
26 explevit West ex Hesych. (cf. fr. 242)    29 οὐκ [ἔχει
πόθων Austin, οὐ κ[ατέσχε πω M.-W.    30 ἄτ]ης Snell
32 ἐφεῖτ᾽ Marcovich, ἐφοῖτ᾽ West, ἐφεστα[ί]η Koenen
35 fin. πάρος M.-W., λαβεῖν Slings    38 fin. M.-W., δόλους
Bonanno    42 εφωνενν pap.    46-47 εὔγ]ματι παρ-
[φ]αμένην . . . νεβρ[ὸν εἱλόμην Slings    49 ἤιπε]ρ Page

   since you are neither untrustworthy nor two-
faced, whereas she is quite precipitous and makes
many (her lovers).
   I'm afraid that if I press on in haste (I may be the
parent) of blind and premature offspring just like
the proverbial bitch."
   So much I said. I took the maiden and laid her
down in the blooming flowers. With a soft
   cloak I covered her, holding her neck with my
arm, . . . as she ceased(?) just like a fawn . . . ,[7]
   and with my hands I gently took hold of her
breasts (where?) she revealed her young flesh, the
approach (bewitchment?) of her prime,
   and caressing all her lovely body I let go my
(white?) force,[8] touching her blond (hair).

[1] I have listed only a few of the many supplements and read-
ings that have been proposed. For a much larger list and a judi-
cious commentary see Slings 24-61. Supplements unidentified
by author's name are those given in the first edition. Some fol-
low the papyrus and print in two-line stanzas.    [2] Presum-
ably Neoboule, the speaker's sister.    [3] Aphrodite.
[4] Sexual intercourse, according to Hesychius' gloss on the phrase.
[5] Perhaps the lacuna contains a reference to some part of the
girl's body, with the verb in the sense of 'to ripen.'
[6] 'Coping,' 'gates' and 'grassy garden' are almost certainly sexual
metaphors, for 'pubic bone,' 'vagina' and 'pubic hair.'
[7] With Slings' proposed text the translation would be: "as she tried
to persuade me with entreaty I caught her just like a fawn."
[8] Clearly a reference to ejaculation.

---

52 λευκ]òν Merkelbach, θερμ]òν West       53 fin. χνοός
Taplin

**197** Hephaest. *Ench*. 6.2 (p. 18 Consbruch)

τρίμετρον δὲ ⟨τροχαϊκὸν⟩ καταληκτικόν, οἷόν ἐστι τὸ
Ἀρχιλόχου, ὅ τινες ἀκέφαλον ἰαμβικὸν καλοῦσι·

Ζεῦ πάτερ, γάμον μὲν οὐκ ἐδαισάμην.

**198-199** = testt. 51-52

**200** *Et. Gen*. (pp. 41-42 Calame) = *Et. Mag*. 689.1 = *Suda*
(iii.55.23 Adler) = Zonaras p. 1573 T.

προίκτης· . . . τινὲς δὲ παρὰ τὸ ἵξεσθαι, ὅ ἐστι δωρεάν
τινα λαμβάνειν, ὡς Ἀρχίλοχος· (Ἀριστοφάνης
Casadio)

ἐμέο δὲ κεῖνος οὐ καταπροΐξεται.

ἐμεῦ vel ἐμοῦ codd. (εὖ *Suda*), corr. West

**201** Zenob. 5.68 (*Paroem. Gr*. i.147.7 L.-S.)

πόλλ᾽ οἶδ᾽ ἀλώπηξ, ἀλλ᾽ ἐχῖνος ἓν μέγα.

μέμνηται ταύτης Ἀρχίλοχος ἐν ἐπῳδῇ, γράφει δὲ καὶ
Ὅμηρος τὸν στίχον . . . λέγεται δὲ ἡ παροιμία ἐπὶ
τῶν πανουργοτάτων.

**197**  Hephaestion, *Handbook of Meters*

And the catalectic trochaic trimeter, such as that of Archilochus, which some call an acephalous iambic (trimeter):

> Father Zeus, I had no wedding feast

**200**  Etymologica

προίκτης: . . . according to some from ἵξεσθαι,[1] to receive some gift, as in Archilochus:

> he will not get off scot-free from me

[1] The *Et. Gen.* goes on to cite a second etymology (see fr. 296).

**201**  Zenobius

> The fox knows many tricks, the hedgehog one, but
> it's a big one.[1]

Archilochus mentions this proverb in an epode and Homer also writes the line[2] . . . The proverb is said of the greatest scoundrels.

[1] Some identify the fox with Archilochus, but it is more probably the hedgehog, unless neither refers to the poet himself.
[2] West prints the verse also as "Homer," *Margites* (fr. 5).

IAMBIC POETRY

**202** Schol. Nic. *Th*. 322 (p. 142 Crugnola), *"κεράων*
*ἔμπλην δέμας ἄμμορον"*

τὸ δὲ ἔμπλην δύο σημαίνει, τὸ χωρὶς καὶ τὸ πλησίον·
ἀντὶ τοῦ χωρὶς παρ᾽ Ἀρχιλόχῳ·

ἔμπλην ἐμέο τε καὶ φίλου.

cf. Apoll. Soph. p. 67.30 Bekker

φίλου, φόλου, ἐφ᾽ ὅλου schol., φίλου Apoll.

**204** Steph. Byz. (p. 507.5 Meineke) = Herodian. (i.189.26
Lentz)

Πάρος· νῆσος, ἣν (v.l. ἢ) καὶ πόλιν Ἀρχίλοχος {αὐτὴν}
καλεῖ ἐν τοῖς ἐπῳδοῖς.

### 205-295. Incerti Generis

**205** Ath. 15.688c

τῷ δὲ τοῦ μύρου ὀνόματι πρῶτος Ἀρχίλοχος κέχρηται
λέγων

οὐκ ἂν μύροισι γρηῦς ἐοῦσ᾽ ἠλείφεο.

καὶ ἀλλαχοῦ δ᾽ ἔφη· (fr. 48.5-6)

cf. Plut. *Pericles* 28.7

γραῦς Ath., corr. Schneidewin          ἠλείφεο Plut., -ετο Ath.

218

**202** Scholiast on Nicander, *Theriaca* ("its deadly body is
without horns")

ἔμπλην has two meanings, 'without' and 'near'; in Archi-
lochus it means 'without':

near[1] me and a (my) friend[2]

[1] In its one Homeric occurrence (*Il.* 2.526) the preposition
means 'near' and so probably in Archilochus too. The Alexandri-
ans may have assumed a connection with πλήν.     [2] Some
read Φόλον and see a reference to the myth of Heracles and the
centaur (cf. Stes. fr. 181 = S 19).

**204** Stephanus of Byzantium, *Lexicon of Place Names*

Paros: an island which Archilochus also calls a city in his
epodes.

*205-295. Of Uncertain Classification*

**205** Athenaeus, *Scholars at Dinner*

Archilochus is the first to use the word μύρον ('perfume'),
saying:

you, an old woman, would not be anointing yourself
with perfume[1]

And also elsewhere he said (fr. 48.5-6).

[1] Presumably something like "if you had not lost your senses"
is to be understood.

**206**

περὶ σφυρὸν παχεῖα, μισητὴ γυνή

περίσφυρος? West (v. Bossi 216-19)

Eust. in Hom. *Od.* 10.114 (1651.1)

ἄλλοι δὲ μισήτην βαρυτόνως, πρὸς διαστολὴν τῆς ὀξυτονουμένης, τὴν κοινὴν καὶ ῥᾳδίαν, λέγοντες καὶ χρῆσιν αὐτῆς εἶναι παρὰ Κρατίνῳ (fr. 354 K.-A.) καὶ Σώφρονι (fr. 130 Kaibel). χρᾶται δὲ αὐτῇ καὶ παροιμία ἐν τῷ "περὶ σφυρὸν παχεῖα μισήτη γυνή."

Herenn. Philo *de diversis verborum significationibus* (p. 194 Palmieri, 83 Nickau *Ammonius*)

μισητὴ ὀξυτόνως καὶ μισήτη βαρυτόνως διαφέρει παρὰ Ἀττικοῖς, ὥς φησι Τρύφων (fr. 10 Velsen) ἐν δευτέρῳ Περὶ Ἀττικῆς προσῳδίας. ἐὰν μὲν γὰρ ὀξυτονήσωμεν, φησίν, τὴν ἀξίαν μίσους δηλοῖ, ἐὰν δὲ βαρυτονήσωμεν, καταφερὴς πρὸς συνουσίαν. τὴν <δὲ> διαφορὰν τ[ῶν σημαινο]μένων καὶ παρὰ Δωριεῦσί φησι φυλάττεσθαι καὶ παρ' Ἴωσιν· "μισήτη γυνή" ὁ Ἀρχίλοχος.

Eust. in Hom. *Il.* 23.775 (iv.836.1 V.d.Valk)

... Ἀρχίλοχος δὲ παχεῖαν καὶ δῆμον ἤγουν κοινὴν τῷ δήμῳ, καὶ ἐργάτιν, ἔτι καὶ μυσάχνην πρὸς ἀναλογίαν τοῦ ἁλὸς ἄχνη, καὶ εἴ τι τοιοῦτον.

**206**

a revolting woman, fat about the ankles[1]

[1] Only a selection of the many testimonia is recorded here. For the others see West's edition.

Eustathius on Homer, *Odyssey*

Others record μισήτη without oxytone accent in distinction from the word with it, i.e., a common woman of easy morals, mentioning its use in Cratinus and Sophron. It is also used in the proverb, "a lewd woman fat about the ankles."

Herennius Philo, *On the Different Meanings of Words*

μισητή with oxytone accent and μισήτη without it are different in Attic, as Tryphon says in the second book of his *On Attic Prosody*. For if we accent it with oxytone, he says, it indicates one who is deserving of hatred, but if we do not so accent it, it is one who is lewd. The distinction in meanings, he says, is preserved in Doric and in Ionic. Cf. Archilochus, "lewd woman."

Eustathius on Homer, *Iliad*

And Archilochus (spoke abusively of a prostitute) as "fat" and a "public woman," i.e., common property of the people, and a "worker for hire" and in addition "froth of defilement" on the analogy of froth of the sea, and such like.

Hesych.

ἐργάτις· τὴν Νεοβούλην (-λιαν cod.) λέγει. καὶ παχεῖαν.

**207** V. Eust. in Hom. *Il.* ad fr. 206

δῆμος

**208** Ut supra

ἐργάτις

**209** Ut supra

μυσαχνή

**210** *Et. Gen.* (p. 44 Calame) + *Et. Sym.* cod. V marg. (Gaisford ad *Et. Mag.* 752.17) + *Epimer. in Hom.* (p. 697 Dyck)

τοῦτο τὸ τέο τετόλμηκεν Ἀρχίλοχος καὶ τεοῦ, οἷον

τίς ἆρα δαίμων, καὶ τέου χολούμενος

ἀντὶ τοῦ καὶ τίνος.

ἄρα codd., corr. Dübner τεοῦ Etym. (τέ *Epimer.*), corr. Bergk

**211** Ammon. in Porph. *isag.* (*Comm. in Arist. Graeca* iv(3).9.8, cf. addenda p. 134)

ἐπειδὴ γὰρ ἐκεῖνοι σοφὸν ὠνόμαζον τὸν ἡντιναοῦν

Hesychius, *Lexicon*

A worker for hire: the reference is to Neoboule. Also (she is called) fat.

**207**  Eustathius on Homer, *Iliad*

   a public woman

**208**  As above

   a worker for hire

**209**  As above

   froth of defilement[1]

[1] We should not assume that these three words occurred in the nominative or even in the same poem.

**210**  Etymologica

Archilochus has ventured on this τέο and τεοῦ, as in

   what god and in anger at whom

instead of τίνος.

**211**  Ammonius on Porphyry, *Introduction to Aristotle's Categories*

For they called σοφός ('skilled') one who pursued every

ἐπιόντα τέχνην· ὧν εἷς ἦν καὶ Ἀρχίλοχος λέγων

τρίαιναν ἐσθλὸς καὶ κυβερνήτης σοφός.

ἐσθλὸς cod. D, ἐσθλὴν cett.

**212** Et. Gen. (p. 28 Calame) = Et. Mag. 424.18

ἠκή· ἡ ὀξύτης τοῦ σιδήρου· Ἀρχίλοχος·

ἴστη κατ' ἠκὴν κύματός τε κἀνέμου.

ἤκην et ἠκὴν codd.

**213** Schol. Ar. Ran. 704 (p. 296 Dübner), "τὴν πόλιν καὶ
ταῦτ' ἔχοντες κυμάτων ἐν ἀγκάλαις"

Δίδυμός (p. 249 Schmidt) φησι παρὰ τῷ Αἰσχύλῳ (cf.
Cho. 587): ἔστι δὲ ὄντως παρ' Ἀρχιλόχῳ·

ψυχὰς ἔχοντες κυμάτων ἐν ἀγκάλαις.

**214** Hesych. s.v. σάλπιγξ

σιγὴν ἡ σάλπιγξ· ἀντὶ τοῦ κῆρυξ (cf. Aesch. Eum. 566-
71). τινὲς δὲ ὄρνιν ποιόν, καὶ ὄργανον πολεμικόν,
καὶ θαλασσίαν σάλπιγγα· παρ' Ἀρχιλόχῳ δὲ τὸν
στρόμβον ἐκδέχονται· <ἔστι> (suppl. Bossi) δὲ καὶ
Σάλπιγγος Ἀθηνᾶς ἱερὸν παρὰ Ἀργείοις.

σιγηνοσάλπιγξ Hesych., corr. Heinsius

craft, and among them was Archilochus who says

> good with fishing spear and a skilled helmsman

**212** *Etymologicum Genuinum* and *Magnum*

ἠκή, the sharpness of iron, cf. Archilochus:

> he set[1] (the ship?) against the edge of wave and
> wind[2]

[1] Or imperative.       [2] Possibly imagery for a critical situation.

**213** Scholiast on Aristophanes, *Frogs* ("and this too
when we have the city in the embrace of the
waves")

Didymus says that this occurs in Aeschylus, but it actually
occurs in Archilochus:

> with their lives in the embrace of the waves

**214** Hesychius, *Lexicon*

σάλπιγξ: the trumpet creates silence in place of a herald.
Some explain σάλπιγξ as a kind of bird, and as an instrument of war, and as a trumpet of the sea[1] (i.e., a conch).
And in Archilochus it is explained as a conch. There is also
a temple of Athena of the Trumpet among the Argives.

[1] θαλασσίαν (corrected to -ίην) is attributed by some to Archilochus, but Bossi 220-22 is probably right to assign it to Hesychius, and also to explain the accusative σάλπιγγα as determined
by the wording of the gloss rather than necessarily as the case
found in Archilochus.

**215** Tzetz. *alleg. Hom.* Ω 125 sqq.

ποιεῖ ὅπερ καὶ ὕστερον Ἀρχίλοχος ἐκεῖνος· σφῆς
ἀδελφῆς γὰρ σύζυγον πνιγέντα τῇ θαλάσσῃ περιπα-
θῶς ὠδύρετο, γράφειν μὴ θέλων ὅλως, λέγων πρὸς
τοὺς βιάζοντας συγγράμμασιν ἐγκύπτειν·

καί μ᾿ οὔτ᾿ ἰάμβων οὔτε τερπωλέων μέλει.

Quae sequuntur v. ad fr. 11.

**216** Schol. Plat. *Lach*. 187b (p. 117 Greene), "ἐν τῷ Καρὶ
ὑμῖν ὁ κίνδυνος"

παροιμία, ἐπὶ τῶν ἐπισφαλέστερον καὶ ἐν ἀλλοτρίοις
κινδυνευόντων. Κᾶρες γὰρ δοκοῦσι πρῶτοι μισθο-
φορῆσαι, ὅθεν καὶ εἰς πόλεμον αὐτοὺς προέταττον . . .
μέμνηται δ᾿ αὐτῆς Ἀρχίλοχος λέγων

καὶ δὴ ᾿πίκουρος ὥστε Κὰρ κεκλήσομαι.

**217** *Et. Gen.* (p. 24 Calame)

ἐγκυτί . . . ὀξυτόνως τὸ ἐγκυτὶ ἐπίρρημα γέγονε,
κείμενον παρ᾿ Ἀρχιλόχῳ·

χαίτην ἀπ᾿ ὤμων ἐγκυτὶ κεκαρμένος.

ἐγκυτὶς Bergk

**215** Tzetzes, *Homeric Allegories*

He does what that Archilochus did later; for when his sister's husband was drowned at sea, he mourned intensely, refusing to compose at all and saying to those who were pressuring him to devote himself to his compositions:

> and I have no interest in iambi[1] or amusements

[1] See Introduction.

**216** Scholiast on Plato, *Laches* ("your risk is put on the Carian")

A proverb, used of those who run a particularly dangerous risk on behalf of others. For the Carians seem to have been the first mercenaries and as a result they used to be assigned the front rank in war . . . Archilochus mentions the proverb when he says

> and what's more I shall be called an auxiliary like a Carian

**217** *Etymologicum Genuinum*

The adverb ἐγκυτί has an oxytone accent, present in Archilochus:

> with hair shorn away from the shoulders close to the skin

**218** Schol. Pind. *Ol*. 12.10 (i.351.19 Dr.), "σύμβολον"

a. σύμβολον ἀρσενικῶς καὶ οὐδετέρως. b. συμβόλους δὲ λέγομεν πταρμούς, ἢ φήμας, ἢ ἀπαντήσεις, ὡς Ἀρχίλοχος·

μετέρχομαί σε σύμβολον ποιεόμενος.

cf. schol. bT Hom. *Il*. 23.199

ποιούμενος, -μένη, -μαι codd. schol. Pind., πονεύμενος schol. T Hom. (om. b)

**219** P. Hibeh 173 = P. Lond. inv. 2946

Ὁμήρ[ου· "τεῖ]χος δ᾽ οὐ χραίσμ[ησε τετυγμένον οὐδέ τι τάφος" (*Il*. 14.66).]
Ἀρχι[λόχου·]

χραίσμησε δ᾽ οὔτεπ[

π[ύργος οὔτε (Lasserre) τείχεα (Slings)

**220**

Ὁμήρου· "ὥς π[οτ]έ τις ἐρέει· τότε μοι χ[άνοι εὐρεῖα χθών" (*Il*. 4.182).]
Ἀρχιλόχου·

]. ἐμοὶ τόθ᾽ ἥδε γῆ χ[

χ[άνοι Lasserre, χ[ασμωμένη West

**218** Scholiast on Pindar, *Olympian* 12

a. There is a masculine σύμβολος and a neuter σύμβολον.
b. We use the term σύμβολοι for sneezes or sayings or meetings, as in Archilochus:

I go in search of you, considering it an omen[1]

[1] Translation uncertain. Perhaps the meaning is, 'I consider my meeting you an omen.'

**219** Hibeh papyrus (3rd c. B.C.)

Homer: "Neither the wall that had been constructed nor the ditch provided a defence." Archilochus:

neither the (tower nor the wall?) provided a defence

**220** Same papyrus

Homer: "Thus one will say; then may the wide earth gape open for me." Archilochus:

. . . then may this earth (gape open?) for me

**221**

Ὁμήρου· [....... ἀ]θανάτοισι θεο[ῖς ] Ἀρχιλόχου·

ἐξουδένιζ̣· ἔπειτα σὺν θεοῖ[ς

κ̣ονδ̣ε̣ισδ leg. Turner, ξουδ̣ε̣νιζ West (redarguit Slings)

**222**  *Et. Gud.* col. 390.42 Sturz

μήδεα· τὰ αἰδοῖα. παρὰ τὸ μέδειν καὶ ἄρχειν τῆς
γενέσεως, <*μέδεα,> καὶ μέζεα κατὰ μετάθεσιν τοῦ δ
εἰς ζ. ἢ *μέδεα καὶ κατὰ τροπὴν τοῦ ε εἰς η μήδεα . . .
ἢ καὶ <μέζεα τὰ> μέσα τοῦ σώματος· <Ἡσίοδος> (Op.
512), "οὐρὴν δ' ὑπὸ μέζε' ἔθεντο," ὡς καὶ Ἀρχίλοχος·

　　ἶνας δὲ μελέων <τῶν μέσων> ἀπέθρισε.

<τῶν μέσων> add. West

**223**

　　τέττιγος ἐδράξω πτεροῦ

e Leone et Constant. restituit Diels　　πτερῶν e Constant.
Wilamowitz　　τέττιγα δ' εἴληφας πτεροῦ e Luciano Bergk

Luc. *Pseudolog.* 1 (iii.133.6 Macleod)

τὸ δὲ τοῦ Ἀρχιλόχου ἐκεῖνο ἤδη σοι λέγω, ὅτι τέττιγα
τοῦ πτεροῦ συνείληφας, εἴπερ τινὰ ποιητὴν ἰάμβων
ἀκούεις Ἀρχίλοχον, Πάριον τὸ γένος, ἄνδρα κομιδῇ

**221** Same papyrus

Homer: ". . . immortal gods . . ." Archilochus:

. . . then with the gods . . .

**222** *Etymologicum Gudianum*

μήδεα: the genitals. From μέδειν ('to rule over') and to begin procreation we have ‹*μέδεα›, and, with exchange of delta and zeta, μέζεα. Either *μέδεα and, with eta for epsilon, μήδεα . . . or also ‹μέζεα the› middle parts of the body. Cf. Hesiod, "they put their tails under their genitals," and Archilochus:

severed the sinews of (the middle) parts[1]

[1] Text of source and fragment uncertain. I have followed West, but with no great confidence. Cf. West, *Studies* 136, and Bossi 224-25.

**223**

you caught[1] a cicada by the wing

Lucian, *The Mistaken Critic*

I now say to you what Archilochus said, that you have caught a cicada by the wing, if in fact you have heard of an iambic poet Archilochus, a Parian by birth, a man who was

ἐλεύθερον καὶ παρρησίᾳ συνόντα, μηδὲν ὀκνοῦντα
ὀνειδίζειν, εἰ καὶ ὅτι μάλιστα λυπήσειν ἔμελλε τοὺς
περιπετεῖς ἐσομένους τῇ χολῇ τῶν ἰάμβων αὐτοῦ.
ἐκεῖνος τοίνυν πρός τινος τῶν τοιούτων ἀκούσας κακῶς
τέττιγα ἔφη τὸν ἄνδρα εἰληφέναι τοῦ πτεροῦ, εἰκάζων
ἑαυτὸν τῷ τέττιγι ὁ Ἀρχίλοχος φύσει μὲν λάλῳ ὄντι
καὶ ἄνευ τινὸς ἀνάγκης, ὁπόταν δὲ καὶ τοῦ πτεροῦ
ληφθῇ, γεγωνότερον βοῶντι. "Καὶ σὺ δή," ἔφη, "ὦ
κακόδαιμον ἄνθρωπε, τί βουλόμενος ποιητὴν λάλον
παροξύνεις ἐπὶ σεαυτὸν αἰτίας ζητοῦντα καὶ ὑποθέσεις
τοῖς ἰάμβοις;"
(2) Ταῦτά σοι καὶ αὐτὸς ἀπειλῶ, οὐ μὰ τὸν Δία τῷ
Ἀρχιλόχῳ εἰκάζων ἐμαυτόν—πόθεν; πολλοῦ γε καὶ
δέω—σοὶ δὲ μυρία συνειδὼς ἰάμβων ἄξια βεβιωμένα,
πρὸς ἅ μοι δοκεῖ οὐδ᾽ ἂν ὁ Ἀρχίλοχος αὐτὸς διαρ-
κέσαι, προσπαρακαλέσας καὶ τὸν Σιμωνίδην καὶ τὸν
Ἱππώνακτα συμποιεῖν μετ᾽ αὐτοῦ κἂν ἕν τι τῶν προσ-
όντων σοι κακῶν, οὕτω σύ γε παῖδας ἀπέφηνας ἐν
ἁπάσῃ βδελυρίᾳ τὸν Ὀροδοκίδην καὶ τὸν Λυκάμβην
καὶ τὸν Βούπαλον, τοὺς ἐκείνων ἰάμβους.

cf. Leon. Philosoph. (*Anecd. Gr.* p. 557.26 Matranga) τέττιγος
ἐδράξαντο τοῦ πτεροῦ, Constant. Rhod. (ib. p. 628.36) ἐπεὶ
πτερῶν τέττιγος ἐδράξω

**224** Ath. 9.388f

πέρδιξ . . . ἔνιοι συστέλλουσι τὴν μέσην συλλαβήν,
ὡς Ἀρχίλοχος·

quite independent, outspoken and not at all reluctant to be abusive, even if he was going to inflict the greatest pain on those who would encounter the bitterness of his iambics. Well, when one such person spoke ill of him, Archilochus said that the man had caught a cicada by the wing, likening himself to the cicada which is by nature vociferous even without any compulsion and which cries out more loudly whenever it is caught by the wing. "Ill-starred fellow," he said, "what reason do you have for provoking against you a vociferous poet who is in search of themes and subject matter for his iambics?"

These same threats I make to you, not, by Zeus, likening myself to Archilochus (how could I? I am far from doing that!), but aware that in your life you have done countless things deserving of iambics. Not even Archilochus, I think, could have responded adequately, though he invited both Semonides and Hipponax to help him in dealing with just one of your evil traits, such children in every kind of abominable behaviour did you make Orodocides[2] and Lycambes and Bupalus, who were the butts of their iambics.

[1] The verb used by Archilochus is uncertain. For a full discussion of the fragment see Bossi 226-34.     [2] The name of Semonides' enemy is judged corrupt by many on metrical grounds and the MSS offer variant readings. See Degani, *Studi* 111 n. 213.

**224** Athenaeus, *Scholars at Dinner*

Partridge . . . Some shorten the middle syllable, as does Archilochus:

IAMBIC POETRY

πτώσσουσαν ὥστε πέρδικα.

**225** Ath. 14.653d

γενναῖα λέγει τὰ εὐγενῆ ὁ φιλόσοφος (Plat. *Leges* 844d), ὡς καὶ Ἀρχίλοχος·

πάρελθε, γενναῖος γάρ εἰς.

**226** Phot. *lex.* s.v. λεωκόρητος

λεωκόρητος (λεώλεθρος Naber)· ἐξωλοθρευμένος. τὸ γὰρ λέως ἐστὶ τελέως. Ἀρχίλοχος·

λέως γὰρ οὐδὲν ἐφρόνεον.

**227** Schol. Hom. *Od.* 15.534, "καρτεροί"

ἐγκρατεῖς, τὸ κράτος ἔχοντες. καὶ Ἀρχίλοχος·

ὁ δ᾽ Ἀσίης καρτερὸς μηλοτρόφου.

cf. Eust. in *Od.* 15.534 (1790.7), schol. Eur. *Med.* 708 (ii.179 Schwartz)

Ἀσίη τε schol. Eur.     κρατερὸς schol. Hom.

cowering like a partridge[1]

[1] West suggests a reference to the fox's cub carried off by the eagle (frr. 174-181), but comparison with a woman seems likelier. On the length of the middle syllable see Slater, *Arist. Byz. Fragmenta* p. 119.

**225** Athenaeus, *Scholars at Dinner*

By γενναῖα the philosopher means 'first-rate,' as also Archilochus:

go ahead, for you are noble[1]

[1] West suggests a reference to the fox bidding the monkey take the treasure he had found (frr. 185-187).

**226** Photius, *Lexicon*

λεωκόρητος: utterly destroyed, since λέως means 'completely.' Cf. Archilochus:

for they were (I was) completely[1] without sense

[1] Some sources record λέως, others λείως.

**227** Scholiast on Homer, *Odyssey*

καρτεροί means 'powerful,' 'having power.' Cf. Archilochus:

he has power over sheep-rearing Asia[1]

[1] Often assumed to refer to Gyges (cf. fr. 19).

# IAMBIC POETRY

**228** Eust. in Hom. *Od.* 5.306 (1542.45)

ἰστέον δὲ ὅτι αἱ συνθέσεις τοῦ τρίς ἐπιρρήματος ποτὲ
μὲν . . . αὐτόχρημα τριάδα δηλοῦσιν . . . ποτὲ δὲ
πλῆθος σημαίνουσιν, ὡς . . . καὶ ἐν τῷ "ἀλλ' ὦ
τρισκεκορημένε Σμερδίη" παρ' Ἀνακρέοντι (fr. 366
PMG), ἤγουν πολλάκις ἐκσεσαρωμένε, καὶ

Θάσον δὲ τὴν τρισοιζυρὴν πόλιν

παρ' Ἀρχιλόχῳ, ἤτοι λίαν ὀϊζυράν.

**229** Porphyrius in Hom. *Il.* 5.568 (p. 58 Sodano)

καὶ "ἔγχεα ὀξυόεντα" τὰ ἐξ ὀξύης τοῦ δένδρου, ὡς καὶ
Ἀρχίλοχος·

ὀξύη ποτᾶτο,

ἀλλ' οὐ τὰ ὀξέα, ὡς οἱ γραμματικοὶ ἀποδεδώκασιν.

ὀξείας et ὀξείη codd., corr. Villoison          'ποτᾶτο Bergk

**230** *Et. Gen.* (p. 17 Calame)

αὐόνη· ξηρότης. Ἀρχίλοχος, οἷον

κακήν σφιν Ζεὺς ἔδωκεν αὐονήν.

**231** Schol. Nic. *Th.* 158 (p. 91 Crugnola), "ἀμυδρότατον
δάκος ἄλλων"

ἀμυδρὸν νῦν τὸ χαλεπὸν λέγεται, ὡς καὶ Ἀρχίλοχος·

236

**228** Eustathius on Homer, *Odyssey*

Know that compounds of the adverb τρίς ('thrice') some-
times . . . indicate exactly the number three . . . and some-
times signify a large number, as in "thrice-swept Smerdies"
in Anacreon, i.e., often swept out, and

Thasos the thrice-wretched city

in Archilochus, i.e., exceedingly wretched.

**229** Porphyry on Homer, *Iliad*

Also, ἔγχεα ὀξυόεντα are spears made from the beech
tree, as in Archilochus,

the beech spear was flying,

and not sharp spears as the grammarians have explained it.

**230** *Etymologicum Genuinum*

αὐόνη[1] means 'dryness,' as in Archilochus:

Zeus gave them an evil drought

[1] Both breathing and accent are disputed.

**231** Scholiast on Nicander, *Theriaca* ("the most
dangerous(?) of all snakes")

ἀμυδρόν here means 'dangerous'(?), as in Archilochus:

237

ἀμυδρὴν χοιράδ᾽ ἐξαλεόμενος.

ἀμυδρὰν et -ῶν codd., corr. Bergk    ἐξαλεύμενος,
-ενάμενος, -εύμενον codd.

**232** Heraclides Lembus π. πολιτειῶν 14 (p. 18 Dilts)

ὅτι δὲ ἀρχαιοτάτη τῶν πολιτειῶν ἡ Κρητική, ἐμφαίνει
καὶ Ὅμηρος λέγων τὰς πόλεις αὐτῶν "εὖ ναιεταώσας"
(Il. 2.648), καὶ Ἀρχίλοχος ἐν οἷς ἐπισκώπτων τινάς (v.l.
τινά) φησιν

   νόμος δὲ Κρητικὸς διδάσκεται.

νόμους δὲ Κρητικοὺς Cragius

**233** Plut. de garrulitate 2.503a

προσκεῖται γὰρ ἀπανταχοῦ τῶν ἱματίων ἀντιλαμ-
βανόμενος, τοῦ γενείου, τὴν πλευρὰν θυροκοπῶν τῇ
χειρί.

   πόδες δὴ κεῖθι τιμιώτατοι,

κατὰ τὸν Ἀρχίλοχον, καὶ νὴ Δία κατὰ τὸν σοφὸν
Ἀριστοτέλην. καὶ γὰρ αὐτὸς ἐνοχλούμενος ὑπ᾽ ἀδο-
λέσχου . . . λέγοντος "οὐ θαυμαστόν, Ἀριστότελες;"
"οὐ τοῦτο," φησί, "θαυμαστόν, ἀλλ᾽ εἴ τις πόδας ἔχων
σὲ ὑπομένει."

avoiding a dimly seen[1] reef

[1] Whatever the adjective means in Nicander, its basic meaning 'faint' or 'indistinct' is appropriate in Archilochus. Perhaps an infinitive has been lost after χαλεπὸν, so that the scholiast may have said ἀμυδρὸν means something like 'hard to detect.'

**232** Heraclides Lembus, *On Constitutions*

That the constitution of the Cretans is the most ancient is shown both by Homer who speaks of their cities as "well situated" and by Archilochus who, in ridicule of some (someone), says

the Cretan law teaches[1]

[1] Emendation to the accusative plural is attractive, "he is learning Cretan laws."

**233** Plutarch, *On Talkativeness*

For (the garrulous man) attaches himself to you everywhere, grasping your cloak and beard and knocking on your ribs with his hand as though they were a door.

Feet are most valuable there,

according to Archilochus and by Zeus according to the wise Aristotle. For when he was being annoyed by a babbler . . . who kept saying, "Isn't it surprising, Aristotle?," he replied, "This is not surprising, but it is if anyone who has feet puts up with you."

# IAMBIC POETRY

**234**  Ath. 3.107f

δασυντέον . . . τὸ ἧπαρ, καὶ γὰρ ἡ συναλοιφή ἐστιν
παρ᾽ Ἀρχιλόχῳ διὰ δασέος. φησὶ γάρ·

  χολὴν γὰρ οὐκ ἔχεις ἐφ᾽ ἥπατι.

**235**  Pollux 10.135

καὶ ἶπος τὸ πιέζον τὰς ἐσθῆτας ἐν τῷ κναφείῳ, ὡς
Ἀρχίλοχος·

  κέαται δ᾽ ἐν ἴπῳ.

cf. Poll. 7.41

**236**  *Epim. in Hom.* (p. 745 Dyck) = Herodian. (ii.277.30
  Lentz)

ἡ φθειρσί δοτικὴ συνέστη παρὰ Ἀρχιλόχῳ,

  φθειρσὶ μοχθίζοντα.

**237**  Erotian. *lex. Hippocr.* σ 25 (p. 79 Nachmanson)

σκύτα· τὸ μεταξὺ τῶν τενόντων τοῦ τραχήλου . . . καὶ
Ἀρχίλοχος λέγων

  πῶς †ἀπέπρησεν τὰν σκύταν†

ἀπέπρισε tacite Eustacchi    σκύτα vel σκύτεα vel σκύτην
Bergk

240

**234** Athenaeus, *Scholars at Dinner*

The word ἧπαρ ('liver') should be given a rough breathing, since Archilochus elides with an aspirate. For he says:

for you have no gall[1] in your liver

[1] I.e., bitter anger.

**235** Pollux, *Vocabulary*

And ἷπος is that which presses clothes in a fuller's shop, as in Archilochus:

they lie in a press[1]

[1] Perhaps a metaphor for those who are 'squeezed' in some way rather than a literal reference to clothes.

**236** *Homeric Parsings*

The dative φθειρσί[1] occurs in Archilochus,

afflicted by lice

[1] The point made by the source is that the dative of φθείρ, unlike that of χείρ, always retains the diphthong.

**237** Erotian, *Lexicon on Hippocrates*

σκύτα: the part between the tendons of the neck . . . Cf. Archilochus who says:

how he sawed off(?) the nape of the neck

**238** Pollux 2.23

καὶ οὐλότριχες παρ' Ἡροδότῳ (2.104). Ἀρχίλοχος δὲ
ἀναστρέψας τρίχουλον εἴρηκεν.

**239** Pollux 2.27

βόστρυχος· ἀφ' οὗ καὶ τὸ διαβεβοστρυχωμένον παρ'
Ἀρχιλόχῳ.

διαβεβοστρυχωμένον, βεβ-, -ημένον, -ασμένον codd.

**240** Pollux 2.34

καὶ διεκτενισμένον μὲν εἴρηκεν Ἀρχίλοχος

ἐκτενισμένοι cod. A

**241** Ath. 2.49e

κοκκύμηλα οὖν ἐστι ταῦτα, ὧν Ἀρχίλοχός (ἄλλος
codd., corr. Bergk) τε μέμνηται καὶ Ἱππῶναξ· (fr. 60)

**242** Hesych.

δὶς τόση

τῇ ἡλικίᾳ. Ἀρχίλοχος.

**238** Pollux, *Vocabulary*

And οὐλότριχες occurs in Herodotus, but Archilochus reversed the order and said

> curly-haired

**239** Pollux, *Vocabulary*

βόστρυχος ('curl'), from which we find the word

> with hair all in ringlets

in Archilochus.

**240** Pollux, *Vocabulary*

And Archilochus said

> thoroughly combed

**241** Athenaeus, *Scholars at Dinner*

These are κοκκύμηλα[1] ('plums'), which are mentioned by Archilochus and Hipponax.

[1] Pollux 1.232 attributes the word to Archilochus and cites it in the genitive plural.

**242** Hesychius, *Lexicon*

> twice as great[1]

with reference to age. Archilochus.

[1] West, probably correctly, inserts this in fr. 196a.26.

**243** Hesych.

ἥμισυ τρίτον

δύο ἥμισυ. Ἀρχίλοχος.

**244** Cyril. *lex.*, cod. Bodl. Misc. gr. 211 f. 233ᵛ (W. Bühler, *Hermes* 96 [1968] 232-36)

ὀθνεῖος· ξένος, ἀλλότριος, ἀλλογενής. ⟨καὶ⟩ ὀθνέος, ἐπεὶ καὶ Ἀρχίλοχος

ὀθνέην ὁδόν.

⟨καὶ⟩ ὀθνέος West (ὀθνεῖος cod.)      ἀρχίλογος ὀθένοδον cod., corr. Bühler

**245** Schol. Nic. *Th.* 213 (p. 107 Crugnola), "ἀργίλιπες"

ἤτοι ἔκλευκοι, ὡς Ἀρχίλοχος·

ἀργιλιπὴς δ' ἐφάνη.

δὲ φάνη, δὲ φάσις, δ' ἐφᾶ, φησιν codd.

**246** *Et. Gen.* (p. 16 Calame) = *Et. Mag.* 152.47

ἀσελγαίνει· . . . Ἐπαφρόδιτος δὲ παρὰ τὸ λέχος λεχαίνειν, τὸ λέχους ἐπιθυμεῖν καὶ κατὰ τροπὴν λε-γαίνειν, ἔνθεν Ἀρχίλοχος·

λέγαι δὲ γυναῖκες

ἀντὶ τοῦ ἀκόλαστοι.

**243** Hesychius, *Lexicon*

a half third

means two and a half. Archilochus.


**244** Cyril, *Lexicon*

ὀθνεῖος: foreign, strange, of another race. Also ὀθνέος, since Archilochus has

foreign road


**245** Scholiast on Nicander, *Theriaca*

ἀργίλιπες means 'very white,' as in Archilochus:

he(?) appeared all in white


**246** *Etymologicum Genuinum* and *Magnum*

behaves licentiously: . . . and Epaphroditus derives from λέχος ('bed') λεχαίνειν ('to desire the bed') and by a change λεγαίνειν, whence Archilochus:

and λέγαι women

with the meaning 'lewd.'[1]

---

[1] The etymology is implausible and the text may be corrupt.

**247** Eust. in Hom. *Il.* 11.385 (iii.218.2 V.d.Valk)

Ἀριστοτέλης δέ, φασί (Arist. Pseudepigraphus p. 166 Rose), κέραι ἀγλαὸν (*Il.* 11.385) εἶπεν ἀντὶ τοῦ αἰδοίῳ σεμνυνόμενον . . . καὶ ἔοικεν ὁ σκορπιώδης τὴν γλῶσσαν Ἀρχίλοχος ἁπαλὸν κέρας τὸ αἰδοῖον εἰπὼν ἐντεῦθεν τὴν λέξιν πορίσασθαι.

**248** Hesych.

Καρπάθ<ι>ος τὸν μάρτυρα· παροιμία "Καρπάθιος δὲ <τὸν> λαγών" (κατ᾽ ἔλλειψιν τοῦ ἐπηγάγετο). διὰ γὰρ τὸ μὴ εἶναι λαγωοὺς ἐν τῇ χώρᾳ ἐπηγάγοντο αὐτοί, καὶ τοσοῦτοι ἐγένοντο ὥστε τόν τε σῖτον αὐτῶν καὶ τὰς ἀμπέλους ὑπ᾽ αὐτῶν βλάπτεσθαι. ὁ γοῦν Ἀρχίλοχος παρὰ ταύτην τὴν παροιμίαν ἔφη

  Καρπάθιος τὸν μάρτυρα.

Καρπάθ<ι>ος Alberti    <τὸν> Bossi e paroemiogr.

**249** Phot. *lex.* = *Suda* (iii.422.17 Adler)

  μυδαλέον

δίυγρον, παρ᾽ Ἀρχιλόχῳ, διάβροχον.

**250** Eust. in Hom. *Od.* 17.455 (1828.9)

ἐνταῦθα δὲ χρήσιμα ἐκ τῶν παλαιῶν καὶ τὸ κίμβιξ

**247** Eustathius on Homer, *Iliad*

And Aristotle, they say, claimed that κέρᾳ ἀγλαὸν meant he was proud of his penis[1] . . . And it seems that when the scorpion-tongued Archilochus called the penis

a soft horn

he derived the expression from there.

[1] The Homeric passage is almost certainly a reference to hair-style. Cf. fr. 117.

**248** Hesychius, *Lexicon*

A Karpathian (introduced) his witness. There is a proverb "A Karpathian (introduced) the hare," with ellipse of the word 'introduced.' For because there were no hares in the land they introduced them, and they became so numerous that the grain and vines were damaged by them. At any rate Archilochus, with a play on this proverb, said:

a Karpathian[1] (introduced) his witness

[1] Karpathos is an island between Rhodes and Crete.

**249** Photius, *Lexicon* = *Suda*

μυδαλέον, meaning 'moist,' 'sodden,' occurs in Archilochus.

**250** Eustathius on Homer, *Odyssey* (on miserly people)

Words used in this sense by the ancients are κίμβιξ

. . . καὶ ῥυποκόνδυλος, καὶ συκοτραγίδης παρ' Ἱπ-
πώνακτι (fr. 167) καὶ Ἀρχιλόχῳ διὰ τὸ εὐτελές, φασί,
τοῦ βρώματος.

**251** V. test. 3

> ὁ Διόνυσος τ[
> ουλαστναζ[
> ὄμφακες α[
> σῦκα μελ[
> 5  Οἰφολίωι ερ[

4 μελ[ιχρὰ Peek

**252** Choerob. *can.* i.158.9 Hilgard = Herodian. *Anecd.
Ox.* iii.231.5 Cramer (i.61.6, ii.679.5 Lentz)

(μύκης) σημαίνει δὲ καὶ τὸ αἰδοῖον τοῦ ἀνθρώπου,
ὅπερ καὶ ἰσοσυλλάβως ἔκλινεν Ἀρχίλοχος εἰπὼν

> ἀλλ' ἀπερρώγασι μύκεω τένοντες.

ἀπερρώγασί <μοι> Cobet, <οἱ> Hauvette

**253** Philod. *de musica* (p. 20 Kemke)

τὸ μέλος καὶ [. . . . . .]ᾳι ταραχῶν εἶν[αι κ]αταπ[α]υ-
στικόν, ὡς ἐπι[. . . .]των καὶ τῶν ζώι[ων . . . .]σθαι
καταπραϋνο[μένω]ν· διὸ καὶ τὸν Ἀρχίλο[χον λ]έγειν.

248

('skinflint') . . . and ῥυποκόνδυλος ('with dirty knuckles')
and συκοτραγίδης ('son of a fig-eater'[1]) in Hipponax and
Archilochus, because, as they say, it was cheap food.

[1] A mock patronymic, perhaps with obscene connotation,
since σῦκον ('fig') can be a metaphor for the vagina (see on fr.
251.4).

**251** Inscription of Mnesiepes

Dionysus . . . unripe grapes . . . sweet(?) figs[1] . . .
Oipholios[2] . . .

[1] Grapes and figs may be sexual metaphors, for young or small
breasts and vaginas.     [2] Presumably an epithet of Dionysus
and derived from the root οἰφ-, denoting sexual intercourse. On
vv. 1-2 see W. Luppe, *Glotta* 71 (1993) 143-45.

**252** Choeroboscus, *On the Canons of Theodosius*

μύκης means the male sex organ and Archilochus declined
it with the same number of syllables[1] when he said:

but the sinews of (his, my) cock were ruptured

[1] Rather than the trisyllabic μύκητος.

**253** Philodemus, *On Music*

Song has the power to cause . . . disturbances to cease,
since . . . and animals are pacified. Therefore Archilochus
says:

κηλωταιδοτισ[..(..)..]ων ἀοιδαῖς

κηλεῖται Kemke (sed cf. Hesych. κηλόω· κηλέω)    δέ τις
Sitzler    κηλῶ‹ν›ται δ᾽ ὅτις / [ἀστ]ῶν Gigante, κηλῶται δ᾽ ὅ
τι / σ[ειρήν]ων (hoc cum Sitzler) Pizzocaro

**254**  Schol. Arat. 1 (p. 37.6 Martin), "ἀρχώμεσθα"

τὸ δὲ ἀρχώμεσθα μετὰ τοῦ σ· ἔστι γὰρ καὶ ἀρχαϊσ-
μός. Ὅμηρος· "δόρπα τ᾽ ἐφοπλισόμεσθα" (Il. 8.503,
al.). καὶ Ἀρχίλοχος·

οὗτοι τοῦτο δυνησόμεσθα.

**255**  Hesych. s.v. Θαργήλια

Θαργήλια· Ἀπόλλωνος ἑορτή. καὶ ὅλος ὁ μὴν ἱερὸς
τοῦ θεοῦ. ἐν δὲ τοῖς Θαργηλίοις τὰς ἀπαρχὰς τῶν
φαινομένων ‹καρπῶν› (add. Liebel) ποιοῦνται καὶ
περικομίζουσι, ταῦτα δὲ θαργηλιά φασι. καὶ μὴν
Θαργηλιών. καὶ τὴν εὐετηρίαν ἐκάλουν ‹θαργήλια,
καὶ ἄρτον› (add. West) θάργηλον. καὶ Ἀρχίλοχός
φησιν

†ὡς φαίε νῦν ἄγει τὰ θαργήλια.†

fort. ὡς Hesychii est    Ταργήλια pro τὰ Θ. ci. Schmidt

**256**  Schol. Plat. Hipp. mai. 295a (p. 177 Greene) =Anecd.
Par. iv.84.11 Cramer

(ἃ) σημαίνει δὲ καὶ τὸ πολὺ καὶ τὸ μέγα, ὡς παρ᾽ Ἀρχι-
λόχῳ,

250

ARCHILOCHUS

. . . is charmed by songs of . . .¹

¹ There is a full discussion of the text by M. Gigante, "Filodemo e Archiloco," *BCPE* 23 (1993) 5-10.


**254** Scholiast on Aratus, *Phaenomena* ("let us begin")

ἀρχώμεσθα with a sigma is an archaism. Cf. Homer: "let us prepare our meal." And Archilochus:

we shall not be able to do this


**255** Hesychius, *Lexicon*

Thargelia: a festival of Apollo. And the whole month is sacred to the god. At the Thargelia they offer and carry round the first-fruits of the ripening (grain), and these are called *thargelia*. And there is the month Thargelion. They called a good season (*thargelia* and bread) made from the first-fruits *thargelos*. And Archilochus says:

. . . now he celebrates the Thargelia(?)


**256** Scholiast on Plato, *Hippias Maior*

ᾶ also means 'much' and 'big,' as in Archilochus:

†ἇ ἔαδε εἷς† τε ταύρους

ἀθαλέας West, ἀειλέας Bossi

**257** Herodian. π. διχρόνων (ii.9.30 Lentz)

τὰ εἰς υψ μονοσύλλαβα ἐκτείνεται . . . τὰ δὲ ὑπὲρ μίαν συλλαβὴν συστέλλεται. θέλουσι δὲ πεδότριψ ἐκτείνειν, πλανώμενοι ἐκ τοῦ παρ᾽ Ἀρχιλόχῳ

†ἄνδρες ὡς† ἀμφιτρίβας.

ἄνδρες codd. ABC, ἄνδρας D     ὡς BCD, ἐς A

**258** *Et. Gen.* (p. 34 Calame)

†κοπάεν† ξίφος

παρὰ τῷ Ἀρχιλόχῳ ἀπὸ τοῦ κοπάειν.

cf. *Et. Mag.* 529.13, *Et. Sym.* cod. V (Gaisford ad *Et. Mag.* loc. cit.) κοπόεν· κόπος κοπόεις κοπόεν, ὡς στόνος στονόεις στονόεν

κοπτάεν *Et. Mag.* cod. M, κοπόεν Edmonds et Lasserre ex *Et. Sym.*, κωπῆεν Sylburg     τὸ Ἀρχιλόχου *Et. Gen.* A, τὸ Ἀντιλόχου B, corr. Calame     κοπάγειν *Et. Mag.*, fort. κοπάζειν West

**259** Aristid. *or.* 45 (ii.137.17 Dindorf)

καὶ ὁ μέν γε κατ᾽ ἰσχὺν προφέρων, εἰ καὶ ἑνὸς εἴη κρείττων, ὑπὸ δυοῖν γ᾽ ἂν αὐτὸν κατείργεσθαί φησι καὶ Ἀρχίλοχος καὶ ἡ παροιμία.

. . . and . . . bulls


**257**  Herodian, *On Doubtful Quantities*

Monosyllables in -υψ have a long iota . . . But it is short in
words exceeding one syllable. They wish to lengthen the
iota in πεδότρυψ, misled by the passage in Archilochus:

> men(?) worn all round[1]

[1] Sense uncertain. LSJ translate by 'practised knave,' compar-
ing Hesychius s.v., but the word need not be derogatory. For the
corruption and meter see West, *Studies* 137.

**258**  *Etymologicum Genuinum*

> the sword (that cuts?, grows weary?)

in Archilochus from κοπάειν.[1]

[1] No such verb is known.


**259**  Aelius Aristides, *Orations*

Both Archilochus and the proverb state that he who is
superior in strength, even though he should be stronger
than one, would be overcome by two.

Schol. ad loc. (iii.429.17 Dindorf)

ἡ μὲν παροιμία φησίν "οὐδὲ Ἡρακλῆς πρὸς δύο·" τὸ δὲ Ἀρχιλόχου ῥητὸν οἷον μέν ἐστιν οὐκ ἴσμεν, ἴσως δὲ ἂν εἴη τοιοῦτον.

**261** Eust. in Hom. *Il.* 2.654 (i.489.3 V.d.Valk)

ἀγέρωχοι δὲ οἱ ἄγαν γέρας ἔχοντες . . . δηλοῖ δέ, φασίν, οὕτως ἡ λέξις τοὺς σεμνούς, ὡς Ἀλκμὰν βούλεται (cf. *PMGF* 5 fr. 1(b).4, 10(b).15). Ἀλκαῖος δέ, φασί (fr. 402 V.), καὶ Ἀρχίλοχος ἀγέρωχον τὸν ἄκοσμον καὶ ἀλάζονα οἶδε.

**262** Hesych.

ἀζυγέα

ἄζευκτον. Ἀρχίλοχος.

ἀζυγία cod., corr. Latte    ἄζυγα Salmasius

**263** Hesych.

ἀηδόνιον· . . . ἀηδόνος νεοσσός. καὶ τὸ τῆς γυναικὸς αἰδοῖον παρὰ Ἀρχιλόχῳ.

ἀηδόνιον Perizonius (ἀηδόνων cod.)

**264** Schol. Hom. *Il.* 7.76 (P. Oxy. viii.1087.22 sqq.), "ἐπὶ μάρτυρας ἔστω"

τὸ δὲ μάρτυρος παρώνυμον [τῆι γ]ενικῆ[ι] τοῦ

254

Scholiast on the passage

The proverb states: "Not even Heracles against two." We do not know what Archilochus' words were, but probably they were something like this.

**261** Eustathius on Homer, *Iliad*

ἀγέρωχοι are the over privileged . . . And so, they say, the word clearly denotes the proud, as in Alcman. Alcaeus, they say, and Archilochus know that ἀγέρωχος is one who is unruly and boastful.

**262** Hesychius, *Lexicon*

ἀζυγέα means 'unyoked,' as in Archilochus.

**263** Hesychius, *Lexicon*

ἀηδόνιον[1] . . . is the nightingale's young and in Archilochus a woman's genitals.

[1] For the problems associated with Hesychius' text see Bossi 253-56.

**264** Scholiast on Homer, *Iliad* ("let him be witness thereto")

The word μάρτυρος (nom.) is derived from the genitive

255

πρωτοτύπου συμ[πέ]πτωκεν, ὡς . . . τὸ ἄτμενος παρ᾽
Ἀρχιλόχῳ.

Hesych.

ἄτμενος (ἀγόμενος cod., corr. Nauck)· δοῦλος παρ᾽
Ἀρχιλόχῳ.

**265** Hesych.

γυμνόν· ἀνυ‹πό›δητον, ἢ ἀπεσκυθισμένον ὡς Ἀρχί-
λοχος.

**266** Hesych.

ἔτρεψεν· ἐπέτρεψεν, ἠπάτησεν, παρέτρεψεν. Ἀρχί-
λοχος.

**267** Cyril. *lex.* apud *Anecd. Par.* iv.183.21 Cramer

†θριαθρίκη· Ἀρχίλοχος. καὶ ὅτι ἀπὸ Θριῶν τῶν Διὸς
θυγατέρων διωνομάσθησαν, ὡς Φερεκύδης (*FGrHist* 3
F 49) ἱστορεῖ. ἐπεὶ τρίαι εἰσίν, οἶον τρισσαὶ κατὰ τὸν
ἀριθμόν.

**268** *Epim. in Hom.* (p. 449 Dyck) = Herodian. (i.494.13
Lentz)

παρὰ τὸ ἐκεῖθι κεῖθι καὶ

κεῖ

παρὰ Ἀρχιλόχῳ,

of the original form (μάρτυρ), as . . . the word ἄτμενος[1] ('slave') in Archilochus.

Hesychius, *Lexicon*

ἄτμενος: slave in Archilochus.

[1] I.e., the nominative ἄτμενος is derived from ἀτμένος, genitive of ἀτμήν. See also Ananius fr. 6.

**265** Hesychius, *Lexicon*

γυμνόν means 'barefoot' or, as in Archilochus, 'shaved bare.'

**266** Hesychius, *Lexicon*

ἔτρεψεν means 'entrusted'(?), 'deceived,' 'misled.' Cf. Archilochus.[1]

[1] Only the last two glosses, it seems, refer to Archilochus.

**267** Cyril, *Lexicon*

†θριαθρίκη: Archilochus. They (sc. θριαί) were named after the Thriae, daughters of Zeus, as Pherecydes relates. (Or) because they were τρίαι, i.e., three in number.[1]

[1] Text and meaning highly uncertain. It seems that the etymology of θριαί, pebbles used in divination, is being discussed.

**268** *Homeric Parsings*

Besides ἐκεῖθι and κεῖθι we find κεῖ

there

in Archilochus.

# IAMBIC POETRY

**269** Pollux 4.71 (i.222 Bethe)

ὁ δὲ τοῖς αὐλοῖς χρώμενος αὐλητής, καὶ κεραύλης κατὰ τὸν Ἀρχίλοχον.

**270** Schol. Lyc. 771 (ii.245.3 Scheer), "μύκλοις"

οἱ δὲ μύκλους φασὶ τοὺς κατωφερεῖς εἰς γυναῖκας· εἴρηται δὲ ἀπὸ ἑνὸς Μύκλου αὐλητοῦ κωμῳδηθέντος ὑπ᾽ Ἀρχιλόχου ἐπὶ μαχλότητι.

**271** Steph. Byz. (p. 383.21 Meineke) = Eust. in Dion. Per. 498 (ii.310.31 Müller) = Herodian. (i.342.16, ii.226.7 Lentz)

Κρήτη· ἡ μεγίστη νῆσος. ἣν Κρεήτην ἔφη Ἀρχίλοχος κατὰ πλεονασμὸν ⟨τοῦ ε⟩.

Ἀρχίας in Eust. pro Ἀρχίλοχος

**272** Schol. A in Hom. *Il*. 6.507 (ii.217 Erbse), "πεδίοιο κροαίνων"

ἡ διπλῆ ὅτι ἐλλείπει ἡ διά, καὶ ⟨ὅτι⟩ τὸ κροαίνων οὐκ ἔστιν ἐπιθυμῶν, ὡς Ἀρχίλοχος ἐξέλαβεν, ἀλλ᾽ ἐπικροτῶν τοῖς ποσὶ διὰ τοῦ πεδίου. ἄλλως. οἱ νεώτεροι ἐπιθυμεῖν τὸ κροαίνειν. καὶ Ἀρχίλοχος.

**269** Pollux, *Vocabulary*

The one who performs on the pipes is called a piper and, according to Archilochus, a

horn blower

**270** Scholiast on Lycophron

They call μύκλοι those who have a propensity for women. The word is derived from one named Myclus, a piper satirized by Archilochus for his lewdness.

**271** Stephanus of Byzantium, *Lexicon of Place Names*

Crete (Κρήτη): the largest island. It is called Κρεήτη by Archilochus with pleonastic epsilon.

**272** Scholiast on Homer, *Iliad*

The marginal note is used because there is an ellipse of the preposition διά and because κροαίνων does not mean 'desiring,' as Archilochus understood it, but clattering with hooves over the plain. A different explanation. Later authors use κροαίνειν to mean 'desire.' So Archilochus.

**273**  Pollux 10.160 (ii.238 Bethe)

ἀλλὰ μὴν καὶ κύρτη {σιδηρᾶ} ἀγγεῖόν τι οἷον οἰκίσκος
ὀρνίθειος, παρὰ Ἡροδότῳ (1.191) καὶ Ἀρχιλόχῳ.

σιδηρᾶ del. Reitzenstein      Κρατῖνος Ἀρχιλόχοις Mar-
zullo

**274**  Schol. Ar. *Pl.* 476 (p. 89 Chantry) = *Suda* (iii.223.6
Adler)

κύφων δὲ δεσμός ἐστι ξύλινος . . . ἔνθεν καὶ ὁ πον-
ηρὸς ἄνθρωπος κύφων· τάσσεται δὲ καὶ ἐπὶ πάντων
τῶν δυσχερῶν καὶ ὀλεθρίων . . . Ἀρχίλοχος δὲ ἀντὶ
τοῦ κακὸς καὶ ὀλέθριος.

**275**  Pollux 6.79 (ii.23 Bethe)

τὰ δὲ ἐπιδορπίσματα . . . ἦν δὲ τρωγάλια, κάρυα,
μυρτίδες, μέσπιλα ἃ καὶ ὅα καλεῖται· καὶ τοὔνομά
ἐστι παρὰ Πλάτωνι τοῦτο (τὰ ὅα, *Conv.* 190d), ὡς παρ'
Ἀρχιλόχῳ ἐκεῖνο.

**276**  Hesych.

μουνόκερα

τὸ μηκέτι ἔχον τὴν ἀλκήν, ὡς Ἀρχίλοχος.

**277**  Phot. *lex.* a 808 (Theodoridis)

σημαίνει δὲ τὸ ὀργᾶν ⟨τὸ⟩ πάνυ ἐπαίρεσθαι πρὸς τὸ

**273** Pollux, *Vocabulary*

But κύρτη is a receptacle such as a birdcage in Herodotus and Archilochus.

**274** Scholiast on Aristophanes, *Plutus*

κύφων is a wooden constraint (i.e., a pillory) . . . and hence a wicked man is called κύφων. It is also used of all who are disagreeable and harmful. And in Archilochus it means evil and harmful.

**275** Pollux, *Vocabulary*

Food for dessert . . . this consisted of fruits, nuts, myrtle-berries, and medlars (μέσπιλα) which are also called sorb-apples (ὄα). The latter name is found in Plato, the former in Archilochus.

**276** Hesychius, *Lexicon*

one-horned

of that which no longer has its strength, as in Archilochus.[1]

[1] Perhaps a reference to Heracles' fight with Achelous in bull-form. Cf. frr. 286-87.

**277** Photius, *Lexicon*

ὀργᾶν means to be highly excited to do or hear something.

IAMBIC POETRY

πρᾶξαί τι ἢ ἀκοῦσαι. καθόλου δὲ ποικίλως χρῶνται
τῷ ὀνόματι. καὶ γὰρ ἐπὶ τοῦ βρέξαι, ὡς Ἀρχίλοχος,
Αἰσχύλος (fr. 435a Radt) δὲ κτλ.

**278** Lex. Messan. de iota adscripto (ed. Rabe, *RhM* 47
[1892] 408) ex Ori *Orthographicis*

ὀρεσκῷος . . . ὁτὲ γοῦν γίνεται ὀρέσκοος ὡς παρ᾽
Ἀρχιλόχῳ, καὶ προπαροξύνεται.

**279** Pollux 10.27 (ii.197 Bethe)

Ἀριστοφάνης (*Lys.* 265) "προπύλαια πακτοῦν," ἢ
πάλιν (fr. 737 K.-A.) "κἀπιπακτοῦν τὰς θύρας," ἢ ὡς
Ἀρχίλοχος

πακτῶσαι

τὸ κλεῖσαι.

**280** Eust. in Hom. *Il.* 8.248 (ii.575 V.d.Valk)

λέγει δὲ <ὁ> αὐτὸς (Arist. Byz. u.v., fr. 186 Slater) καὶ τὰς
πρόκας παρ᾽ Ἀρχιλόχῳ ἐπὶ ἐλάφου τεθεῖσθαι, παρ᾽ ᾧ
καί τις διὰ δειλίαν προσωνομάσθη πρόξ.

Generally the word is used in a variety of senses. It has the force of

> to moisten

in Archilochus,[1] and Aeschylus etc.

[1] The entire extract suggests that Archilochus may have used some form of ὀργάζειν rather than ὀργᾶν.

**278**  Lexicon Messanense, *On the iota adscript*

ὀρεσκῷος . . . sometimes it is used in the form ὀρέσκοος

> mountain-dwelling

as in Archilochus, and it has the proparoxytone accent.

**279**  Pollux, *Vocabulary*

Aristophanes has "to make fast the propylaea" or again "to shut close the door" or as in Archilochus where πακτῶσαι means

> to lock

**280**  Eustathius on Homer, *Iliad*

The same one states that πρόκες ('roe deer') are regarded as meaning 'red deer' in Archilochus who gave the name

> red deer

to someone because of his cowardice.

**281** Choerob. *can.* (i.296.5 Hilgard) = Herodian. (ii.744.22 Lentz)

ῥὰξ δ' ἐστιν ὁ κόκκος τῆς σταφυλῆς. εὑρίσκομεν δὲ καὶ ἐπὶ τῆς σταφυλῆς διὰ τοῦ ω λεγόμενον, οἷον ῥώξ ῥωγός παρ' Ἀρχιλόχῳ.

**282** Hesych.

σκελήπερον

νήπιον. Ἀρχίλοχος.

**283** Erotian. *lex. Hippocr.* τ 13 (p. 85.7 Nachmanson)

τράμιν· τὸν ὄρρον, ὄνπερ καὶ ὑποταύριον καλοῦμεν, ὡς καὶ Ἱππῶναξ φησιν· (fr. 114a) . . . μέμνηται καὶ Ἀρχίλοχος.

**284** Herodian. apud Eust. in *Od.* 13.401 (1746.9) = i.445.17 Lentz (cf. i.393.31, ii.903.14)

. . . φλύος παρ' Ἀρχιλόχῳ ἐπὶ φλυαρίας.

**285** Ath. 3.86a-b

ἐν δὲ τῷ ἐπιγραφομένῳ Ὡλιεὺς (Sophron fr. 44 Kaibel) τὸν ἀγροιώταν (κόγχον) χηράμβας ὀνομάζει. καὶ Ἀρχίλοχος δὲ τῆς χηράμβης μέμνηται.

**281** Choeroboscus, *On the Canons of Theodosius*

ῥάξ is the seed of a grape. And we also find it with an omega (ῥώξ ῥωγός) with reference to the

grape

in Archilochus.

**282** Hesychius, *Lexicon*

σκελήπερον means

foolish

in Archilochus.

**283** Erotian, *Lexicon on Hippocrates*

τράμις is what we call the perineum, as Hipponax says . . . Archilochus also mentions it.

**284** Herodian in Eustathius on Homer, *Odyssey*

. . . φλύος in Archilochus for φλυαρία ('nonsense')

**285** Athenaeus, *Scholars at Dinner*

In the mime entitled *The Fisherman* Sophron calls the wild conch χηράμβη. And Archilochus also mentions the χηράμβη.

# IAMBIC POETRY

**286** Dio Chrys. 60.1

ἔχεις μοι λῦσαι ταύτην τὴν ἀπορίαν, πότερον δικαίως ἐγκαλοῦσιν οἱ μὲν τῷ Ἀρχιλόχῳ, οἱ δὲ τῷ Σοφοκλεῖ, περὶ τῶν κατὰ τὸν Νέσσον καὶ τὴν Δηιάνειραν, ἢ οὔ; φασὶ γὰρ οἱ μὲν τὸν Ἀρχίλοχον ληρεῖν ποιοῦντα τὴν Δηιάνειραν ἐν τῷ βιάζεσθαι ὑπὸ τοῦ Κενταύρου πρὸς τὸν Ἡρακλέα ῥαψῳδοῦσαν, ἀναμιμνήσκουσαν τῆς τοῦ Ἀχελῴου μνηστείας καὶ τῶν τότε γενομένων, ὥστε πολλὴν σχολὴν εἶναι τῷ Νέσσῳ ὅτι ἐβούλετο πρᾶξαι· οἱ δὲ τὸν Σοφοκλέα πρὸ τοῦ καιροῦ πεποιηκέναι τὴν τοξείαν, διαβαινόντων αὐτῶν ἔτι τὸν ποταμόν (*Tr.* 562 sqq.).

**287** Schol. Hom. *Il.* 21.237, "μεμυκὼς ἠΰτε ταῦρος"

ἐντεῦθεν ὁρμηθέντες τὸν Ἀχελῷον ἐταύρωσαν Ἡρακλεῖ ἀγωνιζόμενον. Ἀρχίλοχος μὲν οὐκ ἐτόλμησεν Ἀχελῷον ὡς ποταμὸν Ἡρακλεῖ συμβαλεῖν, ἀλλ' ὡς ταῦρον, Ὅμηρος δὲ πρῶτος ποταμοῦ καὶ ἥρωος ἠγωνοθέτησε μάχην. ἑκάτερος οὖν τὴν αὐτὴν ὑπόθεσιν ἐμέτρησε τῇ δυνάμει.

**288** Schol. Ap. Rhod. 1.1212-1219a (p. 110 Wendel)

φεύγων οὖν τὸν φόνον καὶ σὺν τῇ γαμετῇ στελλόμενος ἀνεῖλεν ἐν Εὐήνῳ ποταμῷ Νέσσον Κένταυρον, ὡς καὶ Ἀρχίλοχος ἱστορεῖ.

**286** Dio Chrysostom, *Orations*

Can you solve this problem for me, whether or not some are right to find fault with Archilochus and others with Sophocles for their treatment of Nessus and Deianeira? For some say that Archilochus is talking nonsense when he makes Deianeira speak at length to Heracles while she is being sexually assaulted by the centaur, as she reminds him of the wooing of Achelous and of the events that took place then, with the result that Nessus had ample time to do what he wanted. And others say that Sophocles introduced the shooting of the arrow too early, while they were still crossing the river.

**287** Scholiast on Homer, *Iliad* ("bellowing like a bull")

From this starting point they represented Achelous as a bull in his fight with Heracles. Archilochus did not dare to pit Achelous as a river against Heracles, but as a bull, whereas Homer was the first to make river and hero contend in battle. Each therefore adapted the same topic to his own talent.

**288** Scholiast on Apollonius Rhodius

Fleeing then from the murder (of Cyathus) and setting out with his wife (Deianeira) Heracles killed the centaur Nessus in the river Euenus, as Archilochus relates.

**289**  Plut. *de Herod. malign.* 14.857f

καίτοι τῶν παλαιῶν καὶ λογίων ἀνδρῶν οὐχ Ὅμηρος, οὐχ Ἡσίοδος, οὐκ Ἀρχίλοχος, οὐ Πείσανδρος, οὐ Στησίχορος, οὐκ Ἀλκμάν, οὐ Πίνδαρος Αἰγυπτίου ἔσχον λόγον Ἡρακλέους ἢ Φοίνικος, ἀλλ' ἕνα τοῦτον ἴσασι πάντες Ἡρακλέα τὸν Βοιώτιον ὁμοῦ καὶ Ἀργεῖον.

**290**  Ath. 1.30f

Ἀρχίλοχος τὸν Νάξιον (οἶνον) τῷ νέκταρι παραβάλλει. Sequitur fr. 2.

**291**  Harpocr. s.v. Στρύμη (p. 242 Keaney)

μνημονεύει τῶν Θασίων πρὸς Μαρωνείτας περὶ τῆς Στρύμης ἀμφισβητήσεως Φιλόχορος ἐν ε' (*FGrHist* 328 F 43), Ἀρχίλοχον ἐπαγόμενος μάρτυρα.

**292**  Plut. *Marius* 21

Μασσαλιήτας μέντοι λέγουσι τοῖς ὀστέοις περιθριγκῶσαι τοὺς ἀμπελῶνας, τὴν δὲ γῆν, τῶν νεκρῶν καταναλωθέντων ἐν αὐτῇ καὶ διὰ χειμῶνος ὄμβρων ἐπιπεσόντων, οὕτως ἐκλιπανθῆναι καὶ γενέσθαι διὰ βάθους περίπλεω τῆς σηπεδόνος ἐνδύσης ὥστε καρπῶν ὑπερβάλλον εἰς ὥρας πλῆθος ἐξενεγκεῖν, καὶ μαρτυρῆσαι τῷ Ἀρχιλόχῳ λέγοντι πιαίνεσθαι πρὸς τοῦ τοιούτου τὰς ἀρούρας.

ARCHILOCHUS

**289**  Plutarch, *On the Malice of Herodotus*

And yet of the ancient storytellers neither Homer nor
Hesiod nor Archilochus nor Pisander nor Stesichorus nor
Alcman nor Pindar made mention of an Egyptian or Phoe-
nician Heracles,[1] but they all know this one Heracles who
is both Boeotian and Argive.

[1] Cf. Herodotus 2.43 f.

**290**  Athenaeus, *Scholars at Dinner*

Archilochus compares Naxian wine to nectar.

**291**  Harpocration, *Lexicon of the Ten Attic Orators*

Philochorus in Book 5, adducing Archilochus as witness,
mentions the contention between the Thasians and the
Maronites[1] over Stryme.[2]

[1] Maroneia is a coastal town in Thrace N-E of Thasos.
[2] Stryme is an island which, according to Harpocration, served as
a trading post for the Thasians.

**292**  Plutarch, *Life of Marius*

Nevertheless they say that the people of Massalia fenced
their vineyards round with the bones and that the land,
when the corpses had been consumed in it and the rains
had fallen throughout the winter, became so rich and so
full of putrified matter that sank deeply into it that as a
result it produced an exceptional harvest for season after
season and bore witness to Archilochus who said that fields
are fattened by such a means.

IAMBIC POETRY

**293** Ath. 4.167d

τοιοῦτος ἐγένετο καὶ Αἰθίοψ ὁ Κορίνθιος, ὥς φησι
Δημήτριος ὁ Σκήψιος (fr. 73 Gaede)· οὗ μνημονεύει
Ἀρχίλοχος. ὑπὸ φιληδονίας γὰρ καὶ ἀκρασίας καὶ
οὗτος, μετ᾽ Ἀρχίου πλέων εἰς Σικελίαν ὅτε ἔμελλε
κτίζειν Συρακούσας, τῷ ἑαυτοῦ συσσίτῳ μελιτούττης
ἀπέδοτο τὸν κλῆρον ὃν ἐν Συρακούσαις λαχὼν ἔμελ-
λεν ἕξειν.

**294** Oenomaus apud Euseb. *praep. ev.* 5.33.5

τί πράττειν κελεύεις ἡμᾶς; ἢ δηλαδὴ τὰ Ἀρχιλόχου,
εἰ μέλλομεν ἄξιοι φανεῖσθαι τῆς ὑμετέρας ἑστίας,
λοιδορῆσαι μὲν πικρῶς τὰς οὐκ ἐθελούσας ἡμῖν
γαμεῖσθαι, ἅψασθαι δὲ καὶ τῶν κιναίδων, ἐπειδὴ τῶν
ἄλλων πονηρῶν πολὺ πονηρότεροί εἰσιν, οὐχὶ δίχα
μέτρου; . . . (13) εἰσὶ καὶ νῦν ἕτοιμοι κωμῳδεῖσθαι καὶ
†Σαβαῖοι (Σαπαῖοι?, cf. fr. 93b) καὶ Λυκάμβαι κτλ.

**295** = test. 33

**295a** (v. Hippon. fr. 29a)

ARCHILOCHUS

**293** Athenaeus, *Scholars at Dinner*

Such (a spendthrift) too, as reported by Demetrius of Scepsis, was Aethiops of Corinth whom Archilochus mentions. For because of his love of pleasure and his lack of self-control Aethiops, while sailing with Archias to Sicily at the time when the latter was going to found Syracuse, sold to his messmate for a honey cake the share which he had drawn by lot and was to have in Syracuse.

**294** Oenomaus in Eusebius, *Evangelical Preparation*

What then do you bid us do? Clearly, if we are going to show ourselves worthy of your hearth, to revile bitterly in meter in the manner of Archilochus those who are unwilling to marry us and also to attack pathics, since they are by far the most wicked of all? . . . Even now the Sapaeans(?) and Lycambeses are ready subjects of comedy etc.[1]

[1] On this passage see J. Hammerstaedt, *Die Orakelkritik des Kynikers Oenomaus* (Frankfurt am Main 1988) 112-17.

## 296-321. Dubia

*These fragments, as well as those judged spurious by West (frr. 322-33), are discussed in detail by V. Casadio, I "dubbi" di Archiloco (Ospedaletto 1996). He defends the authenticity of frr. 296-97, 299-303, 314-21, 323-24, 331 and 333, and in the process he assigns fr. 200 to Aristophanes and 273, in all probability, to Cratinus.*

**296** *Et. Gen.* (pp. 41 sq. Calame)

. . . ὁ δὲ Ἡρωδιανὸς (i.xxxii Lentz) παρὰ τὸ ἴσσω, ὡς Ἀρχίλοχος

προτείνω χεῖρα καὶ προΐσσομαι.

**297** Orion, *etym.* (col. 37.4 Sturz) = *Et. Mag.* 184.49 = *Et. Gen.* et *Sym.* β 3 (pp. 1-2 Berger)

βάβαξ· λάλος, φλύαρος . . . Ἀρχίλοχος·

κατ᾽ οἶκον ἐστρωφᾶτο μισητὸς βάβαξ.

Ἀρχίλοχος Orion, Ἀριστοφάνης *Et. Gen.* et *Mag.* μισητὸς *Et. Gen.* et *Mag.*, δυσμενὴς Orion

**298** Aristides, *or.* 45 (ii.51.17 Dindorf)

οὐ γὰρ ὁμοίως, οἶμαι, οἵ τε θεοὶ τὰ μέλλοντα ἴσασι καὶ τῶν ἀνθρώπων ὅσοι φάσκουσιν. οἱ μὲν γὰρ ἃ μέλλουσι ποιεῖν ἐπίστανται καὶ πρόκειται τὰ πράγματα αὐτοῖς ὥσπερ ἐν ὀφθαλμοῖς· διὰ τοῦτο

## 296-321. *Doubtful Works*

**296** *Etymologicum Genuinum*

. . . but Herodian derives προΐκτης from ἴσσω,[1] as in Archilochus:

> I stretch forth my hand and beg

[1] For the etymology cited previously, see on fr. 200.

**297** Orion, *Etymologicum*

βάβαξ: talker, babbler . . . Archilochus:

> the loathsome babbler roamed about the house

**298** Aelius Aristides, *Orations*

The gods, I think, do not know the future in the same way as men claim to. For the gods know what they are going to do and events lie before them as though before their eyes. Because of this

# IAMBIC POETRY

Ζεὺς ἐν θεοῖσι μάντις ἀψευδέστατος,

καὶ ὅτι γε δι᾽ αὐτὸ τοῦτο, ὁ αὐτὸς οὗτος ποιητὴς
μαρτυρεῖ· τὸ γὰρ δεύτερόν ἐστιν αὐτῷ

καὶ τέλος αὐτὸς ἔχει.

**302** Ael. *V.H.* 4.14

πολλάκις τὰ κατ᾽ ὀβολὸν μετὰ πολλῶν πόνων συν-
αχθέντα χρήματα κατὰ τὸν Ἀρχίλοχον εἰς πόρνης
γυναικὸς ἔντερον καταίρουσιν. ὥσπερ γὰρ ἐχῖνον λα-
βεῖν μὲν ῥᾴδιον, συνέχειν δὲ χαλεπόν, οὕτω καὶ τὰ
χρήματα.

cf. Nicet. Chon. *Hist*. (p. 230 van Dieten)

καταρρέει pro καταίρουσιν Jacobs (μεταρρνῖσκεσθαι
Nicetas)    ἔχιν Hercher (prob. West)

**303** Eustrat. in Arist. *Eth. Nic.* 6.7 (*Comm. in Arist.
Graeca* xx.320.36)

παράγει δ᾽ εἰς μαρτυρίαν τοῦ εἶναι τὸν ὅλως σοφὸν
ἕτερον παρὰ τόν τινα σοφὸν καί τινα ποίησιν Μαρ-
γίτην ὀνομαζομένην Ὁμήρου. μνημονεύει δ᾽ αὐτῆς οὐ
μόνον αὐτὸς Ἀριστοτέλης ἐν τῷ πρώτῳ περὶ ποιητικῆς
(1448b30), ἀλλὰ καὶ Ἀρχίλοχος καὶ Κρατῖνος (fr. 368

Zeus is the most truthful prophet among the gods,

and this same poet testifies to this as follows, since his second verse is

and he himself holds the fulfilment[1]

---

[1] Blass assigned these verses to Archilochus. A scholiast on the passage named Euripides as author, but the meter, which is the same as that of frr. 182-87, is unlikely to have been used by Euripides. Attribution to Euripides, however, is defended by V. Casadio, *MCr* 25-27 (1990-93) 31-35.

## 302  Aelian, *Historical Miscellanies*

Often money amassed with much toil obol by obol goes down into the intestines of a prostitute, according to Archilochus. For money is like a hedgehog, easy to catch but difficult to hold on to.[1]

---

[1] See West, *Studies* 138, on Archilochian authorship.

## 303  Eustratius on Aristotle, *Nicomachean Ethics*

And he brings in a poem of Homer entitled *Margites* as evidence of another who is wholly wise in comparison with one who is wise in such and such. The poem is mentioned not only by Aristotle himself in the first part of his *Poetics*, but also by Archilochus[1] and Cratinus and Callimachus in

## IAMBIC POETRY

K.-A.) καὶ Καλλίμαχος ἐν τοῖς ἐπιγράμμασιν (fr. 397 Pf.), καὶ μαρτυροῦσιν εἶναι Ὁμήρου τὸ ποίημα.

**304** Hesych.

πυρριχίζειν· τὴν ἐνόπλιον ὄρχησιν καὶ σύντονον πυρρίχην ἔλεγον. οἱ μὲν ἀπὸ Πυρρίχου τοῦ Κρητός ... οἱ δὲ ἀπὸ Πύρρου τοῦ Ἀχιλλέως· ἐφησθέντα γὰρ τῷ Εὐρυπύλου φόνῳ ὀρχήσασθαί φησιν Ἀρχίλοχος.

**305** Malalas, *chron.* 4 (p. 68.1 Dindorf)

τῶν δὲ Ἀργείων μετὰ τὸν Ἴναχον ἐβασίλευσεν ὁ Φορωνεὺς καὶ ἄλλοι πολλοὶ ἕως τῆς βασιλείας Λυγκέως τοῦ ἀγαγομένου τὴν Ὑπερμνήστραν γυναῖκα τῶν Δαναοῦ θυγατέρων. ὅστις Λυγκεὺς πολεμήσας τῷ Δαναῷ βασιλεῖ τοῦτον ἐφόνευσε καὶ ἔλαβε τὴν βασιλείαν καὶ τὴν θυγατέρα αὐτοῦ, καθὼς Ἀρχίλοχος ὁ σοφώτατος συνεγράψατο.

**307** Phot. *lex.*

εὕδοντι δ' αἱρεῖ κύρτος.

παροιμία. καθεύδουσι γὰρ καθέντες τοὺς κύρτους. παρὰ τοῦτο ἐποίησε Κρατῖνος Ἀρχιλόχοις (fr. 3 K.-A.) "εὕδοντι δ' αἱρεῖ πρωκτός."

276

his epigrams, and they testify that the poem is Homer's.

[1] Cf. fr. 201.

**304** Hesychius, *Lexicon*

πυρριχίζειν: they gave the name πυρρίχη to a vigorous, martial dance. Some derive the word from Pyrrhicus the Cretan . . . others from Pyrrhus the son of Achilles. Archilochus[1] says that Pyrrhus danced for joy at the slaying of Eurypylus.

[1] An error for Aristophanes? So Casadio pp. 37-38.

**305** Malalas, *Chronography*

After Inachus Phoroneus and many others ruled over the Argives until the kingship of Lynceus who married Hypermnestra, one of the daughters of Danaus. This Lynceus made war on king Danaus, slew him, and took the kingship and his daughter, according to the account of the wise Archilochus.[1]

[1] An error for Aeschylus? So Casadio pp. 39-42.

**307** Photius, *Lexicon*

The fish trap does the catching while one sleeps.

A Proverb. For after letting down the fish traps they sleep. As a parody of this Cratinus in *Archilochi* composed "his anus does the catching while he sleeps."[1]

[1] The proverb may have occurred in Archilochus, given the title of Cratinus' play.

**308** Hesych.

ἐπ' Αἰννύρων ὁδῶν· Αἴννυρα χωρίον τῆς ‹Θάσου κατ-
εναντίον τῆς Σαμο›θράκης, ἀπὸ Αἰννύρου ὀνομασθέν.

‹Θάσου—Σαμο› inseruit West ex Herodoto 6.47

**309** Hesych.

μύσχης· †εὖρος, ὡς Ἀρχίλοχος.
μύσχον· τὸ ἀνδρεῖον καὶ γυναικεῖον μόριον.

**310** Pollux 6.100

ὁλκαίου δὲ (μέμνηται) Ἀντίοχος· ἔστι δ' ὁλκαῖον ᾧ τὰ
ἐκπώματα ἐναπονίπτουσιν.

Ἀρχίλοχος pro Ἀντίοχος Ruhnken

**311** Hesych.

πάγη δέ τις· παγὶς δέ τις

**312** Hesych.

ψαυστά· †ψαυστά. Ἀρχίας.

## ARCHILOCHUS

**308**  Hesychius, *Lexicon*

On the roads of Aennyra.[1] Aennyra is a place in (Thasos opposite Samo)thrace, named after Aennyrus.

[1] Or "Roads in the direction of Aennyra."

**309**  Hesychius, *Lexicon*

The first gloss, a corrupt definition of μύσχης, gives Amphilochus, emended by Alberti to Archilochus, as a source. The second gloss defines μύσχον as the male and female genitals.

**310**  Pollux, *Vocabulary*

Antiochus[1] mentions ὁλκαῖον. It is a basin in which cups are washed.

[1] Meineke proposed Ἀντίδοτος for Ἀντίοχος and the fragment is printed by Kassel-Austin as Antidotus fr. 5 (dubium). An Antiochus is cited as the author of *Anth. Pal.* 11.412 and 422.

**311**  Hesychius, *Lexicon*

πάγη is defined as παγίς, both words meaning 'trap' or 'snare.' Bergk assigned the gloss to Archilochus, comparing frr. 185-87.

**312**  Hesychius, *Lexicon*

A corrupt gloss on ψαυστά, emended by Musurus to ψαιστά "ground up." The source, Archias, was emended to Archilochus by Bergk.[1]

[1] There were several poets named Archias: see Gow-Page, *GP* ii.432-35.

**313**

πύγαργος

Tzetz. in Lyc. 91 (ii.50.23 Scheer)

**314-321** Testimonia de metris (v. testt. 53-60)

*322-333. Spuria*

**322** Hephaest. *Ench.* 15.16 (pp. 52 sq. Consbruch)

ἄλλο ἀσυνάρτητον κατὰ τὴν πρώτην ἀντιπάθειαν, ἐξ
ἰαμβικοῦ διμέτρου ἀκαταλήκτου καὶ τροχαϊκοῦ ἐφθη-
μιμεροῦς τοῦ καλουμένου Εὐριπιδείου, οἷόν ἐστι τὸ ἐν
τοῖς ἀναφερομένοις εἰς Ἀρχίλοχον Ἰοβάκχοις

Δήμητρος ἁγνῆς καὶ Κόρης
τὴν πανήγυριν σέβων.

**323** Steph. Byz. p. 166.11 Meineke

Βέχειρ· ἔθνος Σκυθικόν, ὡς Σάπειρ . . . Λίγειρ ποτα-
μὸς περὶ Γαλατίαν,

χρυσοέθειρ

παρ' Ἀρχιλόχῳ ἐν Ἰοβάκχοις, ὅπερ ἀποκέκοπται τοῦ
χρυσοέθειρος.

**313**

white-rumped

See Tzetzes on fr. 178.

*322-333. Spurious Works*

*See introduction to "Doubtful Works" (frr. 296-321).*

**322** Hephaestion, *Handbook of Meters*

Another unconnected meter involving the first opposition is constructed from an iambic dimeter acatalectic (× – ∪ – × – ∪ –) and a trochaic hephthemimer (– ∪ – ∪ – ∪ –), called Euripidean, as in the *Iobacchi* ascribed to Archilochus

celebrating the festival of pure Demeter and Core

**323** Stephanus of Byzantium, *Lexicon of Place Names*

Becheir, a Scythian tribe, like Sapeir . . . Ligeir, a river in Galatia, χρυσοέθειρ

golden-haired

a shortened form of χρυσοέθειρος, as in the *Iobacchi* of Archilochus.

τήνελλα καλλίνικε
Χαῖρε ἄναξ Ἡράκλεις,
αὐτός τε καἰόλαος, αἰχμητὰ δύω.

Pind. Ol. 9.1-4

τὸ μὲν Ἀρχιλόχου μέλος / φωνᾶεν Ὀλυμπίᾳ, καλλί-
νικος ὁ τριπλόος κεχλαδὼς, / ἄρκεσε Κρόνιον παρ'
ὄχθον ἀγεμονεῦσαι / κωμάζοντι φίλοις Ἐφαρμόστῳ
σὺν ἑταίροις.

Schol. ad loc. (i.268.14-23 Dr.)

Ἐρατοσθένης δέ (FGrHist 241 F 44) φησι μὴ ἐπινίκιον
εἶναι τὸ Ἀρχιλόχου μέλος ἀλλ' ὕμνον εἰς Ἡρακλέα·
"τριπλόον" δὲ (οὐ διὰ τὸ ἐκ τριῶν στροφῶν συγκεῖσ-
θαι ἀλλὰ) διὰ τὸ τρὶς ἐφυμνιάζεσθαι τὸ "καλλίνικε."
περὶ δὲ τοῦ "τήνελλα" Ἐρατοσθένης φησὶν ὅτι ὅτε ὁ
αὐλητὴς ἢ ὁ κιθαριστὴς μὴ παρῆν, ὁ ἔξαρχος αὐτὸ
μεταλαβὼν ἔλεγεν ἔξω τοῦ μέλους, ὁ δὲ τῶν κωμα-
στῶν χορὸς ἐπέβαλλε τὸ "καλλίνικε," καὶ οὕτω συνει-
ρόμενον γέγονε τὸ "τήνελλα καλλίνικε." ἡ δὲ ἀρχὴ τοῦ
μέλους ἐστίν· "ὦ καλλίνικε χαῖρε ἄναξ Ἡράκλεες."

**324**

*The text of this fragment is highly uncertain and ascription to Archilochus improbable. For discussion see West, Studies 138-39, and for variant readings see his edition. I have printed the text as in West and translated the major sources. The first two sources reflect the explanation offered by Eratosthenes, the next three that by Aristarchus, and the last seems to be independent of either critic.*

> Tenella gloriously triumphant, hail lord Heracles, both you and Iolaus, a pair of warriors.

Pindar, *Olympian* 9.1-4

The song of Archilochus that is uttered at Olympia, the triumphal song that rings out thrice sufficed to lead the way past the hill of Cronus for Epharmostus as he celebrated with his dear companions.

Scholia on the passage

Eratosthenes says that the song of Archilochus is not an epinician but a hymn to Heracles, and that the word τριπλόος does not result from the song's being composed of three strophes but from the triple refrain καλλίνικε. With regard to τήνελλα Eratosthenes says that when the piper or lyre player was not present, the choral leader took it up and uttered it outside the song and the chorus of revellers followed with καλλίνικε. In this way the combination τήνελλα καλλίνικε arose. The beginning of the song is ὦ καλλίνικε χαῖρε ἄναξ Ἡράκλεες.

# IAMBIC POETRY

Schol. ad loc. (i.267.1-12 + 268.2-5 Dr.)

ὁ Ἀρχίλοχος, πρὸ τούτων τῶν λυρικῶν γενόμενος, θελήσας ὕμνον ἀναβαλέσθαι εἰς Ἡρακλέα ἐν τῇ Ὀλυμπίᾳ, ἀπορήσας κιθαρῳδοῦ διά τινος λέξεως μιμήσασθαι τὸν ῥυθμὸν καὶ τὸν ἦχον τῆς κιθάρας ἐπεχείρησε. συντάξας οὖν τοῦτο τὸ "τήνελλα," οὕτω τὰ ἑξῆς ἀνεβάλλετο. καὶ αὐτὸς μὲν τὸν ἦχον τῆς κιθάρας ὑποκρινόμενος ἔλεγεν ἐν μέσῳ τὸ "τήνελλα," καὶ ⟨ὁ χόρος⟩ τὰ ἐπίλοιπα, οἷον "καλλίνικε χαῖρε ἄναξ Ἡράκλεις," καὶ εἴ τι ἕτερον, οἷον "αὐτός τε καὶ Ἰόλαος, αἰχμητὰ δύο." {τήνελλα} τὸ λοιπὸν οἱ ἀποροῦντες κιθαρῳδοῦ τούτῳ τῷ κόμματι ἐχρῶντο, τρὶς αὐτὸ ἐπιφωνοῦντες. κεκράτηκεν οὖν ἐπὶ πάντων νικηφόρων παρ᾽ αὐτὸν τὸν καιρὸν τῆς νίκης ἐπάδεσθαι τὸ κόμμα. . . . ἔθος δὲ ἦν κωμάζειν τὴν νίκην ἑσπέρας τοῖς νικηφόροις μετὰ αὐλητοῦ· μὴ παρόντος δὲ αὐλητοῦ εἷς τῶν ἑταίρων ἀνακρουόμενος ἔλεγε "τήνελλα καλλίνικε."

Schol. ad loc. (i.269.11-12 Dr.)

"τριπλόος" δὲ ἤτοι ὁ τρὶς ἐπᾳδόμενος, ἢ τρίστροφος ὢν κατὰ Ἀρίσταρχον.

Schol. ad loc. (i.268.5-10 + 12-14 Dr.)

τὸ μὲν Ἀρχιλόχου μέλος, ὃ τοῖς νικῶσι τὰ Ὀλύμπια ἐπῄδετο, ἦν τρίστροφον, κοινῶς δυνάμενον ἁρμόζειν ἐπὶ παντὸς νικηφόρου διὰ τὸ κατὰ τῆς πράξεως αὐτῆς

284

Additional scholia

Archilochus, who was born before these lyric poets, wished to strike up a hymn to Heracles at Olympia, but lacking a lyre-player he tried to imitate the rhythm and sound of the lyre by means of a word. He therefore composed this word τήνελλα and in this way struck up what followed. And he himself in imitation of the sound of the lyre uttered the word τήνελλα in the middle of the song and the chorus sang the rest, such as καλλίνικε χαῖρε ἄναξ Ἡράκλεες, and whatever else there was such as αὐτός τε καὶ Ἰόλαος, αἰχμητὰ δύο. Afterwards those who lacked a lyre-player made use of this coinage, speaking it three times. Consequently it has been the practice for all winners to sing out the coinage right at the moment of victory . . . It was customary for winners to celebrate the victory in the evening with a piper. But if a piper was not present, one of the companions struck up the words τήνελλα καλλίνικε.

Additional scholia

τριπλόος refers either to threefold singing or according to Aristarchus to three strophes.

Additional scholia

The song of Archilochus, which was sung at Olympia for the winners, consisted of three strophes and was able to suit every winner alike since it did not mention the event

ψιλὸν ἔχειν τὸν λόγον, μήτε δὲ ὄνομα μήτε ἰδίωμα
ἀγωνίσματος. ἐφυμνίῳ δὲ ἐχρῶντο τούτῳ, "τήνελλα
καλλίνικε." . . . τὸ δὲ "τριπλόος" ὅτι τρὶς ἐπεκελάδουν
τὸ "καλλίνικε·" οὐ καθόλου δὲ τρίς, ἀλλ᾽ ὅτι τριπλῆν
ἔχει τὴν στροφὴν καὶ πάλιν ἀναλαμβάνεται.

Schol. Pind. *Nem.* 3.1 (iii.41.16-20 Dr.)

ὁ μὲν οὖν Ἀρίσταρχός φησιν, ἤτοι τὸν χορὸν ὑπὸ τὸν
καιρὸν τῆς νίκης αὐτοσχέδιόν τινα ἐπίνικον ᾆσαι, ἢ
τὸν Ἀρχιλόχου καλλίνικον, οὗ καὶ τὸν Πίνδαρον μνη-
μονεύειν διὰ τούτων· "τὸ μὲν Ἀρχιλόχου μέλος φω-
νᾶεν" καὶ τὰ ἑξῆς.

Schol. Ar. *Aves* 1764 (p. 241 Holwerda), "τήνελλα"

τὸ "τήνελλα" μίμησίς ἐστι φωνῆς κρούματος αὐλοῦ
ποιᾶς, ἀπὸ τοῦ ἐφυμνίου ὃ εἶπεν Ἀρχίλοχος εἰς τὸν
Ἡρακλέα μετὰ τὸν μέγιστον τῶν ἄθλων αὐτοῦ (μετὰ
τὸν ἆθλον αὐτοῦ V, μεγιστῶν ἄθλων αὐτοῦ R: correxit
West)· "τήνελλα—δύω." δοκεῖ δὲ πρῶτος Ἀρχίλοχος
νικήσας ἐν Πάρῳ τὸν Δήμητρος ὕμνον ἑαυτῷ τοῦτο
ἐπιπεφωνηκέναι.

**325** *Anth. Pal.* 7.441 (538-39 Page, *FGE*)

Ἀρχιλόχου·

  ὑψηλοὺς Μεγάτιμον Ἀριστοφόωντά τε Νάξου
    κίονας, ὦ μεγάλη γαῖ᾽, ὑπένερθεν ἔχεις.

or the name of the winner or the nature of the contest. And they used this refrain τήνελλα καλλίνικε . . . The word τριπλόος occurs because they sing out καλλίνικε three times, not three times one after the other, but it's the strophe that is threefold and the refrain is picked up again (in each strophe).

Scholia on Pindar, *Nemean* 3.1

Aristarchus says that either the chorus sang an improvised epinician at the moment of victory or the triumphal song (καλλίνικον) of Archilochus and that Pindar alludes to the latter with these words τὸ μὲν Ἀρχιλόχου μέλος φωνᾶεν etc.

Scholia on Aristophanes, *Birds*

The word τήνελλα is an imitation of a certain musical sound of the pipe, derived from the refrain which Archilochus uttered in honour of Heracles after the greatest of his exploits: τήνελλα—δύω. It seems that Archilochus was the first to apply this refrain to himself after his victory in the contest for the hymn to Demeter in Paros.

**325** *Palatine Anthology*

From Archilochus:

> Great earth, you hold beneath you Megatimus and
> Aristophon, lofty pillars of Naxos.

**326** *Anth. Pal.* 6.133 (536-37 Page, *FGE*)

Ἀρχιλόχου·

Ἀλκιβίη πλοκάμων ἱερὴν ἀνέθηκε καλύπτρην
Ἥρῃ, κουριδίων εὖτ' ἐκύρησε γάμων.

**327** Cod. Vat. Barb. gr. 69 f. 104r (G. Tarditi, *RCCM* 3 [1961] 311-16)

Ἀρχιλόχου·

σίδηρός ἐστι μοῦνος ὃν στέργει Κάπυς,
τὰ δ' ἄλλα λῆρος ἦν ἄρ' αὐτῷ πλὴν πέους
ὀρθοστάδην δύνοντος ἐς γλουτῶν μυχούς·
καὶ μέχρι τοῦδ' ἐραστὴν ἀσμένως ὁρᾷ,
5      ἕως ὑπ' αὐτοῦ τέρπεται κεντούμενος.
ἐπὰν δὲ λήξῃ τοῦτο, τὸν πάρος φίλον
ἀφεὶς ὀχευτὰς εὗρε νευρωδεστέρους.
ὄλοιτο τοίνυν κἀξόλοιτο, Ζεῦ, γένος
ἄπιστον ἄστοργόν τε τῶν κινουμένων.

**328** Ibidem

Ἀρχιλόχου·

ἴσος κιναίδου καὶ κακῆς πόρνης ὁ νοῦς·
χαίρουσιν ἄμφω λαμβάνοντες κέρματα
κινούμενοί τε καὶ διατρυπώμενοι
βινούμενοί τε καὶ διεσπεκλωμένοι
5      γομφούμενοί τε καὶ διασφηνώμενοι

**326** *Palatine Anthology*

From Archilochus:

> Alcibia dedicated to Hera the sacred veil of her
> tresses, when she met with a lawful marriage.

**327** Vatican manuscript

From Archilochus:

> It is only the sword[1] that Capys loves. After all, he
> considers everything else trifling except for an up-
> right cock plunging into the recesses of his but-
> tocks. And he looks fondly on a lover only as long
> as he finds pleasure in being stabbed by him. But
> whenever the pleasure ceases, he discards his for-
> mer friend and finds better-hung mounters. And so,
> Zeus, may the treacherous and loveless race of pa-
> thics be destroyed, utterly destroyed.

[1] Here a metaphor for the penis.

**328** Same manuscript

From Archilochus:

> The mind of a pathic and a foul whore is the same.
> Both delight in taking cash, in being screwed and
> bored through, fucked and penetrated,[1] doweled

χορδούμενοί τε καὶ κατασποδούμενοι.
ἀμφοῖν δ' ὀχευτὴς οὐκ ἀπέχρησέν ποθ' εἷς,
ἀλλ' αἰὲν ἄλλο κἄλλο λασταύρων ὅλον
†εἰδήνον† ἐκφοροῦντες ἥδονται πέος,
10  πειρώμενοί τε μειζόνων καὶ πασσόνων
νεύρων κυβιστώντων τε διφώντων θ' ὁμοῦ
ἅπαντα τἄνδον σύν τε δῃούντων βαθὺ
δεινοῦ βερέθρου χάσμα, καὶ διαμπερὲς
μέσου προκοπτόντων παράχρις ὀμφαλοῦ.
15  τοιγὰρ καπρῶσα μαχλὰς ἄρδην ἐρρέτω
πασχητιώντων εὐρυπρώκτων σὺν γένει·
ἡμῖν δὲ Μουσῶν καὶ βίου σαόφρονος
μέλοι †φρέαρ τε†, τοῦτο γινώσκουσ', ὅτι
ἥδ' ἐστὶ τέρψις, ἥδ' ἀκίβδηλος χαρά,
20  ἥδ' ἡδονὴ πέφυκε, μὴ συνειδέναι
αἰσχρᾷ ποθ' ἡδυνθεῖσιν αὐτοῖς ἡδονῇ.

8 λαυσταύρων cod., corr. Garzya      9 ἐσδῦνον Garzya

**329** *Et. Gen.* a 149 (cod. B), *Mag.* a 394 L.-L. =
Herodian. (ii.523.8 Lentz)

ἀθῷος· . . . ἔχει δὲ τὸ ι ἐκ παραδόσεως, ἐπειδὴ εὕρηται
θωϊή, ὡς παρ' Ἀρχιλόχῳ·

ὡς δ' ἄν σε θωϊὴ λάβοι.

ὡς *Et. Gen.* et *Mag.*, ὣς Norsa et Vitelli

and wedged apart, stuffed[1] and pounded. For both
of them one mounter is never enough, but they al-
ways derive pleasure from gulping down all the way
one plunging(?)[2] cock after another of their fuck-
ers,[3] from trying for bigger and thicker rods which
plunge about, seek out all their insides, rend the
gaping depths of the dread pit, and advance right
to the middle of the navel. Therefore to hell with the
randy[4] slut together with the wide-assed race of pa-
thics. May our concern be for the Muses and a
chaste life . . .[5] in the knowledge that this is delight,
this is genuine joy, this is pleasure, never to be
acquainted with those who indulge in shameful
pleasure.

[1] The precise meaning of both verbs is uncertain.    [2] A
translation of Garzya's emendation.    [3] Elsewhere of pathics,
but here the word must have an active force.    [4] Literally,
"boar-seeking."    [5] The obelized words ("and a well") seem
to be corrupt, since neither sense nor grammar is suitable.

**329** *Etymologicum Genuinum* and *Magnum*

ἀθῷος: . . . it has the iota in accordance with the tradition,
since θωϊή is found, as in Archilochus:[1]

you would thus receive punishment

[1] Archilochus is an error for Callimachus: cf. Callim. fr.
195.22 Pf.

**330** *Et. Gen.* (Miller, *Mélanges* 210)

μακκοᾶν· . . . οἶον

βίος δ' ἀπράγμων τοῖς γέρουσι συμφέρει,
μάλιστα δ' εἰ τύχοιεν ἁπλοῖ τοῖς τρόποις
ἢ μακκοᾶν μέλλοιεν ἢ ληρεῖν ὅλως,
ὅπερ γερόντων ἐστίν.

**331** Ath. 13.594c-d (540-41 Page, *FGE*)

ἐφ' οἷς Ἴωνες ἀγασθέντες, ὥς φησι Μενέτωρ ἐν τῷ
περὶ ἀναθημάτων (*FHG* iv.452), Πασιφίλαν ἐκάλεσαν
τὴν Πλαγγόνα. μαρτυρεῖ δὲ καὶ †Ἀρχίλοχος† περὶ
αὐτῆς ἐν τούτοις·

συκῆ πετραίη πολλὰς βόσκουσα κορώνας,
εὐήθης ξείνων δέκτρια Πασιφίλη.

**332** Hesych.

ἄκομψον· ἀπάνουργον, ἁπλοῦν. Ἀρχίλοχος. οὐκ εὖ
διακείμενον.

⟨Κρατῖνος⟩ Ἀρχιλόχοις Schmitt

**333** Syrianus in Hermog., i.47.21 Rabe (*Rhet. Gr.* vii.
984.11 Walz)

καὶ μέλη δέ τινα ἐκάλουν ἰθυφαλλικά, εὐφημίας
περιέχοντα τοῦ θεοῦ (Διονύσου), οἶα καὶ Ἀρχίλοχος
γέγραφεν.

## 330 *Etymologicum Genuinum*[1]

An idle life suits the elderly, and especially if they happen to be simple in their ways or are likely to be stupid or to speak utter nonsense, as is typical of the elderly.

[1] The source explains μακκοῶ ('be stupid') as derived from an unattested ἀκκοῶ, related to ἀκκίζομαι ('feign ignorance'), and with a pleonastic μ. The Byzantine historian Cedrenus (ii.612.5 Bekker) cites Archilochus for the general subject matter of these verses, but they are probably comic (fr. adesp. 174 K.-A.).

## 331 Athenaeus, *Scholars at Dinner*

From admiration of these acts the Ionians, as Menetor says in his work *On Votive Offerings*, called Plangon Pasiphila. And Archilochus bears witness to her in these verses:

Like a fig tree[1] on rocky ground that feeds many crows, good-natured Pasiphile takes on strangers.[2]

[1] An erotic metaphor, since the fig (σῦκον) can denote the female genitals (see note on fr. 250).  [2] Ascription to Archilochus is frequently rejected: see West, *Studies* 139-40, and M. S. Silk, *Eos* 73 (1985) 239-46. The couplet is probably Hellenistic.

## 332 Hesychius, *Lexicon*

ἄκομψον: naive, simple. Archilochus.[1] Not elegantly presented.

[1] Kassel and Austin print as Cratinus fr. 15. One of Cratinus' comedies was entitled *Archilochoi*.

## 333 Syrianus on Hermogenes

And they called some songs containing praise of Dionysus, ithyphallic, songs such as Archilochus composed.

# SEMONIDES

## TESTIMONIA

**1** *Suda* (iv.363.1 Adler)

Σιμωνίδης Κρινέω, Ἀμοργῖνος, ἰαμβογράφος. ἔγρα-
ψεν ἐλεγείαν ἐν βιβλίοις β΄ , ἰάμβους. γέγονε δὲ καὶ
αὐτὸς μετὰ Ϙ΄ καὶ υ΄ ἔτη τῶν Τρωικῶν. ἔγραψεν ἰάμ-
βους πρῶτος αὐτὸς κατά τινας.

**2** *Suda* (iv. 360.7 Adler)

Σιμμίας Ῥόδιος, γραμματικός. ἔγραψε Γλώσσας,
βιβλία γ΄· ποιήματα διάφορα, βιβλία δ΄. ἦν δὲ τὸ ἐξ
ἀρχῆς Σάμιος, ἐν δὲ τῷ ἀποικισμῷ τῆς Ἀμοργοῦ
ἐστάλη καὶ αὐτὸς ἡγεμὼν ὑπὸ Σαμίων. ἔκτισε δὲ
Ἀμοργὸν εἰς τρεῖς πόλεις, Μινῴαν, Αἰγιαλόν, Ἀρκε-
σίνην. γέγονε δὲ μετὰ υϛ΄ ἔτη τῶν Τρωικῶν. καὶ

# SEMONIDES

## TESTIMONIA

**1** *Suda*

Semonides, son of Crines, from Amorgos, an iambic poet.
He wrote elegiac poetry in two books[1] and iambics. He
flourished 490 years after the Trojan War.[2] According to
some he was the first writer of iambics.

[1] See n. 4 on test. 2.    [2] I.e., 693 B.C., if Eratosthenes'
dating of the war is being followed. Perhaps here, in contrast
to the *Suda*'s common practice, γέγονε means 'was born' rather
than 'flourished,' since this would make the date agree with those
sources which assign the poet's *floruit* to the 660s (see test. 3).

**2** *Suda*

Simmias of Rhodes, a grammarian. He wrote *Glosses* in
three books and a variety of poems in four books.[1] In origin
he was from Samos, but in the colonization of Amorgos he
was sent out as leader by the Samians. In Amorgos he
founded three cities, Minoa,[2] Aegialos and Arcesine. He
flourished (was born?) 406 years after the Trojan War.[3]

ἔγραψε κατά τινας πρῶτος ἰάμβους, καὶ ἄλλα διά-
φορα, Ἀρχαιολογίαν τε τῶν Σαμίων.

**3** Cyrill. *contra Iulian*. 1.14 (p. 132 Burguière & Évieux)

εἰκοστῇ ἐννάτῃ Ὀλυμπιάδι Ἱππώνακτα καὶ Σιμωνίδην
φασὶ γενέσθαι καὶ τὸν μουσικὸν Ἀριστόξενον.

**4** Ath. 14.620c

Λυσανίας δ᾽ ἐν τῷ πρώτῳ Περὶ ἰαμβοποιῶν Μνασίωνα
τὸν ῥαψῳδὸν λέγει ἐν ταῖς δείξεσι τῶν Σιμωνίδου
τινὰς ἰάμβων ὑποκρίνεσθαι.

**5** Choerob. ap. *Et. Mag.* 713.17

Σιμωνίδης· ἐπὶ τοῦ ἰαμβοποιοῦ διὰ τοῦ η γράφεται

According to some he was the first writer of iambics, and he wrote various other kinds of poetry, including a *History of Samos*.[4]

[1] It is clear that what follows pertains to Semonides and has been erroneously included under Simmias.      [2] Stephanus of Byzantium s.v. Ἀμοργός states that Semonides came from Minoa, perhaps suggesting a tradition which associated the poet only or primarily with this settlement. The other two cities were actually founded by Naxos (*Klio* 21 [1927] 313-14).      [3] I.e., 777 B.C., but one MS provides the same date as in the entry above (693).
[4] This may have been in elegiacs, but nothing of this or of any other elegy has survived.

## 3 Cyril, *Against Julian*

They say that Hipponax, Semonides, and the musician Aristoxenus flourished in the 29th Olympiad (664-661 B.C.).[1]

[1] Hipponax is presumably an error for Archilochus. Eusebius ap. Hieron. (p. 94b Helm) dates Semonides to 664-663 and in the Armenian version (p. 86 Schöne-Petermann) to 665-664. For other references to his date see Arch. testt. 6 and 8.

## 4 Athenaeus, *Scholars at Dinner*

In the first book of his *On the Iambic Poets* Lysanias states that the rhapsode Mnasion in his public performances declaimed some of the iambics of Semonides.

## 5 Choeroboscus in *Etymologicum Magnum*

Semonides: with reference to the iambic poet the name is

(καὶ ἴσως παρὰ τὸ σῆμα ἐστίν), ἐπὶ δὲ τοῦ λυρικοῦ διὰ τοῦ ι (καὶ ἴσως ἐπειδὴ παρὰ τὸ σιμός ἐστιν). Χοιρο-βοσκός.

# FRAGMENTA

**1** Stob. 4.34.15

Σιμωνίδου·

   ὦ παῖ, τέλος μὲν Ζεὺς ἔχει βαρύκτυπος
   πάντων ὅσ' ἐστὶ καὶ τίθησ' ὅκῃ θέλει,
   νοῦς δ' οὐκ ἐπ' ἀνθρώποισιν, ἀλλ' ἐπήμεροι
   ἃ δὴ βοτὰ ζώομεν, οὐδὲν εἰδότες
5   ὅκως ἕκαστον ἐκτελευτήσει θεός.
   ἐλπὶς δὲ πάντας κἀπιπειθείη τρέφει
   ἄπρηκτον ὁρμαίνοντας· οἱ μὲν ἡμέρην
   μένουσιν ἐλθεῖν, οἱ δ' ἐτέων περιτροπάς·
   νέωτα δ' οὐδεὶς ὅστις οὐ δοκεῖ βροτῶν
10   πλούτῳ τε κἀγαθοῖσιν ἵξεσθαι φίλος.
   φθάνει δὲ τὸν μὲν γῆρας ἄζηλον λαβὸν
   πρὶν τέρμ' ἵκηται, τοὺς δὲ δύστηνοι βροτῶν
   φθείρουσι νοῦσοι, τοὺς δ' Ἄρει δεδμημένους
   πέμπει μελαίνης Ἀΐδης ὑπὸ χθονός·
15   οἱ δ' ἐν θαλάσσῃ λαίλαπι κλονεόμενοι

spelled with an eta (perhaps derived from *sema*, 'sign'), but with reference to the lyric poet it is spelled with an iota (perhaps because it is derived from *simos*, 'snub-nosed'). So Choeroboscus.[1]

[1] With rare exceptions (see Pellizer-Tedeschi p. 10) our sources give Σιμ-, but to avoid confusion with Simonides of Ceos, the lyric poet, I have consistently used the spelling Sem-.

*For the name of Semonides' presumed enemy see Arch. fr. 223 with n. 2.*

# FRAGMENTS

**1** Stobaeus, *Anthology*

From Semonides:

> Boy, loud-thundering Zeus controls the outcome of everything there is and disposes it as he wishes. There is no intelligence among men, but we live like grazing animals, subject to what the day brings, with no knowledge of how the god will bring each thing to pass. Yet hope and confidence nourish all in our eagerness for the impossible. Some wait for the morrow to come, others for the revolving seasons, and there is no one who does not expect that he will arrive at the next year as the friend of wealth[1] and prosperity. But unenviable old age comes first and seizes one man before he reaches his goal, while the miserable illnesses that beset mortals destroy others, and Hades sends beneath the dark earth others laid low by the war god. Others die at sea tossed

καὶ κύμασιν πολλοῖσι πορφυρῆς ἁλὸς
θνήσκουσιν, εὖτ' ἂν μὴ δυνήσωνται ζόειν·
οἱ δ' ἀγχόνην ἅψαντο δυστήνῳ μόρῳ
καὐτάγρετοι λείπουσιν ἡλίου φάος.
20  οὕτω κακῶν ἄπ' οὐδέν, ἀλλὰ μυρίαι
βροτοῖσι κῆρες κἀνεπίφραστοι δύαι
καὶ πήματ' ἐστίν. εἰ δ' ἐμοὶ πιθοίατο,
οὐκ ἂν κακῶν ἐρῷμεν, οὐδ' ἐπ' ἄλγεσιν
κακοῖς ἔχοντες θυμὸν αἰκιζοίμεθα.

2 ὅπη(ι) codd., corr. Ahrens    3 ἐφημέριοι codd., corr.
Grotius (ἐφ-), Fick    4 δὴ βροτοὶ et ἀΐδη (ἄδη A) βοτὰ
codd., ἃ δὴ Ahrens    ζώομεν codd., ζώουσιν Ahrens, ζόουσιν
West, ζώομεν Fick (omnia metri causa)    12-13 νόσοι
φθείρουσι θνητῶν codd. SM, ν. φ. βροτῶν cod. A, corr. Ahrens
17 ζώειν codd., corr. Porson (fort. iniuria)

**2** Stob. 4.56.4

Σιμωνίδου·

τοῦ μὲν θανόντος οὐκ ἂν ἐνθυμοίμεθα,
εἴ τι φρονοῖμεν, πλεῖον ἡμέρης μιῆς.

2 ἡμέρας μιᾶς codd., corr. Welcker et Schneidewin

**3** Stob. 4.53.2

Σιμωνίδου·

πολλὸς γὰρ ἧμιν ἐστὶ τεθνάναι χρόνος,

about by a gale and the turbulent sea's many waves,
whenever they are unable to gain a livelihood (on
land), and others fasten a noose in a wretched death,
leaving the sun's light by their own choice. Thus
nothing is without misery, but countless death spir-
its and unforeseen sorrows and disasters exist for
mortals. But if they were to take my advice, we
would not long for misfortune nor would we tor-
ment ourselves by having our hearts set on bitter
pain.[2]

[1] Some personify, the god of wealth.    [2] Many argue that
the poet must have gone on to give some positive advice, an obvi-
ously possible but not necessarily correct assumption.

**2** Stobaeus, *Anthology*

From Semonides:

If we had some sense, we would not concern our-
selves with the dead for more than a single day.

**3** Stobaeus, *Anthology*

From Semonides:

For we have a long time to be dead, but we live years

ζῶμεν δ᾽ ἀριθμῷ παῦρα †κακῶς ἔτεα.

1 ἡμῖν codd., corr. West    2 ⟨καὶ⟩ κακῶς Welcker, ⟨παγ⟩κακῶς Meineke, alii alia

**4** Stob. 4.41.7

Σιμωνίδου·

πάμπαν δ᾽ ἄμωμος οὔ τις οὐδ᾽ ἀκήριος.

**5** Plut. *de prof. virt.* 14.84cd

ἄθηλος ἵππῳ πῶλος ὡς ἅμα τρεχ-

ἀλλ᾽ ὅ γε προκόπτων ἀληθῶς μᾶλλον ἔργοις καὶ πράξεσιν ἀνδρὸς ἀγαθοῦ καὶ τελείου παραβάλλων ἑαυτὸν . . . καὶ μεστὸς ὢν ὁρμῆς οὐκ ἠρεμούσης οἷός τ᾽ ἐστὶ κατὰ τὸν Σιμωνίδην "ἄθηλος—τρέχειν," τῷ ἀγαθῷ μονονουχὶ συμφῦναι γλιχόμενος.

cf. Plut. *de tuenda san.* 24.136a, *de virt. moral.* 7.446de, *an seni gerenda resp.* 12.790f, *de esu carn.* 2.2.997d, fr. 210 Sandbach ap. Stob. 4.50.19 = *Paroem. Gr.* ii.541.20 L.-S.

τρέχειν, τρέχει, τρέχῃ Plut.

**6** Clem. *Strom.* 6.13.1

Ἡσιόδου δὲ εἰπόντος (*Op.* 702 sq.) "οὐ μὲν γάρ τι γυναικὸς ἀνὴρ ληΐζετ᾽ ἄμεινον / τῆς ἀγαθῆς, τῆς δ᾽ αὖτε κακῆς οὐ ῥίγιον ἄλλο," Σιμωνίδης εἶπεν

few in number and we live them badly.[1]

[1] Some combine frr. 2 and 3.


**4** Stobaeus, *Anthology*

From Semonides:

No one is utterly free from blame or affliction.


**5** Plutarch, *Progress in Virtue*

(to) run(s)[1] like an unweaned colt beside its mother

But the one who is truly making progress, comparing himself rather with the deeds and actions of a good and perfect man . . . and being filled with an urging that does not rest, is able in the words of Semonides "to run—mother," craving virtually to unite with the good man.

[1] Since Plutarch accommodates the verb to his various contexts, we cannot tell what form Semonides used. The fragment became a proverbial recommendation to the young to follow the example of their elders.


**6** Clement of Alexandria, *Miscellanies*

Hesiod said, "for a man carries off nothing better than a good wife and in turn nothing more horrible than a bad one," and Semonides:

γυναικὸς οὐδὲν χρῆμ᾽ ἀνὴρ ληΐζεται
ἐσθλῆς ἄμεινον οὐδὲ ῥίγιον κακῆς.

Porph. ap. Euseb. *praep. ev.* 10.3.18

ἢ ὡς Ἡσιόδου "οὐ μὲν γάρ—ἄλλο," ταύτην τὴν διά-
νοιαν Σιμωνίδης ἐν τῷ †ἑνδεκάτῳ† μετήνεγκε λαβὼν
οὕτως· "γυναικὸς—κακῆς."

(Porph.) ἐν τῷ α′ Welcker, ἐν ἰά<μβοις> Schmidt

**7** Stob. 4.22.193

Σιμωνίδου·

χωρὶς γυναικὸς θεὸς ἐποίησεν νόον
τὰ πρῶτα. τὴν μὲν ἐξ ὑὸς τανύτριχος,
τῇ πάντ᾽ ἀν᾽ οἶκον βορβόρῳ πεφυρμένα
ἄκοσμα κεῖται καὶ κυλίνδεται χαμαί·
αὐτὴ δ᾽ ἄλουτος ἀπλύτοις ἐν εἵμασιν
ἐν κοπρίῃσιν ἡμένη πιαίνεται.
    τὴν δ᾽ ἐξ ἀλιτρῆς θεὸς ἔθηκ᾽ ἀλώπεκος
γυναῖκα πάντων ἴδριν· οὐδέ μιν κακῶν
λέληθεν οὐδὲν οὐδὲ τῶν ἀμεινόνων·
τὸ μὲν γὰρ αὐτῶν εἶπε πολλάκις κακόν,
τὸ δ᾽ ἐσθλόν· ὀργὴν δ᾽ ἄλλοτ᾽ ἀλλοίην ἔχει.
    τὴν δ᾽ ἐκ κυνός, λιτοργόν, αὐτομήτορα,
ἣ πάντ᾽ ἀκοῦσαι, πάντα δ᾽ εἰδέναι θέλει,
πάντη δὲ παπταίνουσα καὶ πλανωμένη
λέληκεν, ἢν καὶ μηδέν᾽ ἀνθρώπων ὁρᾷ.

A man carries off nothing better than a good wife
nor more horrible than a bad one.[1]

[1]For other sources of the fragment and for parallel passages
see fr. 1 Pellizer-Tedeschi.

## Porphyry in Eusebius, *Evangelical Preparation*

Or how, when Hesiod said "for a man—bad one,"
Semonides took up this sentiment in his . . . and altered it
as follows: "a man—bad one."

## 7 Stobaeus, *Anthology*

From Semonides:

In the beginning the god[1] made diverse the female
mind.[2] One woman he created from a long-bristled
sow. Throughout her house everything lies in disor-
der, befouled with mud, and rolls about on the floor,
and she herself unwashed, in clothes unwashed, sits
in the dung and grows fat.

Another the god made from a wicked vixen, a
woman who has expertise in everything. Nothing of
what is bad escapes her notice, nor even of what is
good, since she often calls the latter bad and the
former good. Her mood is different at different
times.

Another is from a bitch, ill-tempered, her mother
all over again. She wants to hear everything and to
know everything and peering and prowling every-
where she yaps even if she sees no one. A man can't

[1] I.e., Zeus (cf. vv. 72, 96).      [2] Some prefer, "made the
female mind different (from the male)."

παύσειε δ' ἄν μιν οὔτ' ἀπειλήσας ἀνήρ,
οὐδ' εἰ χολωθεὶς ἐξαράξειεν λίθῳ
ὀδόντας, οὐδ' ἂν μειλίχως μυθεόμενος,
οὐδ' εἰ παρὰ ξείνοισιν ἡμένη τύχῃ,
20    ἀλλ' ἐμπέδως ἄπρηκτον αὐονὴν ἔχει.
      τὴν δὲ πλάσαντες γηΐνην Ὀλύμπιοι
ἔδωκαν ἀνδρὶ πηρόν· οὔτε γὰρ κακὸν
οὔτ' ἐσθλὸν οὐδὲν οἶδε τοιαύτη γυνή·
ἔργων δὲ μοῦνον ἐσθίειν ἐπίσταται.
25    κὤταν κακὸν χειμῶνα ποιήσῃ θεός,
ῥιγῶσα δίφρον ἄσσον ἕλκεται πυρός.
      τὴν δ' ἐκ θαλάσσης, ἣ δύ' ἐν φρεσὶν νοεῖ·
τὴν μὲν γελᾷ τε καὶ γέγηθεν ἡμέρην·
ἐπαινέσει μιν ξεῖνος ἐν δόμοις ἰδών·
30    "οὐκ ἔστιν ἄλλη τῆσδε λωΐων γυνὴ
ἐν πᾶσιν ἀνθρώποισιν οὐδὲ καλλίων."
τὴν δ' οὐκ ἀνεκτὸς οὐδ' ἐν ὀφθαλμοῖς ἰδεῖν
οὔτ' ἄσσον ἐλθεῖν, ἀλλὰ μαίνεται τότε
ἄπλητον ὥσπερ ἀμφὶ τέκνοισιν κύων,
35    ἀμείλιχος δὲ πᾶσι κἀποθυμίη
ἐχθροῖσιν ἶσα καὶ φίλοισι γίνεται·
ὥσπερ θάλασσα πολλάκις μὲν ἀτρεμὴς
ἕστηκ', ἀπήμων, χάρμα ναύτῃσιν μέγα,
θέρεος ἐν ὥρῃ, πολλάκις δὲ μαίνεται
40    βαρυκτύποισι κύμασιν φορεομένη.
ταύτῃ μάλιστ' ἔοικε τοιαύτη γυνὴ
ὀργήν· φυὴν δὲ πόντος ἀλλοίην ἔχει.

stop her with threats, nor even if in anger he should knock out her teeth with a stone, nor can he by speaking to her soothingly, not even if she happens to be sitting among guests, but she constantly keeps up her yapping which nothing can be done about.

Another the Olympians fashioned from earth and gave her maimed to her man; for such a woman knows neither what is bad nor what is good. The only thing she knows how to do is to eat. And whenever the god sends harsh winter, she shivers and draws her chair nearer the fire.[3]

Another is from the sea, a woman with a twofold mind. One day she sparkles and is happy. A guest who sees her in the house will praise her: "there is no other woman better than this among all mankind nor one more beautiful." But another day she is unbearable even to look at or come close to; then she rages, unapproachable as a bitch round her pups, implacable and at odds with everyone, friends and enemies alike. Just as the sea often stands without a ripple, harmless, a great joy to sailors, in the season of summer, but often rages, tossed about by the loud-crashing waves, such a woman seems very much like this in temperament. The sea has a variable nature.[4]

---

[3] If Schneidewin's emendation is accepted, the earth-woman is even more inert: "not even if the god sends a harsh winter does she feel the cold and draw her chair nearer the fire."  [4] The line has been variously emended and is excised by some. See H. Lloyd-Jones, *Females of the Species* (London 1975) 72-73 and Pellizer-Tedeschi 129-30.

τὴν δ' ἔκ †τε σποδιῆς† καὶ παλιντριβέος ὄνου,
ἣ σύν τ' ἀνάγκῃ σύν τ' ἐνιπῇσιν μόγις
45  ἔστερξεν ὧν ἅπαντα κἀπονήσατο
ἀρεστά· τόφρα δ' ἐσθίει μὲν ἐν μυχῷ
προνὺξ προῆμαρ, ἐσθίει δ' ἐπ' ἐσχάρῃ.
ὁμῶς δὲ καὶ πρὸς ἔργον ἀφροδίσιον
ἐλθόντ' ἑταῖρον ὁντινῶν ἐδέξατο.
50  τὴν δ' ἐκ γαλῆς, δύστηνον οἰζυρὸν γένος·
κείνῃ γὰρ οὔ τι καλὸν οὐδ' ἐπίμερον
πρόσεστιν οὐδὲ τερπνὸν οὐδ' ἐράσμιον.
εὐνῆς δ' ἀληνής ἐστιν ἀφροδισίης,
τὸν δ' ἄνδρα τὸν παρεόντα ναυσίῃ διδοῖ.
55  κλέπτουσα δ' ἔρδει πολλὰ γείτονας κακά,
ἄθυστα δ' ἱρὰ πολλάκις κατεσθίει.
τὴν δ' ἵππος ἁβρὴ χαιτέεσσ' ἐγείνατο,
ἣ δούλι' ἔργα καὶ δύην περιτρέπει,
κοὔτ' ἂν μύλης ψαύσειεν, οὔτε κόσκινον
60  ἄρειεν, οὔτε κόπρον ἐξ οἴκου βάλοι,
οὔτε πρὸς ἱπνὸν ἀσβόλην ἀλεομένη
ἵζοιτ'. ἀνάγκῃ δ' ἄνδρα ποιεῖται φίλον·
λοῦται δὲ πάσης ἡμέρης ἄπο ῥύπον
δίς, ἄλλοτε τρίς, καὶ μύροις ἀλείφεται,
65  αἰεὶ δὲ χαίτην ἐκτενισμένην φορεῖ
βαθεῖαν, ἀνθέμοισιν ἐσκιασμένην.
καλὸν μὲν ὦν θέημα τοιαύτη γυνὴ
ἄλλοισι, τῷ δ' ἔχοντι γίνεται κακόν,
ἢν μή τις ἢ τύραννος ἢ σκηπτοῦχος ᾖ,
70  ὅστις τοιούτοις θυμὸν ἀγλαΐζεται.

Another is from an ash-coloured (?) ass that is the object of repeated blows. When forced and berated she with difficulty consents to everything and does acceptable work. But meanwhile all day and all night she eats in an inner room and eats at the hearth. And similarly with regard to lovemaking she accepts any companion who comes along.[5]

Another is from the weasel, a wretched and sorry creature, since there is nothing associated with her that is fair, desirable, pleasing or lovable. She is mad for the bed of love, but she turns the stomach of the man who is at her side. She does much harm to her neighbours by her thieving and she often eats up sacrifices left unburned.

Another a dainty, long-maned mare engendered. She pushes servile tasks and trouble onto others, and she wouldn't touch a millstone, lift a sieve, throw dung out of the house, or sit by the oven since she avoids soot. And she forces a man to be her lover.[6] Twice every day, sometimes three times, she washes the dirt off her and anoints herself with scents, and she always wears her hair combed out and long, shaded with flowers. Such a woman is a beautiful sight to others, but for the man who has her as wife she is a plague, unless he is some tyrant or sceptre bearer whose heart delights in such things.

[5] The meaning seems to be that her appetite for sex is as strong as her appetite for food and is equally undiscriminating.

[6] I.e., a man cannot resist her beauty, however much he may disapprove of her behaviour. According to some the sentence is ironical: "and she makes a man the friend of Necessity."

τὴν δ' ἐκ πιθήκου· τοῦτο δὴ διακριδὸν
Ζεὺς ἀνδράσιν μέγιστον ὤπασεν κακόν.
αἴσχιστα μὲν πρόσωπα· τοιαύτη γυνὴ
εἶσιν δι' ἄστεος πᾶσιν ἀνθρώποις γέλως·
75 ἐπ' αὐχένα βραχεῖα· κινεῖται μόγις·
ἄπυγος, αὐτόκωλος. ἆ τάλας ἀνὴρ
ὅστις κακὸν τοιοῦτον ἀγκαλίζεται.
δήνεα δὲ πάντα καὶ τρόπους ἐπίσταται
ὥσπερ πίθηκος· οὐδέ οἱ γέλως μέλει·
80 οὐδ' ἄν τιν' εὖ ἔρξειεν, ἀλλὰ τοῦτ' ὁρᾷ
καὶ τοῦτο πᾶσαν ἡμέρην βουλεύεται,
ὅκως τι κῶς μέγιστον ἔρξειεν κακόν.

τὴν δ' ἐκ μελίσσης· τήν τις εὐτυχεῖ λαβών·
κείνῃ γὰρ οἴῃ μῶμος οὐ προσιζάνει,
85 θάλλει δ' ὑπ' αὐτῆς κἀπαέξεται βίος,
φίλη δὲ σὺν φιλέοντι γηράσκει πόσει
τεκοῦσα καλὸν κὠνομάκλυτον γένος.
κἀριπρεπὴς μὲν ἐν γυναιξὶ γίνεται
πάσῃσι, θείη δ' ἀμφιδέδρομεν χάρις.
90 οὐδ' ἐν γυναιξὶν ἥδεται καθημένη
ὅκου λέγουσιν ἀφροδισίους λόγους.
τοίας γυναῖκας ἀνδράσιν χαρίζεται
Ζεὺς τὰς ἀρίστας καὶ πολυφραδεστάτας·
τὰ δ' ἄλλα φῦλα ταῦτα μηχανῇ Διὸς
95 ἔστιν τε πάντα καὶ παρ' ἀνδράσιν μένει.
Ζεὺς γὰρ μέγιστον τοῦτ' ἐποίησεν κακόν,
γυναῖκας· ἤν τι καὶ δοκέωσιν ὠφελεῖν
ἔχοντι, τῷ μάλιστα γίνεται κακόν·

310

Another is from a monkey. This is absolutely the worst plague that Zeus has given to men. Her face is extremely ugly; such a woman is an object of laughter to everyone as she goes through the town. She is short of neck, moves awkwardly, has no rump, and is all legs. Ah, pity the man who embraces such a plague. She knows every trick and scheme, just like a monkey. Being laughed at doesn't bother her and she wouldn't do anyone a good turn, but she has her eyes on and plots every day how she can do the greatest harm possible.

Another is from the bee. The one who gets her is lucky, since on her alone blame does not settle. Under her management his livelihood flourishes and increases, and she grows old in love with a loving husband, the mother of a handsome and distinguished family. She stands out among all women and a divine grace surrounds her. She takes no pleasure in sitting among women in places where they talk about sex. Such women are the best and the most sensible whom Zeus bestows as a favour on men.

But by the contrivance of Zeus all these other species exist and remain among men. For the greatest plague that Zeus has created is this—women; if they seem to be of some benefit to the one who has them, to him especially do they turn out to be a

οὐ γάρ κοτ' εὔφρων ἡμέρην διέρχεται
100 ἄπασαν, ὅστις σὺν γυναικὶ †πέλεται,
οὐδ' αἶψα Λιμὸν οἰκίης ἀπώσεται,
ἐχθρὸν συνοικητῆρα, δυσμενέα θεῶν.
ἀνὴρ δ' ὅταν μάλιστα θυμηδεῖν δοκῇ
κατ' οἶκον, ἢ θεοῦ μοῖραν ἢ ἀνθρώπου χάριν,
105 εὑροῦσα μῶμον ἐς μάχην κορύσσεται.
ὅκου γυνὴ γάρ ἐστιν οὐδ' ἐς οἰκίην
ξεῖνον μολόντα προφρόνως δεκοίατο.
ἥτις δέ τοι μάλιστα σωφρονεῖν δοκεῖ,
αὕτη μέγιστα τυγχάνει λωβωμένη·
110 κεχηνότος γὰρ ἀνδρός, οἱ δὲ γείτονες
χαίρουσ' ὁρῶντες καὶ τόν, ὡς ἁμαρτάνει.
τὴν ἣν δ' ἕκαστος αἰνέσει μεμνημένος
γυναῖκα, τὴν δὲ τουτέρου μωμήσεται·
ἴσην δ' ἔχοντες μοῖραν οὐ γινώσκομεν.
115 Ζεὺς γὰρ μέγιστον τοῦτ' ἐποίησεν κακόν,
καὶ δεσμὸν ἀμφέθηκεν ἄρρηκτον πέδην,
ἐξ οὗ τε τοὺς μὲν Ἀΐδης ἐδέξατο
γυναικὸς εἵνεκ' ἀμφιδηριωμένους.

cf. Ath. 5.179d (v. 56), Ael. H.A. 16.24 (vv. 57-70), Ael. H.A. 11.36 (v. 64)

5 ἄπλυτος codd., corr. Valckenaer      6 εἱμένη codd., corr. Trincavelli      18 μυθεύμενος codd., corr. Fick      19 εἱμένη codd., corr. Trincavelli      20 αὐονὴν West      25 χ' οταν cod. S, κοῦτ' ἂν codd. MA, κοὐδ' ἢν Schneidewin, κῶταν Ahrens      26 ἄσσον codd., corr. Jacobsohn      29 μὲν codd., corr. Valckenaer      30 λώϊον codd., corr. Gesner

plague. For whoever lives (?) with a woman never goes through a whole day in good spirits, nor will he quickly thrust from the house Hunger, a hostile housemate, enemy of the gods. And whenever a man seems to be especially enjoying himself in his home, either through divine dispensation or the kindness of men, she finds fault and puts on her helmet for battle. For where there is a woman, men may not readily welcome even a stranger who has come to the house.[7] I tell you, the woman who seems most respectable, she's the very one who commits the greatest outrage. For while her husband stands open-mouthed,[8] the neighbours delight in seeing how he too is mistaken. Each man will be mindful to praise his own wife, but will find fault with another's. We do not realize that we have an equal lot. For this is the greatest plague that Zeus has created, and he has placed round us in bondage fetters unbreakable, ever since Hades received those who fought on account of a woman.[9]

[7] I.e., let alone a neighbour.    [8] An open mouth can denote lack of attention (through carelessness he does not notice how she behaves) or gullibility (he is so naïve that her behaviour leaves him incredulous) or a strong desire (he is so infatuated with her that he is blind to her real nature).

[9] Generally assumed to be Helen. Many treat the poem as incomplete, assuming that at least one τοὺς δέ followed. This is possible, but not obligatory.

40 φορευμένη codd., corr. Fick      42 [ὀργὴν] φυὴν δὲ
πόντος ‹ἄλλοτ᾽› ἀλλοίην Renehan, alii alia      43 τε τεφρῆς
Meineke, τεφρῆς τε Brunck      45 ὧν codd., corr. Gesner καὶ
πον- codd., corr. Ahrens      49 ὀντινοῦν codd., corr. Bergk
54 παρόντα codd., corr. Renner      διδεῖ et δίδει codd., corr.
Trincavelli      57 χαιτάεσσ᾽ Aelian., χαιτείης Stob. cod.
S, χαιτήεις codd. MA, corr. Meineke      61 ἀλευμένη codd.,
corr. Fick      65 ἀεὶ codd., corr. Hertel      67 οὖν codd.,
corr. Brunck      76 αὐόκωλος Haupt      82 τί χ᾽ ὡς codd.,
corr. West, τιν᾽ ὡς Meineke      86 φιλεῦντι codd., corr. Fick
87 κοὺν- codd., corr Smyth      95 μενεῖ Bergk      97 δοκῶσιν
codd., corr. Ahrens      102 θεόν Grotius      106 οἰκίαν
codd., corr. Koeler      107 μολῶντα codd., corr. Trincavelli
δεχ- codd., corr. Schneidewin      116 πέδη(ι) codd.,
(κἄρρηκτον) πέδην Crusius, πέδης Koeler (+ ἀρρήκτου Bothe)

**8**  Ath. 7.299c

Σιμωνίδης δ᾽ ἐν ἰάμβοις·

  ὥσπερ ἔγχελυς κατὰ γλοιοῦ

**9**  Pergit Ath.

καὶ τὴν αἰτιατικήν·

  ἐρωδιὸς γὰρ ἔγχελυν Μαιανδρίην
  τρίορχον εὑρὼν ἐσθίοντ᾽ ἀπείλετο.

2 ἀφείλετο cod., corr. Fick

314

SEMONIDES

**8** Athenaeus, *Scholars at Dinner*

And Semonides in his iambics:

> like an eel[1] down in the slime

[1] Athenaeus cites this passage and the next in his discussion of the declension of the word for eel. For possible explanations of the fragment see *Phoenix* 33 (1979) 22-23.

**9** Athenaeus continues

And the accusative:

> For a heron found a buzzard eating a Maeandrian eel[1] and took it away.

[1] Eels from the river Maeander in Caria were a prized delicacy.

**10** Schol. Eur. *Phoen.* 207 (i.277.17 Schwartz), "κατε-
νάσθην"

τινὲς ἀντὶ τοῦ κατανασθήσομαι· καὶ Σιμωνίδης ἰάμ-
βοις

⟨× – ᴜ –⟩ τί ταῦτα διὰ μακρῶν λόγων
ἀνέδραμον;

ἀντὶ τοῦ ἀναδραμεῖν μέλλω.

**10a** Herennius Philo, *de diversis verborum significa-
tionibus* (p. 186 Palmieri, 73 Nickau, *Ammonius*)

κομᾶν τοῦ γαυριᾶν διαφέρει. ⟨κομᾶν γὰρ⟩ ἐπί τινι
ἔλεγον οἱ ἀρχαῖοι, φησὶ Τρύφων (fr. novum), τὸ δὲ νῦν
κομᾶν κουριᾶν, ὡς Σιμωνίδης ἐν πρώτῳ ἰάμβῳ·

καὶ μήτ᾽ ἄλουτος γαυρία σύ, μήτ᾽ ὕδωρ
θαύμαζε, μηδὲ κουρία γενειάδα,
μηδὲ ῥύπῳ χιτῶνος ἔντυε χρόα.

(Herenn.) ⟨κομᾶν γὰρ⟩ suppl. Nickau, ⟨κομᾶν μὲν τὸ
γαυριᾶν⟩ Palmieri          κουριᾶν, ὡς West (κυρίως cod.),
κυρίως ⟨τὸ κουριᾶν⟩ Palmieri          (Sem.) 1 καὶ μήτ᾽ ἀλλ᾽ οὕτως
γὰρ ἂν εὖ μεθ᾽ ὕδωρ cod., corr. West          2 κούρη cod., corr.
West          3 μηδὲ ῥυποχίτων ἔσῃ ἔν τε χώρα cod., corr. West,
ῥύπο⟨υ⟩ χιτῶνα ἔσσον ἐν χροΐ Palmieri

316

**10** Scholiast on Euripides, *Phoenissae* ("I dwelled")

According to some this is equivalent to 'I shall dwell.' And Semonides says in his iambics

> Why did I recount this with a lengthy discourse?

which is equivalent to 'I am going to recount.'[1]

[1] Without a context we cannot comment on the scholiast's explanation of the aorist. The text is disputed on metrical grounds, but if printed as two verses (so Pellizer-Tedeschi following West's suggestion), the caesura is restored. The resolved iambus (-α διὰ) is not found elsewhere in Semonides, but it occurs in other early iambographers.

**10a** Herennius Philo, *On the Different Meanings of Words*

κομᾶν differs from γαυριᾶν.[1] For in ancient times, according to Tryphon,[2] ‹κομᾶν meant 'to put on airs'› over something, but now κομᾶν has the meaning of κουριᾶν 'to need a haircut,' as in the first book of Semonides' iambics:

> Don't take pride in being unwashed, don't stand in
> awe of water, don't let your beard need trimming,
> and don't deck out your body in a filthy tunic.

[1] γαυριᾶν is presumably an error for κουριᾶν. See West, *Maia* 20 (1968) 196.    [2] A grammarian of the time of Augustus.

IAMBIC POETRY

**11** Ath. 2.57d = Eust. in Hom. *Od.* 11.299 (1686.51)

"ὤεα" δὲ ἔφη Ἐπίχαρμος (fr. 152 Kaibel), "ὤεα χανὸς
κἀλεκτορίδων πετεηνῶν." Σιμωνίδης ἐν δευτέρῳ ἰάμ-
βων·

οἷόν τε χηνὸς ὤεον Μαιανδρίου.

**12** Choerob. *can.* (i.267.10 Hilgard) = Herodian.
(ii.626.30 Lentz)

ἴκτινος ἡ εὐθεῖα . . . τούτου ἡ γενικὴ ἰκτίνου, ὡς παρὰ
Σιμωνίδῃ·

σπλάγχ᾽ ἀμπέχοντες αὐτίκ᾽ ἰκτίνου δίκην.

ἀμφέποντες Bergk

**13**

⟨× –⟩ τὸ δ᾽ ἥμιν ἑρπετὸν παρέπτατο
τὸ ζῴων κάκιστον ἔκτηται βίον.


*Et. Gen.* (p. 28 Calame) = *Et. Mag.* 413.20 = Zon. (p. 967
T.; hinc Herodian. ii.516.7 Lentz)

ζῶιον· . . . γράφεται δὲ διὰ τοῦ ι, ἐπειδὴ εὕρηται κατὰ
διάστασιν, ὡς παρὰ Σιμωνίδῃ· φησὶ γὰρ "τὸ δ᾽ ἡμῖν
ἑρπετὸν παρέπτατο ζῶιον κάκιστον."

318

**11** Athenaeus, *Scholars at Dinner*

Epicharmus said ὤεα (for ᾠά), "eggs of a goose and winged hens." Cf. Semonides in the second book of his iambics:

> like the egg of a Maeandrian goose

**12** Choeroboscus, *On the Canons of Theodosius*

The nominative is ἴκτινος . . . its genitive ἰκτίνου, as in Semonides:

> straightway embracing[1] the entrails like a kite

[1] Perhaps a colourful way of describing the greedy seizure of entrails, but many adopt Bergk's emendation, "being busy with."

**13**

> and there flew to us that beetle[1] which among (all) creatures leads the worst way of life

[1] The scarab or dung beetle. Some assume a fable is being related.

*Etymologicum Genuinum*

ζῷιον: it is written with an iota, since it occurs with diaeresis, as in Semonides. For he says τὸ δ'—κάκιστον.

Schol. T Hom. *Il.* 18.407b (iv.515 Erbse), "ζωάγρια"

χαριστήρια τοῦ εἰς τὸ ζῆν ἦχθαι. μετὰ δὲ τοῦ <ι>, ἐπεὶ καὶ Σιμωνίδης φησὶ "τὸ ζώιον κάκιστον κέκτηται βίον," περὶ τοῦ κανθάρου.

1 ἡμῖν libri, corr. West     2 ζώιον Etym., ζῶον schol.
Hom., corr. Bekker     κέκτηται schol., corr. Bekker

**14** Galen. in Hippocr. *epid.* 6.2.1 (*CMG* v.10.2(2) p. 60.8)

διὸ καὶ τὴν δευτέραν συλλαβὴν τοῦ "στενυγρῶσαι" ψιλοῦντας, οὐ δασύνοντας, ἀναγνωστέον ἐστίν· οὐ γὰρ ἔγκειται τὸ ὑγρὸν ἐν τῇ λέξει, καθάπερ ἄν τις οἰηθείη μὴ γινώσκων ὑπὸ τῶν Ἰώνων τὸ στενὸν ὀνομάζεσθαι στενυγρόν· ἀλλὰ τούτο<υ> γε μαρτύριόν ἐστιν αὔταρκες τὸ παρὰ τῷ Σιμωνίδῃ γεγραμμένον ἐν τοῖσδε τοῖς ἔπεσιν·

οὐκ ἄν τις οὕτω δασκίοις ἐν οὔρεσιν
ἀνὴρ λέοντ' ἔδεισεν οὐδὲ πάρδαλιν
μοῦνος στενυγρῇ συμπεσὼν ἐν ἀτραπῷ.

cf. Galen. in Hippocr. *de artic.* (xviii(1).411 Kühn)

1 οὔπω τις *de artic.*     3 στενυγρῷ συντυχὼν *de artic.*

**15** Ath. 3.106d

κουρίδας δὲ τὰς καρῖδας εἴρηκε Σώφρων ἐν Γυναικείοις (fr. 26 Kaibel) . . . Ἐπίχαρμος δ' ἐν Γᾷ καὶ Θαλάσσᾳ (fr. 31 Kaibel), ἐν δὲ Λόγῳ καὶ Λογίνᾳ (fr. 89)

320

Scholiast on Homer, *Iliad* ("reward for a life saved")

Thank-offerings for one's life. The word has an iota, since Semonides says τὸ ζώϊον—βίον, concerning the beetle.

**14** Galen on Hippocrates, *Epidemics*

Therefore one must read the second syllable of στεννγ-ρῶσαι with a smooth, not rough breathing. For ὑγρόν is not part of the word, as might be thought if one did not realize that στενόν ('narrow') is called στεννγρόν by the Ionians. But there is self-sufficient evidence of this in what has been written by Semonides in the following verses:

> a man who all alone met up with a lion or a leopard
> on a narrow path in the shadowy mountains would
> not have been so afraid

**15** Athenaeus, *Scholars at Dinner*

Sophron in *Women's Mimes* called καρῖδες κουρίδες as did Epicharmus in *Land and Sea*, but in *Logos and Logina*

διὰ τοῦ ω εἴρηκεν . . . Σιμωνίδης δέ·

θύννοισι τευθίς, κωβιοῖσι κωρίδες.

**16** Clem. *Paed.* 2.8.64.3-4

τούτων δὲ τῶν μύρων ἄπειροι διαφοραί, βρένθειον καὶ
μετάλλιον καὶ βασίλειον, πλαγγόνιόν τε καὶ ψάγδας
Αἰγύπτιος. Σιμωνίδης δὲ ἐν τοῖς ἰάμβοις οὐκ αἰδεῖται
λέγων·

κἀλειφόμην μύροισι καὶ θυώμασιν
καὶ βακκάρι· καὶ γάρ τις ἔμπορος παρῆν.

cf. Ath. 15.690c

1 κηλ- et ηλ- Ath.    θυμιάμασιν Clem.    2 βάκκαριν
Clem.

**17** *Et.Gen.* (p. 40 Calame) = *Et. Mag.* 633.58

ὀρσοθύρη· θυρὶς δι' ἧς εἰς ὑπερῷον ὑπάρχει ἀνάβασις
. . . λέγει δὲ καὶ Σιμωνίδης κακοσχόλως·

καί τῆς ὄπισθεν ὀρσοθύρης < > ἠλσάμην.

κὰτ Hemsterhuys    ὀρσοθυρίδος Sylburg, ὀρθύρης Bergk,
alii alia    ⟨δι⟩ηλσάμην Lobeck

he used the form with omega, as did Semonides:

for tunny squid, for gudgeons shrimps[1]

[1] The point of the collocation is unknown. Perhaps one creature is a meal for the other.

**16** Clement of Alexandria, *The Schoolmaster*

And of these unguents there are countless varieties, *brentheion, metallion, basileion, plangonion,* and Egyptian *psagdas*.[1] And Semonides does not blush at saying in his iambics:

and I was anointing myself[2] with unguents and scents and *baccaris*;[3] for in fact a merchant was present

[1] Passages in which these various unguents occur are cited by Athenaeus 15.690d-691a.    [2] It cannot be determined whether the speaker is a woman (hetaera?) or the poet himself.
[3] A Lydian unguent made from hazelwort.

**17** *Etymologicum Genuinum* and *Magnum*

ὀρσοθύρη: a little door which gives access to an upper storey ... Semonides gives a vulgar meaning to the word:

and I drove through (?) the back door[1]

[1] The 'back door' is no doubt the anus, but the text is highly uncertain. ὀρσοθύρης is suspect on metrical and other grounds (see West, *Studies* 179).

# IAMBIC POETRY

**18** *Et. Gen.* (pp. 22-23 Calame) = *Et. Mag.* 270.44 = Zon. (p. 539 T.)

διασαυλούμενος· ἀβρυνόμενος καὶ διαθρυπτόμενος
. . . παρὰ τὸν σαῦλον τὸν τρυφερὸν καὶ γαῦρον. Σιμω-
νίδης ἐν ἰάμβοις·

καὶ σαῦλα βαίνων ἵππος ὡς †κορωνίτης.

κορωνιᾷς, -ιᾷ dub. West, alii alia

**19** Pollux 2.65

σκνιπὸν δὲ τὸν ἀμυδρῶς βλέποντα Σιμωνίδης ὁ ἰαμ-
βοποιός·

ἢ τυφλὸς ἤ τις σκνιπὸς ἢ μέγα βλέπων.

μόγις pro μέγα West, alii alia

**20** Schol. Hom. *Od.* 14.435, "τὴν μὲν ἴαν Νύμφῃσι"

ὡς ποιμενικοῖς προστάταις καὶ Σιμωνίδης θύειν
αὐτούς φησι Νύμφαις καὶ

Μαιάδος τόκῳ·
οὗτοι γὰρ ἀνδρῶν αἷμ' ἔχουσι ποιμένων.

cf. Eust. ad loc. (1766.2)

1 θύουσι Νύμφαις τῷ τε suppl. Barnes (ἠδὲ Ahrens)

**18** *Etymologicum Genuinum*

διασαυλούμενος: putting on airs and having an affected
manner . . . from σαῦλος which means effeminate and
haughty. Cf. Semonides in iambics:

> with mincing gait and arched neck like a horse's[1]

[1] Cf. Anac. frr. 452, 458 *PMG*. Whatever the correct reading
of the last word is, the fragment presumably describes a man who
puts on airs.

**19** Pollux, *Vocabulary*

σκνιπός is used by the iambic poet Semonides of one who
has weak eyesight:

> one who is blind or has weak eyesight or sees well

**20** Scholiast on Homer, *Odyssey* ("one portion for the
    Nymphs")

as guardians of shepherds. And Semonides says that they
sacrifice to the Nymphs and

>           to the son of Maia;
> for they[1] have in their care the race of shepherds

[1] I.e., the Nymphs and Hermes. I have followed the explana-
tion of Eustathius, but according to West 'they' are those sacri-
ficing: "for they are of shepherd stock."

# IAMBIC POETRY

**21** Strabo 13.2.6

τὰς δὲ δυσφημίας τῶν ὀνομάτων φεύγοντές τινες ἐν-
ταῦθα μὲν (sc. Πορδοσελήνη) Ποροσελήνην δεῖν
λέγειν φασίν, τὸ δὲ Ἀσπόρδηνον ὄρος τὸ περὶ Πέρ-
γαμον, τραχὺ καὶ λυπρὸν ὄν, Ἀσπόρηνον, καὶ τὸ ἱερὸν
τὸ ἐνταῦθα τῆς Μητρὸς τῶν θεῶν Ἀσπορηνῆς. τί οὖν
φήσομεν τὴν πόρδαλιν καὶ τὸν Σαπέρδην καὶ τὸν
Περδίκκαν; ‹ἀλλὰ ἕτερον σημαίνει, ὅπερ› (add. West)
καὶ τὸ Σιμωνίδου

    (a) σὺν πορδακοῖσιν ἐκπεσόντες εἵμασιν,

ἀντὶ τοῦ διαβρόχοις, καὶ ἐν τῇ ἀρχαίᾳ που κωμῳδίᾳ
(Ar. *Pax* 1148) "πορδακὸν τὸ χωρίον" τὸ λιμνάζον.

Schol. Ar. ad loc. (p. 164 Holwerda)

παρδακὸν (ita codd. Ar.) δὲ δίυγρον· οὕτω γὰρ καὶ
Ἀρχίλοχος, "παρδακὸν δ᾽ ἐπείσιον" (fr. 40), καὶ παρὰ
Σιμωνίδῃ τῷ Ἀμοργίῳ·

    (b) σὺν παρδακοῖσιν εἵμασιν σεσαγμένοις

παρδακῇσιν schol. Ar.    ἱμάσιν libri utrimque, corr. Toup
et Tyrwhitt    σεσαγμένοι Welcker

326

# SEMONIDES

**21** Strabo, *Geography*

So as to avoid the indecency of the names some state that one ought to say here Poroselene (for Pordoselene), and Asporenon for Aspordenon, the rugged and wretched mountain round Pergamum, and that the temple there belongs to the Asporene Mother of the Gods. What then shall we say of *pordalis* ('leopard') and Saperdes and Perdiccas?[1] <But a different meaning> is found in Semonides

    (a) cast forth (on the shore?) with *pordakoisin* clothing,

instead of sodden, and somewhere in early comedy "the area is *pordakon*," i.e., marshy.


Scholiast on Aristophanes, *Peace*

*pardakon* means wet; so too in Archilochus (fr. 40) and in Semonides of Amorgos:

    (b) weighed down by sodden clothing[2]

[1] The point of what precedes is that such changes avoid the roots *pord-* and *perd-* which occur in words denoting the act of farting. Although Strabo mentions only the roots *pord-* and *perd-*, he seems to imply that *pard-* could also be considered indecent, since all three roots occur in the various tenses of πέρδομαι, 'fart.'

[2] Many, probably correctly, treat (a) and (b) as one fragment, reading (with Welcker) σὺν παρδακοῖσιν ἐκπεσόντες εἵμα-σιν / σεσαγμένοι, "cast forth weighed down by sodden clothing." It seems likely that the correct form of the adjective is *pardakos*.

**22** Ath. 14.658b

(τυρὸς Τρομιλικός) οὗ καὶ Σιμωνίδης μνημονεύει ἐν
ἰάμβῳ οὗ ἡ ἀρχή

&lt;ἦ&gt; πολλὰ μὲν δὴ προυκπονέαι, Τηλέμβροτε,

γράφων

**23**

ἐνταῦθα μέν τοι τυρὸς ἐξ Ἀχαΐης
Τρομίλιος θαυμαστός, ὃν κατήγαγον.

ἦ (22) add. Hemsterhuys     προεκπονῇ cod., προυκ- Fick,
-έαι Hiller

**24** Ath. 14.659d-f

οὐδὲν οὖν ἦν παράδοξον εἰ καὶ θυτικῆς ἦσαν ἔμπειροι
οἱ παλαίτεροι μάγειροι. προίσταντο γοῦν καὶ γάμων
καὶ θυσιῶν . . . καὶ παρὰ Σιμωνίδῃ δέ φησιν ἕτερος
(μάγειρος)·

κὼς &lt;ὗν&gt; ἀπεῦσα κὼς ἐμίστυλα κρέα
ἱρωστί· καὶ γὰρ οὐ κακῶς ἐπίσταμαι.

1 χως ἄφευσα χως cod., κὼς . . . κὼς Schnewidewin     &lt;ὗν&gt;
add. Bergk     ἄπευσα Fick, corr. Hiller     2 εἰδώς· τί cod.,
corr. Hecker

**22**  Athenaeus, *Scholars at Dinner*

(Tromilian cheese) which Semonides mentions in the iambic poem whose beginning is

> Much indeed is the work you do in advance, Telembrotus,

where he writes

**23**

> here, take note, is wonderful Tromilian cheese from
> Achaea, which I brought back

**24**  Athenaeus, *Scholars at Dinner*

There's nothing surprising, therefore, if the cooks of old were skilled in the art of divining. At any rate they managed both weddings and sacrifices . . . and another cook says in Semonides:

> and how I singed off the hair of a pig and how I cut
> up the meat in the manner prescribed by ritual; for
> in fact I'm quite knowledgeable in that

**25** Ath. 10.424c

καλοῦνται δὲ (οἱ κύαθοι) καὶ ἀρυστῆρες καὶ ἀρύστι-
χοι. Σιμωνίδης·

ἔδωκεν οὐδεὶς οὐδ᾽ ἀρυστῆρα τρυγός.

**26** Ath. 11.460b

ποτήρια δὲ πρῶτον οἶδα ὀνομάσαντα τὸν Ἀμόργιον
ποιητὴν Σιμωνίδην ἐν ἰάμβοις οὕτως·

ἀπὸ τράπεζαν εἷλε †νιν ποτήρια.

καὶ pro νιν Meineke, εἷλεν ἢ dub. West, alii alia

**27** Schol. Hom. *Il.* 2.219 (i.230 Erbse), "φοξός"

εἴρηται ἀπὸ τῶν κεραμικῶν ἀγγείων, τῶν ἐν τῇ καμίνῳ
ἀπὸ τοῦ φωτὸς ἀπωξυμμένων, καθά φησι καὶ Σιμω-
νίδης·

αὕτη δὲ φοξὴ χεῖλος Ἀργείη κύλιξ.

cf. Apoll. Soph. (p. 164.19 Bekker), *Et. Gen.* (p. 46 Calame),
*Et. Mag.* 798.17, *Et. Gud.* (col. 560.20 Sturz), Zon. (p. 1817 T.),
Epimer. in Hom. (p. 720.18 Dyck), Orion *etym.* (col. 159.12
Sturz), Ath. 11.480cd, Eust. in Hom. *Il.* 2.219 (i.316.1 V. d. Valk)

φοξὴ χεῖλος Vat. gr. 28 (schol. Hom.), Apoll. Soph. (χειρὸς),
φοξίχειλος schol. Hom. primarii, *Et. Gen.*, *Et. Mag.*, Ath., Eust.,
φοξύχειλος *Et. Gud.*, φοξόχειλος Zon.

**25** Athenaeus, *Scholars at Dinner*

κύαθοι ('ladles') are also called ἀρυστῆρες and ἀρύστι-
χοι. Cf. Semonides:

no one gave even a ladleful of dregs

**26** Athenaeus, *Scholars at Dinner*

I know that the term ποτήρια was first used by the poet
Semonides of Amorgos in his iambics as follows:

(s)he cleared away the table . . . cups

**27** Scholiast on Homer, *Iliad* ("pointed")

The word is said of vessels made from pottery which have
been brought to a point in the kiln from the fire, as
Semonides says:

this is an Argive cup with tapered lip[1]

[1] Some prefer the reading φοξίχειλος, but the meaning will
be the same.

**28** Schol. Ar. *Ach.* 740 (p. 97 Wilson), "τὰς ὁπλὰς τῶν χοιρίων"

οὐ μόνον Ἀριστοφάνης ἐπὶ τῶν χοίρων τὰς ὁπλὰς εἴρηκεν, ἀλλὰ καὶ Σιμωνίδης ὁμοίως ἐπὶ χοίρου·

ὁπλὰς ἐκίνει τῶν ὀπισθίων ποδῶν.

**29** Bergk = 514 *PMG*

**30** *Et. Gen.* (Miller, *Mélanges* 82) = *Et. Mag.* 250.18

δαύω· τὸ καίω, παρὰ Σιμωνίδῃ·

μηρίων δεδαυμένων.

παρὰ τὸ δαίω, τροπῇ τοῦ ι εἰς υ.

**31a** *Et. Gen.* (p. 26 Calame)

ἔπληντ' ἀλλήλῃσι. ἐκ τοῦ *πλῶ τοῦ σημαίνοντος τὸ πλησιάζω. ὁ παρακείμενος πέπληκα, λέγεται δὲ καὶ πέπλακα· ὁ παθητικὸς πέπλημαι πέπληται, καὶ παρὰ Σιμωνίδῃ πεπλήαται·

τὰ δ' ἄλλα πεπλέαται ξύλα.

cf. *Et. Mag.* 367.37, Zon. (p. 850 T.)

πεπλήαται *Et. Gen.* et *Et. Mag.*, corr. Renner

**31b** Schol. Lyc. 634 (p. 212.16 Scheer), "σισυρνοδῦται"

σίσυρνα δὲ παχὺ περιβόλαιον ἢ δερμάτινον ἱμάτιον,

# SEMONIDES

**28** Scholiast on Aristophanes, *Acharnians* ("the hooves of the pigs")

Not only does Aristophanes use ὁπλαί ('hooves') with regard to pigs, but so does Semonides:

> it moved the hooves of its back feet[1]

[1] Perhaps said of a pig being sacrificed. Cf. fr. 24.

**30** *Etymologicum Genuinum* and *Magnum*

δαύω means 'burn' in Semonides:

> of burnt thigh bones

Equivalent to δαίω ('burn'), with iota changed to upsilon.

**31a** *Etymologicum Genuinum*

They (sc. shields) came near one another (*Il.* 4.449). From *πλῶ meaning 'come near.' The perfect is πέπληκα and also πέπλακα, the passive πέπλημαι πέπληται and in Semonides πεπλήαται:

> and the other wood has come near (the fire?)

**31b** Scholiast on Lycophron ("wearers of leather coats")

σίσυρνα is a thick mantle or leather coat, the so-called

333

ἡ λεγομένη γοῦννα, ἥντινα Σιμωνίδης ὑποκοριστικῶς
εἶπε "σίσυν παχεῖαν."

παχείην et παχείαν codd., corr. Bergk

**32** Schol. AB Hom. *Il.* 13.103

ἤϊα δὲ τὰ βρώματα, οὐ τὰ ἐν οἴκῳ δὲ ἐσθιόμενα, ἀλλὰ
τὰ ἐν ὁδῷ καὶ πλῷ. "δεῦτε φίλοι, ἤϊα φερώμεθα" (*Od.*
2.410). Σιμωνίδης.

**33** Hesych.

κάρκαρα· †οὖλα ὁ διήτω† καὶ τὰ ποικίλα τῇ ὄψει καὶ
†ἐπιτυρὰ† παρὰ Σιμωνίδῃ (-δει cod., corr. Musurus).
ἔνιοι τοὺς μάνδρας.

**34** Suet. *de blasph.* (pp. 53-54 Taillardat)

Κέρκωπες οἱ πανοῦργοι ἀπατηλοί . . . καὶ κερκωπία
ἡ ἀπάτη κατὰ τὸν Σιμωνίδην.

**35** Antiattic. (*Anecd. Gr.* i.105.3 Bekker)

κορδύλη· τὸ ἔπαρμα. Σιμωνίδης δευτέρῳ.

γοῦννα, which Semonides used in diminutive form

a thick leather coat

## 32 Scholiast on Homer, *Iliad*

ἤϊα are victuals, not those eaten at home, but on a journey or voyage. "Come here, friends, let us carry the provisions" (*Od.* 2.410). Cf. Semonides.[1]

[1] The citation has not been preserved, but clearly some form of the word was contained in it. The poet is probably the iambographer, since the word is also found in Arch. fr. 79.1, with long iota as sometimes in Homer.

## 33 Hesychius, *Lexicon*

The gloss is too corrupt to be translated. If Musurus' emendation of ἐπιτυρά to πίτυρα is accepted, it seems that Semonides (or the lyric poet) used κάρκαρα with the meaning 'bran.'

## 34 Suetonius, *On Defamatory Words*

Κέρκωπες are deceitful scoundrels . . . and κερκωπία means 'deceit' in Semonides.[1]

[1] Perhaps the lyric poet.

## 35 Anti-Atticist

κορδύλη means a 'swelling.'[1] Cf. Semonides in his second book.

[1] According to the scholiast on Arist. *Clouds* 10 κορδύλη is properly a swelling on the head as the result of a blow.

**36** Phot. *lex.* (i.355 Naber)

κύβηβον· Κρατῖνος Θρᾴτταις (fr. 87 K.-A.) τὸν θεοφό-
ρητον. Ἴωνες δὲ τὸν μητραγύρτην καὶ γάλλον νῦν
καλούμενον· οὕτως Σιμωνίδης.

**37** Harpocr. (pp. 178 sq. Keaney)

Μυσῶν λείαν· Δημοσθένης ἐν τῷ ὑπὲρ Κτησιφῶντος
(18.72). παροιμία τίς ἐστιν οὕτω λεγομένη, ἥν φησι
Δήμων ἐν αʹ περὶ παροιμιῶν τὴν ἀρχὴν λαβεῖν ἀπὸ
τῶν καταδραμόντων ἀστυγειτόνων τε καὶ λῃστῶν τὴν
Μυσίαν κατὰ τὴν Τηλέφου τοῦ βασιλέως ἀποδημίαν
(*FGrHist* 327 F 4). κέχρηνται δὲ τῇ παροιμίᾳ ἄλλοι τε
καὶ Στράττις ἐν Μηδείᾳ (fr. 36 K.-A.) καὶ Σιμωνίδης ἐν
ἰάμβοις.

**38** *Et. Gud.* (col. 408.40 Sturz)

νῆστις· οὕτως εἴρηται παρὰ Σιμωνίδῃ. παρὰ τὸ ἔδω
. . . τὸ ἐσθίω, οὗ ὁ μέλλων \*ἔσω, \*ἐστής, καὶ μετὰ τοῦ
νε στερητικοῦ \*νεέστης, οὗ παρώνυμον νῆστης. οὕτως
Ἡρωδιανὸς ἐν ἐπιμερισμοῖς (i.xxxi Lentz).

**39** *Et. Mag.* 764.25

τρασιά· παρὰ τὸ τέρσω τὸ ξηραίνω, τερσιά, καὶ ταρ-
σιά, ὡς παρὰ Σιμωνίδῃ, καὶ καθ᾽ ὑπέρθεσιν τρασιά.

cf. Hesych. ταρσιήν· τὴν τρασιάν

# SEMONIDES

**36** Photius, *Lexicon*

κύβηβος is said of one possessed by a god in Cratinus, *Thracian Women*. But the Ionians use the word of what is now called μητραγύρτης ('begging priest of Cybele') and γάλλος ('priest of Cybele' or 'eunuch'). So Semonides.

**37** Harpocration, *Lexicon of the Ten Attic Orators*

Booty of the Mysians. Demosthenes in his speech *On behalf of Ctesiphon*. There is a proverb in this form which Demon, in Book 1 of his *On Proverbs*, says originated from the raids into Mysia by the neighbouring peoples and robbers during the absence of king Telephus. Others use the proverb, including Strattis in *Medea* and Semonides in his iambics.[1]

1 The proverb, said of anything that can be plundered with impunity, is frequently cited (see West ad loc.). Presumably Semonides used the Ionic form λητίη(ν), as Hoffmann proposed.

**38** *Etymologicum Gudianum*

νῆστης: so in Semonides. It is from ἔδω ('eat') . . . ἐσθίω, whose future is *ἔσω, *ἐστής, and with the privative νε, *νεέστης, the by-form of which is νήστης ('one who fasts'). So Herodian in *Parsings*.

**39** *Etymologicum Magnum*

τρασιά: from τέρσω meaning 'dry' we get τερσιά, and ταρσιά as in Semonides, and by transposition τρασιά ('crate for drying figs').[1]

1 Semonides would have used the Ionic form ταρσιή, but Hesychius' gloss need not mean that it occurred in the accusative.

**40** Orion *etym.* (col. 168.9 Sturz)

ψηνὸς ὁ φαλακρὸς εἴρηται. Σιμωνίδης.

**41** Zenob. Ath. 3.70 cod. A, ed. Kugéas apud O. Crusius, Paroemiographica, *Sitz.-Ber. bay. Ak.* 1910 (4), p. 23 (= *Corp. Paroem. Suppl.* [1961] V)

ὁ Λέσβιος Πρύλις· ταύτῃ καθ᾽ ὁμοίωσιν Σιμωνίδης κέχρηται·

†ἐν εὐδετέω† ὥσπερ Λέσβιος Πρύλις.

δοκεῖ δὲ ὁ Πρύλις Ἑρμοῦ παῖς γενέσθαι καὶ μάντις. ὀνομάζουσι δὲ αὐτόν τινες Πυρσόν.

cf. *Paroem. Gr.* i.327.18 L.-S.

ἐνεύδετ(ε) Crusius, ἐν δευτέρῳ Pellizer (libro altero frag. tribuens)

**42** Stob. 2.1.10

Σιμωνίδου·

ῥεῖα θεοὶ κλέπτουσιν ἀνθρώπων νόον.

**40** Orion, *Lexicon*

ψηνός means 'bald headed.' Cf. Semonides.

**41** Zenobius, *Proverbs*

The Lesbian Prylis. Semonides used this proverbial expression in a comparison:

... like Lesbian Prylis

It seems that Prylis was the son of Hermes and a seer.[1]
Some call him Pyrsus.

[1] According to Lycophron 219 and the scholia ad loc.,
Agamemnon sailed off to Lesbos and Prylis revealed to him the
stratagem of the wooden horse.

**42** Stobaeus, *Anthology*

From Semonides:

Gods easily deceive the mind of mortals.[1]

[1] Attribution to Semonides has been doubted or denied by
many (it is Sim. fr. 525 *PMG*), but the only cause for suspicion is
the choriambic anaclasis in the first metron and this has been
adequately defended, both here and in fr. 1.4, by R. Renehan,
*HSCP* 87 (1983) 5-11.

*Dubium*

**43**  Ar. *Pax* 697-699

Τρ. ἐκ τοῦ Σοφοκλέους γίγνεται Σιμωνίδης.
Ερ. Σιμωνίδης; πῶς;
Τρ.                                   ὅτι γέρων ὢν καὶ σαπρὸς
κέρδους ἕκατι κἂν ἐπὶ ῥιπὸς πλέοι.

Schol. ad loc. (p. 108 Holwerda)

χαριέντως πάνυ τῷ αὐτῷ λόγῳ διέσυρε τῆς β′ τοῦ
ἰαμβοποιοῦ καὶ μέμνηται ὅτι σμικρολόγος ἦν. ὅθεν
Ξενοφάνης "κίμβικα" αὐτὸν προσαγορεύει (Xenoph.
fr. 21 West).

## SEMONIDES

### Doubtful Work

**43** Aristophanes, *Peace*

Trygaeus: He's changing from Sophocles to Simonides.
Hermes: Simonides? How so?
Trygaeus: Because now that he's old and decayed, he'd
even sail on a mat of wickerwork for the sake of profit.

Scholiast on the passage

Aristophanes very elegantly ridiculed Simonides with the
same words of the second book of the iambic poet and
records that Simonides was miserly. Hence Xenophanes
calls him a skinflint.[1]

[1] E. Pellizer, *QUCC* n.s. 9 (1981) 47-51, argues that the scho-
liast is attributing *Peace* 699 to Semonides, since Simonides is
never called an iambic poet. This appears as fr. 4 in the edition
of Semonides by Pellizer and Tedeschi, with κέρδους ἔκατι
emended to κέρδεος ἔκητι. Holwerda's edition of the scholia
prints τοὺς δύο for τῆς βʹ, but Pellizer informs me that the latter is
the correct reading. Holwerda assumes a lacuna in front of
μέμνηται and West supplies Χαμαιλέων on the basis of
Athenaeus 656d.

# HIPPONAX

## TESTIMONIA

### Chronology

**1** Plin. *NH* 36.4.11

fuerat in Chio insula Melas scalptor, dein filius eius Micciades ac deinde nepos Archermus, cuius filii Bupalus et Athenis vel clarissimi in ea scientia fuere Hipponactis poetae aetate, quem certum est LX Olympiade fuisse.

**2** Ps.-Plut. *de musica* 6.1133d

ἔνιοι δὲ πλανώμενοι νομίζουσι κατὰ τὸν ⟨αὐτὸν⟩ χρόνον Τερπάνδρῳ Ἱππώνακτα γεγονέναι. φαίνεται δ' Ἱππώνακτος καὶ Περίκλειτος ὢν πρεσβύτερος.

---

¹ See n. 1 on Arch. test. 9.    ² A Lesbian cithara singer who won at the Carneia in Sparta c. 600 (Lasserre, *Plutarque, De la musique* p. 34).    ³ On Hipponax's date see also Arch. test. 6 and Sem. test. 3.

# HIPPONAX

## TESTIMONIA

### *Chronology*

**1** Pliny, *Natural History*

There lived in the island of Chios a sculptor Melas who was succeeded by his son Micciades and his grandson Archermus;[1] the latter's sons, Bupalus and Athenis, had the very greatest fame in that art (i.e., sculpture) at the time of the poet Hipponax who was clearly alive in the 60th Olympiad (540-537).[2]

[1] Archermus and his father Micciades had their names inscribed on the pedestal of a statue (now lost) in Delos, dated to c. 550-530. See Hansen, *CEG* I no. 425.     [2] The Parian Marble, although only partially preserved at the mention of Hipponax, dates the poet to 541-540 according to Jacoby, *Das Marmor Parium* p. 171.

**2** Pseudo-Plutarch, *On Music*

Some erroneously think that Hipponax lived at the same time as Terpander.[1] But even Periclitus[2] was clearly older than Hipponax.[3]

# IAMBIC POETRY

## Life and Physique

**3** *Suda* (ii.665.16 Adler)

Ἱππῶναξ· Πυθέω καὶ μητρὸς Πρώτιδος, Ἐφέσιος,
ἰαμβογράφος· ᾤκησε δὲ Κλαζομενὰς ὑπὸ τῶν τυράν-
νων Ἀθηναγόρα καὶ Κωμᾶ ἐξελαθείς. γράφει δὲ πρὸς
Βούπαλον καὶ Ἄθηνιν ἀγαλματοποιούς, ὅτι αὐτοῦ
εἰκόνας πρὸς ὕβριν εἰργάσαντο.

**4** Plin. *NH* 36.4.12

Hipponacti notabilis foeditas vultus erat; quamobrem
imaginem eius lascivia iocosam hi proposuere ridentium
circulis, quod Hipponax indignatus destrinxit amaritudi-
nem carminum in tantum ut credatur aliquis ad laqueum
eos compulisse; quod falsum est, complura enim in finiti-
mis insulis simulacra postea fecere, sicut in Delo, quibus
subiecerunt carmen, non vitibus tantum censeri Chion sed
et operibus Archermi filiorum.

# HIPPONAX

## *Life and Physique*

### 3 *Suda*

Hipponax, son of Pytheas[1] and Protis, from Ephesus, an iambic poet. Banished by the tyrants Athenagoras and Comas, he settled in Clazomenae. He wrote against the sculptors Bupalus and Athenis,[2] because they made insulting likenesses of him.

[1] It may be significant that in Herodas 1.76 Metriche gives Pytheas as her father, since Herodas was obviously indebted to Hipponax and actually names him in 8.78.   [2] On Athenis see also Arch. test. 30. In contrast to Bupalus, who figures prominently in the remains of Hipponax's poetry, there is only one reference to Athenis (fr. 70.11).

### 4 Pliny, *Natural History*

The face of Hipponax was notoriously ugly; on account of this they[1] impudently exhibited a humorous likeness of him to a circle of laughing spectators. In anger at this Hipponax unsheathed such bitter verses that some believe he drove them to the noose.[2] This is untrue, since later they made several statues in neighbouring islands, for example in Delos,[3] and set under them verses to the effect that Chios was to be celebrated not only for its vines, but also for the works of the sons of Archermus.

[1] I.e., the sculptors Bupalus and Athenis, sons of Archermus. [2] Presumably on the analogy of Lycambes and his daughters (Arch. testt. 19-32).   [3] See n. 1 on test. 1.

## IAMBIC POETRY

**5** Ath. 12.552c-d; hinc Eust. in Hom. *Il.* 23.844 (iv.847.55 V.d.Valk)

Μητρόδωρος δ' ὁ Σκήψιος (*FGrHist* 184 F 6) ἐν δευτέρῳ
Περὶ ἀλειπτικῆς Ἱππώνακτα τὸν ποιητὴν οὐ μόνον
μικρὸν γενέσθαι τὸ σῶμα, ἀλλὰ καὶ λεπτόν, ἀκρό-
τονον δ' οὕτως ὡς πρὸς τοῖς ἄλλοις καὶ κενὴν λήκυθον
βάλλειν μέγιστόν τι διάστημα, τῶν ἐλαφρῶν σωμά-
των διὰ τὸ μὴ δύνασθαι τὸν ἀέρα τέμνειν οὐκ ἐχόντων
βιαίαν τὴν φοράν.

### The Verdict of Antiquity

**6** Callim. fr. 191.1-4 Pf.

Ἀκούσαθ' Ἱππώνακτος· οὐ γὰρ ἀλλ' ἥκω
ἐκ τῶν ὅκου βοῦν κολλύβου πιπρήσκουσιν,
φέρων ἴαμβον οὐ μάχην ἀείδοντα
τὴν Βουπάλειον [

**7** Theocr. *epig.* 19 Gow = *HE* 3430-33 (*Anth. Pal.* 13.3)

ὁ μουσοποιὸς ἐνθάδ' Ἱππῶναξ κεῖται.
εἰ μὲν πονηρός, μὴ προσέρχευ τῷ τύμβῳ·
εἰ δ' ἐσσὶ κρήγυός τε καὶ παρὰ χρηστῶν,
θαρσέων καθίζευ, κἢν θέλῃς ἀπόβριξον.

346

**5**  Athenaeus, *Scholars at Dinner*

Metrodorus of Scepsis[1] in the second book of his *On the Art of Training* says that the poet Hipponax was not only small of body but also thin[2] and yet was so muscular that in addition to other feats he threw even an empty oil flask a very great distance,[3] although light objects because of their inability to cleave the air do not have a strong momentum.

[1] A philosopher and rhetorician, born c. 160 B.C.
[2] Aelian (*VH* 10.6) also records that Hipponax was small and thin, but adds that he was ugly (αἰσχρός). [3] R. M. Rosen, *Eikasmos* 1 (1990) 11-15, suggests that this anecdote is based on a poem of Hipponax which "illustrated the unreliability of physical appearance as a judge of reality" and that his model was the Euryalus-Odysseus scene in *Od.* 8.158-90.

### The Verdict of Antiquity

**6**  Callimachus, *Iambi*

Listen to Hipponax, for it is I in fact who have come[1] from the place where they sell an ox for a penny,[2] bearing iambics that do not sing of the fight with Bupalus.

[1] See n. 1 on fr. 1.  [2] I.e., from Hades.

**7**  Theocritus, *Epigrams*

Here lies the poet Hipponax. If you are a scoundrel, do not approach the tomb; but if you are honest and from worthy stock, sit down in confidence and, if you like, fall asleep.

**8** *Anth. Pal.* 7.405 = *GP* 2861-66 (Φιλίππου)

ὦ ξεῖνε, φεῦγε τὸν χαλαζεπῆ τάφον
τὸν φρικτὸν Ἱππώνακτος, οὗ τε χὰ τέφρα
ἰαμβιάζει Βουπάλειον ἐς στύγος,
μή πως ἐγείρῃς σφῆκα τὸν κοιμώμενον,
ὃς οὐδ' ἐν Ἅιδη νῦν κεκοίμηκεν χόλον,
σκάζουσι μέτροις ὀρθὰ τοξεύσας ἔπη.

**9** *Anth. Pal.* 7.408 = *HE* 2325-30 (Λεωνίδα)

ἀτρέμα τὸν τύμβον παραμείβετε, μὴ τὸν ἐν ὕπνῳ
πικρὸν ἐγείρητε σφῆκ' ἀναπαυόμενον·
ἄρτι γὰρ Ἱππώνακτος ὁ καὶ τοκεῶνε βαΰξας
ἄρτι κεκοίμηται θυμὸς ἐν ἡσυχίη.
ἀλλὰ προμηθήσασθε· τὰ γὰρ πεπυρωμένα κείνου
ῥήματα πημαίνειν οἶδε καὶ εἰν Ἀίδη.

**10** *Anth. Pal.* 7.536 = *HE* 76-81 (Ἀλκαίου)

οὐδὲ θανὼν ὁ πρέσβυς ἑῷ ἐπιτέτροφε τύμβῳ
βότρυν ἀπ' οἰνάνθης ἥμερον, ἀλλὰ βάτον
καὶ πνιγόεσσαν ἄχερδον ἀποστύφουσαν ὁδιτῶν
χείλεα καὶ δίψει καρφαλέον φάρυγα.
ἀλλά τις Ἱππώνακτος ἐπὴν παρὰ σῆμα νέηται,
εὐχέσθω κνώσσειν εὐμενέοντα νέκυν.

**8** *Palatine Anthology* (Philip of Thessaloniki)

Stranger, flee from the grave with its hailstorm of verses, the frightful grave of Hipponax, whose very ashes utter invective to vent his hatred of Bupalus, lest somehow you arouse the sleeping wasp who has not even now in Hades put to sleep his anger, he who shot forth his words straight to the mark in limping meter.

**9** *Palatine Anthology* (Leonidas of Tarentum)

Go quietly past the tomb, lest you arouse the bitter wasp who is resting. For the wrath of Hipponax that snarled even at his parents has just been stilled in peace. But take care, since his fiery verses know how to injure even in Hades.

**10** *Palatine Anthology* (Alcaeus of Messene)

Even after his death the old man does not rear upon his tomb cultivated clusters of grapes from the vine, but brambles and the choking wild pear that constricts the lips of travellers and their throat parched with thirst. But whenever anyone goes past the tomb of Hipponax, let him pray that his corpse be kindly disposed and sleep.

**11** Pseudacronis schol. (i.404 Keller) ad Hor. *epod.* 6.14
(v. Arch. test. 25)

Hipponactem significat qui Bupali filiam nuptum petiit et
pro deformitate contemptus est. illud tamen verius volunt
fuisse: Bupalum pictorem fuisse apud Clazomenas, civita-
tem Asiae. hic Hipponactem quendam poetam deformem
pro risu pinxit: quo ille furore commotus tali eum carmine
perculit ut se laqueo suspenderet. unde nunc similis
carminis vim maledico minatur Horatius.

*Meter*

**12** Demetr. *de eloc.* 301

καὶ ὥσπερ τὸ διαλελυμένον σχῆμα δεινότητα ποιεῖ,
ὡς προλέλεκται, οὕτω ποιήσει ἡ διαλελυμένη ὅλως
σύνθεσις. σημεῖον δὲ καὶ τὸ Ἱππώνακτος. λοιδορῆσαι
γὰρ βουλόμενος τοὺς ἐχθροὺς ἔθραυσεν τὸ μέτρον καὶ
ἐποίησεν χωλὸν ἀντὶ εὐθέος καὶ ἄρυθμον, τουτέστι
δεινότητι πρέπον καὶ λοιδορίᾳ· τὸ γὰρ ἔρρυθμον καὶ
εὐήκοον ἐγκωμίοις ἂν πρέποι μᾶλλον ἢ ψόγοις.

**13** Hephaest. *Ench.* 5.4 (p. 17.1 Consbruch)

ἔστιν ἐπίσημον ἐν τοῖς ἀκαταλήκτοις καὶ τὸ χωλὸν
καλούμενον, ὅπερ τινὲς μὲν Ἱππώνακτος, τινὲς δὲ
Ἀνανίου εὕρημά φασι, διαφέρει δὲ τοῦ ὀρθοῦ, ᾗ ἐκεῖνο
μὲν τὸν τελευταῖον ἴαμβον ἔχει ἢ πυρρίχιον διὰ τὴν

**11**  Pseudo-Acron on Horace, *Epodes*

He means Hipponax who sought the daughter of Bupalus
in marriage and was scorned because of his ugly features.
But people are of the opinion that the following is closer to
the truth, that Bupalus, a painter in Clazomenae, a city in
Asia, painted a certain poet Hipponax as ugly in order to
rouse laughter. The latter, incensed by this, assailed him
with such verses that he hanged himself.[1] Whence now
Horace threatens an evildoer with the violence of similar
poetry.

[1] See n. 2 on test. 4. See also Arch. test. 31.

*Meter*

**12**  Demetrius, *On Style*

And just as the disjointed form of speech produces a vig-
orous effect, as has already been said, so will disjointed
composition in general. The poetry of Hipponax provides
an example. In his desire to abuse his enemies he shattered
the meter, making it lame instead of straightforward, and
unrhythmical, i.e., suitable for vigorous abuse, since what
is rhythmical and pleasing to the ear would be more suit-
able for words of praise than blame.

**13**  Hephaestion, *Handbook of Meters*

Worthy of mention among the acatalectic (iambic) meters
is also the one called 'lame,' an invention of Hipponax
according to some, of Ananius according to others. It dif-
fers from the straight (i.e., pure iambic) meter, which has
as its last foot an iambus or a pyrrhic because of the indif-

351

ἀδιάφορον, τοῦτο δὲ ἢ σπονδεῖον ἢ τροχαῖον. Quae
sequuntur v. ad fr. 84.17.


# FRAGMENTA

**1** Iuba Artigraphus ap. Rufinum, *comm. in metra Terent.*
(vi.562.19 Keil)

est autem proceritatis eiusdem versus qui unius pedis
differentia nomen amittit. nam quod sexto loco . . . non
iambus sed spondeus vel trochaeus accipitur et a longa
syllaba incipit, claudum carmen facit et choliambus nomi-
natur, ut est:

ὦ Κλαζομένιοι, Βούπαλος κατέκτεινεν.

ἀκούσαθ' Ἱππώνακτος, οὐ γὰρ ἀλλ' ἥκω (Callim. fr.
191.1 Pf.)

cf. Mar. Plot. Sac. (vi.522.15 Keil)

κάτεινε et κάθηινε Plot., unde ⟨τε⟩ κάθηνις Bergk


**2** Tzetz. *Chil.* 10.370-374 (pp. 402 sq. Leone)

περὶ τῶν Μιλησίων μὲν ἔφαν πολλοὶ ἐρίων·
περὶ ἐρίων Κοραξῶν ἐν πρώτῳ δὲ ἰάμβῳ
Ἱππῶναξ οὕτως εἴρηκε μέτρῳ χωλῶν ἰάμβων·

Κοραξικὸν μὲν ἠμφιεσμένη λῶπος.

ferent (final syllable), by having a spondee or trochee (in this position).

See also Arch. fr. 223, Arch. test. 61, and Anan. test. 2.

## FRAGMENTS

**1** Juba in Rufinus, *Commentary on the Meters of Terence*

But there is a verse of the same length (as the iambic trimeter) which differs in one foot and so loses its name. For because a spondee or a trochee rather than an iambus is admitted in the sixth position . . . and begins with a long syllable, this makes the poem lame and it is called a choliambus, such as:

People of Clazomenae, Bupalus has killed

Listen to Hipponax, for it is I in fact who have come.[1]

[1] Plotius cites the verses in reverse order and some follow him, treating them as contiguous. Critics disagree on whether Callimachus might have taken over his fr. 191.1 intact from Hipponax. See Degani, *Studi* 241-43, and E. Redondo, *Veleia* 7 (1990) 258-64, who assigns both verses to Hipponax. Hephaestion also cites the verse of Callimachus in conjunction with Hipp. fr. 84.17.

**2** Tzetzes, *Chiliads*

Many have mentioned Milesian wool, but Hipponax mentions Coraxian wool in the first book of his iambics, using the choliambic meter as follows:

she clad in a Coraxian mantle

353

τοὺς Κοραξοὺς δὲ καὶ Σινδοὺς ἔθνη τυγχάνειν νόει.

**2a** Schol. Ap. Rhod. 4.321 (p. 284.5 Wendel)

τὸ δὲ Σίνδοι Ἡρωδιανὸς ἐν τῷ ϛ′ τῆς Καθόλου (i.142.20 Lentz) βαρυτονεῖν φησι δεῖν· τινὲς δὲ ὀξυτονοῦσιν, οὐκ εὖ. καὶ Ἱππῶναξ δὲ μνημονεύει πρώτῳ·

Σινδικὸν διάσφαγμα.

(Schol.) πρώτῳ pro πρὸς τὸ Meineke, probb. Degani et al.

**3** Tzetz. in Lyc. 219 (p. 102.16 Scheer)

Μαίας δὲ καὶ Διὸς Ἑρμῆς, ὡς Ὀρφεύς φησιν ἐν τῇ ἀρχῇ τῶν Λιθικῶν . . . καὶ ὁ Ἱππῶναξ ἐν τῷ κατὰ Βουπάλου πρώτῳ ἰάμβῳ·

ἔβωσε Μαίης παῖδα, Κυλλήνης πάλμυν.

ἐβόησε codd., corr. Dindorf

**3a** Tzetz. ad *Chil.* 1.147 (p. 547 Leone)

τὸ δὲ Κανδαύλης Λυδικῶς τὸν σκυλοπνίκτην λέγει, ὥσπερ Ἱππῶναξ δείκνυσι γράφων ἰάμβῳ πρώτῳ·

Be aware that the Coraxi and Sindi[1] are tribes.

[1] Both are Scythian tribes.

**2a** Scholiast on Apollonius of Rhodes

In the sixth book of his *Universal Prosody* Herodian says that Σίνδοι should have a paroxytone accent, but some wrongly make it oxytone. Hipponax also mentions the Sindi in his first book:

> Sindian fissure[1]

[1] Hesychius glosses the same two words with τὸ τῆς γυναικός, 'female genitals.' Similarly Stephanus of Byzantium s.v. Σίνδοι. Some retain πρὸς τὸ of the scholiast, assign it to Hipponax, supply γυμνὴ δὲ in front of it ("naked up to the Sindian fissure") and combine the line with fr. 2. But see Degani, *Studi* 243 f.

**3** Tzetzes on Lycophron

Hermes is the son of Maia and Zeus, as Orpheus says at the beginning of his *On Stones* . . . and Hipponax in his first book of iambics against Bupalus:

> he called upon Maia's son, sultan[1] of Cyllene[2]

[1] πάλμυς is a Lydian word with the general meaning of 'king.' West's 'sultan' catches well the comic tone. [2] A mountain in Arcadia where Hermes was born.

**3a** Tzetzes on *Chiliads*

Candaules is a Lydian word meaning 'dog throttler,' as Hipponax shows when he writes in his first book of iambics:

Ἑρμῆ κυνάγχα, Μηιονιστὶ Κανδαῦλα,
φωρῶν ἑταῖρε, δεῦρό μοι σκαπαρδεῦσαι.

fragmento 3 subiunxit Schneidewin    2 τί μοι codd.,
corr. Dübner    σκαπερδεῦσαι Meineke, συμμαχῆσαι sscr.

**4** Tzetz. *exeg. Il.* A 14 (p. 76.8 Hermann)

ἦν δάφνην οἱ ἱερεῖς τοῦ ἡλίου, ἤτοι μάντεις καὶ μάγοι,
οἷος ἦν καὶ ὁ Χρύσης, στεφανούμενοι ἐπορεύοντο,
καθὼς δηλοῖ καὶ Ἱππῶναξ ἐν τῷ κατὰ Βουπάλου
ἰάμβῳ·

Κίκων δ' ὁ πανδάλητος ἄμμορος καύης
†τοιόνδε τι δάφνας κατέχων

**4a** Hesych.

Κίκων· ὁ Κίκων Ἀμυθάονος ἦν,

οὐδὲν αἴσιον προθεσπίζων.

---

1 Amythaon was the father of the seer Melampous and various attempts have been made to emend Hesychius' Ἀ. ἦν so as to incorporate it as a mock patronymic in the fragment (see Degani's fr. 188). The fragment has been plausibly assigned to Hipponax because of the name Cicon (cf. frr. 4, 78.7).

Hermes, dog throttler,[1] Candaules in Maeonian,[2]
companion of thieves, come give me a hand(?).[3]

[1] So as to overcome guard-dogs.    [2] Maeonian = Lydian.
Tzetzes' evidence for Candaules as 'dog throttler' is probably
based solely on Hipponax and the word may instead be simply a
Lydian equivalent of Hermes.        [3] Text and meaning of the
verb are much disputed. Many see a connection with σκαπέρδα,
a kind of tug-of-war, and adopt Meineke's emendation. If the verb
is cognate with σκάπτειν ('dig'), it may allude to the practice of
thieves digging through the wall of a house.

**4** Tzetzes on Homer, *Iliad*

Laurel which the priests of the sun, i.e., prophets and wise
men, like Chryses, wore as a wreath when they walked
about, as Hipponax makes clear in his iambics against Bu-
palus:

> Cicon the . . .[1] ill-starred priest[2]
> (with his laurel)

[1] The word πανδάλητος is not found elsewhere and has been
variously interpreted or emended. It may be a patronymic, 'son of
Pandales.'        [2] καύης seems to be a Lydian word for 'priest.'
Tzetzes elsewhere glosses it with λάρος, a sea bird which often
served as a metaphor for greedy or foolish people, presumably
suggesting a connection with κήξ, another sea bird.

**4a** Hesychius, *Lexicon*

Cicon: Cicon was the son of Amythaon,[1]

> prophesying nothing auspicious

357

**5** Tzetz. *Chil.* 5.728 sqq. (pp. 196 sq. Leone)

ὁ φαρμακὸς τὸ κάθαρμα τοιοῦτον ἦν τὸ πάλαι.
ἂν συμφορὰ κατέλαβε πόλιν θεομηνία,
εἴτ᾿ οὖν λιμὸς εἴτε λοιμὸς εἴτε καὶ βλάβος ἄλλο,
τὸν πάντων ἀμορφότερον ἦγον ὡς πρὸς θυσίαν
εἰς καθαρμὸν καὶ φάρμακον πόλεως τῆς νοσούσης·
εἰς τόπον δὲ τὸν πρόσφορον στήσαντες τὴν θυσίαν,
τυρόν τε δόντες τῇ χειρὶ καὶ μᾶζαν καὶ ἰσχάδας,
ἑπτάκις τε ῥαπίσαντες ἐκεῖνον εἰς τὸ πέος
σκίλλαις συκαῖς ἀγρίαις τε καὶ ἄλλοις τῶν ἀγρίων,
τέλος πυρὶ κατέκαιον ἐν ξύλοις τοῖς ἀγρίοις,
καὶ τὴν σποδὸν εἰς θάλασσαν ἔρραινον εἰς ἀνέμους
εἰς καθαρμὸν τῆς πόλεως, ὡς ἔφην, τῆς νοσούσης . . .
ὁ δὲ Ἱππῶναξ ἄριστα σύμπαν τὸ ἔθος λέγει·

πόλιν καθαίρειν καὶ κράδῃσι βάλλεσθαι.

**6** Pergit Tzetzes

καὶ ἀλλαχοῦ δέ πού φησι πρώτῳ ἰάμβῳ γράφων·

βάλλοντες ἐν χειμῶνι καὶ ῥαπίζοντες
κράδῃσι καὶ σκίλλῃσιν ὥσπερ φαρμακόν.

1 λειμῶνι Schneidewin

**5** Tzetzes, *Chiliads*

The *pharmakos* was an ancient form of purification as follows. If a disaster, such as famine or pestilence or some other blight, struck a city because of divine wrath, they led the ugliest man of all as if to a sacrifice in order to purify and cure the city's ills. They set the victim in an appropriate place, put cheese, barley cake and dried figs in his hand, flogged him seven times on his penis with squills, wild fig branches, and other wild plants, and finally burned him on wood from wild trees and scattered his ashes into the sea and winds in order to purify the city of its ills, as I said . . . But Hipponax describes the whole custom[1] best:

> to purify the city and to be struck with fig branches

[1] On the ritual see also fr. 118E with n. 1.

**6** Tzetzes continues

And somewhere else he says in his first book of iambics:

> in winter[1] striking and flogging him with fig branches and squills as though a scapegoat[2]

[1] Many adopt Schneidewin's emendation ('in a meadow'), perhaps rightly (cf. *Chil.* 5.733 on fr. 5).     [2] Photius (ii.256 Naber) says that the Ionians lengthen the penultimate syllable in φαρμακός and he names Hipponax as proof.

**7** Pergit Tzetzes

καὶ πάλιν ἄλλοις τόποις δὲ ταῦτά φησι κατ᾽ ἔπος·

δεῖ δ᾽ αὐτὸν ἐς φαρμακὸν ἐκποιήσασθαι.

**8** Pergit Tzetzes

κἀφῆ παρέξειν ἰσχάδας τε καὶ μᾶζαν
καὶ τυρόν, οἷον ἐσθίουσι φαρμακοί.

1 κἄφη (= καὶ ἔφη) Welcker

**9** Pergit Tzetzes

πάλαι γὰρ αὐτοὺς προσδέκονται χάσκοντες
κράδας ἔχοντες ὡς ἔχουσι φαρμακοῖς.

1 προσδέχονται codd., corr. Schneidewin    2 ἔχοντας
codd., corr. Meursius

**10** Pergit Tzetzes

καὶ ἀλλαχοῦ δέ πού φησιν ἐν τῷ αὐτῷ ἰάμβῳ·

λιμῷ γένηται ξηρός· ἐν δὲ τῷ θυμῷ
φαρμακὸς ἀχθεὶς ἑπτάκις ῥαπισθείη.

1 θύμῳ Schneidewin    2 ὁ ante φ. del. Blomfield

**7** Tzetzes continues

And again in other places he says word for word:

it is necessary to make[1] him into a scapegoat

[1] Translation of the infinitive is doubtful and emendations are numerous (see Degani's fr. 27).

**8** Tzetzes continues

and to provide within his grasp dried figs, barley cake and cheese, such as scapegoats eat

**9** Tzetzes continues

for they have long been waiting for them,[1] open-mouthed,[2] holding fig branches as they do for scape-goats

[1] Assumed by some to be the poet's enemies, Bupalus and Athenis. [2] I.e., in eager anticipation.

**10** Tzetzes continues

And somewhere else he says in the same book of iambics:

(so that?, until?) he become withered from hunger, and led like a scapegoat may he be flogged seven times on his manhood[1]

[1] Many adopt Schneidewin's emendation (there is some evidence that θῦμος can mean 'penis'), but θυμῷ may be an ironic substitute for penis (see Degani's fr. 30).

**12** Tzetz. ad *Posthom.* 687, "θήπεον"

ἐθαύμαζον. τὸ θέμα θήπω. καὶ Ἱππῶναξ·

τούτοισι θηπέων τοὺς Ἐρυθραίων παῖδας
ὁ μητροκοίτης Βούπαλος σὺν Ἀρήτῃ
†καὶ ὑφέλξων τὸν δυσώνυμον ἄρτον.†

1 θήπων codd., corr. ten Brink        2 ὁ ματροκοίτης HV,
οὕς φησι μητροκοίτας L, corr. Masson        3 κνίζων ὑφέλξον
H, καὶ φελίζων L, ὑφέλξων V        δαρτόν Masson

**13** Ath. 11.495c-d = Eust. in Hom. *Od.* 5.244 (1531.57)

πέλλα ἀγγεῖον σκυφοειδὲς πυθμένα ἔχον πλατύτερον,
εἰς ὃ ἤμελγον τὸ γάλα . . . τοῦτο δὲ Ἱππῶναξ λέγει
πελλίδα·

ἐκ πελλίδος πίνοντες· οὐ γὰρ ἦν αὐτῇ
κύλιξ, ὁ παῖς γὰρ ἐμπεσὼν κατήραξε,

δῆλον οἶμαι ποιῶν ὅτι ποτήριον μὲν οὐκ ἦν, δι᾽ ἀπο-
ρίαν δὲ κύλικος ἐχρῶντο τῇ πελλίδι.

# HIPPONAX

**12**  Tzetzes on *Posthomerica*

θήπεον means 'they marveled.' The primary form is θήπω.
Cf. Hipponax:

> Bupalus, the mother-fucker with Arete,[1] fooling[2]
> with these words (by these means?) the Ery-
> thraeans,[3] preparing to draw back[4] his damnable
> foreskin[5]

[1] Presumably the name of Bupalus' mother.  [2] Tzetzes'
explanation of the verb makes little sense here. Hesychius glosses
θηπῶν with ἐξαπατῶν ('deceiving').  [3] Erythrae is on the
mainland opposite Chios. For a possible sexual allusion in the
name, as well as in Βούπαλος = Βού-φαλλος, see R. M. Rosen,
*TAPA* 118 (1988) 35-37.  [4] The future participle is difficult
and there are many emendations.  [5] Translating Masson's
emendation.

**13**  Athenaeus, *Scholars at Dinner*

πέλλα is a cup-shaped vessel with a rather broad base
which was used as a milk pail . . . Hipponax calls this
πελλίς:

> drinking (plural) from a pail; for she had no cup,
> since the slave had fallen on it and smashed it,

making it clear, I think, that it was not a drinking cup, but
that they used it for lack of a cup.

363

**14** Pergit Ath.

καὶ πάλιν·

ἐκ δὲ τῆς πέλλης
ἔπινον· ἄλλοτ' αὐτός, ἄλλοτ' Ἀρήτη
προύπινον.

**15** Choerob. *can.* (i.268.32 Hilgard) = Herodian. (ii.301.11 et 628.3 Lentz)

ὅτι δὲ καὶ τοῦ τάλας "τάλαντος" ἦν ἡ γενική, δηλοῖ ὁ Ἱππῶναξ εἰπών·

τί τῷ τάλαντι Βουπάλῳ συνοίκησας;

συνῴκησας NC, -οικήσας V, corr. Bergk

**16** Herodian. π. μον. λέξ. (ii.924.14 Lentz)

(ἐρῳδιός) λέγεται δὲ ἔσθ' ὅτε καὶ τρισυλλάβως, ὥσπερ καὶ τὸ παρ' Ἱππώνακτι·

ἐγὼ δὲ δεξιῷ παρ' Ἀρήτην
κνεφαῖος ἐλθὼν 'ρῳδιῷ κατηυλίσθην.

cf. *Epimer. in Hom.* (p. 743.18 Dyck)

1 παρὰ ῥητὴρ cod., corr. Schneidewin    2 ῥόδην συνηυλίσθην *Epimer.*

**14** Athenaeus continues

And again:

> they were drinking from the pail; now he and now
> Arete were drinking a toast

**15** Choeroboscus, *On the Canons of Theodosius*

And that also the genitive of τάλας was τάλαντος is clear from Hipponax who says:

> Why did you[1] cohabit with the wretched Bupalus?

[1] Perhaps Arete (cf. fr. 12).

**16** Herodian, *On Anomalous Words*

Sometimes ἐρῳδιός is trisyllabic, as the passage in Hipponax shows:

> with a heron on the right[1] I went to Arete in the dark
> and took up lodging

[1] I.e., as a favourable sign. Several sources associate the heron with Aphrodite.

**17** *Et. Gen.* λ 156 Adler-Alpers (p. 36 Calame)

λέγεται ἀρσενικῶς καὶ οὐδετέρως, ὁ λύχνος καὶ τὸ λύχνον. Ἱππῶναξ·

κύψασα γάρ μοι πρὸς τὸ λύχνον Ἀρήτη.

**19** Herodian. π. παθῶν ap. *Et. Gen.* A (Reitzenstein, *Index lect. in Acad. Rostock.* 1890/91, 7; p. 16 Calame)

ἀσκαρίζειν σημαίνει τὸ κινεῖσθαι. Ἱππῶναξ·

τίς ὀμφαλητόμος σε τὸν διοπλῆγα
ἔψησε κἀπέλουσεν ἀσκαρίζοντα;

**20** Choerob. in Hephaest. (p. 199.12 Consbruch)

περὶ δὲ τῶν ἀφώνων ἐστὶν εἰπεῖν ὅτι ἀσθενέστερά εἰσι μᾶλλον τῶν ἄλλων στοιχείων, καὶ εὑρέθη ποιοῦντα σπανίως κοινὴν ἐν αὐτοῖς τὸ πτ καὶ τὸ κτ, οἷον παρὰ τῷ ποιητῇ· "Αἰγυπτίη, τῇ πλεῖστα φέρει ζείδωρος ἄρουρα" (*Od.* 4.229). καὶ πάλιν παρὰ Ἱππώνακτι ἐν τῷ πρώτῳ ἰάμβων (ita Hoffmann pro τῷ τρόπῳ ἴαμβον):

δοκέων ἐκεῖνον τῇ βακτηρίῃ κόψαι.

ἐκτεῖνον cod., corr. Hörschelmann, ἰκτῖνον Maas (def. Medeiros)     βακτηρίᾳ cod., corr. Hoffmann, βατηρίῃ Knox

**17** *Etymologicum Genuinum*

There is both the masculine λύχνος and the neuter λύχνον. Cf. Hipponax:

> for Arete, having stooped over[1] for me towards the lamp[2]

[1] Probably a reference to the sexual position in which the woman is on her hands and knees or at least bent over.
[2] The lamp is frequently mentioned in erotic scenes.

**19** Herodian, *On Inflexions*

ἀσκαρίζειν means 'to move.' Cf. Hipponax:

> What navel-snipper[1] wiped and washed you as you squirmed about, you crack-brained creature?

[1] I.e., midwife.

**20** Choeroboscus on Hephaestion

Concerning mute consonants one can say that they are weaker than other consonants, and among them the combinations ππ and κτ are rarely found making a syllable either long or short, as in Homer: "Of Egypt where the fertile earth produces the greatest number (of medicines)." And again in Hipponax in the first book of his iambics:

> thinking to whack him with my (his) stick[1]

[1] Many adopt, perhaps rightly, Knox's emendation, primarily on the basis of Herodas 8.60 τῇ βατηρίῃ κό[ψω. But see Degani, *Studi* 245 f.

**21** Pergit Choerob.

καὶ πάλιν παρὰ τῷ αὐτῷ·

ἡμίεκτον αἰτεῖ τοῦ φάλεω κολάψαι ἑ.

κολάψαιε cod., dist. West, κολάψασα Knox, alii alia

**22** Tzetz. ad π. μέτρων (Anecd. Ox. iii.308.19 Cramer)

τὸ μέτρον τὸ Δωρικὸν παρέλειψα λήθῃ. δέχεται δὲ
πλεῖον τῶν ἄλλων ἰαμβικῶν μέτρων κατὰ τὴν β΄
χώραν ἢ καὶ δ΄ ἢ ϛ΄ σπονδεῖον, σπανιάκις δὲ καὶ
δάκτυλον ὡς ἰσόχρονον τῷ σπονδείῳ. Δωρικὸν Ἱπ-
πώνακτος·

{καὶ} τὴν ῥῖνα καὶ τὴν μύξαν ἐξαράξασα.

καὶ del. Schneidewin

**23** Prisc. de metr. Ter. (iii.426.22 Keil) ex Heliodoro (quae
praecedunt v. ad fr. 35)

in eodem:

τοὺς ἄνδρας τούτους ὀδύνη †πιαλλιρειτιαε†

iste iambus habet in secundo loco spondeum, et in ‹tertio
et in› quarto dactylum.

(Prisc.) ‹tertio et in› Bergk et Diehl

---

[1] The end of the citation contains several variant readings (see
Degani's fr. 11) and is hopelessly corrupt, but it seems likely that

**21** Choeroboscus continues

And again in the same poet:

> he asks eight obols[1] for pecking him[2] on his prick

[1] According to Pollux 9.62 ἡμίεκτον, lit. 'half a sixth (of a medimnus),' can also signify eight obols. Rather than an initial dactyl, as Choeroboscus assumes, the iota may be consonantalized.     [2] I have translated West's text, but the reading is highly uncertain. With Knox's emendation the subject is a woman.

**22** Tzetzes on *On Meter*

I forgot and omitted the Doric meter. More than other iambic meters it admits a spondee in the second, fourth, or sixth position and rarely a dactyl with the same time units as a spondee. A Dorian verse[1] of Hipponax:

> she, bashing her (his?) nose and knocking out the mucus[2]

[1] It seems that Tzetzes (wrongly) treated the final syllable of μύξαν as long.     [2] ῥίς can occasionally stand for 'penis' and μύξα for 'wick,' but I doubt that West (*Studies* 143) is right in seeing a connection with fr. 17.

**23** Priscian, *On the Meters of Terence*, citing Heliodorus in the same book:

> these men pain . . .[1]

That iambic verse has a spondee in the second position and a dactyl in the third and fourth.

we have a hexameter or partial hexameter in a choliambic poem (cf. fr. 35).

# IAMBIC POETRY

**24**  Erot. *lex. Hippocr.* σ 10 (p. 77.17 Nachmanson)

σαπρά· σεσηπότα, ὡς καὶ Ἱππῶναξ ἐν πρώτῳ ἰάμβων
(-ῳ v.l.) φησί·

μυδῶντ᾽ ἤδη
καὶ σαπρόν.

μαδῶντα δὴ codd., corr. et dist. Degani (μυδῶντα iam
Stephanus)

**25**  Tzetz. *exeg. Il.* A 25 (p. 83.25 Hermann) "ἐπὶ μῦθον
ἔτελλεν"

ὑπερβατόν. ἔστι δὲ καὶ τοῦτο Ἰωνικόν, ὥς φησι καὶ
Ἱππῶναξ·

"ἀπό σ᾽ ὀλέσειεν Ἄρτεμις."—"σὲ δὲ κὠπόλλων."

Sequitur fr. 47. Cf. Tzetz. ad fr. 70.7-8.

**26**  Ath. 7.304b

Ἱππῶναξ δέ, ὡς Λυσανίας ἐν τοῖς περὶ ἰαμβοποιῶν
παρατίθεται, φησίν·

ὁ μὲν γὰρ αὐτῶν ἡσυχῇ τε καὶ ῥύδην
θύνναν τε καὶ μυσσωτὸν ἡμέρας πάσας
δαινύμενος ὥσπερ Λαμψακηνὸς εὐνοῦχος

370

**24** Erotian, *Glossary on Hippocrates*

σαπρά means 'rotted,' as Hipponax says in his first book of iambics:

> already clammy and putrid[1]

[1] Probably of a corpse.

**25** Tzetzes, *Commentary on Iliad* ("laid a command upon him")

Transposition of words (i.e., tmesis). This is also an Ionic practice, since Hipponax says:

> "May Artemis damn you"—"And Apollo you."[1]

[1] Presumably uttered in turn by a female and a male. Some emend so as to remove the fifth-foot anapaest because Hephaestion (p. 17.5 Consbruch) says that choliambics do not admit a trisyllabic fifth foot. But Tzetzes (*Anecd. Ox.* iii.309.23 Cramer) explicitly refutes him, citing frr. 25, 40 and 42, although he does not realize that synizesis removes the anapaest in the last two.

**26** Athenaeus, *Scholars at Dinner*

And Hipponax, as Lysanias[1] mentions in his books on the iambic poets, says:

> For one of them, dining at his ease and lavishly every day on tuna and savoury sauce[2] like a eunuch from Lampsacus,[3] ate up his inheritance; as a result

371

κατέφαγε δὴ τὸν κλῆρον· ὥστε χρὴ σκάπτειν
5    πέτρας {τ'} ὀρείας, σῦκα μέτρια τρώγων
καὶ κρίθινον κόλλικα, δούλιον χόρτον.

2 μυττωτὸν codd., corr. Bergk        4 σκληρόν cod., corr.
Dalecampius        5 τ' del. Schweighäuser, γ' Marzullo

**26a** Ath. 14.645c

τοῦ δὲ ἀττανίτου Ἱππῶναξ ἐν τούτοις μνημονεύει·

οὐκ ἀτταγέας τε καὶ λαγοὺς καταβρύκων,
οὐ τηγανίτας σησάμοισι φαρμάσσων,
οὐδ' ἀττανίτας κηρίοισιν ἐμβάπτων.

cf. Ath. 9.388b (v. 1), Tzetz. (v. ad fr. 70.7-8)

1 ατται Ath. 645c, ἀτταγᾶς 388b, corr. Knox        λαγὼς
645c, λαγοὺς Tzetzes        διατρώγων 388b        2 τηγανίας
cod., corr. Casaubon

**27** Anon. π. βαρβ. καὶ σολοικ. (pp. 177 sq. Valckenaer,
      ed. Ammon.[2] 1822) = *Anecd. Gr.* ii.177 Villoison =
      anon. Mutin. (ed. Bühler, *MCr* 4 [1969] 11)

σολοίκους δὲ ἔλεγον οἱ παλαιοὶ τοὺς βαρβάρους. ὁ
γὰρ Ἀνακρέων φησί· "κοίμισον δὲ Ζεῦ σόλοικον
φθόγγον" (fr. 423 *PMG*). καὶ Ἱππῶναξ·

καὶ τοὺς σολοίκους ἢν λάβωσι περνᾶσι,
Φρύγας μὲν ἐς Μίλητον ἀλφιτεύσοντας.

cf. Eust. in Hom. *Il.* 2.867 (i.580.2 V.d.Valk)

1 ἵν' ἐθέλουσι Eust.        2 εἰς codd., corr. Bergk

372

he has to dig a rocky hillside, munching on cheap[4]
figs and coarse barley bread, fodder for slaves.

[1] An Alexandrian scholar of the 2nd cent. B.C. Athenaeus is
here citing passages on the tuna as a delicacy.        [2] See note 4
on Ananius fr. 5.        [3] Lampsacus is a town in the Troad on the
Hellespont. Why a eunuch from this area should be mentioned is
unclear.        [4] Or "a few."

**26a** Athenaeus, *Scholars at Dinner*

And Hipponax mentions the waffle in these verses:

not champing on partridges and hares, not season-
ing pancakes with sesame, and not dipping waffles
in honey[1]

[1] Many consider this a continuation of fr. 26, with or without
an intervening lacuna.

**27** Anonymous, *On Non-Greek Words and Solecisms*

The ancients called barbarians 'soloeci.' For Anacreon
says: "Zeus, put to rest solecian speech." And Hipponax
says:

and if they catch the soloeci they sell them, Phry-
gians[1] to Miletus to grind barley

[1] Often a generic term for slaves, but in view of $\mu\acute{\epsilon}\nu$ the poem
probably went on to list at least one other non-Greek race.

# IAMBIC POETRY

**28** Tzetz. ad *Antehom.* 168 (Morelli, *Iliacum carmen* p. 8
+ ten Brink, *Philologus* 6 [1851] 36)

παράδειγμα δέ σοι δασέως ἐκτείνοντος ἐξ Ἱππώνακ-
τος ἐν παραθήσω, ἐκ τῶν κατὰ Μιμνῆ τοῦ ζωγράφου
χωλιάμβων, τὰ ἐξ ἔθους (v.l. ἑτέρων) παραδείγματα
εἰακώς·

    Μιμνῆ κατωμόχανε, μηκέτι γράψῃς
    ὄφιν τριήρεος ἐν πολυζύγῳ τοίχῳ
    ἀπ' ἐμβόλου φεύγοντα πρὸς κυβερνήτην·
    αὕτη γάρ ἐστι συμφορά τε καὶ κληδών,
5    νικύρτα καὶ σάβαννι, τῷ κυβερνήτῃ,
    ἢν αὐτὸν ὄφις τὠντικνήμιον δάκῃ.

cf. Tzetz. *exeg. Il.* A 273 (Masson, *PP* 5 [1950] 74 sq.), Tzetz.
in Lyc. 425 (p. 156.22 Scheer); (v. 6) Tzetz. in Lyc. 234 (p. 107.20)
et in *Epist.* 1 (p. 158.14 Leone)

1 vv.ll. κατωμήχανε, κακομήχανε, sim.    2 ὄφιν West
    4 ἔσται Bergk    5 vv.ll. σάμ(μ)αννι, σαβαννί,
σάβωνι, σάμαννι: σαρωνί (cf. fr. 82.3) Tarditi coll. Hesych.
σάρων· λάγνος. τινὲς δὲ τὸ γυναικεῖον    6 ὄφις Bergk
δήκη Tzetz. in Lyc. 234 cod. H (cf. *Et. Mag.* 260.56 δήκω τὸ
δάκνω), δάκνῃ Hermann

**29a** Phot. *lex.* ined.

χύτραν· καὶ Ἰώνων τινές, ὥσπερ Ἀρχίλοχος (fr. 295a).
Ἱππῶναξ κύθραν·

    ἐβορβόρυζε δ' ὥστε κύθρος ἔτνεος.

ἐβορβόριζεν et ἔτνε cod., corr. West

374

**28** Tzetzes on *Antehomerica*

I shall provide you with one example of an aspirate that lengthens [i.e., ὄφις v. 6] from the choliambics of Hipponax against the painter Mimnes, omitting the customary examples:

> Mimnes, you who gape open all the way to the shoulders,[1] don't paint again on a trireme's many-benched side a serpent that runs from the ram to the helmsman; for this is a dangerous omen for the helmsman, you slave born of a slave[2] and . . . ,[3] if the serpent bites him on the shin.[4]

[1] An hyperbole for εὐρύπρωκτος 'wide-arsed.' [2] A translation of Hesychius' gloss νικύρτας· δουλέκδουλος. [3] Neither σάβαννι nor any of the variant readings occurs elsewhere. [4] Perhaps a complete poem.

**29a** Photius, *Lexicon*

χύτραν: also some of the Ionians, such as Archilochus. κύθραν in Hipponax:

> (his stomach) gurgled like a pot of soup

**30** Tzetz. ad π. μέτρων (*Anecd. Ox.* iii.308.26 Cramer); quae praecedunt v. ad fr. 22

δέχονται καὶ τρισυλλάβους εἰς ς′, πλὴν τοὺς ἀπὸ
βραχείας ἀρχομένους, τὸν χορεῖόν φημι καὶ τὸν ἀνά-
παιστον, ὡς ὁ Ἱππῶναξ·

οὔ μοι δικαίως μοιχὸς ἁλῶναι δοκεῖ
Κριτίης ὁ Χῖος ἐν †τῷ κατωτικῷ† δούμῳ.

1 δοκέει codd., corr. Fick      2 τῷ κατωτικῷ ut glossema secl. Masson      δούλῳ codd., corr. Masson

**32**

Ἑρμῆ, φίλ᾽ Ἑρμῆ, Μαιαδεῦ, Κυλλήνιε,
ἐπεύχομαί τοι, κάρτα γὰρ κακῶς ῥιγῶ
καὶ βαμβαλύζω . . .
δὸς χλαῖναν Ἱππώνακτι καὶ κυπασσίσκον
5    καὶ σαμβαλίσκα κἀσκερίσκα καὶ χρυσοῦ
στατῆρας ἑξήκοντα τοὐτέρου τοίχου.

**30**  Tzetzes on *On Meters*

They admit also words of three syllables in the sixth position except for those beginning with a short, I mean the tribrach and the anapaest, as Hipponax shows:

> I don't think that Critias the Chian was justly apprehended as an adulterer in the . . . assembly of women[1]

[1] δοῦμος is a Phrygian word which according to Hesychius s.v. δοῦλος (corr. Wackernagel) denotes a gathering of women (συν-έλευσιν τῶν γυναικῶν). West suggests something like κατώγεῳ τῷ ('underground') for the preceding corruption to account for Tzetzes' citation, τῷ δούμῳ being a trisyllabic word-group.

**32**

> Hermes, dear Hermes, son of Maia, Cyllenian,[1] I pray to you, for I am shivering violently and terribly and my teeth are chattering . . . Give Hipponax a cloak, tunic, sandals, felt shoes[2] and 60 gold staters[3] on the other side.[4]

[1] Cf. fr. 3.     [2] The force of the diminutives for tunic, sandals and shoes is perhaps to minimize their value for humorous effect.     [3] Value unknown. The numeral is presumably generic (cf. fr. 36.3).     [4] Variously interpreted. Perhaps best explained as referring to the other side, i.e., scale pan of the balance. In Tzetzes' text the phrase is glossed with τοῦ νερτέρου μέρους, "the lower part" (of the scales?). If this is correct, Hipponax is in effect asking that his accounts be balanced. Or does he hope to dig through to the other side of a wall and steal the objects?

Prisc. *de metr. Terent.* (iii.428.24 Keil) ex Heliodoro

Hipponactem etiam ostendit Heliodorus iambos et choliambos confuse protulisse: "Ἑρμῆ—ῥιγῶ." nam ῥιγῶ spondeus est.

Tzetz. in Lyc. 855 (quae praecedunt v. ad fr. 34)

ἢ χρεία σοι καὶ ἑτέρας μαρτυρίας; ἄκουσον. "ὦ φίλ᾽ Ἑρμῆ—Κυλλήνιε," καὶ μετά τινά φησιν "δὸς—τοίχου."

confuse Plut. *Sto. paradox.* 6.1058d

ὁ δ᾽ ἐκ τῆς Στοᾶς βοῶν μέγα καὶ κεκραγώς "ἐγὼ μόνος εἰμὶ βασιλεύς, ἐγὼ μόνος εἰμὶ πλούσιος," ὁρᾶται πολλάκις ἐπ᾽ ἀλλοτρίαις θύραις λέγων "δὸς χλαῖναν Ἱππώνακτι, κάρτα—βαμβαλύζω."

1 Ἑρμῆ φίλ᾽ Prisc., ὦ φίλ᾽ Tzetzes    Μαιαδεῦ Prisc., Μαιάδευσος, -δερος, -δος codd. Tzetz.    3 βαμβακύζω codd. Plut., corr. Schneidewin; cf. fr. adesp. iamb. 60    4 κυπασίσκον codd., corr. Gaisford

**34** Tzetz. in Lyc. 855 (p. 277.10 Scheer)

ἀσκέραι δὲ κυρίως τὰ ἐν τοῖς ποσὶ πιλία ἤτοι ἀρτάρια λέγονται. ὦ Λύκοφρον, γίνωσκε ὅτι τὰς μὲν λέξεις ἀπὸ Αἰσχύλου κλέπτεις, ἐξ Ἱππώνακτος δὲ πλέον. ἐπιλήσμων δὲ ὢν ἢ μὴ νοῶν ταύτας ἄλλην ἄλλως τίθησιν· ἀλλ᾽ ἀναμνήσω τοῦτον ἐγὼ τὸν σοφὸν ποιητήν. οὐκ οἶσθα, ὦ Λύκαφρον, ὅτι, ὅτε σὺ τὴν Ἱπ-

Priscian, *On the Meters of Terence*

Heliodorus has shown that Hipponax also produced a mixture of iambic and choliambic lines: "Hermes—I am shivering." For ῥιγῶ is a spondee.

Tzetzes on Lycophron

Or do you need additional proof? Listen. "Dear Hermes—Cyllenian," and after a bit he says "Give—side."

Plutarch, *The Stoics talk more paradoxically than the poets*

The Stoic philosopher, shouting in a loud voice and crying "I alone am king, I alone am rich," is often seen at other people's doors saying "Give a cloak to Hipponax, for I am shivering violently and terribly and my teeth are chattering."

**34**  Tzetzes on Lycophron

ἀσκέραι properly mean felt shoes or ἀρτάρια. Lycophron, realize that you are stealing words from Aeschylus, but more so from Hipponax. Either from forgetfulness or ignorance of these words he uses another wrongly; but I shall remind this clever poet. You did not know, Lycophron, that

πώνακτος κατεῖχες βίβλον, κατόπιν σου ἑστηκὼς ἐγὼ
ἑώρων σε τὰς αὐτοῦ λέξεις ἀναλεγόμενον. καὶ τὸ
ἀσκέρας δὲ ἐκεῖσε εὕρηκας, καὶ οὕτω τέθεικας μὴ
προ‹σ›σχὼν (corr. West) μηδ᾽ εἰς νοῦν ἔχων τὰ ῥή-
ματα. ἀλλ᾽ ἄκουε πῶς φησιν Ἱππῶναξ, καὶ μάθε
ὅτι ἀσκέραι οὐ τὰ ὑποδήματα ἀλλὰ πιλία ἤτοι τὰ
ἀρτάρια λέγονται, ὡς καὶ Ἱππῶναξ·

> ἐμοὶ γὰρ οὐκ ἔδωκας οὔτε κω χλαῖναν
> δασεῖαν ἐν χειμῶνι φάρμακον ῥίγεος,
> οὔτ᾽ ἀσκέρῃσι τοὺς πόδας δασείῃσιν
> ἔκρυψας, ὥς μοι μὴ χίμετλα ῥήγνυται.

ἔγνως ὅτι διὰ τὸ εἰπεῖν δασείας τὰς ἀσκέρας τὰ
ἀρτάριά φησιν;

1 χωλεύαν, χωδαῖνε, χλαῖναν, τὴν χλαῖναν codd., corr.
Schneidewin (πω iam Scaliger)    4 μή μοι codd., corr. Har-
tung caesurae causa    ῥήγνυται codd. dett. (ῥίγνυται cod.
H), γίγνηται codd. potiores

**35** Prisc. *de metr. Terent.* (iii.426.16 Keil) ex Heliodoro

Heliodorus metricus ait: Ἱππῶναξ πολλὰ παρέβη τῶν
ὡρισμένων ἐν τοῖς ἰάμβοις, hoc est: Hipponax multa
praeteriit, id est praetermisit, praefinita in iambis. Hip-
ponax in primo:

> ἐρέω γὰρ οὕτω· "Κυλλήνιε Μαιάδος Ἑρμῆ."

iste enim versus cum sit choliambus, in quarto loco et

when you were holding the book of Hipponax I was stand-
ing behind you and watching you as you read his words.
You found ἀσκέραι there and so you used it, without pay-
ing attention or keeping in mind what was being said. But
listen to what Hipponax says and know that ἀσκέραι do
not mean sandals but felt shoes or ἀρτάρια, as Hipponax
shows:

> For you haven't yet given me a thick cloak[1] as a
> remedy against the cold in winter nor have you cov-
> ered my feet with thick felt shoes, so that my chil-
> blains not burst.

Do you realize that by calling the ἀσκέραι thick he means
ἀρτάρια?

[1] A thick cloak was the prize awarded to the victor in the games
at Pallene in honour of Hermes (see the proverb cited under Sim.
fr. 514 in Campbell's Loeb edition and the app. crit. to Degani's
fr. 43). Some, perhaps rightly, combine frr. 32 and 34

**35** Priscian, *On the Meters of Terence*, citing Heliodorus

Heliodorus the metrician says: "Hipponax over-stepped
many of the boundaries in his iambics," i.e., Hipponax
passed over, that is neglected, many of the limitations in
his iambics. Cf. Hipponax in his first book:

> for I'll speak thus: "Cyllenian Hermes, son of Maia"[1]

For although that verse is a choliambus, it has dactyls in

# IAMBIC POETRY

quinto habuit dactylos, cum in utroque debuerit a brevi in-
cipiens pes poni.

οὕτω· Κυλλήνιε Putschen (vv.ll. in codicibus: v. Degani fr. 10)

**36**  Tzetz. in Ar. *Pl.* 87 (p. 30ᵇ1 Massa Positano)

τυφλὸν δὲ τὸν Πλοῦτόν φησιν ἐξ Ἱππώνακτος τοῦτο
σφετερισάμενος. φησὶ γὰρ οὕτως Ἱππῶναξ·

> ἐμοὶ δὲ Πλοῦτος—ἔστι γὰρ λίην τυφλός—
> ἐς τῷκί᾽ ἐλθὼν οὐδάμ᾽ εἶπεν "Ἱππῶναξ,
> δίδωμί τοι μνέας ἀργύρου τριήκοντα
> καὶ πόλλ᾽ ἔτ᾽ ἄλλα·" δείλαιος γὰρ τὰς φρένας.

1 λίαν cod., corr. Herwerden    3 μνᾶς cod., corr. Meister
ἀργυρίου cod., corr. Bergk

**37**  Choerob. in Hephaest. (p. 195.22 Consbruch); quae
praecedunt v. ad frr. 43-44

εἶτα πάλιν ὁ αὐτός·

> ἐκέλευε βάλλειν καὶ λεύειν Ἱππώνακτα,

τὴν λευ ἐν τετάρτῳ ποδί· λεύειν δέ φησιν ἀντὶ τοῦ
λιθοβολεῖν.

HIPPONAX

the fourth and fifth positions, whereas a foot beginning
with a short syllable ought to have been placed in both
positions.

1 Both here and in fr. 23 the mixture of rhythms is for comic
effect. We can assume that the surrounding verses were normal
choliambics.

**36** Tzetzes on Aristophanes, *Plutus*

Aristophanes says that Plutus is blind, borrowing this from
Hipponax. For Hipponax speaks as follows:

Wealth—for he is exceedingly blind[1]— never came
into my house and said: "Hipponax, I'm giving you
30 minas of silver[2] and much else besides." For he
has a coward's mind.[3]

1 After Aristophanes the blindness of Plutus is a common-
place.    2 Value unknown. The numeral is generic as in fr.
32.6.    3 Some take the last phrase to mean that Plutus is
dim-witted.

**37** Choeroboscus on Hephaestion

Then again the same poet says:

gave orders to pelt and stone Hipponax,

with λευ in the fourth foot.[1] He says λεύειν instead of
λιθοβολεῖν ('pelt with stones').

1 The line is cited to illustrate the correption of the diphthong
ευ in λεύειν, but there may be the same correption in ἐκέλευε,
since initial tribrach is much commoner than an anapaest.

**38**  Tzetz. in Lyc. 690 (p. 227.25 Scheer)

ἡ δὲ λέξις ὁ πάλμυς ἐστὶν Ἰώνων, καὶ χρῆται ταύτῃ
Ἱππῶναξ λέγων·

> ὦ Ζεῦ, πάτερ ⟨Ζεῦ⟩, θεῶν Ὀλυμπίων πάλμυ,
> τί μοὐκ ἔδωκας χρυσόν, ἀργύρου †πάλμυ;

1 Ζεῦ alterum add. Meineke          2 πάλμυν codd. PH

**39**  Tzetz. ad π. μέτρων (*Anecd. Ox.* iii.308.30 Cramer);
    praecedit fr. 30

καὶ πάλιν (ita Meineke pro καὶ πᾶ, sim.)·

> κακοῖσι δώσω τὴν πολύστονον ψυχήν,
> ἢν μὴ ἀποπέμψῃς ὡς τάχιστά μοι κριθέων
> μέδιμνον, ὡς ἂν ἀλφίτων ποιήσωμαι
> κυκεῶνα πίνειν φάρμακον πονηρίης.

3 ἄλφιτον codd. (def. Degani ut dupl. accus.), corr. Bergk
4 πίνων codd., corr. Ahrens          πονηρίης A, πονηρίοις BC

**38** Tzetzes on Lycophron

The word πάλμυς belongs to the Ionians and Hipponax uses it when he says:

> Zeus, father Zeus, sultan[1] of the Olympian gods,
> why have you not given me gold, . . .?[2]

[1] See n. 1 on fr. 3.    [2] The ending, 'sultan of silver,' gives implausible sense and both words have been variously emended. If the last word is an instance of dittography, it may have replaced something totally dissimilar.

**39** Tzetzes on *On Meters*

And again:[1]

> I will surrender my grieving soul to an evil end,[2] if you do not send me a bushel of barley as quickly as you can, so that I may make a potion[3] from the groats to drink as a cure for my suffering.

[1] Tzetzes wrongly assumes that κριθέων in v. 2 is trisyllabic.
[2] Apparently a way of saying that he will lose all hope and commit suicide.    [3] On κυκεών see R. M. Rosen, *AJP* 108 (1987) 416-26.

**40** Tzetz. ad π. μέτρων (*Anecd. Ox.* iii.308.30 Cramer);
quae praecedunt v. ad frr. 25 et 42

καὶ πάλιν (ita Meineke pro καὶ πᾶσα)·

{Ἀθηνᾶ} Μαλὶς †κονισκε†, καί με δεσπότεω
    βεβροῦ
λαχόντα λίσσομαί σε μὴ ῥαπίζεσθαι.

1 Ἀθηνᾶ del. Bergk, Ἀθηναίη / Μαλὶς dub. Bergk (prob.
Degani)    ]νισκε sscr. χαιρε A, κονὶς κελαῖρε B, κονίσκε C,
fort. μ᾿ ὄνισκε West    δεσπότεα codd., corr. Schneidewin

**41** *Et. Gen.* (p. 16 Calame)

δεῖ γινώσκειν ὅτι ἀρειῶ ἀρειᾷ· σημαίνει δὲ τὸ ἀπειλῶ,
ὡς παρ᾽ Ἱππώνακτι·

καὶ νῦν ἀρειᾷ σύκινόν με ποιῆσαι,

τουτέστιν ἀπειλεῖ σύκινόν με ποιῆσαι.

cf. *Et. Sym.* cod. V (Gaisford ad *Et. Mag.* 139.36) = Herodian.
(i.454.11 Lentz)

ἀρειᾷς (et ἀπειλεῖς) *Et. Sym.* (prob. Degani)

**42** Tzetz. ad π. μέτρων (*Anecd. Ox.* iii.310.19 Cramer);
quae praecedunt v. ad fr. 25

καὶ πάλιν (ita Meineke pro καὶ πᾶ)·

†τέαρε[. . . . .]δεύειε† τὴν ἐπὶ Σμύρνης
ἴθι διὰ Λυδῶν παρὰ τὸν Ἀττάλεω τύμβον

**40** Tzetzes on *On Meters*

And again:[1]

> O Malis,[2] help me (?), and since it is my lot to have
> a demented[3] master I beg of you that I not get a
> beating.

[1] Tzetzes wrongly assumes that -πότεω is trisyllabic.
[2] Hesychius glosses Μαλίς with ᾿Αθηνᾶ and Malis may be a Lydian goddess identified with Athena.     [3] βεβρός appears elsewhere only in Hesychius who glosses it with ψυχρός ('cold-hearted') and τετυφωμένος ('demented').

**41** *Etymologicum Genuinum*

It should be realized that ἀρειῶ means 'I threaten,' as in Hipponax:

> and now he (she?) threatens to make me a weakling[1]

[1] σύκινον is literally 'of a fig tree,' but is often glossed with ἀσθενής ('weak'), ἀχρεῖος ('useless') etc. because of the poor quality of the wood. Without a context its precise significance cannot be determined here.

**42** Tzetzes on *On Meters*

And again:[1]

> . . .[2] go along the road to Smyrna through Lydia past
> the tomb of Attalus[3] and the gravestone of Gyges[4]

καὶ σῆμα Γύγεω καὶ †μεγάστρυ† στήλην
καὶ μνῆμα Τωτος, Μυτάλιδι πάλμυδος,
5    πρὸς ἥλιον δύνοντα γαστέρα τρέψας.

1 ὅδενε Schneidewin     2 ἰθὺ Knox, rec. West (cf. *Studies*
86)     3 γήγεω codd., corr. Cramer     Σεσώστριος
Bergk, rec. West (μεγάστρυ ex gloss. μεγάλου ad μυτάλιδι, cf.
Hesych. μυττάλυτα· μεγάλου)     4 τ' ὦτος codd., corr.
Bergk (Τῶτος vel Τωτὸς)     Μυταλίδεω Masson

**43** Choerob. in Hephaest. (p. 195.15 Consbruch)

ὁμοίως καὶ τὴν ευ (δίφθογγον) εὑρίσκομεν ποιοῦσαν
κοινήν, οἷον ἐν τῷ πρώτῳ ἰάμβῳ Ἱππώνακτος ἔνθα
φησί·

    μάκαρ ὅτις < > θηρεύει †πρήσας.

τὴν ρευ ἐν τετάρτῳ ποδὶ συνέστειλε.

μάκηρ' ὅτις U, μακάριος ὅστις K, corr. Perrotta     <τι>
θηρεύει μὴ τηρήσας e.g. West

**44** Pergit Choeroboscus

καὶ πάλιν ὁ αὐτὸς ἐν δευτέρῳ ποδὶ τὴν ευ·

    καί τοί γ' εὔωνον αὐτὸν εἰ θέλεις δώσω.

καί τι γ' εὔγονον U, καίτοι γ' εὔωνον K, corr. Latte

388

and the column of . . .⁵ and the memorial of Tos,⁶ sultan at Mytalis,⁷ turning your belly towards the setting sun.

¹ Tzetzes wrongly assumes that -άλεω (v. 2) is trisyllabic.
² The poet is giving directions to someone travelling from the interior to Smyrna on the coast. The first word has been variously explained or emended, some treating it as a proper noun. If the second word is emended to ὅδευε ('travel'), it will be necessary to read Knox's ἰθὺ ('straight') in v. 2.     ³ Brother of king Alyattes, the father of Croesus.     ⁴ Cf. Arch. fr. 19. The schol. on Nic. *Th.* 633 says that Hipponax mentions the gravestone of Gyges in his first book.     ⁵ For the Sesostris of Bergk's emendation cf. Hdt. 2.106.     ⁶ Person unknown.     ⁷ Place unknown (or with Masson's genitive, person unknown).

## 43 Choeroboscus on Hephaestion

Similarly we find the diphthong ευ treated as either long or short, as in the first book of Hipponax's iambics where he says:

blessed is he who hunts . . .

He has shortened ρευ in the fourth foot.

## 44 Choeroboscus continues

And again the same poet shortens ευ in the second foot:

and if you like I'll give him to you cheap

IAMBIC POETRY

**47** Tzetz. *exeg. Il.* A 25 (p. 84.1 Hermann); quae praecedunt v. ad fr. 25

καὶ ἀλλαχοῦ·

παρ' ᾧ σὺ λευκόπεπλον ἡμέρην μείνας
πρὸς μὲν κυνήσεις τὸν Φλυησίων Ἑρμῆν.

2 κυνήσειν codd., corr. Welcker        "Φλυησίων obscurum, cf. Hesych. Φλυήσιος· ὁ Ἑρμῆς, unde possis τὸν Φλυήσιον πάλμυν" West        Φλυήσιον < > / Ἑρμῆν Degani

**48** Ath. 3.78b = Eust. in Hom. *Od.* 24.341 (1964.14 sqq.)

Φερένικος δὲ ὁ ἐποποιός, Ἡρακλεώτης δὲ γένος, ἀπὸ
Συκῆς τῆς Ὀξύλου θυγατρὸς προσαγορευθῆναι (τὴν
συκῆν)· Ὄξυλον γὰρ τὸν Ὀρείου Ἁμαδρυάδι τῇ ἀδελ
φῇ μιγέντα μετ' ἄλλων γεννῆσαι Καρύαν, Βάλανον,
Κράνειαν, Μορέαν, Αἴγειρον, Πτελέαν, Ἄμπελον,
Συκῆν, καὶ ταύτας Ἁμαδρυάδας νύμφας καλεῖσθαι
καὶ ἀπ' αὐτῶν πολλὰ τῶν δένδρων προσαγορεύεσθαι.
ὅθεν καὶ τὸν Ἱππώνακτα φάναι

συκῆν μέλαιναν, ἀμπέλου κασιγνήτην.

μελαίνης dub. Degani, cl. Babr. 19.1 μελαίνης ἀμπέλου

**49** P. Berol. 12605 (ostr., III a.c.), ed. Wilamowitz, *Sitz.-
Ber. preuss. Akad.* (1918) 739 sqq.

ὧρος· ἐνιαυτός. "ἐννέωροι γὰρ τοί γε" (*Od.* 11.311).
Ἱππώνακτος·

**47** Tzetzes, *Commentary on Iliad*

And elsewhere:

> after awaiting at his side the dawn of white-robed
> day you will make obeisance to Hermes of the
> Phlyesians[1]

[1] Not attested elsewhere.

**48** Athenaeus, *Scholars at Dinner*

Pherenicus the epic poet and a Heracleot by birth says
that the fig tree got its name from Syke, the daughter of
Oxylus; for he says that Oxylus, the son of Oreius, had
intercourse with his sister Hamadryas and begat among
others Carya (hazel), Balanus (walnut), Craneia (cornel),
Morea (mulberry), Aegeirus (poplar), Ptelea (elm), Am-
pelus (vine), and Syke (fig tree), that these are called
Hamadryad nymphs, and that many trees got their names
from them. Hence, he states, Hipponax spoke of

> the black fig tree, sister of the vine[1]

[1] For the figure of speech cf. frr. 103.10 and 144 (also Aesch.
*Agam.* 494 f., *Septem* 494). Elsewhere it is rare.

**49** Potsherd

ὧρος means 'year.' "For nine years old" (*Od.* 11.311). Cf.
Hipponax:

πονηρὸς [            ].·[. . .].οι πᾴντας
Ἀσωποδώρου παῖδα κ[

1 πονηρὸς [ὥρους Wilamowitz

**50** Strabo 14.1.4 (quae praecedunt v. ad Callini frr. 2-2a)

Σμύρνα δ᾽ ἦν Ἀμαζὼν ἡ κατασχοῦσα τὴν Ἔφεσον,
ἀφ᾽ ἧς τοὔνομα καὶ τοῖς ἀνθρώποις καὶ τῇ πόλει, ὡς
καὶ ἀπὸ Σισύρβης Σισυρβῖταί τινες τῶν Ἐφεσίων
ἐλέγοντο. καὶ τόπος δέ τις τῆς Ἐφέσου Σμύρνα ἐκα-
λεῖτο, ὡς δηλοῖ Ἱππῶναξ·

οἴκει δ᾽ ὄπισθε τῆς πόλιος †ἐν Σμύρνῃ
μεταξὺ Τρηχέης τε καὶ Λεπρῆς Ἀκτῆς.

ἐκαλεῖτο γὰρ Λεπρὴ μὲν ἀκτὴ ὁ Πριὼν ὁ ὑπερκείμενος
τῆς νῦν πόλεως, ἔχων μέρος τοῦ τείχους αὐτῆς· τὰ
γοῦν ὄπισθεν τοῦ Πριῶνος κτήματα ἔτι νῦν λέγεται ἐν
τῇ Ὀπισθολεπρίᾳ. Τραχεῖα δ᾽ ἐκαλεῖτο ἡ ὑπὲρ τὸν
Κορησσὸν παρώρειος. ἡ δὲ πόλις ἦν τὸ παλαιὸν περὶ
τὸ Ἀθήναιον τὸ νῦν ἔξω τῆς πόλεως ὂν κατὰ τὴν
καλουμένην Ὑπέλαιον· ὥστε ἡ Σμύρνα ἦν κατὰ τὸ νῦν
γυμνάσιον, ὄπισθεν μὲν τῆς νῦν πόλεως, μεταξὺ δὲ
Τρηχέης τε καὶ Λεπρῆς Ἀκτῆς.

1 ὤκει codd., corr. Schneidewin     ἐπὶ vel ἐν ⟨τῇ⟩ prop.
West     2 Τρηχείης codd., corr. Knox

bad . . . all the son of Asopodorus . . .[1]

[1] It must be assumed that Hipponax used some form of ὧρος 'year.' West suggests that the sense may have been: "may misfortune befall the son of Asopodorus all his years."

## 50 Strabo, *Geography*

Smyrna was an Amazon who took possession of Ephesus and both the people and the city derived their name from her, just as some of the Ephesians were called Sisyrbitae after Sisyrbe. And also a certain place in Ephesus was called Smyrna, as Hipponax makes clear:

> he (she) lived behind the city in Smyrna between Tracheia[1] and Lepra Acte.[2]

For Lepra Acte was the name given to Prion[3] which lies above the present city and contains a portion of the city wall. At any rate the property behind Prion is still to the present day said to be in Opistholepria (Behind Lepra). And the district on the side of the mountain above Coressus was called Tracheia. In ancient times the city was round the Athenaeum which is now outside the city opposite what is called the Hypelaeus, with the result that Smyrna was opposite the present gymnasium, behind the present city, but between Tracheia and Lepra Acte.

[1] Lit., 'Rugged (Height).'    [2] Lit., 'Scabby Height.'
[3] The precise form is uncertain. The MSS of Strabo record both Πριών and Πρηών and Pausanias 7.5.10 has Πίων.

**51** Harpocr. s.v. μάλθη (p. 169 Keaney)

ὁ μεμαλαγμένος κηρός. Δημοσθένης ἐν τῷ κατὰ Στεφάνου (46.11). Ἱππῶναξ·

ἔπειτα μάλθη τὴν τρόπιν παραχρίσας.

τρόπην et τρόπιν codd.

**52** Schol. Plat. *Gorg.* 494b (p. 157 Greene) = Schol. marg. in Olympiod. ad loc. (p. 157.25 Westerink)

χαραδριὸς ὄρνις τις ὃς ἅμα τῷ ἐσθίειν ἐκκρίνει· εἰς ὃν ἀποβλέψαντες, ὡς λόγος, οἱ ἰκτεριῶντες ῥᾷον ἀπαλλάττονται. ὅθεν καὶ ἐγκρύπτουσιν αὐτὸν οἱ πιπράσκοντες, ἵνα μὴ προῖκα ὠφελῶνται οἱ κάμνοντες.

καί μιν καλύπτει· μῶν χαραδριὸν περνάς;

ὥς φησιν Ἱππῶναξ.

cf. schol. Ar. *Av.* 266d (p. 47 Holwerda), *Sud.* iv.787.10 Adler

μιν schol. Plat., μὴν schol. Ar. et *Suda*      καλύπτη (καλύπτει codd. G et B) *Suda*, καλύπτει schol. Plat. et Ar., καλύπτεις Ruhnken, καλύπτεαι West      ὡς pro μῶν schol. Ar.      περνᾷς *Suda*

**53** *Et. Gen.* (p. 25 Calame) = *Et. Mag.* 334.1 = *Et. Sym.* (Gaisford ad *Et. Mag.* 334.1) = Zonaras (p. 706 T.)

ἐμβιβάξαντες· παρὰ Ἱππώνακτι,

**51** Harpocration, *Lexicon of the Ten Attic Orators*

μάλθη = softened wax. Cf. Demosthenes *On the Crown* and Hipponax:

then smearing the keel with pitch[1]

[1] μάλθη, here only in a nautical context, is presumably a mixture of wax and pitch. The imagery may be sexual: see Henderson 145 f., 164.

**52** Scholiast on Plato, *Gorgias*

χαραδριός is a bird which defecates while it eats. If those suffering from jaundice look upon it, as the story goes, they gain relief more easily. Consequently those who sell it keep it covered, so that patients may not derive benefit free of cost.

and he keeps it covered; not selling a plover, is he?

as Hipponax says.

**53** *Etymologicum Genuinum*

ἐμβιβάξαντες, in Hipponax,

IAMBIC POETRY

ἀλλ' αὐτίκ' ἀλλήλοισιν ἐμβαβάξαντες,

ἀντὶ τοῦ ἐμβοήσαντες. ἀπὸ τοῦ βάζω βάξω, *βιβάξω,
*βιβάξας *βιβάξαντος, καὶ ἐμβιβάξαντες.

ἐμβιβάξαντες Etym., corr. Schneider

**54** *Et. Gen.* (p. 35 Calame) = *Et. Mag.* 539.1 (ex
Herodiano; ii.803.11 Lentz) = *Et. Gud.* (col. 347.27
Sturz) = *Epimer. in Hom.* (p. 476.72 Dyck) = Zonaras
(p. 1258 T.)

καὶ ῥηματικὸν ὄνομα κριγή, ὡς παρ' Ἱππώνακτος,
οἷον

κρίγη δὲ νεκρῶν ἄγγελός τε καὶ κῆρυξ.

**56** Pollux 6.19

καὶ σίφωνα μὲν ὅτῳ ἐγεύοντο (τὸν νέον οἶνον) Ἱπ-
πῶναξ εἴρηκεν·

σίφωνι λεπτῷ τοὐπίθημα τετρήνας.

τέτρηνας codd., corr. Salmasius

**57** Pollux 10.75

καὶ ὁ σάκος ἐπὶ τοῦ τρυγοίπου εἰρημένος, καὶ ὁ
ὑλιστήρ. Ἱππῶναξ δέ φησι·

στάζουσιν ὥσπερ †ἐκ τροποίιον† σάκκος.

ἐκ τροποίιον, ὥσπερεὶ τροπηίον codd., ἐκτροπηίιον Sal-
masius (rec. West)

396

but straightway yammering at one another,

instead of 'shouting.' From βάζω, βάξω, βιβάξω, βιβά-
ξας βιβάξαντος, and ἐμβιβάξαντες.[1]

[1] The sources have confused the rare βαβάζω with the com-
mon βιβάζω. Cf. Arch. fr. 297.

## 54 Etymologicum Genuinum

There is also a verbal noun κριγή, as in Hipponax:

a screech owl,[1] messenger and herald of the dead

[1] There is disagreement on the accentuation of κριγη. It
seems probable from a gloss in Hesychius s.v. that κρίγη is a
screech owl and κριγή any strident sound. See Degani, *Studi* 257
f. In any event a bird is more appropriate in the context.

## 56 Pollux, Vocabulary

And Hipponax speaks of a siphon with which they tasted
(the new wine):

piercing the lid with a thin pipe[1]

[1] Explained by some as sexual imagery (pipe = penis and lid =
vagina or anus), but without a context this is merely a possibility.

## 57 Pollux, Vocabulary

And σάκος said of a strainer, also ὑλιστήρ ('filter'). Hip-
ponax says:

they are dripping as a strainer drips . . .[1]

[1] With West's text we have a reference to sour wine which he
treats as "a metaphor for the vaginal secretion" (*Studies* 142).

**58** Pollux 10.87

ἐν δὲ τοῖς Δημιοπράτοις λέκος εὑρίσκομεν, Ἱππώνακ-
τος εἰπόντος

κἄλειφα ῥόδινον ἡδὺ καὶ λέκος πυροῦ.

πυρῶν dub. West

**59** Erotian. *lex. Hippocr.* φ 19 (p. 92.6 Nachmanson)

καλοῦσι δὲ φῷδας τὰ ἐκ τοῦ πυρὸς γινόμενα (μάλιστα
δὲ ὅταν ἐκ ψύχους ἐν τῷ πυρὶ καθίσωσι) στρογγύλα
ἐπιφλογίσματα . . . καὶ Ἱππῶναξ δέ φησι·

πρὸς τὴν μαρίλην τὰς φοῖδας θερμαίνων
οὐ παύεται.

cf. Tzetz. in Ar. *Pl.* 535 (p. 130.2 Massa Positano)

1 τὰς φωῖδας Tzetz. (φο- Hoffmann), τοὺς παῖδας codd.
Erot. (πόδας cod. K)

**60** Ath. 2.49e

κοκκύμηλα οὖν ἐστι ταῦτα· ὧν Ἀρχίλοχός τε (fr. 241)
μέμνηται καὶ Ἱππῶναξ·

†στέφανον εἶχον κοκκυμήλων καὶ μίνθης.

<καὶ> στέφανον Gaisford, στέφανον ἔχοντες Bossi

**58** Pollux, *Vocabulary*

And we find λέκος in *The Goods Confiscated and Sold* and in Hipponax:

> and a sweet unguent made from roses and a pan of wheat[1]

[1] G. Tedeschi, *MCr* 13/14 (1978/79) 169 f., plausibly suggests that we have here the ingredients for a medical prescription.

**59** Erotian, *Glossary to Hippocrates*

They use the word φῷδες of the round inflammations caused from fire (and especially whenever people sit by the fire after being cold) . . . and Hipponax also says:

> he doesn't stop warming his blisters by the charcoal embers

**60** Athenaeus, *Scholars at Dinner*

These are κοκκύμηλα, mentioned by Archilochus and Hipponax:

> I (they?) wore a wreath of plums and mint

**61** *Et. Gen.* (p. 40 Calame) = *Et. Mag.* 615.12 (versu omisso)

οὐδὸν ἐς λαύρην (*Od.* 22.127 sq.)· τὴν δημοσίαν ὁδόν. λαύρην δὲ Φιλόξενος (fr. 572 Theodoridis) τὴν ῥύμην φησί . . . τινὲς δὲ τὸν κοπρῶνα, ὡς Ἱππῶναξ·

ἔκρωζεν ⟨ὡς⟩ κύμινδις ἐν λαύρῃ.

⟨ἐλθὼν ὡς⟩ Bergk, ⟨× –⟩ ἔκρ. ⟨ὡς⟩ Hoffmann    ἐν λαύρῃ *Et. Gen.* A (-ρη Reitzenstein), ἐς λαύρην B

**62** *Et. Gen.* (p. 46 Calame)

χαμεύνιον· ἐπὶ τοῦ κραβάτου τάσσεται. Ἱππῶναξ·

ἐν †ταμείῳ τε καὶ χαμευνίῳ γυμνόν.

cf. Did. *lex. Plat.* (Miller, *Mélanges* 402)
ταμείῳ Didymus, μίῳ *Et. Gen.*, φορμίῳ dub. West (cl. fr. 170)

**63** D. L. 1.107

μέμνηται δὲ αὐτοῦ καὶ Ἱππῶναξ εἰπών·

καὶ Μύσων, ὃν Ὡπόλλων
ἀνεῖπεν ἀνδρῶν σωφρονέστατον πάντων.

**61** *Etymologicum Genuinum*

"Threshold to the street," i.e., to the public road. Philoxenus says that λαύρη means 'street' . . . but some say it means 'privy,' as does Hipponax:

> (he?) squawked like a *kymindis*[1] in the privy

[1] The bird cannot be securely identified, but seems to be some kind of owl.

**62** *Etymologicum Genuinum*

χαμεύνιον, a term applied to a mattress. Cf. Hipponax:

> naked on a . . . and a mattress

**63** Diogenes Laertius, *Lives of the Philosophers*

And Hipponax also mentions him (i.e., Myson). saying:

> and Myson[1] whom Apollo proclaimed as the most sensible of all men

[1] A shadowy figure whom Plato (*Prot.* 343a) includes among the Seven Sages. Most of our information about him is derived from Diogenes 1.106-108.

**64** Stob. 3.29.42

Ἱππώνακτος·

χρόνος δὲ φευγέτω σε μηδὲ εἷς ἀργός.

cf. Append. Vat. 2 nr. 53 Sternbach (Ἱππῶναξ ἔφη), Apostol. 18.41d (Δημώνακτος)

**65** Tzetz. *exeg. Il.* A 314 (Masson, *PP* 5 [1950] 74), "καὶ εἰς ἅλα λύματ᾽ ἔβαλλον"

εἰς τὴν θάλασσαν τὸ ἀπολουτήριον ὕδωρ ἔχεον. ἔθος γὰρ ἦν τοῖς διὰ θαλάσσης ἐπὶ θυσίας ἀποιχομένοις οὕτω ποιεῖν, ὡς εἰς θυσίαν δῆθεν τοῦτο τοῦ Ποσειδῶνος ἤτοι τῆς θαλάσσης, καθά φησιν καὶ Ἱππῶναξ·

πρύμνης ἀπ᾽ ἄκρης ἐς θάλασσαν σπένδοντες.

ἄκρας cod., corr. Adrados        σπεύδοντες cod., corr. Maas

**66** Tzetz. *exeg. Il.* A 363 (Masson, *PP* 5 [1950] 74)

καὶ μετὰ ὑποτακτικῶν μορίων οὐχ ὑποτάσσει (ἡ Ἰωνικὴ διάλεκτος), ὡς παρ᾽ Ἱππώνακτι·

κοὐκ ὡς κύων λαίθαργος ὕστερον τρώγει.

κρυφιοδάκτης post κύων cod., del. Masson ut gloss. λάθαργος cod., corr. Masson

**64** Stobaeus, *Anthology*

From Hipponax:[1]

> let no time idly slip by you

[1] Rightly denied to Hipponax by most editors, including West and Degani. Perhaps the work of an Alexandrian choliambic poet or of Demonax of Cyprus, a Cynic philosopher (2nd c. A.D.).

**65** Tzetzes, *Commentary on Iliad* ("and they threw the offscourings into the sea")

They poured into the sea the water used for washing. For it was the custom of those who went across the sea for a sacrifice to do so, as an offering, I suppose, to Poseidon or the sea, as Hipponax says:

> pouring an offering from the tip of the stern into the sea

**66** Tzetzes, *Commentary on Iliad*

The Ionic dialect, as in Hipponax, does not use postpositives:

> and he does not chew to pieces(?) afterwards like a treacherous dog[1]

[1] Meaning obscure.

**67** *Et. Gen.* (p. 46 Calame)

χάλις· ὁ οἶνος.

ὀλίγα φρονέουσιν οἱ χάλιν πεπωκότες.

cf. Tzetz. in Lyc. (p. 199.20 Scheer), in Hes. *Op.* 336 (p. 221.8 Gaisford), in Ar. *Pl.* 435 (p. 109.9 Massa Positano)

φρονοῦσιν testes, corr. Hiller

**68** Stob. 4.22.35 + P. Berol. 9773 verso (*BKT* V(2).130)

Ἱππώνακτος·

δύ᾽ ἡμέραι γυναικός εἰσιν ἥδισται,
ὅταν γαμῇ τις κἀκφέρῃ τεθνηκυῖαν.

**70** P. Oxy. xviii.2174 fr. 1 col. ii (ed. Lobel)

ωσ[
ημε[
ανδ[
ταρσ[
5   φερο[
γρύζουσ᾽ .[
τὸν θεοῖσ[ιν ἐχθρὸν τοῦτον, ὃς κατευδούσης
τῆς μητρ[ὸς ἐσκύλευε τὸν βρύσσον

**67** *Etymologicum Genuinum*

χάλις is wine.

those who drink wine[1] have few wits about them[2]

[1] χάλις is presumably a very potent wine, perhaps from Thrace.　　[2] The fragment is attributed to Hipponax in the citations by Tzetzes.

**68** Stobaeus, *Anthology*

From Hipponax:

Two days in a woman's life are sweetest, whenever she is married and whenever she is carried out dead.[1]

[1] Attribution to Hipponax is rejected by many, but on inadequate grounds.

**70** Oxyrhynchus Papyrus (early 2nd c. A.D.)

. . . she grunting (they are grunting?) . . . this god-forsaken fellow who used to despoil his sleeping mother's sea urchin[1]. . . blind . . . and crippled . . .

[1] Clearly a metaphor for the genitals. Some prefer "despoiled the sea urchin (of the daughter) while the mother slept," but cf. fr. 12.2.

# IAMBIC POETRY

```
      τυφλὸν π[
10    καὶ χωλὸν [
      ───────
      Ὤθηνι κυ[
      ἐπ᾽ ἦισεπ[
      ἔστησα.[
```

Tzetz. *exeg. Il.* A 118 (Masson 72, v. ad fr. 65)

ἀλλ᾽ οἱ Ἴωνες ψιλοῦσι τὰ δασέα ὡς τό· (fr. 72.5) καὶ τό· (fr. 26a.1) καὶ τό· "τὸν θεοῖς—βρύττον" καὶ τό· (fr. 25). καὶ τί τὸν Ἱππώνακτα νῦν λέγω μόνον; πάντας ψιλωτὰς τοὺς Ἴωνας σὺ νόει.

7 θεοῖς cod., corr. Masson    8 ἐσκάλευσε Kassel βρύττον cod., corr. Masson ⟨κάτω⟩ βρύσσον Gallavotti 12 ἦι vel ἦις

**72** P. Oxy. 2174 fr. 3

```
5     ἐπ᾽ ⌊ἁρμάτων τε καὶ Θρεϊκίων πώλων
      λε⌊υκῶν †ὀείους κατεγγὺς† Ἰλίου πύργων
      ἀπ⌊ηναρίσθη Ῥῆσος, Αἰνειῶν πάλμυς
```

Tzetz. ad *Hom.* 190 (Schirach, *Tz. carm. Il.* p. 65)

ὁ δὲ Ῥῆσος Αἰνειῶν Θράκης ἦν βασιλεύς, υἱὸς Στρύμονος ἢ Ἠιονέος καὶ Τερψιχόρης . . . τοὺς ἵππους δὲ Ῥήσου Ὀδυσσεὺς καὶ Διομήδης ἐλήισαν, λευκοὺς ὄντας, ὡς Ὅμηρός φησι· (*Il.* 10.437 sqq.) . . . καὶ Ἱππῶναξ· "ἐπ᾽ . . . πάλμυς."

Athenis[2] . . . I (they?) set up . . .

Tzetzes, *Commentary on Iliad*

But the Ionians smooth aspirated consonants as in frr. 72.5, 26a.1, 70.7-8, and 25. And why do I now speak only of Hipponax? Know that all the Ionians do this.

[2] A paragraphus and coronis in the margin indicate the beginning of a new poem. Athenis was the brother of Bupalus (see test. 3 n. 2).

**72** Same papyrus

. . . (while sleeping near?) the towers of Ilium by his chariot and white Thracian foals Rhesus, sultan of the Aeneians, was despoiled of them . . .

Tzetzes on *Homerica*

Rhesus was king of the Aeneians in Thrace, the son of Strymon or Eïoneus and Terpsichore . . . Odysseus and Diomedes carried off Rhesus' horses which were white as Homer says . . . and Hipponax (72.5-7).

Tzetz. *exeg. Il.* A 15 (p. 78.1 Hermann)

καὶ ἀντὶ τῶν δασέων ψιλὰ ἐξεφώνουν ὡς ἔχει ἡ ἀρχαία
Ἰωνική, "ἐπιβρύκων" (fr. 104.15) ἀντὶ τοῦ ἐπιβρύχων,
καὶ τὸ "ἐπ'—πώλων," καὶ "μεταρμόσας" (fr. 161).

cf. Tzetz. ad fr. 70.7-8, Tzetz. ad Hes. *Op.* 157 (ἐπ' ἁρμάτων
tantum)

5 Θρηϊκίων Tzetz., corr. Fick     6 Tzetz. ad Hom. ἰὼν
κατεγγὺς (cod. L) et καθεύδων ἐγγύς, unde ἰαύων ἐγγὺς Mayor
7 Αἰνίων ten Brink     πάλμυς Schneidewin, παλάμας cod.
M, βασιλεύς HLV

**73** P. Oxy. 2174 fr. 4

τῶι πλ[
ὤ]μειξε δι' αἷμα καὶ χολὴν ἐτίλησεν·
ἐγὼ δεγ[         ]οἱ δέ μεο ὀδόντες
5 ἐν ταῖς γ[νάθοισι πάντες ⟨ἐκ⟩κεκινέαται.
φοιτῶ δ[
δέδοικ' α[
κεῖνος δ[
καλῶς· .[

*Et. Gen.* (p. 39 Calame) = *Et. Mag.* 624.4

ὀμιχεῖν· σημαίνει δὲ τὸ οὐρεῖν . . . ἔστι δὲ καὶ
βαρύτονον ῥῆμα, ὀμίχω, ὁ μέλλων ὀμίξω, ὡς παρ'
Ἱππώνακτι, οἷον "ὤμιξεν—ἐτίλησεν."

Tzetzes, *Commentary on Iliad*

And instead of aspirated consonants they pronounced them smooth as does ancient Ionic, ἐπιβρύκων for ἐπιβρύχων and (fr. 72.5) and μεταρμόσας (for μεθαρμόσας).

**73** Same papyrus

> . . . he pissed blood and shat bile;[1] but I . . . and all the teeth in my jaws have been dislodged.[2] I roam about . . . I am afraid . . . (but?) he . . . well . . .

*Etymologicum Genuinum*

ὀμιχεῖν means 'to urinate' . . . And there is also the uncontracted form ὀμίχω, future ὀμίξω, as, for example, in Hipponax (73.3).

[1] The line is cited in numerous sources (see Degani's fr. 73).
[2] Degani rejects the insertion of vv. 4-5 here, treating them as a separate fragment (his 132). Instead of 'dislodged' (from blows) perhaps simply 'fallen out' from old age or disease, or if the prefix is incorrectly supplied the verb's literal meaning 'have moved' may be a reference to eating or fear. For other sources of vv. 4-5 see Degani's fr. 132.

# IAMBIC POETRY

*Epimer. in Hom.* (p. 509.37 Dyck)

μεμετρέαται· τοῦτο Ἰωνικόν ἐστιν . . . καὶ παρ᾽ Ἱπ-
πώνακτι· "οἱ δέ—κεκινέαται."

3 ]μῖξεδ[ pap., ὤμιξεν (vel ὤμηξεν) codd., corr. Diehl
4 μευ codd., corr. Fick      5 ταισγ[ pap., τοῖσι codd.
ἐκ- add. Ahrens

**74** P. Oxy. 2174 fr. 5

οδυ[

Ὀδυ[σσε- Lobel

**75** P. Oxy. 2174 fr. 6

                    ].ζων φυκι[
              ]αν αὐτὸν ὅστις ε[
              ]ἐπεὶ τὸν ψωμὸ[ν
              ]ερεῦσι τὴν γενὴ[ν

**77** P. Oxy. 2174 fr. 8

                    ]υψου.[
              ].αιηκασ[
              ]επλοωσεν[
          ]ασιος ὥσπερ βου[
5         ]υτο φρενώλης τ[
          ]θεν διδάξων γ[
          ]ο κορσιππ[

410

# HIPPONAX

*Homeric Parsings*

μεμετρέαται ('have been measured'); this is Ionic . . . and in Hipponax (73.3-4).

**74** Same papyrus

*Apparently a title containing some form of the word Odysseus, and frr. 75 and 77 would suit the context of a poem dealing with the wanderings of Odysseus, presumably in a mock-heroic manner.*

**75** Same papyrus

. . . seaweed . . . him who . . . after . . . the morsel . . . they inquire into his lineage . . .

**77** Same papyrus

. . . Phaeacians(?) . . . like (Bupalus?) . . . frenzied . . . (came?) to teach . . . lotus root . . .

---

2 Φαίακας Lobel    4 Βού[παλος Diehl    6 ἦλ]θεν
Adrados

411

**78** P. Oxy. 2174 fr. 9 + 10 + addit. (xix p. 150)

```
                    ]ομβρ[
                  ]εινος γι[
5          ὥσπερ τραγω[
           ὑ]πέατι καί μιν[
           ὥσπερ Κίκωνα[
                    ]ἐδυσφήμει τε κα.[
           ].ας μαρίλην ἀνθρ[άκων
10       ...]ς δὲ κ[α]ὶ πῦρ οὐκ ἐσέρχε[... π]υρρ[όν
               ἀ]θερίνην ἐς Καβείρ[ων] φοίτε[σκε
           τὸν λ[..]ριῶνα μῆνα κα[ν]θαρο[
           ἐ]λθὼν δ' ἐς οἶκον, συκάμινα δ[ει]π[νήσας,
           καὶ τῶι κιμαίωι τόν[δε] ῥῖνα φοινίξα[ς
15       ἐπιπτύσας τρὶς καὶ τ[
           ἀ]π' ὦν ἐδέψατ' ὡς .[
```

4 κ]εῖνος Adrados    5 τραγὼ[ν Diehl, τράγω[ν δορὰς
vel ἀσκοὺς Miralles    6 suppl. Lobel    7 vel Κίκων α[
8 in fine πολλὴν suppl. Masson e fr. 78a    9 suppl.
Lobel    10 σέλα]ς West    ἐσέρχε[ται π]υρρ[όν Adrados,
-χε[τ' οὖ π]υρρ[όν West    11 ἀ]θερίνην Lobel, in init. θύων
δ' e.g. West    καβιρ[ pap., suppl. Adrados (-βεί- Medeiros)
in fine suppl. West    12 Λ[αυ]ριῶνα Bossi
13 δ[ει]π[νήσας West    14 τόν[δε Adrados    16 ἀ]π'
Diehl    ἐδέψατ' Scheller (εδεψᾶτ' pap.)

**78** Same papyrus[1]

. . . like . . . with an awl and . . . like Cicon[2] . . . he
used indecent language and . . . embers of charcoal
. . . and he did not approach . . . the flaming fire (and
offering?) a smelt he would go to the temple of the
Cabiri[3] throughout the month of . . .[4] dung beetle(s)
. . . , and going into his house he dined on mulber-
ries, and dyeing this[5] red at the nose with the juice
he spat three times and . . . jerked off . . .

[1] Although many of the details are obscure, it seems clear that
the fragment describes magical procedures to cure impotence.
See West, *Studies* 142 f., and Miralles in Miralles-Pòrtulas 9-21.
[2] Cf. frr. 4, 4a.    [3] Divinities somewhat similar to the
Dioscuri in their attributions and worshipped especially in
Samothrace, Lemnos and Miletus. See also n. on fr. 155b.
[4] Bossi's supplement, based on fr. 92.10, is highly probable. If cor-
rect, Laurion is a parody of the month name Taureon known
from several cities in Ionia and a translation might be something
like "throughout the month of Bull Shit."    [5] Presumably his
penis, with 'nose' denoting its tip. For the imagery see Henderson
243.

**78a** Erotian. *lex. Hippocr.* μ 24 (p. 61.10 Nachmanson)

μᾶλλον δὲ ἡ θερμοσποδιὰ μαρίλη λέγεται, ὡς καὶ Ἀριστοφάνης ἐν Ἀχαρνεῦσί φησιν· (350 sq.). καὶ Ἱππῶνάξ φησι·

πολλὴν μαρίλην ἀνθράκων.

**79** P. Oxy. 2174 fr. 11 col. i (1-17)

```
                    ἀ]λοιᾶσθα[ι
              τῆς] ἀνοίης ταύτη[ς
              τὴ]ν γνάθον παρα.[
    5            ]ι κηρίνους ἐποι[
                 ]κἀνετίλησε[
                 ]χρυσολαμπέτωι ῥάβδωι
                 ]αν ἐγγὺς ἑρμῖνος·
       Ἑρμῆς δ᾽ ἐς Ἱππώ]νακτος ἀκολουθήσας
   10         το]ῦ κυνὸς τὸν φιλήτην
                 ]ὡς ἔχιδνα συρίζει
                 ]αξ δὲ νυκτὶ βου[
                 ]καὶ κατεφράσθη[
                 ]δευς κατεσκη.[
   15    ἐμερ]μήριξε· τῶι δὲ κ[η]λητ[ῆι
                 ]ς παῦνι, μυῖαν .[
       ὁ δ᾽ αὐτίκ᾽ ἐλθ]ὼν σὺν τριοῖσι μ[άρτυσιν
       ὅκου τὸν ἕρπιν ὁ σκότος καπηλεύει,
       ἄνθρωπον εὗρε τὴν στέγην ὀφέλλοντα—
   20  οὐ γὰρ παρῆν ὄφελμα—πυθμένι στοιβῆς.
```

**78a** Erotian, *Glossary to Hippocrates*

But rather hot ashes are called μαρίλη, as Aristophanes says in *Acharnians*. And Hipponax says:

> many embers of charcoal

**79** Same papyrus as for frr. 70-78[1]

> . . . to be cudgeled . . . of this foolishness . . . (striking?) his jaw . . . made of wax[2] . . . and he shat upon[3] . . . staff gleaming with gold[4] . . .near the bed post. And Hermes providing an escort to the house of Hipponax . . . the dog-stealer[5] . . . hisses like a viper . . . (Hipponax deliberating?) at night . . . and devised . . . pondered; and to the charmer . . . small(?),[6] (like?) a fly[7] . . . With three witnesses he went at once to the place where the swindler[8] sells wine[9] and found a fellow sweeping the room with a stock of thorn, since no broom was at hand.

[1] See West, *Studies* 143 f., for an attempt to explain the sequence of events.    [2] Probably metaphorical here. Those who are afraid can be described as 'waxen,' i.e., 'soft as wax' or 'pale as wax.'    [3] No doubt from fear, as in Arist. *Ach.* 350 f.
[4] West takes the staff to belong to a seer (Cicon), but the epithet suggests Hermes.    [5] West prefers "(had kept safe) the burglar from the dog."    [6] Hesychius glosses παυνί and παῦνις with 'small,' 'big,' 'good' and 'sufficient.' The word does not occur elsewhere.    [7] With Bossi's supplement 'fly' will describe something of little value.    [8] The meaning of σκότος is uncertain (West renders it as 'bastard'), but Latin *tenebrio*, describing one who works under cover of darkness, is a close parallel.
[9] An Egyptian word, probably for a wine of poor quality.

*Et. Gen.* (p. 13 Calame)

ἀκολουθήσας· "Ἑρμῆς—ἀκολουθήσας," ἔκτασις τοῦ
α. οὕτως Ἡρωδιανός (ii.1240 Lentz)

Tzetz. in Lyc. 1165 (p. 338.27 Scheer), "ὀφελτρεύσωσι"

σαρώσωσι. σάρον γὰρ καὶ ὄφελμα καὶ ὀφελμος ἡ
σκοῦπα λέγεται. καὶ τοῦτο Ἱππῶναξ φησιν· "ὁ δ'—
στοιβῆς."

cf. Eust. in Hom. *Il.* 1.340 (i.178.7 V.d.Valk), Tzetz. in Lyc. 579
(p. 199.24 Scheer), Schol. vet. ad loc. (p. 199.18 Scheer), Tzetz. in
Ar. *Pl.* 435 (p. 109.9 Massa Positano)

2 suppl. Lobel          3 τῆς] Diehl          ταύτη[ς Lobel
4 τὴ]ν Diehl          παρακ[ρούσας e.g. West          5 ἐποί[ησε
Lobel          9 δὲ σιμώνακτος *Et. Gen.*, corr. Lehrs
10 το]ῦ Lobel          12 Ἱππῶν]αξ Diehl          in fine
βου[λεύων e.g. West          14 Μαια]δεὺς κατέσκηψ[ε Lobel
15 suppl. Lobel          16 in fine ᾧ[ς Bossi          18 ἔρπιν codd.,
corr. Masson

**82** P. Oxy. 2174 fr. 14

                    ]οιον στρυμ[
          κυσ]οχήνηι πολλα[
          ἔ]βηξε καὶ σαρων[
          ]ν σελήνην ει[

1 Στρυμ[ Lobel          2-3 suppl. Lobel          3 σαρων[ίσας
Diehl

*Etymologicum Genuinum*

ἀκολουθήσας: (v. 9), with lengthening of the alpha. So Herodian.

Tzetzes on Lycophron

ὀφελτρεύσωσι means 'they will sweep clean.' For a broom is called σάρον and ὄφελμα and ὄφελμος. And Hipponax says (17-20).

**82**  Same papyrus

... Strymon(?)[1] ... gaping anus(?)[2] ... coughed and ...[3] moon ...

[1] If the next word is correctly translated, a pathic's gaping anus may be compared to the river Strymon, but there is also the word στρύμοξ which Hesychius defines as a piece of wood used for crushing grapes.    [2] Another definition given by Hesychius is 'pillory for prostitutes,' but κυσός and compounds of it elsewhere designate the anus (Henderson 131).    [3] Hesychius defines σάρων as 'lecherous' or 'female genitals,' but both the form of the word here and its meaning are obscure.

**84** P. Oxy. 2174 fr. 16 col. ii + addit. (xix p. 150)

```
    .δ’ ἦλθεν οι[
    .]ειου[ .]ακεσ[
    γληχῶνος[
5   κ]αί μ’ εἴρετ’ ὁ[
    ]ε̣ἰπασ .[
    ]κ̣ο̣ὐδιψ[
    ἀλλ’ ἐστεγυ[
    χαμαὶ ’πιφ[
10  ἐκδύντες α[
    ἐδάκνομέν τε κἀφ[ιλέομεν
    διὲκ θυρέων βλέ[ποντες
    μὴ ἥμεας λάβ[
    γυμνοὺς ἐρυ .[
15  ἔσπευδε δ’ ἡ μ[ὲν
    ἐγὼ δ’ ἐβίνε[ον          ]τ̣ε̣ κ̣α̣[ὶ
    ἐπ’ ἄκρον ἔλκ[ων ὥσπε]ρ ἀλλᾶ[ν]τα ψύχων,
    ]κλαίειν κ̣ελεύ[ων Βού]παλο[ν
    ]κ[αί] μ’ αὐτίκ’ ἐξ[..(.)]σεν ἐκ δεπ̣[
20  ]καὶ δὴ ’πὶ τοῖς ἔργοισιν εἴχομ[εν
    ]ἐγὼ μὲν ὥσπ[ερ ῥ]υ̣σὸν ἰστι .[
    σφάζειν ὑπέτ[.......]φαλο̣υ̣τ[
```

Hephaest. *Ench.* 5.4

τὸ δὲ χωλὸν οὐ δέχεται τοὺς παραλήγοντας τρισυλ-
λάβους πόδας, οὔτε δάκτυλον οὔτε πρίβραχυν οὔτε
ἀνάπαιστον, ἀλλὰ μάλιστα μὲν ἴαμβον, ὅτε καὶ

**84** Same papyrus

. . . (she?) came . . . pennyroyal[1] . . . and asked me
. . . saying . . . and not . . . but . . . on the ground . . .
with our clothes off . . . we were biting and kissing(?)
. . . looking through the doors . . . in case we be
caught naked . . . she was in a hurry[2] . . . and I was
fucking . . . pulling out to the tip as though drying(?)
a sausage[3] . . . bidding Bupalus go to hell . . . and at
once she . . . me and I(?) . . . And after our exertions
we had (a rest?). I . . . like a wrinkled sail[4] . . .

[1] Perhaps here a metaphor for the pubic area (see Henderson
135).    [2] Or "she was urging me on."    [3] Chosen pre-
sumably because of its resemblance to a penis, but the participle
('drying by exposure to the breeze') is judged inappropriate by
many. Knox's supplement is rendered by 'skinning a sausage' in
the Supplement to LSJ, not an obvious meaning of the word. See
R. M. Rosen, *TAPA* 118 (1988) 38 f.    [4] Presumably an image
for a detumescent penis.

Hephaestion, *Handbook of Meters*

And the choliambic does not admit penultimate feet of
three syllables, dactyl, tribrach, or anapaest, but prefers an

εὐπρεπές ἐστιν· "ἀκούσαθ᾽ Ἱππώνακτος, οὐ γὰρ ἀλλ᾽
ἥκω" (Callim. fr. 191.1 Pf.)· ἔσθ᾽ ὅτε δὲ καὶ σπονδεῖον,
ὅτε καὶ τραχύτερον γίνεται· "εἰς—ψύχων."

cf. schol. Hephaest. (p. 269.4 Consbruch)

2 in init. ἡ West    5 εἰρεθο[ pap., unde εἴρεθ᾽ ὁ Lobel:
corr. Medeiros    11, 12, 15 suppl. West    16 εβείνε[
pap., corr. et suppl. Lobel    17 εἰς codd. Hephaest., ἐπ᾽ pap.,
codd. schol. Hephaest.    ψήχων Knox (rec. West)
18 κελεύ[ων West    Βού]παλο[ν Lobel    19 ἐξ[έλυ]σεν,
ἐκ δ᾽ ἐπ[λήμυρα e.g. West ("she pushed me out, and I brimmed
over")    20 in fine παῦλαν e.g. West    21 ῥ]υσὸν West
ἱστίον Masson

**85(c)**  P. Oxy. 2174 fr. 17

2 ]ἀπαλλαχθείς[    3 χλαίνας    8 ἐ]ξεδίφησ[

**86**  P. Oxy. 2174 fr. 18

2 ]τιλησας    3 π]εριτρώγων    4 φωλεοί

**92**  P.S.I. 1089 col. ii, ed. Coppola (5-9 frustula P. Oxy.
  2174 fr. 24 + addit. (xix p. 150))

ηὔδα δὲ λυδίζουσα· "βασκ...κρολεα."
πυγιστί· "τὸν πυγεῶνα παρ[        ."
καί μοι τὸν ὄρχιν τῆς φαλ[
κ]ράδηι συνηλοίησεν ὥσπ[ερ φαρμακῶι

iambus when it is fitting. "Listen to Hipponax, for it is I in fact who have come" (see on fr. 1); but sometimes also a spondee, when it becomes rather harsh (v. 17).

**85(c)** Same papyrus

2 set free      3 cloak      8 ferreted out

**86** Same papyrus

2 shat      3 gnawing round about      4 lairs

**92** Papyri[1]

She spoke in Lydian: "*Faskati krolel*,"[2] in Arsish,[3] "your arse . . ." and my balls . . . she thrashed with a fig branch as though (I were a scapegoat) . . . fas-

5     ].τοις διοζίοισιν ἐμπεδ[
      καὶ δὴ δυοῖσιν ἐν πόνοισ[ι
      ἥ τε κράδη με τοὐτέρωθ[εν
      ἄνωθεν ἐμπίπτουσα, κ[
      παραψιδάζων βολβίτωι[
10    ὦζεν δὲ λαύρη· κάνθαρο[ι δὲ ῥοιζέοντες
      ἦλθον κατ᾽ ὀδμὴν πλέον[ες ἢ πεντήκοντα·
      τῶν οἱ μὲν ἐμπίπτοντε[ς
      κατέβαλον, οἱ δὲ τοὺς ὀδ..[
      οἱ δ᾽ ἐμπεσόντες τὰς θύρα[ς
15    τοῦ Πυγέλησι[
      ..]ρυσσον οἷα[....]αροιμο[
      ..]ω δ᾽ ἐς υμν[
         ]εντ[

Tzetz. *exeg. Il.* A 273 (Masson, *PP* 5 [1950] 75) de ευ
Ionico

(fr. 28), καὶ ἀλλαχοῦ· "ὦζεν—πεντήκοντα."

   4 suppl. Coppola     5 ἐμπεδ[ωθέντι Knox
8 κ[άνθεν ὁ πρωκτὸς Latte     9 παραψιάζων Degani
13 ὀδό[ντας ὤξυνον Knox

422

## HIPPONAX

tened securely by forked pieces of wood(?) . . . and
(I was caught?) between two torments . . . On the
one side the fig branch . . . me, descending from
above, (and on the other side my arse?) spattering
with shit . . . and my arse-hole stank. Dung beetles
came buzzing at the smell, more than fifty of them.
Some attacked and struck down(?) . . . , others (whet
their teeth?), and others falling upon the doors[4] . . .
of the Arsenal[5] . . .

Tzetzes, *Commentary on Iliad* (on Ionic ἐυ)

(fr. 28), and elsewhere (vv. 10-11)

[1] It seems that a Lydian woman is treating Hipponax (for im-
potence?, cf. fr. 78) by blows from a fig branch (cf. frr. 5-10) and by
inserting something into his anus which causes him to defecate.
Commentators compare Petronius 138, but the state of the papy-
rus leaves much in obscurity. Opposite v. 14 there is the numeral
800, i.e., of Book 1 or 2.   [2] A rendering in the Greek al-
phabet of something in Lydian. See West, *Studies* 144 f.
[3] West's translation of a word modeled on Δωριστί ('in Doric'),
Ἰαστί ('in Ionic') etc.   [4] Perhaps the dung beetles are at-
tacking three parts of his body. For 'door' as anus see Henderson
199, but the plural is surprising in this sense.   [5] West's ren-
dering. There seems to be a pun on Pygela, a town inland near
Ephesus.

**95** P. Oxy. xxii.2323 + xviii.2174 fr. 27

```
              ]ήσαιτο κα[
              ]κ Βουπάλωι[
              ]υ Βούπαλον[
5             ]νοι τὸν κ[
          ἄλ]λος ἄλλοθεν[
              ]ελθόντες [
          ] ύσοντές τε καλ[
          π]αρεκνημοῦντ|ο
10        ]ων [    ] σικ[
              ]ηκεβ[
              κ]ατεῖλε[
              ]αὐτίκ᾿ ειρ[
              ]ητες ἐγγυ[
15        Βο]υπάλωι κ( )[
```

Tzetz. *exeg. Il.* A 17 (p. 79.21 Hermann)

Ἱππῶναξ "παρεκνημοῦντο" φησὶν ἀντὶ τοῦ ἐπορεύ-
οντο.

14 ἐγγὺ[ς Adrados

**95a** Tzetz. in Lyc. 436 (p. 160.20 Scheer)

ὅτι δὲ ἁγὴς ὁ μυσαρός . . . Ἱππῶνάξ φησιν·

ὡς οἱ μὲν †ἁγεῖ Βουπάλῳ κατηρῶντο.

ὡς Gaisford    ⟨ἐν⟩αγεῖ vel ἀγέι Fix

424

**95** Oxyrhynchus papyri[1]

> ... Bupalus ... Bupalus ... one from one place, one
> from another ... coming ... they were advancing
> ... seized(?) ... at once ... near by ... Bupalus ...

Tzetzes, *Commentary on Iliad*

Hipponax says παρεκνημοῦντο instead of ἐπορεύοντο
('they advanced').

[1] It seems that a crowd of people have come from different
directions to inflict some kind of harm on Bupalus (cf. fr. 95a).

**95a** Tzetzes on Lycophron

Hipponax says that ἀγής denotes one who is polluted:

> Thus some were calling down curses upon the pol-
> luted Bupalus[1]

[1] Some insert this line in fr. 95.15.

**102** P. Oxy. xviii.2175 fr. 1

```
                          ]κωτιλλησ[ ]
                          ]ν ἀποπνίξηι
                            ]υνηκεων
                          ]ν̣ τὸ μήνυτρον
5                         ἄ]λλο τι π[ρ]ῆσσε
                          ]αὐχενοπλῆγα
                          ]ς ἀνθρ[ώ]που
                          πυ]κταλίζουσι
        σπονδῇ τε καὶ σπλάγχνοι]σιν ἀγρίης χοίρου
10                        ]ὕδρον ἐν Λέρνηι
                          κ]α[ρ]κίνον συνέτριψε
                          ]ν̣εσθαι φιλήτην
                          ]κατηρῆσθαι·
                          ]φροναπ[
15                        ]τερην
                          ].⟦ι⟧ν.[.].[
                          ]Κίκων..[
```

Ath. 9.375c

χοῖρον δὲ οἱ Ἴωνες καλοῦσιν τὴν θήλειαν, ὡς Ἱπ-
πῶναξ· "σπονδῇ—χοίρου." (ἐν σπονδῇ A, corr. Dindorf:
ἐν ⟨α'⟩ Bergk)

**102** Oxyrhynchus papyrus (late 2nd or early 3rd c. A.D.)[1]

. . . chatters (wheedles?) . . . throttles[2] . . . the reward for information . . . was doing something else . . . struck on the neck[3] . . . man . . . they box . . . with a libation and entrails of a wild sow . . . serpent at Lerna . . . he crushed the crab . . . thief[4] . . . to curse . . . Cicon . . .

Athenaeus, *Scholars at Dinner*

The Ionians call the female pig χοῖρος, as in Hipponax (v. 9).

[1] It is clear that some of the labours of Heracles are being related, but the connection between them and the seer Cicon (cf. frr. 4, 4a) is obscure.     [2] The Nemean lion?     [3] Geryon?
[4] Of Cerberus?

427

IAMBIC POETRY

**103** P. Oxy. 2175 fr. 2

```
      ]λάσας τὸν τράχ[ηλον
      ]ν ἐς Μίλητον ἐξεκ[
      ]ν νησῖδα τερματιζ[
      ]. σφιν κἀγορη[] πεπο[
5     ].[.]ν οὐκ οἶδ’ ηκ[.]. ειτ[
      ]. ήσαντο καὶ δ.[.]απρ[
       ἐ]γγὺς τῆς θαλά(σ[σ)η]ς αι[
      ]ευς κ[α]ρκίνωι κ[..]ηρα[
      ]ν ἱερευ[.(.)]ν κοτ[..]κατ[
10         ]ἀ[σ]βόλ[ου] κασιγ[νητ
          πασ]πα[λ]ηφάγον γ[ρόμφιν
            ]κυνα[
```

Phot. *lex.* (ii.67 Naber)

πασπάλη· τὸ τυχόν. οἱ δὲ κέγχρον, οἱ δὲ τὰ κέγχρινα ἄλευρα. Ἱππῶναξ· "πασπαληφάγον γρόμφιν."

1 ἀνακ]λάσας Degani     τράχ[ηλον Lobel
2 Λάδη]ν Diehl     4 κἀγορὴ πεπο[ίηται Diehl ("nisi καγορη[ι]" West)     7 θαλατ[ pap.

**104** P. Oxy. 2175 fr. 3 + 4 (xviii p. 184)

```
10         δακ]τύλους μεταστρέψας·
          ]ος τε καὶ ῥύδην
      ]. ων δ’ αὐτὸν ἀσκαρίζοντα
      ]ν ἐν τῆι γαστρὶ λὰξ ἐνώρουσα·
```

428

**103**  Same papyrus

. . . (bending back?) the neck . . . to Miletus . . .
boundary(?) of the islet[1] . . . and an assembly has
been held(?) . . . do(es) not know . . . near the sea . . .
crab . . . sister of soot[2] . . . millet-fed grunter[3] . . .

Photius, *Lexicon*

πασπάλη means a scrap. Some say it is millet, others millet meal. Cf. Hipponax (v. 11).

[1] Perhaps the small island Lade off Miletus.  [2] Cf. frr. 48 and 144, also 138. Lobel suggests that μαρίλην 'charcoal embers' (cf. frr. 59.1, 78.9) preceded.  [3] An onomatopoeic word, defined by Aristophanes of Byzantium (fr. 169 Slater), citing Hipponax, as either any sow or an old sow.

**104**  Same papyrus[1]

. . . bending back his fingers . . . and abundantly . . .
him as he squirmed . . . I jumped on his stomach . . .

[1] More than one poem may be represented in these verses.

```
            ]．ις μὴ δοκῆι με λασθαίνειν
15          ]δευν ἐπιβρύκων
            ]ηιον καταπλ[ί]ξας
            ἐ]ξέδυσα τὴν χλαῖναν
            πό]δας περιψήσας
            τὴν] θύρην ἐπάκτωσα
20          ]．τὸ πῦρ κατακρύψας
            βακκάρ]ι δὲ τὰς ῥῖνας
            ἤλειφον †ἔστι δ'† ο]ἵηνπερ Κροῖσος·
            ]ν Δασκυλείωι
            ]ξιωνν[．]ωι[
25          ]μβολα[．]δοντε[ς
            ]ωιωνα[．．．]
            ]π．χ．σκόρ[．．．]
            ]λόγων κα[．．]κιζ[
            ]οσυλασ[
30          ]ανδροσον[
            ]ται καθη．[．]αι
            ν]εννυχμένωι πρωκτῶ[ι
            ]．ι σημαίνων
            ]σελλη πόρνη
35          ]ε．αλσιν ἐξορύξειαν[
            ]ακι．ρεψει νήσου
            ]ες κατὰ κνίσην
            ]ν κισκυητιμεσναρ．[
            ]．σαμου λοφορρῶγας[
40          ]．αιπαλωντ[．]．σ．σ．[
            ]．．τατον δι．．．．[
```

so that he might not have a mind to curse me . . .
gnashing my teeth . . . with legs apart . . . I took off
my cloak . . . wiping my feet clean . . . I barred the
door . . . covering the fire . . . and I anointed my
nostrils with perfume . . . such as Croesus had . . .
Daskyleion[2] . . . stabbed arse-hole . . . giving a sign
. . . prostitute . . . they dig out . . . island . . . at the
smell of roasted fat . . . with shoulders broken off . . .

[2] There were several towns in Asia Minor with this name
(see Stephanus of Byzantium s.v.). Perhaps it is here the town in
Bithynia a few miles south of the Propontis.

]ντεσενδεξ[
]..ν λαλα[
] θλυ ιέ.[.]ψ[
]λος χορωι[.]..[
]ταραξ[ί]πουν·
ὁ δ' ἐξολισθὼν ἱκέτευ]ε τὴν κρά[μ]βην
τὴν ἑπτάφυλλον, ἣν θύεσ]κε Πανδώρ[ηι
Ταργηλίοισιν ἔγκυθρον] πρὸ φαρμακ[οῦ
μέ]τωπον καὶ πλ[ευράς
]ριοσαυσ[.]πη[

45

50

Ath. 15.690a-b

παρὰ πολλοῖς δὲ τῶν κωμῳδοποιῶν ὀνομάζεταί τι
μύρον βάκκαρις· οὗ μνημονεύει καὶ Ἱππῶναξ διὰ
τούτων· "βακκάρι—Κροῖσος."

Ath. 9.370a

μήποτε δὲ ὁ Νίκανδρος μάντιν κέκληκε τὴν κράμβην
ἱερὰν οὖσαν, ἐπεὶ καὶ παρ' Ἱππώνακτι ἐν τοῖς ἰάμβοις
ἐστί τι λεγόμενον τοιοῦτον· "ὁ δ'—φαρμακοῦ." καὶ
Ἀνάνιος δέ φησιν (fr. 4).

10 suppl. Lobel      15 v. Tzetz. ad fr. 70.5
18-19 suppl. Lobel      22 ἔστι δ' vel ἐσθ' οἵηπερ κρόκ(κ)ος
codd.      32 suppl. Lobel      48 ἦ θ. πανδώρη codd., ἦ θ.
Πανδώρη Casaubon, ἣν θ. Πανδώρη Schmidt
49 θαργιλίοισιν, γαργηλ-, γαργιλ- codd., unde Θαργηλίοισιν
Dalecampius (Ταργ- Schneidewin)      ἔκχυτον codd., ἔγχυτον

feet-tripping . . . Slipping, he besought the seven-leafed cabbage[3] which he used to offer in a pot to Pandora[4] at the Thargelia in front of(?) the scape-goat . . . forehead and ribs . . .

Athenaeus, *Scholars at Dinner*

A certain perfume is called *bakkaris* by many comic poets. Hipponax also mentions it in these words (vv. 21-22).

Athenaeus, *Scholars at Dinner*

Perhaps Nicander (fr. 85.7 Gow-Schofield) has called the cabbage a prophet because it is sacred, since something of this sort is said in the iambics of Hipponax (vv. 47-49). And Ananius also says (fr. 4).

[3] The oath 'by the cabbage' (ναὶ μὰ τὴν κράμβην) is found in the comic poets (Ath. 9.370b), but its significance is unclear.
[4] Presumably here a name for the Earth goddess (cf. Arist. *Birds* 971), but the text is uncertain (see Degani, *Studi* 269) and some treat Pandora as a fictitious name for a woman.

---

Salmasius, ἔγχυντρον Schmidt, ἔγκυθρον West    φαρμάκου cod., corr. Meineke    50 in init. suppl. Lobel, in fine Diehl

**105**  P. Oxy. 2175 fr. 5

3 ϲελλεαν[    6 Βάραγχοϲ ἀρτεμ[    8 κ]αὶ
ϲτατῆραϲ πέν[τε    9 κυνὸϲ    10 μυϲαχνὸν

*Et. Gen.* β 40 (p. 23.4 Berger, 20.5 Calame); cf. *Et. Mag.*
188.8

"Βάραγχοϲ" Ἱππῶναξ μάλιϲτα, οἱ γὰρ ἄλλοι
Βράγχοϲ· Ἱππῶναξ ⟨δὲ⟩ πλεοναϲμῷ τοῦ α. οὕτωϲ
Ἡρωδιανὸϲ ἐν τοῖϲ περὶ παθῶν (ii.220.22 Lentz).

3 Σελλέα Diehl (cf. Arch. fr. 183)    6 Callim. fr. 104.31
Pf. (de Brancho) ἀρτεμέαϲ ἐποίηϲεν cont. Lobel

**114a**  Erotian. *lex. Hippocr.* τ 13 (p. 85.7 Nachmanson)

τράμιν· τὸν ὄρρον, ὅνπερ καὶ ὑποταύριον καλοῦμεν,
ὡϲ καὶ Ἱππῶναξ φηϲιν·

†ἔξ τίλλοι τιϲ αὐτοῦ τὴν τράμιν †ὑποργάϲαι.

μέμνηται καὶ Ἀρχίλοχοϲ (fr. 283).

ἐξ⟨άκιϲ⟩ τίλλοι τιϲ αὐτὸν τὴν τράμιν ⟨θ᾽⟩ ὑποργάϲϲαι
Meineke (-ήϲαι ten Brink, -άζοι Sitzler)

**114b**  Eust. in Hom. *Od.* 17.219 (1817.19)

Ἀριϲτοφάνηϲ γοῦν ὁ γραμματικὸϲ (fr. 197 Slater) ἐν τῷ
περὶ ὀνομαϲίαϲ ἡλικιῶν, εἰπὼν ὅτι τῶν ἀγρίων ὑῶν τὰ
νέα οἱ μὲν κολόβρια οἱ δὲ μολόβρια καλοῦϲιν, ἐπάγει

434

**105**  Same papyrus

> . . . Baranchos (restored them?) to health[1] . . . and
> five staters . . . of a dog . . . debauched[2] . . .

*Etymologicum Genuinum*

Hipponax above all uses the form Baranchos, the others
Branchos. Hipponax has a pleonastic alpha. So Herodian
in *On Inflexions*.

[1] The seer Branchos was said to have founded the oracle of
Apollo at Didyma and to have freed the inhabitants of Miletus
from a pestilence.     [2] Cf. Arch. fr. 209.

**114a**  Erotian, *Lexicon on Hippocrates*

τράμις is what we call the perineum, as Hipponax says:

> may someone pluck his anus (and soften it up?)

Archilochus also mentions it.

**114b**  Eustathius on Homer, *Odyssey*

At any rate Aristophanes the grammarian who says in
his *On Age Names* that some call the young of wild pigs
κολόβρια, others μολόβρια, concludes that Hipponax

IAMBIC POETRY

ὡς καὶ Ἱππῶναξ τὸν ἴδιον υἱὸν μολοβρίτην που λέγει ἐν τῷ

κρέας ἐκ μολοβρίτεω συός.

μολοβρίτου Eust., corr. Schneidewin

**114c** Suet. *de blasph.* (p. 62 Taillardat) = Eust. in Hom. *Od.* 18.55 (1837.42)

μεσσηγυδορποχέστης

ὁ μεσοῦντος τοῦ δείπνου πολλάκις ἀποπατῶν, ὅπως πάλιν ἐμπίμπληται ὁ αὐτός.

μεσηγυ- Renner          -χέστα Knox

*115-118 Epodi*

**115** P. Argent. 3 fr. 1.16, ed. Reitzenstein

κύμ[ατι] πλα[ζόμ]ενος·
5   κἂν Σαλμυδ[ησσ]ῶι γυμνὸν εὐφρονέσ̣[τατα
Θρήϊκες ἀκρό[κ]ομοι
λάβοιεν—ἔνθα πόλλ᾽ ἀναπλήσει κακὰ
δούλιον ἄρτον ἔδων—

436

somewhere speaks of his own son[1] as μολοβρίτης in

the meat of a young pig

[1] Eustathius' text is no doubt corrupt, with υἱὸν ('son') an error for ὗν ('pig').

**114c** Suetonius, *On Defamatory Words*

an interprandial pooper[1]

Of one who often retires to defecate in the midst of a meal so that he may fill himself up again.

[1] West's translation, which catches well the comic flavour. The word is cited anonymously in Suetonius, but attributed to Hipponax by Eustathius.

*115-118 Epodes*

*The authorship of frr. 115-117 is much disputed, some attributing them to Archilochus, some to Hipponax, and some assigning fr. 115 to Archilochus and 117 to Hipponax (fr. 116 is omitted here, since no complete word is preserved).*

**115** Strasburg papyrus

. . .[1] drifting about on the wave. And at Salmydessus[2] may the top-knotted Thracians give him naked a most kindly reception—there he will have full measure of a multitude of woes, eating the bread of slaves—stiff from cold. As he comes out from the

ῥίγει πεπηγότ᾽ αὐτόν· ἐκ δὲ τοῦ χν‹ό›ου
10     φυκία πόλλ᾽ ἐπιχ‹έ›οι,
κροτέοι δ᾽ ὀδόντας, ὡς [κ]ύων ἐπὶ στόμα
κείμενος ἀκρασίηι
ἄκρον παρὰ ῥηγμῖνα κυμα.......
    ταῦτ᾽ ἐθέλοιμ᾽ ἂν ἰδεῖν,
15 ὅς μ᾽ ἠδίκησε, λ[ὰ]ξ δ᾽ ἐφ᾽ ὁρκίοις ἔβη,
    τὸ πρὶν ἑταῖρος [ἐ]ών.

4 κύμ[ατι] Reitzenstein, κύμ[ασι] Cantarella
5 εὐφρονέσ[τατα] Diels, alii alia    7 ἐνθαναπλησει pap.,
sscr. πο]λλαναπλησε[ικα]κα, ἀναπλήσαι West    9 χνου
pap., corr. Masson    10 ἐπέχοι Reitzenstein, probb. West
alii, επιχοι leg. Schwartz, corr. Masson    15 ἐπ᾽ Blass
ὁρκίοις Reitzenstein, ὁρκίοισ᾽ Diehl

**117** P. Argent. 3 fr. 2

ἡ χλαῖν[α ......]αστινη[
    κυρτον ε[.....]φιλεῖς
ἀγχοῦ καθῆσθαι· ταῦτα δ᾽ Ἱππῶνα[ξ ∪ –
5     ο]ἶδεν ἄριστα βροτῶν,
οἶ]δεν δὲ κάρίφαντος· ἆ μάκαρ ὄτ[ις
    μηδαμά κώ σ᾽ ἔϊδε
τ]ρ[άγ]ου πνέοντα φῶρα. τῶι χυτρεῖ [δὲ νῦν
    Αἰσχυλίδηι πολέμει·
10 ἐκεῖνος ἤμερσέ[ν σε ........]ης,
    πᾶς δὲ πέφηνε δό[λος.

4 Ἱππῶνα[ξ Reitzenstein, -α[κτίδης Maas    8 τ]ρ[άγ]ου

foam may he vomit much seaweed and may his teeth
chatter while he lies on his face like a dog at the edge
of the surf, his strength spent, . . . This is what I'd
like him to experience, who treated me unjustly by
trampling on his oaths, he who was formerly my
friend.

¹ Only three letters of what precedes are preserved.
² On the southwest coast of the Black Sea. For more details see J.
P. Stronk, "Wreckage at Salmydessos," *Talanta* 18-19 (1986-87)
63-75.

**117** Same papyrus

. . . the cloak¹ . . . fishing basket(?)² . . . you are in the
habit of sitting nearby. Hipponax . . . knows this
better than anyone and so does Ariphantus.³ Ah,
blessed is he who has never yet seen you, you thief
with the stench of a goat(?). Now wage war with the
potter Aeschylides. He robbed (you?) of . . . and all
your deceit has been revealed.

¹ Perhaps stolen by the thief of v. 8.          ² If accented κύρ-
τον, but probably 'hunchbacked' if accented κυρτόν.          ³ Ap-
parently a friend of Hipponax rather than the name of the thief.

---

Diehl, γ]ρ[άσ]ου Wilamowitz          fin. suppl. Reitzenstein
10 -έ[ν σε Blass          τῆς ἀπαρτί]ης West          11 Diels

**118** P. Oxy. xviii.2176, ed. Lobel

**a**  ὦ Σάνν᾽, ἐπειδὴ ῥῖνα θεό[συλιν ]εις
      καὶ γαστρὸς οὐ κατακρα[τεῖς,
  τοὺς μοι παράσχες, ὦ[            ].ν·
      σύν τοί τι βουλεῦσαι θέ[λω

**b**  λαιμᾶι δέ σοι τὸ ⌊χεῖ⌋λος ὡς ⌊ἐρωι⌋διοῦ

**c**                τοὺς] βρα[χίονας
      καὶ τὸ]ν τράχ[ηλον
  κα[        μή σε γαστρίη[

**d**  πρῶτον μὲν ἐκδὺς νε.[

**e**               ]αὐλήσει δέ σοι
    Κίκων τὸ Κωδάλου [μέλος

**b** Schol. Nic. *Th.* 470, "μαιμώσσων" (p. 191 Crugnola)

. . . γράφεται καὶ λαιμώσσων ἀντὶ τοῦ πεινῶν, ὡς
Ἱππῶναξ "λαιμᾶ δέ σου χεῖλος ὡς ἐρῳδιοῦ."

440

**118** Oxyrhynchus papyrus (2nd c. A.D.)

*The order of the lemmata and of the fragments of the commentary is disputed. For the former I have adopted the order in which Degani prints them (his fr. 129), since this agrees with the commentary, and my text of both lemmata and commentary is essentially that of Degani. Degani's apparatus and Slings' study should be consulted for supplements. Those scraps which contain little or nothing intelligible have been omitted.*

   **a**  O Sannus, since you (sport?) a sacrilegious nose[1] and have no control over your appetite, lend me your ear, O . . . , I want to give you some advice

   **b**  your beak is as ravenous as a heron's

   **c**  your arms and neck (are wasted?) . . . see that you don't (get?) colic

   **d**  first strip . . .

   **e**  Cicon[2] will pipe for you the tune of Codalus

**b** Scholiast on Nicander, *Theriaca* ("being very eager")

. . . λαιμώσσων is also written [i.e., is a variant reading], the equivalent of πεινῶν ('being hungry') as in Hipponax ("your beak—heron's")

**e** Ath. 14.624b

διὸ καὶ τοὺς παρὰ τοῖς ῞Ελλησιν αὐλητὰς Φρυγίους
καὶ δουλοπρεπεῖς τὰς προσηγορίας ἔχειν, οἷός ἐστιν
ὁ παρὰ Ἀλκμᾶνι (fr. 109 *PMGF*, 206 Calame) Σάμβας
καὶ ῞Αδων καὶ Τῆλος, παρὰ δὲ Ἱππώνακτι Κίⲥκⲣων
καὶ Κώδαλος, καὶ Βάβυς, ἐφ' ᾧ καὶ ἡ παροιμία ἐπὶ
τῶν αἰεὶ πρὸς τὸ χεῖρον αὐλούντων, "κάκιον ἢ Βάβυς
αὐλεῖ."

a 1 θεό[συλιν Lobel        φορέ]εις Luppe        2 fin.
Lobel        b λαιμώσσων, λαιμώσσει, λαιμῷ codd., corr.
Schneidewin        c 1,2 suppl. Lobel        2 fin. ἐφθίσαι
suppl. West        3 fin. λάβῃ Snell, Lobel        e 2 fin. Latte

Commentarii fragmenta

**A** (fr. 1 col. i + fr. 9, cf. P. Oxy. xix p. 153)

"ὦ Σάνν', ἐπειδὴ ῥῖνα θεό[συλιν
εις, καὶ γαστρὸς οὐ κατακρα[τεῖς"· κύρι-
ο]ν ὄνομα ὁ Σάννος, ὧⲥιⲣ λοιδορ[εῖται
πεποιῆσθαί φασιν παρὰ τὴ[ν σαννάδα.
5        Κρ[ῆτ]ας δὲ τὰς ἀγρίας αἶγας λέγειν σαν-
νάδας φη]σὶν Πολέμων ἐν τοῖς Πρὸς
Ἀντίγονον κα]ὶ Ἀδαῖον· τὰς δὲ αἶγας ἐπι-
                    ]ποπλήκτους εἶναι καιναι
                    ]καὶ ἐν τῶι βίωι το[ὺ]ς εὐή-
10        θεις        ].μεν[...ἀ]λλ' οὐδὲ του
                    ]ν· "ὦ Σά[ν]ν', ἐπειδὴ ῥῖνα

442

**e**  Athenaeus, *Scholars at Dinner*

For this reason pipers among the Greeks have names that
are Phrygian and appropriate to slaves. Examples are Sam-
bas in Alcman and Adon and Telus and in Hipponax Cicon
and Codalus and Babys who gave rise to the proverb said
of those whose pipe-playing always gets worse, "he pipes
worse than Babys."

¹ Perhaps his penis (see n. 5 on fr. 78), but it's not clear why
it would be called "sacrilegious." Slings (pp. 84 f.) suggests that
Sannus is "one who steals food from altars," but then mention of
his nose seems strange.    ² See frr. 4, 4a, 78.7. Presumably
both the piping and the tune are of poor quality.

Fragments of the Commentary

**A**

"O Sannus, since you (sport?) a sacrilegious nose
and have no control over your appetite." Sannus is a
proper name as a term of abuse. (Some?) say that it
is derived from *sannas* ('wild goat'). Polemon in his
*Address to Antigonus and Idaeus*¹ says that the Cre-
tans call wild goats *sannades*; and . . . that goats are
stupid(?) . . . and in (everyday) life simpletons (are
so called?)² . . . "O Sannus, since you (sport?) a sacri-

θεόσυλιν            ]ς τοὺς μοι παράσχες, ὦ
                   ].ν σύν τοί τι βουλεῦσαι θέ-
λω·                ]ς τὴν ἱερόσυλιν ῥῖνα
15                 ]ννε[.]ακοντος αὐτοῦ
                   ]ν ἀπὸ παν-
                   ]ν τάχα δε
                   ]νετομε

**B**  (frr. 3 + 5 + 4, cf. P. Oxy. xviii p. 184)

                        "]λαιμᾶι δέ σοι τὸ
χεῖ]λος ὡς [ἐρω]διοῦ"· [ἀπὸ] τοῦ λαιμοῦ ωσαν
...].. σει.[.]ε λέγε[ι. ἁρπ]ακτικὸν δὲ τὸ
5    ὄρνεο]ν ὁ ἐρωδιό[ς, ὅθεν] κ[αὶ] τοῖς περὶ τὸν Ὀ-
δυ[σσ]έα ἐν τ[ῆι] νυκτ[ηγρ]εσίαι Ἀθηνᾶ ἐπι-
πέμπ[ε]ι τ[οῦτο]ν τὸν [οἰ]ωνὸν ἁρπασομέ-
νοις δηλονότι γα[
να ὥσπερ καὶ γει[
10   ἐρωδιόν. Παλ(αμήδης) γρά[φει
εὖ. "ὡς ἐρωδιοῦ" ω[
ος ἐκτιθεὶς τα.[
καθηγησαμεν[
νησον ταύτην[

**C**  (fr. 1 col. ii)

                          τοὺς]
βρα[χίονας καὶ τὸ]ν τράχ[ηλον
κα[..........] μή σε γαστρίη [υ –". στρό-

legious nose, lend me your ear, O . . . ; I want to
give you some advice." . . . the sacrilegious nose . . .

[1] Polemon of Ilium (2nd c. B.C.) ascribed the invention of epic
parody to Hipponax (see on fr. 128) and wrote against the art
historians Antigonus and Adaeus.    [2] That Sannus is a nick-
name for an idiot is substantiated by Aristophanes of Byzantium
(fr. 1 Slater).

**B**

. . . "your beak is as ravenous as a heron's"; he derives
'is ravenous' from the word for gullet . . . The heron
is a rapacious bird and hence Athena sent this bird
to Odysseus and his companion [i.e., Diomedes]
who were about to go on a raiding expedition during
the night[1] . . . like . . . heron. Palamedes[2] writes . . .
(not?) well. "A heron's" . . . set forth(?) . . . this is-
land(?)[3] . . .

[1] A reference to *Iliad* 10.274 ff.    [2] According to the
*Suda* s.v., Palamedes of Elea (date uncertain) was a grammarian
who, among other things, was a collector of words (ὀνομα-
τολόγος).    [3] If 'island' is the correct reading, as seems
likely, there may be a reference to the island called Diomedea
where Diomedes' companions were said to have been turned into
herons. See D'A. W. Thompson, *A Glossary of Greek Birds,* pp.
88-91.

**C**

. . . your arms and neck (are wasted?) . . . See that you
don't (get?) colic." (He means?) a twisting of the

5    φο[.........γ]αστρὸς ἀλγηδ.[
    μωι συνεχόμενοι εἰώθασ[ι
    τὴν γαστέρα εἰς ἀπόδ‹ε›ιξιν[    νενε-
    κρῶσθαι. ἴδε σου, φησίν, τοὺς β[ραχίονας
    καὶ τὸν τράχηλον ὅτι ἐφθιν[
10   καὶ κατεσθίεις καὶ μή σε κατα[
    μός. "πρῶτον μὲν ἐκδὺς νε.[    "· παραι-
    νεῖ αὐτῶι πρῶτον χειρονομ[ήσαντι τὸ
    φάρμακον πιεῖν· ῥαιδίως γὰρ ο[ὕτως τὸ
    φάρμακον ποιεῖν καὶ ἀναδοθ[
15   "αὐλήσει δέ σοι Κίκων τὸ Κωδά[λου μέλος"·
    σκευ[άσα]ι δὲ τὸν Κίκωνα κ[

**D** (fr. 6)

                      ]ς χηραμὸν . ποιοι
    ἰπνοὶ κ]αίονται· λέγει δὲ τὰς καμί-
5   νους. ἰπ]νὸς δὲ ἀπὸ τοῦ ἐξιποῦν
    τὸ συνεστρ]αμμέν[ο]ν ἐν τῶι στατὶ ὕ-
    δωρ ......].ν διτουλη ἦ[.] φησιν
             ].εσθαι χ.ορ.[..
          ]ε γυναικ[ο]π[ί]πην· λ[
10         ].ώματα, τὰ ἐναπολ[ειφ-
    θέντα τῶι κλι]βάνωι περικαύμα-
    τα ..... φλυκτ]αίνας, οὓς ἔνιοι ἀττ[α-
    ράγους καλοῦσιν].[..]νισ[.]αρα[..]η[

bowels and stomach pain . . . those afflicted with . . .
are in the habit of . . . their stomach as proof of its
(their?) deathlike state. See, he says, how your arms
and neck are wasted (even though?) you eat up,[1] and
see to it that you don't . . . "First strip . . ."; he ad-
vises him first to do hand exercises and drink the
medicine, for in this way the medicine works more
readily and is spread throughout the body. "Cicon
will pipe for you the tune of Codalus." To get ready
Cicon . . .

[1] It seems that, in spite of the glutton's voracious appetite, he
is becoming emaciated. West, *Studies* 147, compares Erysichthon
in Callim. *Hymn* 6.88-93.

# D[1]

. . . hole . . . *ipnoi* are being fired up. By this he
means ovens. *Ipnos* is derived from squeezing out
(*exipoun*) the water that has collected in dough . . .
he says . . . ogler of women[2] . . . the charred remains
left in the oven . . . blisters which some call *at-
taragoi*[3] . . .

[1] Presumably a commentary on a different poem.     [2] Ap-
parently a continuation of the etymological discussion of *ipnos*.
[3] The name given to the blister-like protrusions on the top of
baked bread. See Degani, *Studi* 274 f.

**E** (frr. 2 + 8 + Addenda + P. Oxy. x.1233 fr. 29; cf. P. Oxy. xviii p. 185, xix p. 153)

τρ[ιτα]ῖον ἐκ κήρυ[κο]s ἀσμε[ν...]έ μιν

Commentarii fragmentum

αὐτοὺς ἐπὶ χρόνο[ν.......] ἕως τ[ὸ
σ]ῶμα ψύχηται· νῦν δ[ὲ ἐ]πὶ ἄμμον θα-
λα]σσίαν ἐ[κ]βάλλουσι. "τρ[ιτα]ῖον ἐκ κήρυ-
5    κο]s ἀσμε[ν...]έ μιν"· πρ[..] αὐτὰ τὰ ἀνδρ[
      [..ήν]εγκεν αὐτ[ὸ]ν τριταῖον
            ]ν προ[σ]κηρυ-
            ]το κἀν τοῖς
            ]νημος δαρ-
10          ἐ]κ κήρυκος ε-
           ]ομοῖον τῶι
           ].τανησαν
           ]ντες ἆσσον
           ]γράφου-
15   σι         ἐγ]γὺς τῆς θα-
   λάσσης      ].ω...ε
          ἐκβά]λλουσι
          ]..πατήρ
          ].s διασκευ-
20         ]ν νεκρὸν ε-
         ]αιωι ὀστέωι
         ].Ἀρ[ι]στοφά-
   ν         ]πολ[.]ανδρει
         ].λονων

448

**E**[1]

    on the third day at the hands of the herald (and?)
gladly him . . .

Commentary

    . . . them for a time . . . until the body grows cold;
and now they cast it forth on the sand of the sea.
"On the third day at the hands of the herald (and?)
gladly him." (To?) the very . . . he [i.e., the herald?]
brought him on the third day . . . also in the . . . at
the hands of the herald . . . (dis)similar to the . . .
nearer,[2] they write . . . near the sea . . . they cast forth
. . . father . . . corpse . . . bone . . . Aristophanes[3] . . .
common burial place(?) . . .

[1] It seems clear from the commentary that the poem dealt
with the *pharmakos* or scapegoat ritual, on which see Slings 89-
91, and cf. frr. 5-10.     [2] Possibly a quotation from Hipponax.
[3] Presumably the grammarian Aristophanes of Byzantium.

IAMBIC POETRY

**118a** Pollux 10.18

τοὔνομα δὲ ἡ ἀπαρτία ἔστι μὲν Ἰωνικόν, ὠνομασ-
μένων οὕτω παρ᾽ αὐτοῖς τῶν κούφων σκευῶν ἃ ἔστι
παραρτήσασθαι . . . εἰ μέντοι ἐν βιβλίῳ τινὶ τοὔνομα
τὴν ἀπαρτίαν εὑρεῖν ἐθέλοις, . . . , εὑρήσεις ἔν τε τῷ
δευτέρῳ τῶν Ἱππώνακτος ἰάμβων,

ἀκήρατον δὲ τὴν ἀπαρτίην ἔχει,

καὶ παρὰ Θεοφράστῳ ἐν τῷ δεκάτῳ Νόμων.

ἀπαρτίαν codd., corr. Bergk

**119** Hephaest. *Ench.* 5.3 (p. 16.16 Consbruch)

καταληκτικὸν . . . τετράμετρον [sc. ἰαμβικὸν] δὲ οἷον
τὸ Ἱππώνακτος·

εἴ μοι γένοιτο παρθένος καλή τε καὶ τέρεινα.

*120-127 Tetrametri*

**120** *Suda* i.487.10 Adler

Βούπαλος· ὄνομα. Ἀριστοφάνης· "εἰ νὴ Δία τις τὰς
γνάθους τούτων δὶς ἢ τρὶς ἔκοψεν ὥσπερ Βουπάλου,

450

**118a** Pollux, *Vocabulary*

The word ἀπαρτία is Ionic, the name given by the Ionians to light utensils which can be fastened at one's side . . . If however you should wish to find the word ἀπαρτία in a book, . . . , you will find it in the second book[1] of Hipponax's iambics,

> he has his utensils undamaged,[2]

and in the tenth book of Theophrastus' *Laws*.

[1] Only here and in fr. 142 is book 2 explicitly given as a source.
[2] Masson, whose enumeration West followed, assigned the line to the epodes because it is a pure trimeter, but there are several examples of such verses among the choliambics.

**119** Hephaestion, *Handbook of Meters*

An example of the iambic tetrameter catalectic is the line of Hipponax:

> If only I might have a maiden who is both beautiful and tender[1]

[1] Perhaps a contamination of Arch. frr. 118 and 196a.6. Since Hephaestion tends to quote from the beginning of a poem, this may be its first verse.

*120-127 Trochaic Tetrameters*

**120** *Suda*

Bupalus, a name. Cf. Aristophanes: "By Zeus, if anyone had struck their jaws two or three times like that of Bu-

451

# IAMBIC POETRY

φωνὴν ἂν οὐκ εἶχον" (*Lys.* 360 sq.). παρὰ τῷ Ἱππώνακτι
(τὸ Ἱππωνάκτειον Degani)

λάβετέ μεο ταἰμάτια, κόψω Βουπάλου τὸν
    ὀφθαλμόν.

cf. *Sud.* iii.155.24 Adler

μοῦ codd., corr. Fick      θοἰμάτιον codd., corr. Schnei-
dewin      Βουπάλῳ *Suda* iii.155, rec. West

**121** Erotian. *lex. Hippocr.* α 31 (p. 15.8 Nachmanson)

ἀμφιδέξιος· Βακχεῖός φησιν ἀμφοτεροδέξιος, ὡς ἀμ-
φήκης ὁ ἀμφοτέρωθεν ἠκονημένος. σαφὲς δ' αὐτὸ
ποιεῖ Εὐριπίδης ἐν Ἱππολύτῳ (780) λέγων "ἀμφιδέξιον
σίδηρον" ἀντὶ τοῦ ἑκατέρωθεν τέμνοντα. ὁ δὲ Ἱπ-
ποκράτης (Aph. 7.43) οὐκ ἐπὶ τοῦ ἀμφήκους ἀλλ' ἐπὶ
τοῦ εὐχρήστου τίθεται κατὰ ἀμφότερα τὰ μέρη.
διδάσκει δὲ καὶ ὁ ποιητής, τὸ μὴ καθ' ἓν μόνον μέρος
εὔχρηστον περιδέξιον λέγων (Il. 21.163). ὁμοίως καὶ ὁ
Ἱππῶναξ φησιν·

ἀμφιδέξιος γάρ εἰμι κοὐκ ἁμαρτάνω κόπτων.

cf. Galen. in Hippocr. *Aph.* (xviii(1).147 sq. Kühn) et *lex. Hip-
pocr.* (xix.78 K.)

καὶ οὐχ codd., corr. ten Brink      κόπτων om. Gal.
utroque loco

452

palus, they wouldn't have any voice." It is a parody of Hipponax,

> take my cloak, I'll hit Bupalus in the eye[1]

[1] Combined by many with fr. 121, perhaps rightly.

**121** Erotian, *Lexicon on Hippocrates*

*amphidexios.* Bacchius says *amphoterodexios*, with the meaning 'two-edged,' i.e., sharp on both sides. Euripides clearly does this in *Hippolytus* when he speaks of an "*amphidexios* sword" instead of a sword that cuts on both sides. In Hippocrates it does not mean 'two-edged' but having ready use of limbs on both sides. And the poet [i.e., Homer] proves this when he uses *peridexios* of what is not readily useful in one part only. Similarly Hipponax says:

> for I have two right hands and I don't miss with my punches

# IAMBIC POETRY

**122** Hephaest. *Ench.* 6.2 (p. 18.16 Consbruch); praecedit
Arch. fr. 88

τοῦτο δὲ τὸ τετράμετρον [sc. τὸ καταληκτικὸν] γίνεται
καὶ χωλόν, τοῦ παρατελεύτου ποδὸς σπονδείου γενο-
μένου, οἷόν ἐστι καὶ τὸ

Μητροτίμῳ δηῦτέ με χρὴ τῷ σκότῳ δικάζεσθαι.

cf. schol. p. 271.13 Consbruch, Io. Sicel. in Hermog. *Rhet. Gr.*
vi.240.13 Walz

Μητρόδημε et κολάζεσθαι Io. Sicel.

**123** Strabo 14.1.12

ἐκ Πριήνης δὲ ἦν Βίας, εἷς τῶν ἑπτὰ σοφῶν, περὶ οὗ
φησιν οὕτως Ἱππῶναξ·

καὶ δικάζεσθαι Βίαντος τοῦ Πριηνέως κρέσσον.

cf. Diog. Laert. 1.84, *Sudam* i.470.19, ii.93.21 Adler

δικάσασθαι Strabo        Πριηνέος Diog. cod. B κρέσσον
Strabo, Diog. Bᵃᶜ, κρεῖσσον Diog., κρείσσων *Suda* (rec. Degani)

**124** Sext. Emp. *adv. math.* 1.275

ἔχοι δ' ἄν τινα, φασίν, [ἡ γραμματική] ἐξαιρέτως καὶ
ταῖς τῶν μανθανόντων αὐτὴν πατρίσιν ἀναγκαῖα. Λε-
βεδίων γοῦν διαφερομένων πρὸς τοὺς ἀστυγείτονας
περὶ Καμανδωλοῦ ὁ γραμματικὸς τὸ Ἱππωνάκτειον
παραθέμενος ἐνίκα·

**122**  Hephaestion, *Handbook of Meters*

This catalectic tetrameter also occurs in 'limping' form,
with the penultimate foot becoming a spondee, as in

> Once again I must take the swindler[1] Metrotimus[2]
> to court[3]

[1] See n. 8 on fr. 79.          [2] Treated by some as a fictitious
name ironically alluding to the μητροκοίτης Bupalus of fr. 12.2.
[3] Although cited anonymously, the verse is commonly assigned to
Hipponax because the same infinitive occurs in fr. 123 and be-
cause a Metrotime appears in the choliambics of Herodas 3.

**123**  Strabo, *Geography*

Bias, one of the Seven Sages, came from Priene. Hipponax
speaks about him as follows:

> and to have a better judge than Bias of Priene[1]

[1] Joined by some to fr. 122. Bias appears also in Callimachus
fr. 191.73 Pf., a poem which begins with an address to Hipponax
(see fr. 1 above).

**124**  Sextus Empiricus, *Against the Professors*

And grammar, they say, can contain some things which are
especially necessary for the countries of those who learn
it. At any rate when the Lebedians were quarreling with
their neighbours over Camandolus, the grammarian won
the day by citing the verse from Hipponax:

μηδὲ μοιμύλλειν Λεβεδίην ἰσχάδ᾽ ἐκ
  Καμανδωλοῦ.

μοι μῦ λαλεῖ(ν) codd., corr. Meineke ex Hesych. μοιμύλλειν·
θηλάζειν, ἐσθίειν      Καμανδωδοῦ in test. et v.l. in versu

**125** Strabo 8.3.8

καὶ τὸ Βουπράσιον μὲν δὴ μέρος ἦν τῆς Ἤλιδος,
ποιητικῷ δέ τινι σχήματι συγκαταλέγειν τὸ μέρος τῷ
ὅλῳ φασὶ τὸν Ὅμηρον ὡς τὸ "ἀν᾽ Ἑλλάδα καὶ μέσον
Ἄργος" (Il. 2.615) . . . χρῶνται δὲ καὶ οἱ νεώτεροι,
Ἱππῶναξ μέν·

  Κυπρίων βέκος φαγοῦσι κἀμαθουσίων πυρῶν

—Κύπριοι γὰρ καὶ οἱ Ἀμαθούσιοι—καὶ Ἀλκμὰν δέ·
(fr. 55 PMGF, 121 Calame).

καὶ Ἀμ. codd., corr. Hermann

**127** Hesych.

Κυβήβη· ἡ μήτηρ τῶν θεῶν, καὶ ἡ Ἀφροδίτη . . . <ὑπὸ
Λυδῶν> (suppl. ten Brink e Phot. i.355 Naber) ἢ (del.
Degani) καὶ Φρυγῶν. παρ᾽ ὃ καὶ Ἱππῶνάξ φησι·

  καὶ Διὸς κούρη Κυβήβη καὶ Θρεϊκίη Βενδῖς.

ἄλλοι δὲ Ἄρτεμιν.

διόσκουρος κυβήκη cod., corr. Bergk      θρηίκη βένδιν
cod., corr. Bergk (Θρε- Fick)

and not to suck on a Lebedian dried fig¹ from
Camandolus²

¹ Probably = vagina (see nn. on Arch. frr. 250, 251.4 and Henderson 22), especially if Bartalucci, *Maia* 16 (1964) 248, is right in analysing μοιμύλλειν as both 'suck' and 'fuck, I pray' (μοι μύλλειν).      ² Site unknown, but presumably in the territory of Lebedos which lay between Teos and Colophon.

## 125 Strabo, *Geography*

And although Buprasium was a part of Elis, they say that by a kind of poetic figure Homer includes the part with the whole, in "throughout Greece and the middle of Argos" . . . And more recent poets also use the figure, as for example Hipponax:

those who ate the bread¹ of Cyprian and Amathusian wheat

—for the Amathusians are also Cyprians—and Alcman.

¹ A Phrygian word according to Herodotus 2.2.

## 127 Hesychius, *Lexicon*

Cybebe: the Mother of the Gods, and identified with Aphrodite by the Lydians and Phrygians. Compare what Hipponax says:

and the daughter of Zeus, Cybebe, and Thracian Bendis.

Others identify her with Artemis.

*128-129a Hexametri*

**128** Ath. 15.698b

Πολέμων δ' ἐν τῷ δωδεκάτῳ τῶν πρὸς Τίμαιον περὶ
τῶν τὰς παρῳδίας γεγραφότων ἱστορῶν τάδε γράφει·
"καὶ τὸν Βοιωτὸν δὲ καὶ τὸν Εὔβοιον τοὺς τὰς παρ-
ῳδίας γράψαντας λογίους ἂν φήσαιμι διὰ τὸ παίζειν
ἀμφιδεξίως καὶ τῶν προγενεστέρων ποιητῶν ὑπερ-
έχειν ἐπιγεγονότας. εὑρετὴν μὲν οὖν τοῦ γένους Ἱππώ-
νακτα φατέον τὸν ἰαμβοποιόν. λέγει γὰρ οὗτος ἐν τοῖς
ἑξαμέτροις·

Μοῦσά μοι Εὐρυμεδοντιάδεω τὴν ποντοχάρυβδιν,
τὴν ἐγγαστριμάχαιραν, ὃς ἐσθίει οὐ κατὰ κόσμον,
ἔννεφ', ὅπως ψηφῖδι ⟨κακῇ⟩ κακὸν οἶτον ὄληται
βουλῇ δημοσίῃ παρὰ θῖν' ἁλὸς ἀτρυγέτοιο.

1 Εὐρυμεδοντιάδεα A (rec. West), corr. Wilamowitz
3 κακῇ suppl. Musurus, κακὸς Cobet, κακῶς Kalinka
ὀλεῖται Cobet (rec. West)

---

[1] See n. 1 on fr. 118A.    [2] On this topic see Athenaeus
15.698a-699c and especially Degani's introduction (pp. 5-36) to
his *Poesia parodica greca* (Bologna 1982).    [3] Boeotus of

# HIPPONAX

## *128-129a Dactylic Hexameters*

**128** Athenaeus, *Scholars at Dinner*

Polemon,[1] inquiring into the composers of parody,[2] writes as follows in the twelfth book of his *Address to Timaeus*: "I should say that both Boeotus and Euboeus[3] who composed parodies are skilled in words because they play with double meanings and, although born later, outstrip the poets who preceded them. It must be said, however, that the iambic poet Hipponax was the founder of the genre.[4] For he speaks as follows in hexameters:

> Tell me, Muse,[5] of the sea swallowing,[6] the stomach carving[7] of Eurymedontiades[8] who eats in no orderly manner, so that through a baneful vote determined by the people he may die a wretched death along the shore of the undraining(?) sea.[9]

Syracuse and Euboeus of Paros wrote in the 4th c. B.C. Almost nothing has survived.        [4] Arist. *Poetics* 1448a12 calls Hegemon of Thasos (5th c.) the founder of parody, but by this he means that Hegemon made parody a profession.        [5] The first of several epic parodies in the poem. For the opening cf. *Hymn to Aphrodite* 1.        [6] Literally 'the sea-Charybdis,' i.e., his drinking is compared to the famous whirlpool which "sucks up the dark water" (*Od.* 12.104).        [7] Literally 'the knife-in-the-stomach,' i.e., he does not take the time to cut up food before eating it, relying on his stomach to perform the function of a knife.

[8] There was a Eurymedon, king of the Giants (*Od.* 7.58 f.), but it is unclear what relevance, if any, this has for identifying the patronymic.        [9] It sems that Hipponax is alluding to the *pharmakos* ritual (cf. fr. 5). For an excellent discussion of the poem see Degani, *Studi* 187-205, 216-225.

IAMBIC POETRY

**129** Gramm. in cod. Voss. gr. Q 20 (Reitzenstein, *Geschichte der gr. Etymologika* 367)

οἱ δὲ Ἴωνες αὐτὴν [sc. τὴν αἰτιατικὴν] εἰς τὴν ουν ἐποίουν, Σαπφοῦν καὶ Λητοῦν, ὡς δηλοῦσιν αἱ χρήσεις . . . ὁμοίως καὶ παρ᾽ Ἱππώνακτι·

πῶς παρὰ Κυψοῦν ἦλθε.

**129a** Suet. π. παιδιῶν (p. 65 Taillardat)

σκιράφεια δ᾽ ἐκάλουν τὰ κυβευτήρια· ὅθεν καὶ τοὺς πανούργους σκιράφους ἐκάλουν Ἱππῶναξ τε καὶ ἕτεροι, ἀπὸ τῆς ἐν τοῖς σκιραφείοις δηλονότι ῥᾳδιουργίας.

Eust. in Hom. *Od.* 1.107 (1397.24)

καὶ ὅτι ἐσπουδάζετο ἡ κυβεία, οὐ μόνον παρὰ Σικελοῖς, ἀλλὰ καὶ Ἀθηναίοις, οἳ καὶ ἐν ἱεροῖς ἀθροιζόμενοι ἐκύβευον, καὶ μάλιστα ἐν τῷ τῆς Σκιράδος Ἀθηνᾶς τῷ ἐπὶ Σκίρῳ. ἀφ᾽ οὗ καὶ τὰ ἄλλα κυβευτήρια σκιράφεια ὠνομάζετο. ἐξ ὧν καὶ πάντα τὰ πανουργήματα διὰ τὴν ἐν σκιραφείοις ῥᾳδιουργίαν σκίραφοι ἐκαλοῦντο. Ἱππῶναξ·

τί με σκιράφοις ἀτιτάλλεις;

**129**  Anonymous Grammarian

The Ionians formed the accusative (of feminine nouns
ending in -ω) in -ουν, e.g. Σαπφοῦν and Λητοῦν, as the
usage shows . . . Similarly also in Hipponax:

how he came to Cypso[1]

[1] Perhaps a parody of Καλυψοῦν (Calypso) with obscene in-
tent (cf. fr. 17 with n. 1 and Arch. fr. 45). The same word may be
present in fr. 77.1. Some treat the fragment as interrogative.

**129a**  Suetonius, *On Greek Games*

They used to call dicing places *skirapheia*. Clearly because
of the trickery that went on in them Hipponax and others
called tricksters *skiraphoi*.

Eustathius on Homer, *Odyssey*

And they say that dice playing was taken seriously not only
by the Sicilians but also by the Athenians who gathered
together and played dice even in temples, and especially
in the temple of Athena Skiras in the district Skiron. As a
result other dicing places were called *skirapheia* and all
acts of trickery were called *skiraphoi* because of the trick-
ery in the *skirapheia*. Cf. Hipponax:

why do you raise me on trickery?[1]

[1] Of the two meanings, trickster and trickery, given by the
sources, the latter seems more appropriate for the fragment.

**130**  Hesych.

ἄβδης· μάστιξ παρ᾽ Ἱππώνακτι.

**131**  Hesych.

Ἀγχαλέη· τόπου ὄνομα παρ᾽ Ἱππώνακτι.

**132**  Eust. in Hom. *Od.* 12.281 (1721.62)

ὅτι δὲ τὸ ἀδῶ ἀδήσω καὶ αὐτόχρημα τὸ ἥδεσθαι δηλοῖ
ποτε, δῆλον ἀπὸ χρήσεως Ἱππώνακτος, ἣν Ἡρα-
κλείδης προφέρει, εἰπόντος

　　ἄδηκε βουλή,

ἤγουν ἤρεσκε τὸ βούλευμα.

**133**  Io. Philop. τονικὰ παραγγέλματα (p. 38.11 Dindorf;
hinc Herodian. i.511.6 Lentz)

τὰ εἰς ας μὴ παραληγόμενα τῷ ε σὺν ἀμεταβόλῳ
ὀξύνεται . . . τὸ δὲ ἅλιας παρ᾽ Ἱππώνακτι ⟨προ⟩πα-
ροξύνεται, ἀπὸ τοῦ ἅλις πλεονάσαν τὸ α.

**130** Hesychius, *Lexicon*

ἄβδης, 'whip,' occurs in Hipponax.

**131** Hesychius, *Lexicon*

Ἀγχαλέη, the name of a place[1] in Hipponax.

[1] Unidentified and hence often emended (see fr. 149 Degani)

**132** Eustathius on Homer, *Odyssey*

That ἀδῶ ἀδήσω and in fact ἤδεσθαι explain it (i.e., ἀδηκότας) is clear from the usage of Hipponax (cited by Heraclides[1]) who said

the plan pleased,[2]

i.e., the resolution was pleasing.

[1] A grammarian from Miletus (1st c. A.D.).    [2] The perfect of ἀνδάνω, formed apparently from the aorist infinitive ἀδεῖν as though it were a present.

**133** Ioannes Philoponus, *Rules of Accentuation*

Words ending in -ας which do not have ε in the penultimate syllable are oxytone without any change . . . But ἅλιας in Hipponax is proparoxytone since it is from ἅλις ('in abundance') with pleonastic α.

**134** Orion, *etym.* col. 30.14 Sturz

ἀλίβας· ὁ νεκρός, παρὰ τὸ λιβάδα καὶ ὑγρότητα μὴ ἔχειν. ἔστι παρ᾽ Ἱππώνακτι καὶ ἐπὶ τοῦ ὄξους.

cf. *Et. Gen.* a 489, *Et. Sym.* a 592, *Et. Mag.* a 847 L.-L., etc.

**135** ἀνασεισίφαλλος

**135a** ἀνασυρτόλις

**135b** βορβορόπη

Eust. in Hom. *Il.* 23.775 (iv.835.13 V.d.Valk)

ἐνταῦθα δὲ οὐκ ἄκαιρον εἰπεῖν καὶ ὅτι στόμα τὸ οὕτως ἀποπτύον ὄνθου λεχθείη ἂν καὶ βορβόρου ὀπή, ὅπερ κατὰ παλαιὰν ἱστορίαν συνθεὶς ὁ βαρύγλωσσος Ἱππῶναξ "βορβορόπην" ὕβρισε γυναῖκά τινα, σκώπτων ἐκείνην εἰς τὸ παιδογόνον ὡς ἀκάθαρτον. ὃς καὶ "ἀνασεισίφαλλον" ἄλλην τινὰ διέσυρεν, ὡς ἀνασείουσαν, φασί, τὸν φάλητα.

**134** Orion, *Etymologicum*

ἀλίβας is 'corpse,' from lack of λιβάς ('moisture') and wetness. In Hipponax[1] it also means 'vinegar.'

[1] Probably Hipponax is an error for Callimachus, since the etymological lexica cite the latter (fr. 216 Pf.) for the meaning 'vinegar' (i.e., dead wine?). Or perhaps Callim. fr. 216, ἔβηξαν οἶον (οἶνον codd., corr., Bentley) ἀλίβαντα πίνοντες, "they coughed as though drinking vinegar," should be assigned to Hipponax.

**135** cock-shaker

**135a** self-exposer

**135b** opening of filth[1]

Eustathius on Homer, *Iliad*

Here it is not inappropriate to say that a mouth that spits out in this way might be described as an opening of dung and filth, a combination which according to ancient information the bitter-tongued Hipponax formed when he insultingly called a woman 'opening of filth,' jeering at her for her impure child-bearing. He also tore to pieces another woman, calling her a 'cock-shaker.'

[1] βορβορόπη is the form given by Eustathius. Other sources give -ώπη, -όπις, -όκη, -ωπός. By 'opening' Hipponax is referring to the vagina. For a full treatment of the other testimonia on these three words see frr. 151, 152, 158 Degani.

# IAMBIC POETRY

*Suda* iii.429.15 Adler

Ἱππῶναξ δὲ "βορβορόπιν" ὡς ἀκάθαρτον ταύτην φησίν, ἀπὸ τοῦ βορβόρου, καὶ "ἀνασυρτό{πο}λιν" ἀπὸ τοῦ ἀνασύρεσθαι.

**135c** Eust. in Hom. *Il.* 9.129 (ii.678.2 V.d.Valk)

Ἀντιφάνης δέ, φασί, "κασωρῖτιν" ἔφη τὴν ἐπὶ τέγους προεστῶσαν (fr. 310 K.-A.). οὕτω δὲ καὶ Ἱππῶναξ.

**136** Antiattic. in Bekker, *Anecd. Gr.* i.82.13

ἀνδριάντα· τὸν λίθινον ἔφη Ἱππῶναξ Βούπαλον ⟨τὸν⟩ (suppl. Diehl) ἀγαλματοποιόν.

**137** *Et. Gen.* (p. 14 Calame) = *Et. Mag.* 99.14

ἀναρριχᾶσθαι· . . . εὑρίσκεται καὶ χωρὶς τῆς αν συλλαβῆς παρ' Ἱππώνακτι, ἀρριχῶμαι. οὕτως Ἡρωδιανὸς ἐν τῷ περὶ παθῶν (ii.387.5 Lentz, cf. 475.27)

**138** Phryn. *praep. soph.* p. 28.1 von Borries (Bekker, *Anecd. Gr.* i.17.22)

ἄσβολος· θηλυκῶς λέγουσιν, Ἱππῶναξ δὲ ἀρσενικῶς. τινὲς δὲ καὶ τὴν ἀσβόλην.

*Suda*[2]

Hipponax calls her 'opening of filth' as of one who is impure, from βόρβορος 'filth,' and 'self-exposer' from ἀνασύρεσθαι 'to pull up one's clothes.'

[2] In what immediately precedes the *Suda* cited Arch. frr. 207-209.

**135c**  Eustathius on Homer, *Iliad*

They say that Antiphanes called a prostitute in a brothel *kasoritis*. So also Hipponax.

**136**  Anti-Atticist

Hipponax called the sculptor Bupalus a statue made of stone.[1]

[1] It is unclear whether 'statue made of stone' (i.e., blockhead?) or only 'statue' is to be attributed to Hipponax.

**137**  *Etymologicum Genuinum* and *Magnum*

ἀναρριχᾶσθαι: it is found also without the syllable αν in Hipponax, ἀρριχῶμαι 'I clamber up with hands and feet.' So Herodian in *On the Modification of Words*.

**138**  Phrynichus, *Sophistic Preparation*

ἄσβολος 'soot' is feminine, but masculine in Hipponax.[1] Some use the form ἀσβόλη.

[1] Perhaps a reference to fr. 103.10, but the gender there cannot be determined.

IAMBIC POETRY

**138a**  Phot. β 68

βαρεῖα χείρ· Ἱππῶναξ τὴν δεξιάν.

**139**  Hesych.

βασαγικόρος· ὁ θᾶσσον συνουσιάζων παρὰ Ἱππώνακτι.

**140**  Antiattic. in Bekker, *Anecd. Gr.* i.85.20

βατταρίζειν· Ἱππῶναξ.

**141**  Hesych.

βεβρενθυμένον παρὰ Ἱππώνακτι ὀργιζόμενον.

βεβρενθυόμενον cod., corr. (dub.) Alberti, βρενθυόμενον Dindorf

**142**  Antiattic. in Bekker, *Anecd. Gr.* i.85.23

βῖκος· Ἱππῶναξ δευτέρῳ. Ἡρόδοτος πρώτῳ (194).

βῖκος pro βίκος Dindorf

**138a** Photius, *Lexicon*

βαρεῖα χείρ ('heavy hand'): Hipponax uses it of the right hand.[1]

[1] A surprising gloss. More natural is Hesychius' gloss of the same two words as μιαιφόνος 'bloodthirsty.'

**139** Hesychius, *Lexicon*

βασαγικόρος[1] is used by Hipponax of one who is quick (too quick?) to have sexual intercourse.

[1] The word is not found elsewhere and various emendations have been suggested (see fr. 154 Degani). Some postulate a Lydian origin, comparing fr. 92.1.

**140** Anti-Atticist

βατταρίζειν ('to stammer') is found in Hipponax.[1]

[1] For a detailed study of this and related words see O. Masson, *Glotta* 54 (1976) 84-98.

**141** Hesychius, *Lexicon*

βεβρενθυμένον meaning 'angry' is found in Hipponax.[1]

[1] Degani (fr. 156) prefers Dindorf's emendation, since only the present and imperfect of this verb are attested elsewhere.

**142** Anti-Atticist

βῖκος occurs in the second book of Hipponax and the first book of Herodotus.[1]

[1] The word, perhaps of Egyptian origin, is used to describe various kinds of containers for liquids or food (see fr. 16 Degani).

**143** Diog. Laert. 4.58

γεγόνασι δὲ Βίωνες δέκα . . . δέκατος ἀγαλματοποιὸς
Κλαζομένιος ἢ Χῖος, οὗ μέμνηται καὶ Ἱππῶναξ.

**144** *Et. Gen.* β 178 = *Et. Sym.* β 151 (pp. 95-96 Berger) =
*Et. Mag.* 204.28 (hinc Herodian. ii.282.7, 482.32
Lentz) = Zonaras (p. 401 T.)

βόλιτον· βόλβιτον δὲ Ἴωνες, οἵ τε ἄλλοι καὶ Ἱπ-
πῶναξ, οἷον

βολβίτου κασιγνήτην.

**144a** Tzetz. *Chil.* 13.636

καὶ δοῦλος δὲ τῷ ποιητῇ κλῆσιν ὑπῆρχε Βύκκων.

Tzetz. ad loc. (p. 602 Leone)

βύκκων δὲ ὁ βρύχων ἤτοι ὁ ὄνος παρά τε Λυδοῖς καὶ
τοῖς κατ᾽ Ἔφεσον Ἴωσι λέγεται.

**145** Ath. 9.374e

(δέλφαξ) ἐπὶ δὲ τῶν θηλειῶν τοὔνομα τάττει Ἀριστο-
φάνης Ταγηνισταῖς (fr. 520.6 K.-A.) . . . καὶ Ἱππῶναξ δ᾽
ἔφη·

†ὥς† Ἐφεσίη δέλφαξ.

ὥσ‹περ› vel ὡς ‹ἂν› Meineke, ὡς ‹. . .› ᾽E. Welcker

HIPPONAX

**143** Diogenes Laertius, *Lives of the Philosophers*

There were ten named Bion . . . The tenth was a sculptor from Clazomenae or Chios, mentioned by Hipponax.

**144** *Etymologicum Genuinum, Symeonis, Magnum,*
  Zonaras

βόλιτον: the Ionians, including Hipponax, use the form βόλβιτον, as in

> sister of cow manure[1]

[1] For the figure cf. frr. 48 and 103.10.

**144a** Tzetzes, *Chiliads*

And also the poet [Homer] had a slave named Byccon.

Tzetzes ad loc.

βύκκων is used by the Lydians and the Ionians in Ephesus of one who eats greedily(?) or of an ass.[1]

[1] It is only a possibility that the word occurred in Hipponax.

**145** Athenaeus, *Scholars at Dinner*

Aristophanes in *The Broilers* treats δέλφαξ as feminine . . . And also Hipponax said:

> (like?) an Ephesian sow[1]

[1] With reference to a woman?

**146** Hesych.

ἐμβάφιον· ὀξύβαφον παρ᾽ Ἱππώνακτι.

**146a** Hesych.

"ἐμπεδὴς ⟨δὲ⟩ γαμόρος ⟨ἔ⟩μαρψεν Ἅιδης" (Trag. adesp.
208 K.-Sn.). ἔμπεδον ἔλεγον τὸν Ἅιδην, ὡς Ἱππῶναξ,
ἀντὶ τοῦ ἐν πέδῳ καὶ χθόνιος.

ἀντίον τοῦ οὖν ἐμπέδου χθόνιος cod., corr. West (ἀντὶ iam
Heinsius), ἀντὶ τοῦ ὁ (vel ὢν) ἐν πέδῳ, χθόνιος Degani (fr. 159)

**146b** Phot. *lex.* i.241 Naber

ἐ⟨μ⟩ψίουσα· τροφὰς διδοῦσα χόνδρου, καὶ τὰ ἑψητά.
Αἰσχύλος ἐν Τροφοῖς (fr. 246b Radt)· "βιοτὴν αὔξιμον
ἐ⟨μ⟩ψίουσα." Ἱππῶναξ.

ἑψιοῦσα cod., corr. Lobeck

**147** Suet. *de blasph.* (p. 63 Taillardat)

παρ᾽ Ἱππώνακτι δὲ καὶ "ἑπτάδουλος."

Ex eodem fonte Eust. in Hom. *Il.* 8.488 (ii.623.9
V.d.Valk); praecedit Arch. fr. 228

Ἱππῶναξ δὲ τὸν τρία ὑπεραναβὰς ἀριθμὸν "ἑπτάδου-
λον" ἔφη τινά.

**146** Hesychius, *Lexicon*

ἐμβάφιον is used by Hipponax[1] of a saucer for vinegar.

[1] Perhaps an error for Hippocrates, since the same gloss appears in Galen, *Lexicon to Hippocrates* (xix.97 Kühn).

**146a** Hesychius, *Lexicon*

"Hades the landowner under the earth seized." They called Hades ἔμπεδος, as did Hipponax, instead of 'in the ground' and 'under the ground.'

**146b** Photius, *Lexicon*

ἐ<μ>ψίουσα: giving food consisting of gruel, and what is boiled. Cf. Aeschylus in *Nurses* (of Dionysus): "feeding gruel as growth-promoting sustenance." So Hipponax.[1]

[1] Presumably only ἐμψιόνσα (or some form of the verb) is to be attributed to Hipponax. The *vox nihili* ἐψιοῦσα is generally emended on the basis of Hesychius' ἐμψιοῦσα (ἐμψίονσα corr. Lobeck)· ἐρέγματα διδοῦσα, i.e., 'giving crushed grain.'

**147** Suetonius, *On Defamatory Words*

And in Hipponax there is also ἑπτάδουλος.

Eustathius on Homer, *Iliad*

And Hipponax, exceeding the number three, called someone ἑπτάδουλος.

Eust. in Hom. *Od.* 5.306 (1542.49)

τρίδουλος ... Ἱππῶναξ δὲ ὑπεραναβὰς τοῦτό φησιν·

ἀφέω τοῦτον

τὸν ἑπτάδουλον;


**148**  *Suda* i.344.22 Adler

ἄρρεν· καὶ ἀρρενικῶς καὶ ἡμίανδρος καὶ ἡμιγύναιξ
καὶ διγενὴς καὶ θηλυδρίας καὶ ἑρμαφρόδιτος καὶ ἴθρις
... Ἱππῶναξ δὲ ἡμίανδρον, τὸν οἷον ἡμιγύναικα.


**148a**  Pollux 4.169 = 10.113

κύπρον δὲ τὸ οὕτω καλούμενον μέτρον εὕροις ἂν παρ'
Ἀλκαίῳ ἐν δευτέρῳ μελῶν (fr. 417A Voigt). καὶ
ἡμίκυπρον παρ' Ἱππώνακτι ἐν τῷ πρώτῳ τῶν ἰάμβων.


**149**  Hesych.

θεύτιν (θεῦτιν Bergk, θευτίν Smyth)· †σκαράδιν.† Ἱπ-
πῶναξ.

474

HIPPONAX

Eustathius on Homer, *Odyssey*

τρίδουλος ('thrice a slave') . . . and Hipponax, exceeding this, says:

> Am I to excuse this sevenfold slave?[1]

[1] Since this sentence occurs in Herodas 5.74, some consider Hipponax an error for Herodas, but it is possible that Hipponax also used the word ἑπτάδουλος.

## 148 *Suda*

male: and in the manner of a male and half-man and half-woman and of doubtful sex and effeminate and hermaphrodite and eunuch . . . and Hipponax calls

> half-man

one who is, as it were, half-woman.

## 148a Pollux, *Vocabulary*

You can find the measure called 'cyprus' in the second book of Alcaeus' lyric poems, the

> half-cyprus

in the first book of Hipponax's iambics.[1]

[1] The 'cyprus' is said to have been a grain measure used by those in the Pontic area. Hesychius s.v. ἡμίκυπρον defines it as half a medimnus, i.e., about 25 litres as an Attic measure.

## 149 Hesychius, *Lexicon*

A corrupt gloss on the word for 'squid.'

**150**  Pollux 10.184

κάνναι δὲ πλεγμάτιόν τι ἐστίν . . . , τὸν μέντοι ταύτας
πλέκοντα †καννηνοποιὸν† Ἱππῶναξ κέκληκεν.

ita CLB, καννακοποιὸν A, ὁ ποιῶν FS, κανητοποιὸν Bergk

**151a**  'Diogen.' 5.69 (*Paroem. Gr.* i.264.13 L.-S.)

Κωδάλου χοῖνιξ· ἐπὶ τῶν μεγάλοις μέτροις κεχρη-
μένων.

**151b**  Erotian. fr. 17 (p. 103 Nachmanson)

κοχώνην οἱ μὲν τὸ ἱερὸν ὀστοῦν, οἱ δὲ τὰς κοτύλας
τῶν ἰσχίων, ἐξ ὧν ἐστιν Ἀριστοφάνης ὁ γραμματικός
(fr. 341 Slater). Γλαυκίας δὲ καὶ Ἰσχόμαχος καὶ Ἱπ-
πῶναξ τὰ ἰσχία.

**152**  Hesych.

κραδησίτης· φαρμακός, ὁ ταῖς κράδαις βαλλόμενος.

**150** Pollux, *Vocabulary*

κάνναι are a kind of wickerwork . . . Hipponax called one who plaits them a

maker of reed mats[1]

[1] The precise form of the word is uncertain, but the meaning is reasonably clear.

**151a** Pseudo-Diogenianus, *Proverbs*

A 'choenix' of Codalus:[1] of those who use large measures.

[1] A 'choenix' was a dry measure, 1/48 of an Attic medimnus (see n. on fr. 148a). Codalus is named in fr. 118e, but that is no guarantee that the proverb was used by Hipponax.

**151b** Erotian, *Lexicon on Hippocrates*

Some take κοχώνη to mean the tail bone, others (among them Aristophanes the grammarian) the sockets of the hip joints. Glaucias, Ischomachus and Hipponax[1] take it to mean the haunches.

[1] Almost certainly not the poet. Perhaps the grammarian mentioned by Athenaeus 11.480f or an error for the medical writer Hippon (see Degani's edition p. 186).

**152** Hesychius, *Lexicon*

κραδησίτης: scapegoat, one struck by fig branches.[1]

[1] Attribution to Hipponax is suggested by frr. 5, 6, 9, 92.4 and 92.7.

IAMBIC POETRY

**153** Ps.-Plut. *de musica* 8.1133f

καὶ ἄλλος δ᾽ ἐστὶν ἀρχαῖος νόμος καλούμενος Κρα-
δίας, ὅν φησιν Ἱππῶναξ Μίμνερμον αὐλῆσαι. ἐν
ἀρχῇ γὰρ ἐλεγεῖα μεμελοποιημένα οἱ αὐλῳδοὶ ᾖδον.

Hesych.

κραδίης νόμος· νόμον τινὰ ἐπαυλοῦσι τοῖς ἐκπεμ-
πομένοις φαρμακοῖς, κράδαις καὶ θρίοις ἐπιραβδι-
ζομένοις.

**154** Prisc. *Inst.* 7.7 (ii.289.5 Keil)

nec mirum, cum Graecorum quoque poetae similiter in-
veniantur protulisse vocativos in supra dicta terminatione.
Ἀνακρέων· ἥλιε καλλιλαμπέτη (fr. 451 *PMG*) posuit pro
καλλιλαμπέτα. Ἱππῶναξ·

    εὔηθες κρίτη

pro κρίτα.

ευητες, ευντες, ευγες, ειτνετες, ειγνετες codd., corr. Krehl
καριτη et καριτα codd., corr. Putschen

**155** Herodian. π. καθολ. προσῳδ. in cod. Vind. hist. gr.
10 f. 5ᵛ (ed. H. Hunger, *JÖByzG* 16 [1967] 23)

κρεκύδειλος ὄνομα προπαροξύνεται ἐπὶ τοῦ (σαύ)ρου
τιθέμενον παρὰ τοῖς Ἴωσιν, ὥσπερ παρ᾽ Ἱππώνακτι·

478

**153**  Pseudo-Plutarch, *On Music*

And there is also another ancient melody called Cradias,[1]
which Hipponax says Mimnermus performed on the pipe.
For in the beginning singers to the pipe sang elegies set to
music.

Hesychius, *Lexicon*

κραδίης νόμος: a melody they pipe over those escorted
out as scapegoats, whipped with fig branches and fig
leaves.

  [1] Literally, 'melody of the fig branch.'

**154**  Priscian, *Grammar*

Nor is it surprising, since Greek poets are also found
to lengthen vocatives in the same way with the above-
mentioned termination. Cf. Anacreon: "fair-shining sun,"
with καλλιλαμπέτη instead of καλλιλαμπέτα. Cf. Hip-
ponax:

   simple-minded judge,

with κρίτη for κρίτα.

**155**  Herodian, *On General Accentuation*

The noun κρεκύδειλος, applied to the lizard by the Ionians
as by Hipponax, has the proparoxytone accent:

## IAMBIC POETRY

κατέπιεν ὥσπερ κρεκύδειλος ἐν λαύρῃ.

(Herod.) τ̣ο̣υ̣ τ̣ . .(.)ρου τιθεμενου cod., suppl. et corr. West
(Hipp.) κατέπιεν West, κατεῖρπεν (= καθεῖρπεν) Tsopanakis
κερκύδιλος West (metri causa)

**155a** Pergit Herodianus

καὶ ἐν ἑτέροις·

ἢ κρεκύδειλον ἢ πίθηκον.

κερκύδιλον West (metri causa)

**155b** Pergit Herodianus

προπερισπᾶται τὸ Κασμῖλος παρ' Ἱππώνακτι . . .
τοιοῦτο (-ῳ cod., corr. West) δὲ καὶ τὸ Καδμῖλος·

οὐ γὰρ μὰ τὸν Καδμῖλον

**156** Tzetz. in Lyc. 1170 (p. 339.15 Scheer), "στερρὰν
κύβηλιν"

ὁ Ἱππῶναξ Κύβηλιν τὴν Ῥέαν λέγει, παρὰ τὸ ἐν
Κυβέλλᾳ πόλει Φρυγίας τιμᾶσθαι.

**156a** Hesych.

κυλλήβην· †κολοβόντα. οἱ δὲ κέρατα κολόβια† παρ'
Ἱππώνακτι

cf. eundem κυληβίς· κολοβή

480

drank like a lizard in a privy[1]

[1] So West (cf. fr. 61) who assumes the lizard is drinking urine (*Studies* 149), but such a simile does not seem very appropriate.

**155a** Herodian continues

And elsewhere:

either a lizard or an ape

**155b** Herodian continues

Κασμῖλος has a circumflex on the penultimate syllable in Hipponax . . . So too Καδμῖλος:

no, by Cadmilus[1]

[1] Ascription to Hipponax is uncertain, but Herodian may have found both spellings (Κασ- and Καδ-) in the source he was using. For these and other spellings see Pfeiffer on Callim. fr. 723. The figure is often identified with Hermes and associated with the mysteries at Samothrace.

**156** Tzetzes on Lycophron, "hard axe"

Hipponax calls Rhea Cybelis,[1] from her being honoured in Cybella, a city in Phrygia.

[1] It is possible that Tzetzes was misled by Lycophron's κύβηλιν ('axe') to record Κύβηλιν rather than Κυβελίν. Both spellings are attested (see fr. 167 Degani).

**156a** Hesychius, *Lexicon*

A highly corrupt gloss on an unknown word which may itself be corrupt. A reference to docked horns is possible.

**157** Schol. Nic. *Alex.* 465b (p. 163 Geymonat), "λαγοῖο"

τοῦ θαλασσίου λαγωοῦ, ὅς ἐστιν εἶδος ἰχθύος, καὶ
Ἱππῶναξ μνημονεύει. ἔστι δὲ καὶ τὴν μὲν ἀσθένειαν
ἀφρῷ παραπλήσιος, μέλας δὲ τὴν ἐπιφάνειαν, θανά-
σιμος δὲ βρωθείς.

**158** *Epim. in Hom.*, p. 473.71 Dyck (hinc Lentz,
Herodian. i.108.6)

τὸ λαὸς ἄτρεπτος ἔμεινε παρ' Ὁμήρῳ, καίτοι τῇ μετα-
γενεστέρᾳ Ἰάδι τραπέν·

    ληὸν ἀθρήσας.

Ἱππῶναξ.

**159** Cyril. *lex.*, *Anecd. Par.* iv.185.30 Cramer (cf. W.
Bühler, *Hermes* 96 [1968] 233 n. 2)

λὶς ὁ λέων, καὶ λιὸς ἡ γενική, ὡς κίς, κιός, ὡς Ἱπ-
πῶναξ.

**160** Hesych.

μαυλιστήριον· παρ' Ἱππώνακτι, Λύδιον †λέμισμα†
λεπτόν τι.

    νόμισμα Palmerius

**157** Scholiast on Nicander, *Alexipharmaca* ("hare")

The sea hare, which is a kind of fish. Hipponax mentions it.[1] It has the weakness of foam, is dark in appearance, and deadly when eaten.

[1] Hipponax would have used some form of λαγός (cf. fr. 26a.1).

**158** *Homeric Parsings*

The word λαός did not undergo change (i.e., to ληός) in Homer, but in later Ionic it did. Cf. Hipponax:

looking at the people

**159** Cyril, *Lexicon*

λίς = λέων ('lion') and the genitive is λιός, like κίς ('weevil'), genitive κιός, as in Hipponax.[1]

[1] It is unclear which word was used by Hipponax, or in which case.

**160** Hesychius, *Lexicon*

μαυλιστήριον: in Hipponax. It is a Lydian coin(?) of little value.[1]

[1] μαυλιστήριον can also mean 'brothel,' but here it seems to be 'prostitute's fee.' Good discussion in Masson's edition (pp. 178 f.).

# IAMBIC POETRY

**161** Tzetz. *exeg. Il.* (v. ad fr. 72.5)

μεταρμόσας

**162** Pollux 2.188

γόνατος δὲ τὸ μὲν τῷ τοῦ μηροῦ τέλει συνηρμοσμένον κνήμης κεφαλή, τὸ δὲ ἔξωθεν ἐπικείμενον πλατὺ καὶ περιφερὲς ὀστοῦν, ὥσπερ φράγμα τοῦ γόνατος, ἐπιγονατίς τε καὶ κόγχη καὶ κόγχος καὶ μύλη, κατὰ δὲ Ἱπποκράτην (μοχλ. I, ii.245.13 Kühlewein) ἐπιμυλίς, κατὰ δὲ Ἱππώνακτα μυλακρίς.

**163** Pollux 4.79

τὸ δὲ νηνίατον (sc. μέλος) ἔστι μὲν Φρύγιον, Ἱππῶναξ δὲ αὐτοῦ μνημονεύει.

**164** Tzetz. in Lyc. 1162 (p. 338.19 Scheer)

τὸ δὲ "παππαλώμεναι" ἀδείᾳ Λυκοφρονείᾳ ἐλέχθη. Ἱππώνακτος γάρ ἐστιν ἡ λέξις, καὶ δηλοῖ τὸ περιβλέπουσαι· ἀλλ' ἐκεῖνος παμφαλῆσαι τὸ ἰδεῖν λέγει, οὐ παππαλῆσαι ὥσπερ νῦν φησιν οὗτος.

Schol. Ap. Rhod. 2.123-129e, "πόλλ' ἐπιπαμφαλό‹ωντες›

πολλὰ ἐπιβλέποντες καὶ μετ' ἐνθουσιασμοῦ· παμφαλᾶν γὰρ τὸ μετὰ πτοιήσεως ἐπιβλέπειν. κέχρηται δὲ τῇ λέξει καὶ Ἱππῶναξ καὶ Ἀνακρέων (fr. 482 PMG).

**161** Tzetzes, *Commentary on Iliad*

μεταρμόσας (for μεθαρμόσας)

making a change[1]

[1] It is not clear from Tzetzes whether he found the word in Hipponax.

**162** Pollux, *Vocabulary*

The part of the knee that is joined to the end of the thigh bone is the top of the shin bone, and the part that lies outside is a broad and curved bone, a defence as it were for the knee, the knee cap, called ἐπιμυλίς by Hippocrates, μυλακρίς by Hipponax.

**163** Pollux, *Vocabulary*

The νηνίατος[1] song, mentioned by Hipponax, is Phrygian.

[1] Presumably a dirge in view of the Latin *nenia*. See J. A. C. Greppin, *AJP* 108 (1987) 487-90.

**164** Tzetzes on Lycophron

παπταλώμεναι was said by Lycophron with his typical excess. For the word occurs in Hipponax and means 'to look around,' but he used παμφαλῆσαι 'to see,' not παπταλῆσαι as Lycophron now does.

Scholiast on Apollonius of Rhodes ("often glancing over")

Often looking at in an ecstatic manner. For παμφαλᾶν means 'to gaze excitedly.' Hipponax and Anacreon used the word.

**165**  Phot. *lex.* ii.137 Naber

ῥυφεῖν· τὸ ῥοφεῖν Ἴωνες. οὕτως Ἱππῶναξ.

**165a**  *Et. Gud.* i.199.16 de Stefani

ἁρμαλιά . . . ἢ παρὰ τὸ αἴρω . . . ὡς δὲ καθαίρω
καθαρμός, σαίρω σαρμός παρὰ Ἱππώνακτι.

**165b**  Ar. *Pax* 481-483

ἕλκουσιν δ᾽ ὅμως / γλισχρότατα σαρκάζοντες ὥσπερ
κυνίδια. /—ὑπὸ τοῦ γε λιμοῦ νὴ Δί᾽ ἐξολωλότες.

Schol. ad loc. (pp. 78 sq. Holwerda)

σαρκάζοντες· ἤτοι ἐξισχνούμενοι καὶ ἠτονηκότες καὶ
διὰ τὸν λιμὸν ἕλκοντες μόλις . . . καλῶς δ᾽ ἂν ἔχοι
τοῦτο τηρῆσαι πρὸς τὸ Ἱππωνάκτειον οὕτως ἔχον,

    †σαρκοκύων λιμόν

οὐ γάρ ἐστι τῶν σαρκῶν, ὥσπερ ἀξιοῦσι τῶν ἐξηγη-
σαμένων τινές· παντάπασι γὰρ ἂν εἴη αὐτὸ ὑπεναν-
τίον ἑαυτῷ. ἔργον γὰρ τοῦ λιμοῦ οὐ σάρκας ἐμποιεῖν,
ἀλλὰ τοὐναντίον ἀπισχνοῦν τὰ σώματα καὶ τῶν
σαρκῶν παραιρεῖσθαι τὸν ὄγκον.

    σαρκῶν . . . ⟨ὡς⟩ κύων λιμῷ tent. West

**165** Photius, *Lexicon*

ῥυφεῖν: Ionic for ῥοφεῖν ('to gulp down'). So Hipponax.

**165a** *Etymologicum Gudianum*

ἁρμαλιά ('food') . . . Or from αἴρω ('raise up') . . . like
καθαρμός from καθαίρω, and σαρμός ('sweepings') in
Hipponax from σαίρω ('sweep').

**165b** Aristophanes, *Peace*

"And yet they are pulling with much tenacity, their mouths
open like puppies."—"Yes, by Zeus, because they are per-
ishing from hunger."

Scholiast on the passage

σαρκάζοντες: i.e., wasting away and exhausted and pull-
ing with difficulty because of hunger . . . And one can
clearly see that this is the meaning from Hipponax,

. . . hunger

For it is not from the word for flesh (σάρκος), as some
commentators claim. This would give exactly the opposite
meaning, since the action of hunger is not to produce flesh,
but the opposite, i.e., to dry out the body and to reduce the
size of the flesh.[1]

---

[1] It seems from the scholiast that Hipponax used a form of
σαρκάω (not σαρκόω 'to make fleshy'), but it is unlikely that it
could mean 'waste away.' Another scholiast on the passage ex-
plains σαρκάζοντες as ὑποσεσηρότες ('open-mouthed') and
Hesychius glosses σαρκῶν in a similar way (σεσηρώς).

**166** Ath. 7.324a; hinc Eust. in Hom. *Il.* 23.31 (iv.676.16
V.d.Valk)

Ἱππώνακτος δὲ ἐν τοῖς ἰάμβοις εἰπόντος

σηπίης ὑπόσφαγμα,

οἱ ἐξηγησάμενοι ἀπέδωκαν τὸ τῆς σηπίας μέλαν· ἔστι
δὲ τὸ ὑπόσφαγμα, ὡς Ἐρασίστρατός φησιν ἐν Ὀψαρ-
τυτικῷ, ὑπότριμμα.

**167** Eust. in Hom. *Od.* 17.455 (1828.9); v. ad Arch. fr. 250

συκοτραγίδης

**168** Ath. 2.69d

Ἱππώνακτα δὲ τετρακίνην τὴν θρίδακα καλεῖν Πάμφι-
λος ἐν Γλώσσαις φησί (fr. xxxiv Schmidt), Κλείταρχος
δὲ Φρύγας οὕτω καλεῖν.

**169** Ath. 7.327b

(ὕκης) Ἕρμιππος δὲ ὁ Σμυρναῖος ἐν τοῖς περὶ Ἱπ-
πώνακτος (fr. 93 Wehrli) ὕκην ἀκούει τὴν ἰουλίδα· εἶναι
δὲ αὐτὴν δυσθήρατον, διὸ καὶ Φιλίταν φάναι "οὐδ᾽
ὕκης ἰχθὺς ἔσχατος ἐξέφυγε" (fr. 20 Powell).

**166** Athenaeus, *Scholars at Dinner*

When Hipponax in his iambics spoke of

the cuttle fish's ὑπόσφαγμα,

commentators explained ὑπόσφαγμα as the cuttle fish's
ink. But, as Erasistratus says in his *Cookbook*, it is a kind of
stew.[1]

[1] Athenaeus goes on to cite Erasistratus' explanation of ὑπό-
σφαγμα as a mixture of cooked meat, blood, honey, cheese, salt,
cummin, silphium, and vinegar.

**167** Eustathius on Homer, *Odyssey*

son of a fig eater[1]

[1] See note on Arch. fr. 250.

**168** Athenaeus, *Scholars at Dinner*

Pamphilus in his *Glosses* says that Hipponax called lettuce
τετρακίνη, and Clitarchus says that it was a word used by
the Phrygians.

**169** Athenaeus, *Scholars at Dinner*

Hermippus of Smyrna in his *On Hipponax* understands
ὕκης[1] to be the rainbow wrasse. He says that it is hard to
catch, as a result of which Philitas says: "not even the last
*hyces* fish escaped."

[1] It is a reasonable assumption that the word occurred in Hip-
ponax.

**170** Schol. Plat. *Lys.* 206e (p. 457 Greene)

φορμίον δὲ πλέγμα τι ψιαθῶδες παρ᾽ Ἱππώνακτι.

**171** Pollux 2.152 (de compositis a χειρο-)

χειροπέδας Ἡρόδοτος (Ἡρώδας Bossi) εἴρηκεν, Ἱππῶναξ δὲ χειρόχωλον τὸν τὴν χεῖρα πεπηρωμένον.

**172** *Suda* iv.797.10 Adler

χελιδόνων φάρμακον·

παρ᾽ Ἱππώνακτι τὸ φίλτρον τὸ διαπινόμενον (διαγινόμενον cod., corr. Degani) ἐπειδὰν χελιδόνα πρῶτόν τις ἴδῃ.

**172a** Cyril. *lex.* in cod. Matr. Univ. Z-22.116 (cf. M. Naoumides, *GRBS* 9 [1968] 276)

χιλιάγρα· ζωύφιον, ὡς Ἱππῶναξ, καὶ νόμισμα.

**173** Pollux 10.99

ἐν δὲ τῷ πρώτῳ τῶν Ἱππώνακτος ἰάμβων εἴρηται χυτροπόδιον, ὥσπερ καὶ παρ᾽ Ἡσιόδῳ (*Op.* 748) "μηδ᾽ ἀπὸ χυτροπόδων ἀνεπιρρέκτων ἀνελόντα." ἀλλὰ τοῦτο μὲν ἕτερόν τι δηλοῖ.

**170** Scholiast on Plato, *Lysis*

φορμίον is a plaited rush mat in Hipponax.

**171** Pollux, *Vocabulary* (on compounds of χειρο- 'hand')

Herodotus (Herodas?) used the word 'handcuffs' and Hipponax used χειρόχωλος of one whose hand is maimed.

**172** *Suda*

a remedy against swallows

In Hipponax the charm that is drunk whenever the first swallow is seen.[1]

[1] Perhaps because the sight of a swallow could portend misfortune. So Degani, *Studi* 287-89, who discusses the passage in detail.

**172a** Cyril, *Lexicon*

χιλιάγρα: a little animal,[1] as in Hipponax, and a coin.

[1] If the word means literally 'with a thousand claws,' Naoumides' identification with the centipede is appropriate.

**173** Pollux, *Vocabulary*

In the first book of Hipponax's iambics χυτροπόδιον[1] ('little pot') is mentioned, as in Hesiod, "and do not take from unconsecrated pots." But this signifies something different.[2]

[1] In Hipponax the form would be κυθροπόδιον (so Renner), as in fr. 29a.     [2] I.e., different from the other meaning of the word, 'stand for a pot.'

IAMBIC POETRY

**174** Tzetz. in Ar. *Ran.* 516 (p. 840.7 Koster), "κἄρτι
παρατετιλμέναι"

νεοξυρεῖς τὸν δορίαλον, τὸ{ν} μύρτον, τὸν χοῖρον, τὸν
κύσθον, καὶ ὅσα τοιαῦτα ὁ Σώφρων καὶ ὁ Ἱππῶναξ
καὶ ἕτεροι λέγουσι.

*175-181 Metra Varia*

**175** Hephaest. *Ench.* 10.2 (p. 32.18 Consbruch)

δίμετρον δὲ ὑπερκατάληκτον (ἀντισπαστικὸν) τὸ καλού-
μενον Σαπφικὸν ἐννεασύλλαβον ἢ Ἱππωνάκτειον,
οἷον

  καὶ κνίσῃ τινὰ θυμιήσας.

**176** Mar. Plot. Sac. *ars gramm.* 3.4 (vi.523.3 Keil)

duplex clodum hipponactium trimetrum acatalectum fit
hoc modo, cum tertii pedis quattuor syllabae sint longae,
ut est exemplum hoc:

**174** Tzetzes on Aristophanes, *Frogs* ("freshly depilated")

Newly shaved as to the δορίαλος,[1] μύρτον, χοῖρος, κύσθος,[2] and all such expressions used by Sophron, Hipponax,[3] and others.

[1] The spelling given by the source (other spellings are δορίαλλος, δορύαλλος, δόριλλος). [2] All four words are colloquialisms for the vagina. [3] None of these words is found in the remains of Sophron and it is unclear whether Tzetzes meant that they were all found in Hipponax.

### 175-181 Various Meters

*These fragments are cited as examples of Hipponactean meters, but those cited in Greek need not be actual quotations from Hipponax. For frr. 178-181 I merely reproduce the metrical schemes deduced by West from the sources.*

**175** Hephaestion, *Handbook of Meters*

And the (antispastic) dimeter hypercatalectic called Sapphic nine-syllable or Hipponactean, such as

and fumigating someone with the steam from burnt fat[1]

[1] Translation uncertain because of the fragment's brevity and lack of context.

**176** Marius Plotius Sacerdos, *Grammar*

The doubly lame hipponactean trimeter acatalectic[1] is composed in this way, since the four syllables of the third foot are long, as in this example:

†ἀναβιος† πλάνητι προσπταίων κώλῳ.

αναβιοσπδδνητιρρροσπταιωνκωλω A, αναβιοσιταδηντιρ-
ροσπιλιονκωλω B    ἀνόλβιος πλάνητι Bergk, προσπ-
ταίων Putschen

**177**  Mar. Plot. Sac. *ars gramm.* 3.4 (vi.525.5 Keil)

tetrametrum clodum brachycatalectum, quod et episca-
zon trimetrum nuncupatur, fit hoc modo, cum quartus pes
debens esse tetrasyllabus duas habeat syllabas, ideo bra-
chycatalectus; clodus propterea, quod ipsum pedem no-
vissimum disyllabum debens habere iambum habeat spon-
deum:

Ἑρμῆ μάκαρ, ⟨ὃς καὶ⟩ κάτυπνον οἶδας
    ἐγρήσσειν.

⟨ὃς καὶ⟩ West, ⟨σὺ γὰρ⟩ Schneidewin post Meineke (τὺ γὰρ)

**178**  Servius (iv.458.18 Keil)

× – ∪ – × – ∪ – ∪ – –

**179**  Servius (iv.464.5 Keil)

× – ∪ ∪ – –

**180**  Marius Plotius Sacerdos (vi.523.10 Keil)

× – – – ∪ – ∪ – × – – –

**181**  Marius Plotius Sacerdos (vi.540.12 Keil)

× – ∪ – –

494

. . . stumbling with wandering foot

[1] The so-called ischiorrhogic, but the diphthong of $\pi\rho o\sigma\pi$-$\tau\alpha\acute{\iota}\omega\nu$ may be short by correption.

**177**  Marius Plotius Sacerdos, *Grammar*

The brachycatalectic lame tetrameter, which is also called the episcazon (limping) trimeter, is composed in this way, since the fourth foot which ought to have four syllables has two, i.e., is brachycatalectic; it is lame because it has a spondee in the last foot when it ought to have an iambus:

Blessed Hermes, (you who) know how to awake[1] the sleeper

[1] If $\dot{\epsilon}\gamma\rho\acute{\eta}\sigma\sigma\epsilon\iota\nu$ here has a unique transitive force. Perhaps the poet went on to state 'and to put to sleep the wakeful,' as in *Iliad* 24.343 f.

**182**  Stob. 4.22.123/124 = Arsenius, *Paroem. Gr.* ii.338.29
L.-S.

Ἱππώνακτος·

γάμος κράτιστός ἐστιν ἀνδρὶ σώφρονι
τρόπον γυναικὸς χρηστὸν ἕδνον λαμβάνειν·
αὕτη γὰρ ἡ προὶξ οἰκίαν σῴζει μόνη.
ὅστις δὲ †τρυφερῶς† τὴν γυναῖκ᾽ ἄγει λαβών
<                                              >
συνεργὸν οὗτος ἀντὶ δεσποίνης ἔχει
εὔνουν, βεβαίαν εἰς ἅπαντα τὸν βίον.

2 ἔνδον codd., corr. Haupt          4 τρυφερὰν Bergk,
τρυφῶσαν (δὲ deleto) Meineke       lac. post v. 4 posuit
Meineke

**183**  Choerob. ad Hephaest. 3.1 (p. 214.8 Consbruch)

Ἴαμβος . . . εἴρηται ἤτοι ἀπὸ Ἰάμβης τῆς Κελεοῦ
θεραπαίνης, ἥτις τὴν Δήμητρα λυπουμένην ἠνάγκασε
γελάσαι γέλοιόν τι εἰποῦσα, τῷ ῥυθμῷ τούτου τοῦ
ποδὸς αὐτομάτως χρησαμένη. ἢ ἀπὸ Ἰάμβης τινὸς
ἑτέρας, γραός, ᾗ Ἱππῶναξ ὁ ἰαμβοποιὸς παρὰ θάλασ-
σαν ἔρια πλυνούσῃ συντυχὼν ἤκουσε τῆς σκάφης
ἐφαψάμενος, ἐφ᾽ ἧς ἔπλυνεν ἡ γραῦς,

ἄνθρωπ᾽, ἄπελθε, τὴν σκάφην ἀνατρέπεις.

καὶ συλλαβὼν τὸ ῥηθὲν οὕτως ὠνόμασε τὸ μέτρον.

**182** Stobaeus, *Anthology*

From Hipponax:[1]

> The best marriage for a sensible man is to get a woman's good character as a wedding gift; for this dowry alone preserves the household. But (and?) whoever gets and marries(?) a spoiled(?) wife, . . . he has a well-disposed helpmate instead of a tyrant, steadfast for ever.

[1] Almost all have rightly treated these verses as spurious. Meter and language suggest a poet of New Comedy, perhaps one whose name resembled that of Hipponax.

**183** Choeroboscus on Hesphaestion

Iambus . . . derived its name either from Iambe, Celeus' maidservant, who compelled the grieving Demeter to laugh by saying something in jest and spontaneously using the rhythm of this meter, or from some other Iambe, an old woman, whom Hipponax the iambic poet met as she was washing wool by the sea and heard her say, as he touched the trough at which the old woman was washing,

> Sir, be gone, you are upsetting the trough.

And grasping what had been said he named the meter after

ἄλλοι δὲ περὶ τοῦ χωλιάμβου τὴν ἱστορίαν ταύτην ἀναφέρουσι, γράφοντες τὸ τέλος τοῦ στίχου

τὴν σκάφην ἀνατρέψεις.

her. But others refer this narrative to the choliambus, writing as the end of the line

you will upset the trough.[1]

[1] C. G. Brown, *Hermes* 116 (1988) 478-81, and R. M. Rosen, *AJP* 109 (1988) 174-79, have shown that the verse, in either its iambic or choliambic form, could have come from a poem of Hipponax, perhaps containing a poetic initiation scene (cf. Arch. test. 3). R. L. Fowler, *ICS* 15 (1990) 1-22, adds two more (partially corrupt) verses from the MS cited by Consbruch on p. 214. For other testimonia in which the verse is cited see 21a-d in Degani's edition.

# ANANIUS

## TESTIMONIA

**1** Tzetz. in Lyc. (ii.18 Scheer)

ἀριπρεπεῖς δὲ ἰαμβογράφοι Ἀνανίας, Ἀρχίλοχος, Ἱππῶναξ.

**2** Tractatus Harleianus (p. 16 Studemund)

τὸ οὖν παλαιὸν ἰαμβικὸν διαιρεῖται εἰς τὸ κωμικόν, τὸ τραγικόν, τὸ σατυρικόν, τὸ Ἱππωνάκτειον τὸ καὶ χωλόν, τὸ τοῦ Ἀνανίου τὸ καὶ ἰσχιορρωγικόν . . . τοῦ δὲ Ἱππωνακτείου (sc. γνώρισμα) τὸ δέχεσθαι ἐν τῇ ἕκτῃ χώρᾳ σπονδεῖον ἢ τροχαῖον· διὸ καὶ χωλαίνειν δοκεῖ κατὰ τὴν βάσιν, ὑπερκατάληκτον ταύτην ἔχον. τοῦ δὲ Ἀνανίου τὸ ἀπὸ τοῦ τετάρτου ποδὸς μέχρι τέλους πέντε συλλαβὰς ἔχειν καὶ ταύτας μακράς. διὸ καὶ ἰσχιορρωγικὸν ὁ στίχος οὗτος λέγεται διὰ τὸ μὴ

# ANANIUS

## TESTIMONIA

**1** Tzetzes on Lycophron

The most distinguished iambic writers are Ananius,[1] Archilochus and Hipponax.

> [1] Only Tzetzes and the source for fr. 1 record Ἀνανίας rather than Ἀνάνιος as the poet's name and the latter has been adopted throughout in my translation. The spelling Ἀνανίας may have resulted from an erroneous interpretation of the genitive Ἀνανίου or been influenced by the New Testament where there are three named Ananias. Tzetzes is the only source to include Ananius instead of Semonides as one of the three early iambographers.

**2** Anonymous Grammarian

The iambic meter of old is divided into comic, tragic, satyric, Hipponactean which is also called 'lame,' that of Ananius which is also called 'broken-hipped' . . . The admittance of a spondee or trochee in the sixth position is the mark of the Hipponactean, and therefore it seems to be lame in its movement, since this is hypercatalectic.[1] The mark of Ananius is the presence of five long syllables from the fourth foot to the end, and therefore this line is called ischiorrhogic ('broken-hipped') because it does not suffer

κατὰ τὸ τέλος πάσχειν τὴν χώλανσιν, ὡς ὁ τοῦ Ἱπ-
πώνακτος, ἀλλ' ἀνωτέρω ἀπὸ τῆς τετάρτης χώρας.

# FRAGMENTA

## 1-4 Trimetri

**1**

Ἄπολλον, ὅς που Δῆλον ἢ Πυθῶν' ἔχεις
ἢ Νάξον ἢ Μίλητον ἢ θείην Κλάρον,
ἵκεο καθ' ἱρὸν ἢ Σκύθας ἀφίξεαι.

cf. Tzetz. in Ar. *Ran.* 659a (p. 874 Koster)

2 θείαν codd., corr. Meineke    3 ἵκου codd., corr.
Meineke    ἱέρ' cod. V, ἱερὸν Θ, ἱερῶν Tzetzes, ἱρὸν Degani

Ar. *Ran.* 659-61

ΔΙΟΝ. Ἄπολλον—ὅς που Δῆλον ἢ Πυθῶν' ἔχεις.
ΞΑ. ἤλγησεν· οὐκ ἤκουσας; ΔΙΟΝ. οὐκ ἔγωγ', ἐπεὶ
ἴαμβον Ἱππώνακτος ἀνεμιμνησκόμην.

lameness at the end, as does the line of Hipponax, but farther back from the fourth position.[2]

[1] The term should mean that the line contains an extra syllable at the end, but that makes little sense here.     [2] Similar comments are made by Tzetzes, *On Metres* (*Anecd. Ox.* iii.309 Cramer). Of the nine iambic trimeters of Ananius that are extant, three (fr. 1) are pure iambic, three are lame (choliambic), and three are ischiorrhogic (fr. 2 and fr. 3.2-3). Of the many more trimeters of Hipponax about 15 are ischiorrhogic and about 10 pure. It seems, therefore, that Ananius was in fact fonder of the ischiorrhogic than Hipponax. A dispute whether Hipponax or Ananius invented the choliambic is recorded in Hipp. test. 13.

## FRAGMENTS

### *1-4 Trimeters*

**1**

Apollo, you who are perhaps residing in Delos or Pytho or Naxos or Miletus or holy Clarus,[1] come to your temple or[2] you will end up among the Scythians.[3]

Aristophanes, *Frogs*

Dionysus. Apollo—you who are perhaps residing in Delos or Pytho.
Xanthus. He felt pain. Didn't you hear?
Dionysus. It wasn't I, since I was recalling an iambic line of Hipponax.

# IAMBIC POETRY

Schol. ad loc.

ὡς ἀλγήσας καὶ συγκεχυμένος οὐκ οἶδε τί λέγει, ἐπεὶ οὐχ Ἱππώνακτος ἀλλ' Ἀνανίου. ἐπιφέρει δὲ ὁ Ἀνανίας αὐτῷ· "ἢ Νάξον—ἀφίξεαι."

**2** Ath. 14.625c

φασὶ δὲ Πύθερμον τὸν Τήιον ἐν τῷ γένει τῆς ἁρμονίας {αὐτοῦ} τούτῳ ποιῆσαι σκολιὰ (σκαιὰ codd., corr. Casaubon) μέλη, καὶ διὰ τὸ εἶναι τὸν ποιητὴν Ἰωνικὸν Ἰαστὶ κληθῆναι τὴν ἁρμονίαν. οὗτός ἐστι Πύθερμος οὗ μνημονεύει Ἀνάνιος <ἢ> Ἱππῶναξ ἐν τοῖς ἰάμβοις· <"—". καὶ> ἐν ἄλλῳ οὕτως·

χρυσὸν λέγει Πύθερμος ὡς οὐδὲν τἆλλα.

λέγει δὲ οὕτως ὁ Πύθερμος (fr. 910 PMG)· "οὐδὲν ἦν ἄρα τἆλλα πλὴν ὁ χρυσός."

Scholia on the passage

Because of his pain and confusion he doesn't know what he is saying, since the line is not from Hipponax but from Ananius.[4] And Ananius adds to it (vv. 2-3).

[1] All important places where Apollo was worshipped. For the purpose of such lists see A. W. Bulloch, *Callimachus, The Fifth Hymn* (Cambridge 1985) 167.    [2] The words "to your temple or" translate a text that is far from certain.    [3] Perhaps a jocular reference to the risk of being scalped by the Scythians.
[4] West (ad loc.) suggests that the confusion may have arisen from the poems of Ananius being included in a collection of the works of Hipponax, a much more famous and apparently more prolific poet. There is a similar confusion in frr. 2 and 3.

## 2 Athenaeus, *Scholars at Dinner*

They say that Pythermus of Teos composed lyric scolia in this kind of tuning and that it was called Ionian because the poet came from Ionia. This is the Pythermus whom Ananius or Hipponax[1] mentions in iambics: ⟨citation lost⟩. And in another passage as follows:

Pythermus says of gold that everything else is nothing.

And Pythermus' words[2] are as follows: "everything else after all is nothing except for gold."

[1] See n. 4 on fr. 1.    [2] No other citation of Pythermus has been preserved.

IAMBIC POETRY

**3** Ath. 3.78f

καὶ Ἀνάνιος δὲ ὁ ἰαμβοποιὸς ἔφη·

εἴ τις καθείρξαι χρυσὸν ἐν δόμοις πολὺν
καὶ σῦκα βαιὰ καὶ δύ' ἢ τρεῖς ἀνθρώπους,
γνοίη χ' ὅσῳ τὰ σῦκα τοῦ χρυσοῦ κρέσσω.

cf. Stob. 4.33.12

1 καθείρξει Stob.        3 γνώη σχάσοντας Stob., unde
γνοίης χ' ὅσον τὰ Schneidewin, fort. recte

**4** Ath. 9.370b

καὶ Ἀνάνιος δέ φησι·

καὶ σὲ πολλὸν ἀνθρώπων
ἐγὼ φιλέω μάλιστα, ναὶ μὰ τὴν κράμβην.

*Tetrametri*

**5** Ath. 7.282ab

ἀνθίας· κάλλιχθυς. τούτου μέμνηται Ἐπίχαρμος ἐν
Ἥβας γάμῳ (fr. 38 Kaibel)· "καὶ σκιφίας χρόμιός θ',
⟨ὃς⟩ ἐν τῷ ἦρι καττὸν Ἀνάνιον / ἰχθύων πάντων
ἄριστος, ἀνθίας δὲ χείματι." λέγει δὲ Ἀνάνιος οὕτως·

ἔαρι μὲν χρόμιος ἄριστος, ἀνθίης δὲ χειμῶνι·
τῶν καλῶν δ' ὄψων ἄριστον καρὶς ἐκ συκέης φύλλου.
ἡδὺ δ' ἐσθίειν χιμαίρης φθινοπωρισμῷ κρέας·

506

**3** Athenaeus, *Scholars at Dinner*

And the iambic poet Ananius said:

> If one were to shut up in a room much gold, a few
> figs, and two or three people, he would recognize
> how much superior figs are to gold.[1]

[1] Some assume, perhaps rightly, that frr. 2 and 3 came from the
same poem. For the general thought of fr. 3 cf. Achaeus fr. 25
Snell: "barley-bread is worth more to a hungry man than gold
and ivory." Stobaeus assigns the fragment to Hipponax. See n. 4 on
fr. 1.

**4** Athenaeus, *Scholars at Dinner*

And Ananius says:

> I love you by far the most of all people, by the cab-
> bage[1]

[1] For what precedes see on Hipponax fr. 104.47-49.

*Trochaic Tetrameters*

**5** Athenaeus, *Scholars at Dinner*

Anthias[1] or beauty fish. Epicharmus mentions this in *The
Marriage of Hebe*: "and skiphias and chromios, which ac-
cording to Ananius is the best of all fish in spring, whereas
the anthias is best in winter." And Ananius speaks as fol-
lows:

> In spring the chromios is best, in winter the anthias,
> but the best of fine delicacies is karis taken from[2] a
> fig leaf. Sweet it is to eat the flesh of a she-goat in

δέλφακος δ᾽ ὅταν τραπέωσιν καὶ πατέωσιν ἐσθίειν,
5   καὶ κυνῶν αὐτὴ τόθ᾽ ὥρη καὶ λαγῶν κἀλωπέκων.
οἰὸς αὖθ᾽, ὅταν θέρος τ᾽ ᾖ κἠχέται βαβράζωσιν·
εἶτα δ᾽ ἐστὶν ἐκ θαλάσσης θύννος, οὐ κακὸν βρῶμα,
ἀλλὰ πᾶσιν ἰχθύεσσιν ἐμπρεπὴς ἐν μυσσωτῷ.
βοῦς δὲ πιανθείς, δοκέω μέν, καὶ μεσέων νυκτῶν
  ἡδὺς
10   κἠμέρης.

τῶν τοῦ Ἀνανίου πλεόνων ἐμνημόνευσα, νομίζων καὶ
τούτων ὑποθήκας τοῖς λάγνοις ⟨ἡδέως⟩ (add. West)
ταύτας ἐκτεθήσεσθαι.

1 ἀνθίας codd., corr. Schneidewin    3 χιμέρης A, corr.
Heringa    φθινοπωρισμῷ susp. West    6 αὖθ᾽ Her-
inga, αὐτοετ᾽ A    8 μυττωτῷ codd., corr. Schneidewin

*Incerti Generis*

**6** Schol. Hom. *Il.* 7.76 (P.Oxy. 1087.22 sqq.); v. ad Arch.
fr. 264

τὸ "σωλῆνος" π[α]ρ᾽ Ἀνανίωι.

autumn, and that of a pig when they turn and tread
the grapes, and then this is the season for dog fish,
sea hare and fox shark.³ Next (it is sweet to eat the
flesh) of a sheep when it is summer and the cicadas
are shrill. And then from the sea there is tuna, no
mean food, but one that stands out among all fish in
a savoury sauce.⁴ But a fattened ox, I think, is sweet
in the middle of the night and in daytime.

I have cited the verses of Ananius at some length, consid-
ering that it will give pleasure to the lecherous to have even
these admonitions set forth.

¹ For details on the various fish see D'A. W. Thompson, *A
Glossary of Greek Fishes* s.vv. Anthias is not securely identified,
skiphias is the Doric form of xiphias, 'swordfish,' chromios is "cel-
ebrated for its grunting voice . . . and for its acute hearing," and
karis is "a small crustacean," prawn or shrimp.      ² I.e.,
'served on.'        ³ It seems unlikely that these three fish were
all eaten, since the sea hare or sea slug was poisonous, although it
was said to serve various medicinal purposes as an ointment.
⁴ Mentioned in conjunction with tuna also in Hipponax fr. 26.2. Its
main ingredients were cheese, leeks, garlic, honey, and vinegar.

*Uncertain Classification*

**6** Scholiast on Homer, *Iliad*

σωλῆνος (for σωλήν) in Ananius.¹

¹ I.e., the nominative σωλῆνος is derived from σωλῆνος, gen-
itive of σωλήν. See on Arch. fr. 264. Without a context the mean-
ing of the word cannot be determined. In Arch. fr. 46 it means
'pipe,' perhaps as a metaphor, but in Epicharmus (fr. 42) it is a
type of shellfish and in view of the introduction to fr. 5 above, this
may be the likelier meaning here.

# SUSARION

**1**

ἀκούετε λεῴ· Σουσαρίων λέγει τάδε
υἱὸς Φιλίνου Μεγαρόθεν Τριποδίσκιος.
κακὸν γυναῖκες· ἀλλ' ὅμως, ὦ δημόται,
οὐκ ἔστιν οἰκεῖν οἰκίαν ἄνευ κακοῦ.
καὶ γὰρ τὸ γῆμαι καὶ τὸ μὴ γῆμαι κακόν.

Stob. 4.22.68. (vv. 1+3-5); Tzetz. prol. in Ar. (p. 26.78
Koster), vv. 1-4

τῆς οὖν κωμῳδίας τῆς καλουμένης πρώτης πρῶτος καὶ
εὑρετὴς γέγονεν ὁ Μεγαρεὺς Σουσαρίων ὁ Τριποδί-
σκιος, υἱὸς ὢν Φιλίνου, ὃς φαύλῃ γυναικὶ συνοικῶν
ἀπολιπούσῃ αὐτὸν Διονυσίων ἠγμένων εἰσελθὼν εἰς
τὸ θέατρον τὰ τέσσαρα ἰαμβεῖα ταυτὶ ἀνεφθέγξατο, ἃ
μόνα τῶν ἐκείνου συγγραμμάτων ἐφεύρηνται, τῶν ἄλ-
λων ἀπάντων ἠφανισμένων· "ἀκούετε—κακοῦ." οὕτως
ἡ πρώτη κωμῳδία τὸ σκῶμμα εἶχεν ἀπαρακάλυπτον.

cf. schol. Dion. Thr. (p. 19.4 Hilgard), Ioan. Diac. in Hermog.
(Rabe, *RhM* 63 [1908] 149), Tzetz. π. κωμῳδίας (p. 39.18 Kos-
ter), Tzetz. schol. π. ποιητῶν (p. 88 Koster), Diom. (*Gramm. Lat.*
i.488.23)

1 λεώς Stob., Ioan. Diac., schol. Dion., Tzetz. π. κωμ.

510

# SUSARION

**1**

> Listen, people. These are the words of Susarion, son
> of Philinus, from Tripodeske in Megara. Women are
> a bane: but nevertheless it's not possible to live in
> a household without bane. For to marry or not to
> marry, either is baneful.[1]

Tzetzes, *Introduction to Aristophanes*
The first poet and inventor of the so-called first comedy
was Susarion of Tripodeske in Megara, the son of Philinus.
Married to a bad wife who had left him, he entered the
theatre at the festival of Dionysus and uttered these four
iambic verses, which alone of his compositions have sur-
vived, all the others having disappeared: (vv. 1-4). Thus the
first comedy had undisguised scurrility.

[1] I agree with West that whatever role Susarion actually had in
the early history of comedy, these verses are not from a comedy.
The Parian Marble (*FGrHist* 239 A 39) dates Susarion to a year
between 581/80 and 562/61. For additional testimonia see West
or *Poetae Comici Graeci* vii.661-63.

---

2 om. Stob., Diom.     Φιλίννου Tzetz. prol. in Ar.
4 εὑρεῖν Ioan. Diac., Tzetz. prol. in Ar. et schol. π. ποιητῶν,
Diom.     5 habet Stob. solus

# HERMIPPUS

*1-3 Trimetri*

**1** Schol. Ar. *Pl.* 701 (p. 162 Massa Positano), "᾽Ιασώ"

ἐπεὶ καὶ Ἕρμιππος ἐν τῷ πρώτῳ ἰάμβῳ τῶν τριμέτρων
᾽Ασκληπιοῦ καὶ Λαμπετίας τῆς Ἡλίου λέγει Μαχάονα
καὶ Ποδαλείριον καὶ ᾽Ιασὼ καὶ Πανάκειαν καὶ Αἴγλην
νεωτάτην. ἔνιοι δὲ προστιθέασιν ᾽Ιανίσκον καὶ ᾽Αλε-
ξήνορα.

**2** Ath. 3.76c

λευκερινεὸς δέ τι εἶδός ἐστι συκῆς, καὶ ἴσως αὕτη
ἐστὶν ἡ τὰ λευκὰ σῦκα φέρουσα. μνημονεύει δὲ αὐτῆς
Ἕρμιππος ἐν ἰάμβοις οὕτως·

  τὰς λευκερινεὼς δὲ χωρὶς ἰσχάδας.

λευκερινεὼ vel -ὼν (gen. sing. / pl.) tent. West

# HERMIPPUS

*Hermippus is best known as an Athenian comic poet active in the latter part of the fifth century. For this aspect of his career see the 10 testimonia and 94 fragments in vol. 5, pp. 561-604, of* Poetae Comici Graeci.

### 1-3 Iambic Trimeters

**1** Scholiast on Aristophanes, *Plutus* ("Iaso")

For Hermippus says in the first iambic poem of his trimeters that the children of Asclepius and Lampetia, daughter of Helius, were Machaon, Podalirius, Iaso, Panacea, and as the youngest Aegle. Some add Ianiscus and Alexenor.

**2** Athenaeus, *Scholars at Dinner*

λευκερινεός is a kind of fig tree, and this is perhaps the one that produces white figs. Hermippus mentions it in his iambics as follows:

    and separately the dried white figs

**3** Schol. Ar. *Av.* 1149b (p. 176 Holwerda), "ὑπαγωγέα"

ὁ ὑπαγωγεύς, ὥς τινες, σιδηροῦν τι οἷον πτυίδιον ᾧ
χρῶνται οἱ κονιαταί· οἱ δὲ ἐργαλεῖον οἰκοδομικόν, ᾧ
ἀπευθύνουσι τὰς πλίνθους πρὸς ἀλλήλας· τινὲς δὲ
αὐτὸ παράξυστον καλοῦσιν. εἰ μὴ ἄρα πηλόν τινα
ὑπαγωγέα καλοῦσιν. τοιοῦτον γάρ τι καὶ Ἕρμιππος
ἐν τοῖς τριμέτροις ἐμφανίζει·

> ξύνεστι γὰρ δὴ δεσμ⟨ί⟩ῳ μὲν οὐδενί,
> †τοῖσι δ᾽ ὑπαγωγεῦσι τοῖς ἑαυτοῦ τρόποις.†

1 δεσμῷ codd., corr. Bergk      2 τούτοισι et αὐτοῦ
Meineke, μόνοισι Bergk

*4-6 Tetrametri*

**4** Ath. 11.461e

κυλικηγορήσων ἔρχομαι, οὐ τῶν Κυλικράνων εἷς
ὑπάρχων, οὓς χλευάζων Ἕρμιππος ὁ κωμῳδοποιὸς ἐν
τοῖς ἰάμβοις φησίν·

> εἰς τὸ Κυλικράνων βαδίζων σπληνόπεδον
>     ἀφικόμην·
> εἶδον οὖν τὴν Ἡράκλειαν, καὶ μάλ᾽ ὡραίαν
>     πόλιν.

Quae sequuntur v. ad Scythinum test. 3.

**3** Scholiast on Aristophanes, *Birds*

According to some the ὑπαγωγεύς¹ is like a little iron winnowing-shovel which plasterers use. Others say it is a house-building tool whereby they keep the bricks in a straight line with one another. And some call it a παράξυστον, unless the ὑπαγωγεύς is a kind of clay (mortar), as Hermippus makes clear in his trimeters:

> for he(?) is held together without any fastening (but only with the mortar of his own habits?)

¹ See Dunbar on *Birds* (pp. 602 f.) for a detailed treatment of the word.

*4-6 Trochaic Tetrameters*

**4** Athenaeus, *Scholars at Dinner*

I am going to give a talk over cups, not as one of the Cylicranians¹ whom the comic poet Hermippus mocks in his iambics:

> On my journey I came to the spleen-land² of the Cylicranians; and so I saw Heracleia,³ a very beautiful city.

¹ Intended as a pun on *cylix* 'cup' ("Cup-heads"). Athenaeus goes on to cite several authorities on the name of this people.
² Presumably a pun, but the force of it is obscure. Various emendations have been suggested.   ³ At the foot of Mt Oeta in southern Thessaly. See Scythinus test. 3.

IAMBIC POETRY

**5** Schol. Ar. *Vesp.* 1169 (pp. 184 sq. Koster), "διασαλα-κώνισον"

ἁβρύνθητι καὶ διαθρύφθητι . . . ὁμοίως δ᾽ ἐστὶ καὶ
παρ᾽ Ἑρμίππῳ ἐν τοῖς τετραμέτροις·

   ὕστερον δ᾽ †αὐτὸν στρατηγὸν οὓς ἀνειλωτημένην†
   καὶ κασαλβάζουσαν εἶδον καὶ
   σεσαλακωνισμένην.

1 αὐτὸν et αὐτὴν codd., αὐτὴν στρατηγῶν οὖσαν εἰλωτισ-
μένην Meineke, αὐτὴν στρατηγόν, ὡς ἂν εἰλωτισμένην Koster

**6** Schol. Ar. *Av.* 304 (p. 56 Holwerda), "κεβλήπυρις"

μήποτε οὐχ ἕν ἐστιν ἀλλὰ δύο, φησὶν ὁ Σύμμαχος.
καὶ γὰρ ἐν τοῖς Καλλιμάχου (fr. 422 Pf.) ἀναγέγραπται
κέβλη . . . Ἑρμίππου τετραμέτροις,

   καὶ Θεμιστοκλέα †τὸν πρωνός τις ὦν†,

κεβλήπυρίς τις ὀνομάζεται, ὥστε ἐνθάδε ἢ ἐκεῖ ἡμάρ-
τηται τὸ ἓν παρὰ τῇ γραφῇ.

**5** Scholiast on Aristophanes, *Wasps*

διασαλακώνισον, i.e., 'put on airs' . . . The word is similarly used by Hermippus in his tetrameters:

> and (but?) afterwards . . .[1] I saw her playing the harlot and strutting about

[1] With αὐτὴν and Meineke's emendation at the end of v. 1 we have an unattested verb (but see the *Suda*, iii.74.17 Adler) which would represent the woman (or the city Heraclea if Meineke is right in joining fr. 5 to fr. 4) as acting like a helot (a Spartan serf). For an attractive analysis of the fragment see R. M. Rosen, *Old Comedy and the Iambographic Tradition* (Atlanta 1988) 10-11.

**6** Scholiast on Aristophanes, *Birds*

According to Symmachus,[1] κεβλήπυρις[2] is not one word but two (i.e., κέβλη and πυρίς). For in Callimachus κέβλη is written[3] . . . (But?) in the tetrameters of Hermippus,

> and Themistocles . . . ,

a κεβλήπυρις is named,[4] so that one or the other is a mistake in writing.

[1] An early commentator on Aristophanes (1st-2nd c. A.D.).
[2] Presumably a bird with a fiery-red head. Dunbar in her commentary on Ar. *Birds* (pp. 252 f.) discusses at length both the form of the word and the bird's identification, preferring Woodchat Shrike. She also suggests that Hermippus "linked Themistokles and κεβλήπυρις simply because he was the red-haired son of an allegedly Thracian mother."      [3] Passage not preserved.
[4] It seems that Hermippus is being contrasted with Callimachus and that he used the longer form, but no emendation is convincing.

## 7-8 Incerti Generis

**7** Ath. 15.667d

ὅτι δὲ ἆθλον προύκειτο τῷ εὖ προεμένῳ τὸν κότταβον
. . . , Ἕρμιππός τε ἐν τοῖς ἰάμβοις.

**8** Ath. 15.700d

Ἕρμιππος δὲ ὁ κωμῳδοποιὸς ἐν ἰάμβοις τὸ στρα-
τιωτικὸν λυχνεῖον σύνθετον οὕτως ὀνομάζει.

**9** P. Oxy. xiii.1611 fr. 1, col. v, 119

κ[αὶ Πλά]των φησὶν ἐν τ[ῶι Μέ]νωνι (94c) οὕτως· ["ὅτι
Θου]κυδίδης δύο [υἱεῖς ἔθρε]ψεν, Μελησία[ν καὶ
Στέ]φανον· τούτου[ς ἐπαίδευ]σεν." καὶ Ἕρμιπ[πος ὁ
ποι]ητὴς ἐν ἰάμβ[

## 7-8 *Uncertain Classification*

**7** Athenaeus, *Scholars at Dinner*

That a prize was offered for a skilful tossing of the cotta-bus[1] . . . , and Hermippus in his iambics.

[1] The cottabus in its various forms involved basically the throwing of wine drops at a target and the player often dedicated his toss to someone with a view to amorous success. For further details see Athenaeus 11.487d-e, 15.665a-69e, and F. Lissarrague, *The Aesthetics of the Greek Banquet* (Princeton 1987) 80-86.

**8** Athenaeus, *Scholars at Dinner*

The comic poet Hermippus in his iambics thus calls the military lampstand a compound.[1]

[1] Sense unclear. Perhaps Athenaeus means that Hermippus described the lampstand as constructed from several components.

**9** Oxyrhynchus papyrus (early 3rd c. A.D.)

And Plato speaks as follows in the *Meno*: "that Thucydides raised two sons, Melesias and Stephanus; he educated them." And Hermippus the poet in iambics (an iambic poem?) . . .

# SCYTHINUS

## TESTIMONIA

**1** St. Byz. (pp. 619 sq. Meineke)

Τέως· πόλις Ἰωνίας . . . ἀφ' οὗ Πρωταγόρας Τήϊος καὶ
Σκυθῖνος ὁ ἰάμβων ποιητὴς Τήϊος.

**2** Diog. Laert. 9.16

Ἱερώνυμος δέ (fr. 46 Wehrli) φησι καὶ Σκυθῖνον τὸν τῶν
ἰάμβων ποιητὴν ἐπιβαλέσθαι τὸν ἐκείνου (sc. Ἡρακ-
λείτου) λόγον διὰ μέτρου ἐκβαλεῖν.

**3** Ath. 11.461e (quae praecedunt v. ad Hermipp. fr. 4)

Ἡρακλεῶται δ' εἰσὶν οὗτοι οἱ ὑπὸ τῇ Οἴτῃ κατοικοῦν-
τες, ὥς φησι Νίκανδρος ὁ Θυατειρηνός (FGrHist 343 F
12), ὀνομασθῆναι φάσκων αὐτοὺς ἀπό τινος Κύλικος
γένος Λυδοῦ, ἑνὸς τῶν Ἡρακλεῖ συστρατευσαμένων.
μνημονεύει δ' αὐτῶν καὶ Σκυθῖνος ὁ Τήϊος (FGrHist 13
F 1) ἐν τῇ ἐπιγραφομένῃ Ἱστορίῃ λέγων οὕτως·
"Ἡρακλῆς λαβὼν Εὔρυτον καὶ τὸν υἱὸν ἔκτεινε φόρους

# SCYTHINUS

## TESTIMONIA

**1** Stephanus of Byzantium, *Lexicon of Place Names*

Teos, a city in Ionia . . . From it came Protagoras of Teos and the iambic poet Scythinus of Teos.

**2** Diogenes Laertius, *Lives of the Philosophers*

Hieronymus says that Scythinus, the iambic poet, undertook to put forth in verse the discourse of Heraclitus.[1]

[1] Diogenes proceeds to quote two epigrams on this topic (= *Anth. Pal.* 7.128, 9.540) and two more are attributed to Scythinus in the *Palatine Anthology* (12.22, 12.232), but all are judged spurious.

**3** Athenaeus, *Scholars at Dinner*

The people of Heracleia are those who dwell at the foot of Oeta, as Nicander of Thyateira says, asserting that they derived their name from a certain Cylix, a Lydian native, one of those who joined with Heracles on his expedition. Scythinus of Teos also mentions them in his work entitled *Inquiry*, speaking as follows: "Heracles captured and killed Eurytus and his son when they were exacting tribute

521

IAMBIC POETRY

πρήσσοντας παρ' Εὐβοέων. ⟨καὶ⟩ Κυλικρῆνας ἐξ-
επόρθησε ληζομένους καὶ αὐτόθι πόλιν ἐδείματο
Ἡράκλειαν τὴν Τρηχινίαν καλεομένην."

FRAGMENTUM

**1** Plut. *de Pyth. orac.* 16.402a

ὕστερον μέντοι (οἱ Μεγαρεῖς) πλῆκτρον ἀνέθηκαν τῷ
θεῷ χρυσοῦν, ἐπιστήσαντες ὡς ἔοικε Σκυθίνῳ λέγοντι
περὶ τῆς λύρας ἣν

ἁρμόζεται
Ζηνὸς εὐειδὴς Ἀπόλλων, πᾶσαν ἀρχὴν καὶ τέλος
συλλαβών, ἔχει δὲ λαμπρὸν πλῆκτρον ἡλίου
φάος.

from the Euboeans. He also sacked the Cylicranians who were engaged in plunder and built there Heracleia called the Trachinian."

## FRAGMENT

**1** Plutarch, *The Oracle at Delphi*

Later, however, the Megarians dedicated to the god a golden plectrum, paying attention as it seems to the words of Scythinus concerning the lyre which

> Zeus's son, comely Apollo, who comprehends every beginning and end, tunes, and he has the bright light of the sun as his plectrum

*I have omitted the corrupt fr. 2 preserved in Stobaeus 1.8.43 and attributed to Scythinus' On Nature. It seems to be a prose version of trochaic tetrameters, which West partially restores.*

# DIPHILUS

## TESTIMONIUM

**1** Schol. ad Arist. *Nubes* 96d (p. 31 Holwerda)

πρῶτον μὲν γὰρ Δίφιλος εἰς Βοίδαν τὸν φιλόσοφον
ὁλόκληρον συνέταξε ποίημα, δι' οὗ †τοὺκ† εἰς δουλείαν
ἐρυπαίνετο <ὁ> φιλόσοφος· οὐ διὰ τοῦτο δὲ ἐχθρὸς ἦν.
ἔπειτα Εὔπολις, εἰ καὶ δι' ὀλίγων ἐμνήσθη Σωκράτους,
μᾶλλον ἢ Ἀριστοφάνης ἐν ὅλαις ταῖς Νεφέλαις αὐτοῦ
καθήψατο.

# DIPHILUS

*Test. 1 suggests that Diphilus is older than, or at least contemporary with, the 5th-century comic poet Eupolis, but, as West ad loc. remarks, a Theseis in choliambics (fr. 1) is unlikely before the Hellenistic period unless it is "ludicra." Either then the Diphilus of test. 1 is different from the Diphilus of fr. 1 or fr. 1 is from a poem that might be similar to the Margites attributed to Homer. G. A. Gerhard,* Phoenix von Kolophon *(Leipzig 1909) 215, tentatively identifies this Diphilus as the Diphilus named by Diogenes Laertius 7.161 as a pupil of the philosopher Ariston (3rd c. B.C.).*

## TESTIMONIUM

**1** Scholiast on Aristophanes, *Clouds*

For first Diphilus composed an entire poem against the philosopher Boidas,[1] in the course of which the philosopher was abused as a slave, though he was not for this reason an enemy. And second Eupolis, even if he mentioned Socrates in (only) a few places, attacked him more than Aristophanes did in the whole of the *Clouds*.

---

[1] Identity and date unknown.

# IAMBIC POETRY

## FRAGMENTA

**1a** Schol. ad Pind. *Ol.* 10.83b (i.332.10 Dr.), "ἀν' ἵπποισι δὲ τέτρασιν ἀπὸ Μαντινέας Σᾶμ(ος) Ἁλιρροθίου"

Σῆμον δέ τινα νῦν νενικηκέναι ἅρματι, ὥς φησι Δίφιλος ὁ τὴν Θησηίδα ποιήσας ἔν τινι ἰάμβῳ (vv. ll. ἰάμῳ, ἰαμβείῳ) οὕτω·

στρέψας δὲ πώλους ὡς ὁ Μαντινεὺς Σῆμος,
ὃς πρῶτος ἅρματ' ἤλασεν παρ' Ἀλφειῷ.

1 τρέψας, τρέψαν codd., corr. Bergk

**1b** Id. 83a (i.331.26 Dr.)

παρατίθεται δὲ καὶ τὸν γράφοντα τὴν Θησηίδα μαρτυροῦντα τῷ ἥρωι τὴν τοῦ ἅρματος ἡνιοχευτικὴν ἀρετήν·

στρωφᾷς δὲ πώλους ὡς ὁ Μαντινεὺς ἥρως.

στρωφᾷς, στρωφάσων, στροφὰς, στροφαὶ codd.
Σῆμος pro ἥρως cod. B

DIPHILUS

FRAGMENTS

**1a** Scholiast on Pindar, *Olympian* 10 ("Samos[1] from Mantinea, the son of Halirrhothius, won the prize in the four-horse chariot race")

A certain Semus had won with the chariot, as Diphilus, the author of a *Theseis*, says in the following iambics:

You wheeled (wheeling?) the horses like Semus from Mantinea who was the first to drive a chariot beside the Alpheus.[2]

**1b** Scholiast on the same passage

He (Aristodemus?) cites as evidence the author of a *Theseis* who attests to the hero's skill in driving the chariot:

You keep wheeling the horses like the hero[3] from Mantinea

[1] The name of one of the first victors at the Olympic games, according to Pindar. Mantinea is in Arcadia. In one version Halirrhothius is the son of Poseidon, in another the grandson of Aeolus. [2] The river at the site of the Olympic games. [3] Possibly an error for Semus. The scholia on the Pindaric passage, only parts of which are quoted here, contain much that is confusing and contradictory.

# PANARCES

**1** Plat. *Resp.* 5.479b-c

"τοῖς ἐν ταῖς ἑστιάσεσιν," ἔφη, "ἐπαμφοτερίζουσιν ἔοικε καὶ τῷ τῶν παίδων αἰνίγματι τῷ περὶ τοῦ εὐνούχου τῆς βολῆς πέρι τῆς νυκτερίδος, ᾧ καὶ ἐφ᾽ οὗ αὐτὸν αὐτὴν αἰνίττονται βαλεῖν."

Schol. ad loc. (p. 235 Greene)

Κλεάρχου γρῖφος (fr. 95 Wehrli)

(a)  αἶνός τίς ἐστιν ὡς ἀνήρ τε κοὐκ ἀνὴρ
     ὄρνιθα κοὐκ ὄρνιθ᾽ ἰδών τε κοὐκ ἰδὼν
     ἐπὶ ξύλου τε κοὐ ξύλου καθημένην
     λίθῳ τε κοὐ λίθῳ βάλοι τε κοὐ βάλοι.

ἄλλως·

(b)  ἄνθρωπος οὐκ ἄνθρωπος, ἄνθρωπος δ᾽ ὅμως,
     ὄρνιθα κοὐκ ὄρνιθα, †ὄρνιθα δ᾽ ὅμως†,
     ἐπὶ ξύλου τε κοὐ ξύλου καθημένην
     λίθῳ βαλών τε κοὐ λίθῳ διώλεσεν.

νυκτερίδα ὁ εὐνοῦχος νάρθηκος κισήρει.

# PANARCES

**1** Plato, *Republic*

"It is like ambiguous statements at banquets," he said, "and like the children's riddle about the eunuch and his throwing at the bat; they riddle about what he pelted it with and on what it was sitting."

Scholiast on the passage

A riddle recorded by Clearchus:

(a)   There is a riddle that a man who is not a man saw and did not see a bird which was not a bird sitting on wood which was not wood struck and did not strike it with a stone which was not a stone.

Another version:

(b)   A man who is not a man, but yet a man, killed a bird which was not a bird . . . , sitting on wood which was not wood, having struck it with a stone which was not a stone.

(Solution) bat (v. 2), eunuch (v. 1), fennel (v. 3), pumice (v. 4) cf. Tryph. *De tropis* 4 (*Rhet. Gr.* iii.194.15 Spengel), Ps.-Choerob. (ibid. iii.253.18), David. (*Comm. in Arist. Gr.* xviii(2). 42.10), Eust. in *Il.* 8.252 (ii.580.12 V.d.Valk)

(a) 3 καθημένην τε καὶ οὐ καθημένην omnes praeter Davidem    4 βάλει . . . βάλει Tryphon    (b) 4 βαλών με κοὐ λίθῳ schol. Plat., τε κοὐ λίθῳ βαλὼν David

Ath. 10.452c

καὶ τὸ Πανάρκους δέ ἐστι τοιοῦτον, ὥς φησι Κλέαρχος ἐν τῷ περὶ γρίφων, ὅτι βάλοι ξύλῳ τε καὶ οὐ ξύλῳ καθημένην ὄρνιθα καὶ οὐκ ὄρνιθα ἀνήρ τε καὶ οὐκ ἀνὴρ λίθῳ τε καὶ οὐ λίθῳ· τούτων γάρ ἐστι τὸ μὲν νάρθηξ, τὸ δὲ νυκτερίς, τὸ δὲ εὐνοῦχος, τὸ δὲ κίσηρις. καὶ Πλάτων δὲ ἐν πέμπτῳ Νόμων μνημονεύει· τοὺς τῶν τεχνυδρίων φιλοσόφους τοῖς ἐν ταῖς ἑστιάσεσιν ἔφη ἐπαμφοτερίζουσιν ἐοικέναι κτλ.

Athenaeus, *Scholars at Dinner*

And there is also a similar riddle by Panarces, as Clearchus says in *On Riddles*, that a man who was not a man struck a bird which was not a bird, sitting on wood which was not wood, with a stone which was not a stone. The solution to this is eunuch, bat, fennel, and pumice. And Plato also mentions it in the fifth book of the *Laws*;[1] he said that philosophers of petty crafts are like those who propound ambiguities at banquets etc.[2]

[1] An error for *Republic*.      [2] Tryphon expands upon the riddle in version (a) by explaining that the man missed because his vision was poor. The ambiguity in $\beta\acute{\alpha}\lambda o\iota$ is that the verb can mean both 'throw at' and 'strike.'

# ADESPOTA IAMBICA

*1-35 Trimetri Recti*

**1** Heracl. Lemb. π. πολιτειῶν (p. 24.22 Dilts)

τὴν δὲ πολιτείαν τῶν Σαμίων Συλοσῶν ἠρήμωσεν· ἀφ᾽
οὗ καὶ ἡ παροιμία·

ἕκητι Συλοσῶντος εὐρυχωρίη.

**2** Cic. *ad Att.* 6.3.1

tu autem abes longe gentium,

πολλὰ δ᾽ ἐν μεταιχμίῳ
Νότος κυλίνδει κύματ᾽ εὐρείης ἁλός.

2 εὐρέης Lobel

**3** Strabo 14.1.30

καὶ ἡ Τέως δὲ ἐπὶ χερρονήσῳ ἵδρυται, λιμένα ἔχουσα.
ἐνθένδε ἐστὶν Ἀνακρέων ὁ μελοποιός, ἐφ᾽ οὗ Τήιοι τὴν

# ANONYMOUS

### 1-35 Iambic Trimeters

**1** Heraclides Lembus, *On Constitutions*

Syloson laid waste the state of the Samians and from this there arose the proverb:

> By the will of Syloson there is wide open space.[1]

[1] The same proverb is recorded by Strabo 14.1.17 who states that after Polycrates, tyrant of Samos, was murdered by the Persians (c. 522), Darius installed Polycrates' brother Syloson as tyrant. According to Strabo the proverb arose from Syloson's ruling so harshly that the state suffered from a lack of men.

**2** Cicero, *Letters to Atticus*

but you are in a far distant land,

> and in the intervening space the South Wind rolls many a wave of the wide sea

**3** Strabo, *Geography*

Teos too is situated on a peninsula and has a harbour. From there came the lyric poet Anacreon in whose day the

πόλιν ἐκλιπόντες εἰς Ἄβδηρα ἀπῴκησαν Θρακίαν
πόλιν, οὐ φέροντες τὴν τῶν Περσῶν ὕβριν· ἀφ' οὗ καὶ
τοῦτ' εἴρηται·

Ἄβδηρα, καλὴ Τηΐων ἀποικίη.

ἀποικία codd., corr. Meineke

**4** *Et. Gen.* (p. 21 Calame) = *Et. Mag.* 230.57, ex
Herodiano (ii.266.7 Lentz)

ἔστι δὲ πρώτης καὶ δευτέρας συζυγίας τὸ γηρᾷς,
ὥσπερ τὸ πιμπλᾷς, οἷον πιμπλῶ πιμπλᾷς καὶ πιμπλῶ
πιμπλεῖς, οἷον "†τὰς Ῥαδάμανθυς πιμπλεῖν βίαν†" (fr.
adesp. 969 *PMG*). οὕτως οὖν καὶ γηρῶ γηρᾷς . . . καὶ
γηρῶ γηρεῖς . . . ἡ μετοχὴ γηρείς,

γηρεὶς ἐν οἰκίοισι.

Quae sequuntur v. ad Xenoph. fr. 9.

οἰκέοισι *Et. Gen.*, οἰκέουσι *Et. Mag.*, corr. Sylburg

**5** Iuba Artigraphus ap. Rufinum (*Gramm. Lat.* vi.561.11
Keil)

iamborum itaque exempla quae maxime frequentata sunt
subdidi: πάτερ Λυκάμβα, ποῖον ἐφράσω τόδε; (Arch. fr.
172.1). Δαναὸς ὁ πεντήκοντα θυγατέρων πατήρ (Eur.
*Archel.* fr. 1.1 Austin).

Ξάνθη παλαιῇ γρη‹ΐ›, πολλῇσιν φίλη.

534

Teians abandoned their city and migrated to Abdera in
Thrace, since they could not endure the insolence of the
Persians; hence there arose the following verse:

Abdera, fair colony of the Teians[1]

[1] Crusius assigned both fr. 1 and fr. 3 to Anacreon.

**4** *Etymologicum Genuinum* and *Magnum*

The verb γηρῶ (2nd sing. γηρᾷς), 'grow old,' belongs to
both the first and the second conjugation, like πιμπλῶ,
'fill,' which has both πιμπλᾷς and πιμπλεῖς, as in (frag-
ment corrupt). Similarly then γηρῶ which has both γηρᾷς
. . . and γηρεῖς . . . the participle is γηρείς:

growing old in the house[1]

[1] R. Stark, *RhM* 99 (1956) 173-75, assigns the fragment to
Alcaeus, with Aeolic accentuation γήρεις.

**5** Juba in Rufinus, *The Meters of Terence*

Accordingly I have supplied the examples most commonly
found of iambic verses: "Father, Lycambes, what did you
mean by this?" "Danaus the father of fifty daughters."

to Xanthe, aged crone, dear to many women

**6** Hesych.

× – Πριηπίδος τε τῆς πρὸ Βοσπόρου

πόλεως Ἑλλησποντιακῆς, ⟨ἣν⟩ τὸν Πρίαπον τὸν Διο-
νύσου καὶ Περκώτης (περικότης cod.) φασὶν οἰκίσαι.

**7-34** P. Oxy. xxii.2318

**35** P. Oxy. xxii.2320, ed. Lobel

```
         ].̣.̣.̣.̣.̣.̣ ·  ̣νειδ  ̣καλὸ̣ν̣ [
         ]ἀκρ[ο]β[η]μάτιζε καὶ β[ι̣
         ]ασ̣ ε̣.̣.̣.τοις· α̣.[.].̣.[
         ].̣.̣.̣.̣ .̣.̣.̣.̣.̣ .̣με̣ α[
    5    ].̣μ̣.̣τ.̣.̣.̣.̣.̣ .̣.̣.̣.̣[
         ]ν ἆρα κἀσεβέως εἰργα[σμέν-
         ].̣εν Φιλάνθη τεύξε[
         ] ̣νεκείνη γ᾽ ἀνδρὸς ἢ ἐρινύω[ν
         ]ῃ τό γ᾽ αὐτὸς ἴσθι· πολλά τοι κακὰ[
    10   ]σσα θεοσύλησιν ἀνδράσιν θ[εοὶ
       διδοῦσιν, ὅ]στις περὶ φίλους ἁμαρτ[άνηι.
       ἀλλ᾽ οὐδέ]πω τις ἄλλος οὔτε μητέρα[
       προδοὺς] μέγ᾽ εὗρε κέρδος οὐδ᾽ ἀδελφ[εήν.
       ἕξει σ᾽ ἀμοι]βή· ταῦτ᾽ [ἐ]γὼ μαντεύο[μαι·
    15      ] ̣μ᾽ αὐτῆς μὴλ᾽ ἐπισφάζει[
```

**6** Hesychius, *Lexicon*

and of Priapis which faces the Bosporus,

a city on the Hellespont which they say was settled by
Priapus, son of Dionysus and Percote.[1]

[1] Strabo 13.1.12, in his account of the city Priapus, states that
the god was worshipped there and was said to be the son of Diony-
sus and a nymph. Homer (*Iliad* 2.835) mentions a place called
Percote, which was on the Hellespont west of Priapus.

**7-34** Scraps of papyrus too mutilated to be translated

**35** Oxyrhynchus papyrus (early 3rd c. A.D.)

. . . strut[1] and . . . Philanthe will meet with (retribu-
tion?) for impious deeds . . . of a man or the Furies
. . . know this on your own; many in truth are the
evils which the gods (give) to sacrilegious men, if
one wrongs his friends. (Not) yet has anyone else
found great profit from (betraying) a mother or sis-
ter. Requital (will get you). This is my prophecy.
(Even if you?) slaughter sheep . . . of her . . . relent-

[1] If Hesychius' gloss refers to this passage, the verb is impera-
tive. The fragment could be the work of Archilochus.

# IAMBIC POETRY

]μοῖρα νηλεὴ[ς] κιχή[σεται
οὐ μ]αλάξεις θυμὸν οὐδεκ[
οὐδὲ]ν ἐοῦσαν αἰτίην ἀπώλεσα[ς
]αντ[.] καιλαοισιν ἀνδα[ν-

2 Hesych. ἀκροβηματιζε· ἐπ᾽ ἄκροις τοῖς βήμασιν ἵστασο

6-7 εἰργα[σμένων / . . . τεύξε[ται τιμωρίης e.g. West
10 θ[εοὶ Peek      11-14 initia suppl. West      12 οὐδέ]πω
Lobel      14 ἀμοι]βή Lobel      15-16 κεῖ πάνθ᾽ ἅ]μ᾽
αὐτῆς μῆλ᾽ ἐπισφάζει[ς γάμῳ, / πάντως σε] e.g. West
17 κ[αρδίην Peek      18 ἐῦσαν pap., corr. West


*36-38 Tetrametri*

**36** Plut. *de cohib. ira* 9.457c

τοὺς δ᾽ ἠπίως καὶ λείως ὁμιλοῦντας ὀργαῖς κάλλιστα
μὲν ἀκούσματα κάλλιστα δὲ θεάματα ποιούμενος
ἄρχομαι καταφρονεῖν τῶν λεγόντων "ἄνδρ᾽ ἠδίκησας,
ἄνδρ᾽· ἀνεκτέον τόδε;" (Trag. adesp. 382 K.-S.) καὶ

βαῖνε λὰξ ἐπὶ τραχήλου, βαῖνε καὶ πέλα χθονί,

καὶ τἆλλα παροξυντικὰ κτλ.

**37** Plut. *non posse suav. viv. sec. Epic.* 21.1101f

ἐν δὲ πομπαῖς καὶ θυσίαις οὐ μόνον "γέρων καὶ
γρηῢς" οὐδὲ πένης καὶ ἰδιώτης, ἀλλὰ καὶ

less fate will catch up with (you) . . . You will (not)
soften the mind or the (heart?) . . . you have ruined
a woman who is in no way culpable . . .

*36-38 Trochaic Tetrameters*

**36** Plutarch, *On the control of anger*

As for those who deal with anger in a mild and gentle way
I offer examples which are very beautiful to hear and to
view, and I begin by scorning those who say "it was a man
you wronged, a man; is this to be borne?" and

  trample his neck (their necks) underfoot, trample
  and bring him (them) to the ground

and other provocative statements etc.

**37** Plutarch, *A pleasant life is impossible according to
Epicurus*

But in processions and at sacrifices not only "an old man
and an old woman"[1] or one who is poor and of low station,
but also

παχυσκελὴς ἀλετρὶς πρὸς μύλην κινουμένη

καὶ οἰκότριβες καὶ θῆτες ὑπὸ γήθους καὶ χαρμοσύνης
ἀναφέρονται.

καὶ potest poetae addi

## 38 P. Oxy. xxii.2317, ed. Lobel

 ....] ἐπικροτέων[
 ..]εβαμβάλυζε· πολλ[ὰ
5 καὶ τὸ μὲν φυγεῖν ὅταν δη[
 ἀνδράσιν κείνοις χολωθεὶ[ς
 δυσμενέων κομῆτα παιδ[
 οὔ σε τοῦτ’ ἤισχυνεν οὐδεν[
 ὡς ἀπ’ εὐεργέα τινάξας ἐτρ[άπης
10 καὶ γὰρ ἀλκιμωτέρους σέο κατα[
 ταῦτ’ ἐπηβόλη[σ]ε· θεοὺς γὰρ οὐκ ἐνίκ[ησεν
  βροτός·
 ἀλλ’ ὀτεύνεκεν πρὸ πάντων εκ[
 ἦλθες ἐκπλ[...]ς ἐφ’ ὑγρὰ κύματ[’ εὑρέης ἁλὸς
 ἀδρυφής, ου[...]νσε[......]εκλεϊ[
15 ἀλλαπαρθε[..... .....]δεμ.[
 .[.. π[όλιν π[..... ..... ]ναγγ[

3 [ὀδόντας suppl. Peek   7 Κομῆτα Peek
παῖδ[ων Latte et Peek  9 ἐτρ[άπης Peek  10 σεῦ
pap., corr. West  11 fin. Peek  13 ἐκπλ[εύσα]ς Peek
fin. Lobel

a stout-legged woman grinding grain, being screwed[2] against the millstone,

and house-born slaves and hired labourers have their spirits lifted in joyful delight.

[1] Words from two anonymous hexameters which Plutarch has just quoted. [2] This seems more probable than a reference to her moving about as she grinds the grain.

**38** Oxyrhynchus papyrus (2nd c. A.D.)[1]

... with chattering (teeth) ... he shivered; many ... and as for flight whenever ... in anger at those men ...; you with the long hair, of enemy ... this brought no shame on you, that you got rid of your well-made ... and were put to flight ... In fact these ... have seized braver men than you; no (mortal) wins out over the gods. But that (because?) before all ... you went (sailing?) over the broad sea's watery waves unscathed ... city ...

[1] The speaker is assuring someone who fled from battle that there is no disgrace in this and that better men have done the same, but little else is clear. V. 9 reminds us of Arch. fr. 5 and the author may be Archilochus.

*39-48 Trimetri vel Tetrametri*

**39** 'Longinus' *de subl.* 34.4

ἀλλ᾽ ἐπειδήπερ, οἶμαι, τὰ μὲν θατέρου καλά, καὶ εἰ πολλά, ὅμως ἀμεγέθη,

  καρδίη νήφοντος ἀργά,

καὶ τὸν ἀκροατὴν ἠρεμεῖν ἐῶντα—οὐδεὶς γοῦν Ὑπερείδην ἀναγιγνώσκων φοβεῖται—ὁ δὲ κτλ.

**39a** Ath. 3.126f

. . . ἵνα μὴ λέγῃς

  ἄκικύς εἰμι κωλιγοδρανέω

**40** St. Byz. (p. 22.3 Meineke)

ἀγρός, τὸ χωρίον . . . καὶ συνθέτως ἄγροικος καὶ ἀγροῖκος, ἀφ᾽ ὧν παρώνυμον τὸ ἀγροικηρός, ὡς σιγηρός, καὶ

  ἀγροικηρὴν φύσιν

**41-48** P. Oxy. 2324, 2325, 2328

## ADESPOTA IAMBICA

### *39-48 Trimeters or Tetrameters*

**39** 'Longinus,' *On the Sublime*

But whereas in my opinion Hyperides' fine points, even if numerous, nevertheless lack grandeur,

> inert in the heart of a sober man,[1]

and allow the listener to remain calm—no one at any rate is frightened while reading Hyperides—Demosthenes etc.

---

[1] D. A. Russell in his edition of 'Longinus' ad loc. suggests that the author may be Anacreon. For the thought cf. Plut. *de garrul.* 4.503f: τὸ γὰρ ἐν τῇ καρδίᾳ τοῦ νήφοντος ἐπὶ τῆς γλώττης ἐστὶ τοῦ μεθύοντος, ὡς οἱ παροιμιαζόμενοί φασιν, "for what is in the heart of one who is sober is on the tongue of one who is drunk, as those who are given to proverbs say."

**39a** Athenaeus, *Scholars at Dinner*

. . . so that you may not say

> I am feeble and have little strength

**40** Stephanus of Byzantium, *Lexicon of Place Names*

ἀγρός, place . . . And in composite form ἄγροικος ('boorish') and ἀγροῖκος ('dwelling in the country'), from which is derived ἀγροικηρός, like σιγηρός ('silent'),

> a rustic (boorish?) nature

**41-48** Scraps of papyrus too mutilated to be translated. Frr. 43–48 contain glosses on some iambic poet.

543

# IAMBIC POETRY

## 49-53 Trimetri Claudi

**49** Arist. *de part. anim.* 3.10.673a17

περὶ δὲ Ἀρκαδίαν οὕτω τὸ τοιοῦτον διεπίστευσαν
ὥστε καὶ κρίσιν ἐποιήσαντο περί τινος τῶν ἐγχωρίων.
τοῦ γὰρ ἱερέως τοῦ Ὁπλοσμίου Διὸς ἀποθανόντος,
ὑφ᾽ ὅτου δὲ δὴ ἀδήλως, ἔφασάν τινες ἀκοῦσαι τῆς κε-
φαλῆς ἀποκεκομμένης λεγούσης πολλάκις

> ἐπ᾽ ἀνδρὸς ἄνδρα Κερκιδᾶς ἀπέκτεινεν.

διὸ καὶ ζητήσαντες ᾧ ὄνομα ἦν ἐν τῷ τόπῳ Κερκιδᾶς,
ἔκριναν.

**50** Io. Alex. τονικὰ παραγγέλματα (p. 32.23 Dindorf)

καὶ τὸ βαύ κατὰ μίμησιν κυνὸς ὀξύνεται·

> × – ∪ "βαύ βαύ" καὶ κυνὸς φωνὴν ἱείς.

ἐξ οὗ καὶ τὸ βαΰζω ῥῆμα.

ἱείς pro ἵεις Dindorf          καὶ—ἵεις; alteri personae dat
Knox

*49-53 Choliambics*

**49** Aristotle, *On Parts of Animals*

In Arcadia they so firmly believed this sort of thing[1] that they actually brought to trial one of the local inhabitants. When a priest of Zeus Hoplosmios[2] had been killed and it was unclear who had done it, some said that they had heard the head, after it had been cut off, repeating again and again

Cercidas has killed man after man.[3]

And so they searched for one bearing the name Cercidas and brought him to trial.

[1] I.e., that a head can speak after being cut off.    [2] Presumably Zeus In Armour. The cult is attested only in Arcadia.
[3] The first two words of the fragment are often deemed corrupt. West suggests ἄνανδρος, with μ᾽ supplied before the verb: "the cowardly Cercidas has killed me a man." All that one actually expects is Κερκιδᾶς μ᾽ ἀπέκτεινεν, "Cercidas has killed me."

**50** John of Alexandria, *Rules of Accentuation*

And the word βαύ in imitation of a dog is accented oxytone:

"bow wow" and emitting the sound of a dog

Hence the verb βαΰζω 'bark.'

**51** Schol. *B in Hom. *Il.* 9.539 (ii.515 Erbse apparatus), "χλούνην"

οἱ μὲν ἀφριστήν, χλουδεῖν γὰρ τὸ ἀφρίζειν τινὲς Δωριέων ἔλεγον. ἄλλοι δὲ κακοῦργον, καὶ γὰρ τῶν ἀρχαίων ἰαμβοποιῶν τινα φάναι·

> ἀνὴρ ὅδ᾽ <        > ἑσπέρης καθεύδοντα
> ἀπ᾽ ὧν ἔδυσε <            > χλούνην

2 ἄπουν ἔδησε cod., corr. Hermann (οὖν), Schneidewin

**52** Schol. Ar. *Av.* 704 (p. 111 Holwerda), "καὶ τοῖσιν ἐρῶσι σύνεσμεν"

Σύμμαχος διὰ τὸ τοὺς ἐραστὰς ὄρνιθας ‹τοὺς› (add. West) εὐγενεῖς χαρίζεσθαι τοῖς ἐρωμένοις. Δίδυμος δέ, ἐπεὶ ἡ σίττη καὶ εἴ τι τοιοῦτον ὄρνεον δεξιὰ πρὸς ἔρωτας φαίνεται·

> ἐγὼ μέν, ὦ Λεύκιππε, δεξιῇ σίττῃ.

cf. *Sud.* i.63.11 Adler

ἐρῶμεν tent. West      ὡς schol.      λευκίππη schol., *Suda*, corr. Bentley      δεξιὴ (-ὰ *Suda*) σίττῃ libri, corr. Meineke

**53** Phot. *lex.* (ii.33 Naber)

ὁ τὸν †πατέρα εὑρὼν χαλκοῦ χρείᾳ†·

>                   ὁ τὸν κυσὸν τρωθεὶς
> †ἤδη αἰσώπου† μάλιστα τοῦ κράνους χρεία

2 ἤδεις ὅπου Dobree      χρείη Bergk

546

**51** Scholiast on Homer, *Iliad*

Some explain χλούνης as the 'foamer,' since some of the Dorians said χλουδεῖν for ἀφρίζειν ('to foam'). Others explain it as 'villain,' since they say that one of the old iambic poets says:

> this fellow . . . while (I?) was sleeping in the evening stripped (me?) . . . the villain[1]

[1] Several assign the fragment to Hipponax (see Degani's fr. 191). In the Homeric passage χλούνης is an epithet of a wild boar, but its meaning is much disputed. In the lacuna preceding 'villain' perhaps something like 'but they caught' has been lost.

**52** Scholiast on Aristophanes, *Birds* ("and we associate with lovers")

According to Symmachus because lovers give fine-bred birds to their beloveds. According to Didymus because the nuthatch and other such birds seem to be a lucky omen for love:

> I (am in love?) with(?) a lucky nuthatch, Leucippus[1]

[1] Attributed by some to Hipponax (see Degani's fr. 192).

**53** Photius, *Lexicon*

(source corrupt)

> you(?), the one wounded[1] in the rump, (you know where there is?) special need of a helmet

[1] In all probability 'wounded' here means 'sexually penetrated,' as in Eubulus fr. 106.4 K.-A.

*54-55 Trimetri vel Tetrametri Claudi*

**54** *Epimerismi* (*Anecd. Ox.* ii.371.19 Cramer)

ζῷον ἐν πυρὶ σκαῖρον·

ἡ σαλαμάνδρα, ἥτις ζῷόν ἐστιν ὡσεὶ σαύρας τὸ μέγε-
θος ἢ μικροῦ κροκοδίλου χερσαίου· ἔστιν δὲ ψυχρότα-
τον ὑπερφυῶς, ὥστε καὶ ἐν πυρὶ εἰσερχόμενον τὴν μὲν
φλόγα σβέννυναι, αὐτὸ δὲ μὴ κατακαίεσθαι.

**55** Zenob. 2.29 (iv.224 Bühler) = *Paroem. Gr.* i.90.5 =
    Schol. Plat. *Leg.* 968e (p. 379 Greene)

"ἢ τρὶς ἓξ ἢ τρεῖς κύβοι." κεῖται ἡ παροιμία παρὰ
Φερεκράτει ἐν τοῖς Μυρμηκανθρώποις (fr. 129 K.-A.)
. . . τοὺς δὲ κύβους τοὺς τοιούτους οἱ Ἴωνες καλοῦσιν
οἴνας, καὶ τὴν παροιμίαν οὕτως ἐκφέρουσιν·

ἢ τρὶς ἓξ ἢ τρεῖς οἴνας

οἶναι Salmasius (ex εἶναι Zenob.)

*55a-57 Epodi*

**55a** Ostr. Edfu 326

ἔπος δ᾽ ἐφώνησεν τόδε·
"σὸν τὸ κράτος βασιλεῦ."

## ADESPOTA IAMBICA

### 54-55 *Choliambic Trimeters or Tetrameters*

**54** *Parsings*

> an animal dancing in the fire

The salamander, which is a creature the size of a lizard or small desert monitor. It is extremely cold so that it quenches fire upon entry,[1] but is not itself burned.

[1] This is also reported by Aristotle, *HA* 5.552b16.

**55** Zenobius, *Proverbs*

"Either treble six or treble one." The proverb occurs in Pherecrates, *The Ant Men* . . . The Ionians call such dice οἶναι and they express the proverb as follows:

> either treble six or treble one[1]

[1] I.e., the highest or lowest score and so a proverb for 'all or nothing.'

### 55a-57 *Epodes*

**55a** Potsherd

> And this is what he said:
> "Yours is the power, O king."[1]

[1] See West, *ZPE* 32 (1978) 1-5 and 91 (1992) 8-9. The potsherd contains an unmetrical third line σὸν τὸ κράτος Ἱέραξ, "yours is the power, Hierax," which West suggests may be a reference to "the power behind the throne," perhaps to the general Hierax who served Ptolemy Euergetes II c. 140 B.C. The first two lines may be from an animal fable of Archilochus.

549

**56** Schol. Aesch. *PV* 400d (p. 132 Herington), "ῥέος"

ῥεῦμα, παρὰ τὸ ῥέω, ῥέος, ὡς κλέπτω κλέπος"

οἴχεται

τὸ κλέπος αὐτὸς ἔχων.


**57** *Suda* (iii.443.13 Adler)

ναὶ ναὶ μὰ μήκωνος χλόην·

ὅρκος ἐπὶ χλευασμῷ.

**56** Scholiast on Aeschylus, *Prometheus Bound*

ῥέος = ῥεῦμα ('stream'), from ῥέω ('flow'), like κλέπος
from κλέπτω ('steal'):

he's gone off with the loot for himself[1]

[1] Recorded also in *SH* fr. 1158. West compares Hipponax fr.
117 for the meter and subject matter.

**57** *Suda*

yes, yes, by the poppy shoot,

a mocking oath.

*Composed in ZephGreek and ZephText by
Technologies 'N Typography, Merrimac, Massachusetts.
Printed in Great Britain by St. Edmundsbury Press Ltd,
Bury St. Edmunds, Suffolk, on acid-free paper.
Bound by Hunter & Foulis Ltd, Edinburgh, Scotland.*